THE PASSENGER
ON THE U

CLAUDE AVELINE

THE PASSENGER
ON THE U

Translated by Mervyn Savill

DOUBLEDAY & COMPANY, INC.

GARDEN CITY, NEW YORK

1969

All of the characters in this book
are fictitious, and any resemblance
to actual persons, living or dead,
is purely coincidental.

Library of Congress Catalog Card Number 69–15188
English text copyright © 1968 Dobson Books Ltd
from the original French, L'ABONNE DE LA LIGNE U,
copyright © 1963 Mercure de France
All rights reserved
Printed in the United States of America
First edition in the United States of America

To Martin Premsela

Part One

BELOT

1

A Murder in the Champs-Elysées

At five minutes to two in the afternoon of Monday, October 3rd 19 . .—the Motor Show had opened its doors that very morning— M. Étienne Tavernier, director of the head agency of Gascogne Motors, got off at the stop Rond-Point des Champs-Elysées from a bus of the U Line—Levallois-Gobelins. He had travelled first class from the Porte de Champerret to the Rond-Point. As he was about to cross the Avenue Victor-Emmanuel another traveller, who had left the bus close on his heels, took out a revolver and fired at his back. M. Tavernier fell to the ground directly in front of a taxi. The taxi stopped, but the driver braked so violently that the truck behind ran into it. The noise of the crash distracted the onlookers' attention from the fatal shots. Alone on his platform (the other passengers had crowded round M. Tavernier) the bus conductor was able to see the murderer put the revolver back in his pocket and slip away without undue haste, to be swallowed up in the crowd. The conductor said later that he had wanted to follow him. Unfortunately a crowd of passers-by besieged his vehicle, the damaged taxi and the victim, forming an almost impassable barrier. The traffic came to a complete standstill. The hooting of stationary cars echoed the furious whistling of the police at the Rond-Point. To restore order they had to call for reinforcements. A police van and an ambulance appeared within five minutes. This brilliant feat took four minutes too long for them to be able to catch the murderer. A black car with two inspectors arrived a few moments later.

When the police and the ambulance men reached the victim, a doctor declared that he was dead. The body was taken away; some of

9

the policemen were sent off in the direction pointed out by the bus conductor, the taxi was pushed over to the pavement and the truck driver, after giving particulars, was allowed to go on his way. The passengers of the bus had to give their names and addresses although they all insisted that they had seen nothing either before or during the crime . . . all of them except two, the first-class passengers, M. and Mme Colet, who provided a few essential details. M. Tavernier had boarded the bus after them, but they could not remember exactly where. He had taken the only free seat in the first-class compartment, opposite Mme Colet and next to a lady. This lady had got off a few stops later. Her seat was taken by a man in a grey suit and hat who, after a moment, turned to M. Tavernier and said "A very good morning to you, monsieur . . ." M. Colet had understood Tabarnier, while his wife thought it was Tavarnier. M. Tavernier, who was reading a paper replied: "Oh, it's you!" The man in grey had bent forward and neither M. nor Mme Colet had heard the rest of the conversation. Actually they had lost interest and had gone on with their own conversation. According to the conductor the man in grey was the murderer. He had only seen his back view after the murder, and figured that he was a little above average height. Mme Colet insisted that he was clean shaven, still young and rather smart, with very ugly hands. She could not say much more because "descriptions were not her strong point," but she would have no difficulty in recognising him again. She had also noticed that he was wearing a tie pin in the form of a large grasshopper, in rather dubious taste.

The detectives thanked the witnesses, with an "Au revoir" that held promise for the future and finally let the bus leave, not without having noted its number—197—and the exact spot where it had stopped. They then proceeded to question the taxi driver—Camus, Fernand, forty-five years old. Camus had heard the shots but said: "I thought it could have been that or something else! I didn't have time to think of anything. I saw the man fall about a yard in front of me and said to myself: Good God, I shall run over him! Actually that would have been better, since he was already dead, but I didn't know that. Look at the back of my cab! Lucky I was empty or my passengers would have been flattened. . . ." He had not even noticed the murderer. He was still trembling.

At the Forensic Institute the inspectors examined the contents of the victim's pockets. They discovered his name, his profession, his home address and that of his firm, after which they went to the Quai des Orfèvres with their booty.

The article in *Le Grand Journal* was the most complete and the most moving of all those which appeared on the day after the crime. The reporter described his visit to the dead man's family, the imposing block of flats on the Boulevard Gouvion-Saint-Cyr and its thick carpets: "the smooth, silent lift speeding up to the fourth floor," the maid "whose red-rimmed eyes proved better than the finest phrases the grief which the violent loss of her unfortunate master had caused." Mme Tavernier had been informed of the murder by the G . . . Agency, (*Le Grand Journal* never gives free advertising) where Chief Inspector Belot had called first of all. Young Roux, the under-manager of the agency, had left his post instantly despite the stream of visitors from the Motor Show and had carried the terrible news to the Boulevard Gouvion-Saint-Cyr. He was consoling Mme Tavernier when Chief Inspector Belot was announced. The three of them were closeted in Mme Tavernier's boudoir, while the reporter of *Le Grand Journal* remained in the gallery. Did they speak loudly? Did the reporter possess a singularly acute sense of hearing? His report gave the minutest details of the dialogue. Endowed with a courage as great as her despair, Mme Tavernier replied without flagging to the inspector's questions. No, she did not know of any enemies M. Tavernier might have had. No, she did not suspect anyone among her husband's relations. True, she knew nothing of his business acquaintances, but here young Roux insisted upon the excellent relations of the dead man with his customers and the employees of various grades, of his own agency and the head office. M. Tavernier held an important position at G . . . Motors—the Champs-Elysées branch was the largest—and he had always carried out his duties in an exemplary manner.

Chief Inspector Belot suddenly asked a question of detail, which was somewhat surprising after these generalities: How was it that the director of a big motor agency did not have his own private car and took a bus?

Mme Tavernier's grief was redoubled.

"When I think," she said, "that he would still be alive if he had listened to me. Naturally, monsieur, we have a car. You can see it through the window. There it is. My husband let me have it to do my shopping. He did not want to be bothered with it on the first day of the Motor Show."

"We have eight company cars parked in front of the showrooms," said M. Roux.

"I said to him," Mme Tavernier went on, "take a taxi for once in a while! My husband was not a miser, Inspector, he was economical, very economical. He replied that it would be ridiculous to see the meter ticking in the traffic jams. He always replied a little sourly, when I suggested spending money. I can still hear him saying 'It's the U I want to take and I shall take the U.' Then he smiled and gave me a kiss. . . ."

On these words, according to *Le Grand Journal*, Mme Tavernier's voice broke.

"I'm sorry, madame," the inspector continued, "to put you through this ordeal so soon after such a misfortune, but time is of the utmost importance."

"I'm listening, monsieur," murmured Mme Tavernier.

"So this bus journey was not a habit? Nobody could have foreseen that *today* M. Tavernier. . . ."

"No, I don't think so, particularly since I could have dropped him in the car as I have done many times before."

"Even during previous Motor Shows?"

Mme Tavernier must have thought for a moment for there was a silence.

"Yes, now I come to think of it he took the bus every year at this time."

"And who, to your knowledge, could have known of it?"

"Apart from me. . . ."

"Me," said young Roux. "And our employees, all four of whom have been with the firm for several years."

"And as a matter of fact," said Mme Tavernier, "all my servants, but none of them comes under suspicion! Then there are my children, my husband's family and mine."

"Alas, madame," said the inspector, "in an inquiry I have to . . . I don't say suspect everybody, but I have to consider that one can reach the suspects through people who are above suspicion. It is not by chance that a murderer sits in a bus next to his future victim."

"But why? Why?" groaned Mme Tavernier. "I haven't seen him

as happy as he was yesterday for ages. We spent such a wonderful Sunday when he got back."

"When he got back?"

"Each year before the Motor Show," said young Roux, "he visited the G . . . branches in Brussels, Amsterdam and London. He came back on Saturday. Yes, he was in a good mood."

"Because normally . . ." Belot asked.

"Oh, Inspector," said Mme Tavernier, "he was the gentlest man in the world, but a little sad, a trifle gloomy. He was very preoccupied with his business."

"He had no reason to be," said young Roux. "The business is going like a house on fire."

"It's too awful," said Mme Tavernier.

Le Grand Journal broke off the conversation on the arrival of the victim's two brothers, to describe in the most flattering terms the character and career of Chief Inspector Frédéric Belot. The eulogy was not exaggerated. All those familiar with crime (on the police side) had occasion to know and appreciate Belot. He was one of those privileged men who at the same time gives the impression of strength and finesse—strength by his square shoulders and finesse by his glance. He expressed himself well and seemed endowed with infinite patience. His successes justified his rank and reputation. Compared to the inquiries which usually fell to him, the Tavernier affair, as far as one could tell on the evening of October 3rd, could be described as an average or even as a mediocre case. He could not foresee that forty-eight hours later it was to become the most extraordinary case of his already long career.

2

Nothing new, but eventually an envelope

Next day M. and Mme Colet, the principal witnesses from the bus were invited by Belot to visit Gascogne Motors in the Champs-Elysées. They were to present themselves as interested visitors. It was possible that they might recognise the murderer among the employees.

"If you recognise him," said Belot, "don't hesitate to shout 'That's him!' You have nothing to fear. I shall have all the men there I need. Besides I shall be there myself."

M. and Mme Colet, who were furniture dealers from Avignon on a short holiday in Paris, accepted this secret mission with alacrity. Belot had summed them both up: M. Colet, 12 out of 20 (he had said: "With his tie pin, he would have been spotted immediately"). Mme Colet, 15 out of 20 (she had replied: "But my dear, a tie pin can easily be removed!"), possibly 17 out of 20, (for she had added: "particularly if it was put on to attract attention"). Mme Colet resembled a sweet little mouse and M. Colet a big cat.

During their visit Mme Colet earned full marks. The showrooms were full of people. The morning and midday papers had devoted almost as much space to the murder of M. Tavernier as to the opening of the Motor Show, to which after all it formed the tragic complement. In the midday papers, the publicity service of Gascogne Motors had had time to go into action. In spite of all the traditions of a well-understood business, the crowd had to be kept on the move. No doubt viewers of the new 19 . . models, the fine chromium plated fittings, the engines displayed in sections, the coachwork gleaming like black lacquer, had one sole topic of conversation, the corpse. Young Roux was distressed. He found such an appetite for crime indecent, and feared that it would have a bad effect on their orders. One of the Gascogne brothers, M. René, who was usually at the stand in the Grand-Palais throughout the whole show, but whom Belot had asked to come to the showrooms that afternoon, scanned the huge crowd tirelessly and whispered in young Roux's ear: "Don't worry, my boy, they'll be buying as usual tomorrow!"

Mme Colet wanted to buy at once. She approached the bemedalled commissionaire who directed her to a salesman. After questioning the salesman she dismissed him on the pretext that she was in no hurry. On seeing a second salesman pass she complained that she was being kept waiting. The second young man who was engaged sent her a third. She asked such a preposterous question of the third that he left open-mouthed, and she was obliged to ask for a fourth salesman. The fourth young man appeared. Mme Colet knew from Belot that there were no more. She said that on second thoughts she preferred to speak to the director. She was taken—M. Colet followed her in silence—to young Roux and M. Gascogne. From a corner of the showroom Belot watched the antics of his voluntary collaborator with a smile. But when he saw her thank young Roux and make for the door he shrugged his shoulders with resignation. He himself now approached M. Gascogne and shook him by the hand. This was the signal for his men that the experiment had drawn a blank and that they could leave.

M. Gascogne accompanied him as far as the door. The previous evening they had discussed M. Tavernier's career, in particular his recent voyage to Brussels, Amsterdam and London.

"We have been in touch with the three police forces," said Belot. "Let's hope there will be no delay in their inquiries."

"Obviously," said M. Gascogne, "an arrest before the end of the Motor Show would be very favourable to . . ."

He bit his lip.

"To . . . ?" asked Belot, who had already guessed.

". . . to your reputation!"

On the avenue, the inspector joined M. and Mme Colet. Night had fallen.

"Allow me to congratulate you, *madame*. A professional could not have done the job better."

Mme Colet blushed, but continued to look crestfallen.

"You're very kind, Inspector, but I'm disappointed all the same. I had all prepared such a lovely shout of: 'That's him!' "

Some passers-by looked round.

"Who's that? What do you mean, him?" asked one of them.

Mme Colet pointed to M. Colet.

"Him, why my husband of course!"

"So what?" asked the stranger.

"So what?" echoed Mme Colet. "What business is it of yours?"

"That's enough, Blondel," said Belot.

"Ah," said the stranger, "I didn't see you, Inspector. I'm sorry."

He walked away.

Mme Colet clapped her hands. "How exciting all this is. Don't you think so, Raymond? Inspector, ask me something else, please. I was thinking we ought to repeat our experiment at the showrooms at the Gascogne stand in the Grand-Palais."

"I was thinking of that, too, madame," said Belot with a smile. "I'm only afraid M. Colet will get tired."

"Oh," replied M. Colet, gloomily, "I'm willing to trail along, but I'm starting to want a car."

"Hmm," said his wife with a laugh, "you're beginning to catch on. So you haven't told us everything, Inspector."

Belot nodded.

"You are an extraordinary woman, *madame*. I was going to ask you to come to the Quai des Orfèvres tomorrow. You'll be shown an album of photographs which I borrowed from Madame Tavernier. I don't hold out great hopes from that quarter, but who knows? In the meantime, I'm still going through the victim's papers."

"And you've found nothing in them?"

"That is a professional secret, *madame*."

"Forgive me, Inspector, but I will answer for you. You have found nothing in them."

Belot returned to the Boulevard Gouvion-Saint-Cyr. He had already spent the whole morning there without, as he remarked, finding anything. He had gone through a great number of drawers and questioned Mme Tavernier again and her two brothers-in-law: Paul, the elder, who was as cold as he was formal and Vincent, the younger, whose tear-stained face showed, on the contrary, deep distress. The brothers placed themselves at his disposal, although both of them insisted, as with one voice, that the murder seemed totally inexplicable. For a second, Paul Tavernier lost his impassive calm. As Belot reached for the photograph album, he cried, "Inspector! They are family portraits!" He recovered his composure immediately however. "Forgive me. Obviously I know nothing of police inquiries."

Some reporters were gossiping in front of the block of flats. They rushed at Belot. But it was he who asked them: "Anything new?"

He learnt that the undertakers had just brought round the body of the victim. It had been placed in a coffin at the Forensic Institute after an autopsy which had established the calibre of the murder weapon.

"Thanks," said Belot. "No need to get out your notebooks or to stay here any longer. I shan't come out again for hours. The inquiry will follow its usual course."

"So will we!" cried a voice.

"And marking time, at that."

Everyone laughed. On entering the fourth-floor flat Belot caught sight of the yellow flame of candles through the glass doors of the drawing-room. In the hall people dressed in black were speaking in undertones. A child sobbed. There were flowers. . . .

Mme Tavernier wore her mourning with dignity, but her features revealed great fatigue.

"My husband is . . . in there," she whispered. "I have had his writing desk put in my boudoir so that you can work in peace. I have questioned all my in-laws. They are all at a loss and no one can think of the slightest reason. . . ."

Paul Tavernier came up. He bore a strange resemblance to the dead man, although his greying hair made him seem twenty years older.

"I'll leave you in the hands of my brother-in-law, Paul," Mme Tavernier said to Belot. "He knows. . . . He knew my poor Étienne even better than I. In any case," she murmured, pointing to the drawing-room door, "I shall not be far away. . . ."

The telephone suddenly rang in the hall. The sound was so shrill among the whispers that even Belot gave a start.

"That must be stuffed with cotton wool at once!" said a distraught old lady.

The maid came running in. "M. Belot is wanted on the telephone."

"Hallo, Belot? It's me." It was Picard, the Chief of the Murder Squad. "Anything new?"

"No, nothing. I've just arrived."

"Will you be long?"

"All evening. Part of the night, too, I expect."

"Forget it. I want you here at once. You can go back there later."

When Belot left the building, cries of indignation rose from the group of reporters. One of them called out: "You didn't tell the truth, M. Belot. You're trying to get rid of us."

A shadow appeared at the foot of the back stairs. It was the reporter from *Le Grand Journal.*

"No, gentlemen, M. Belot did not lie. He has just been called away on the telephone."

"Ha, ha!" said Belot. "A leakage from below stairs." He hailed a taxi. "Quai des Orfèvres!"

The reporters leapt into their cars and everyone drove off to Police Headquarters.

"Look here," said Picard. "This envelope has just been found in one of the U Line buses." He pointed to it on the desk. "I see there's a gleam in your eye. The conductor brought it to me half an hour ago."

"From the same vehicle as yesterday's?"

"Let me speak. No, another—No. 805. It had just arrived at its terminus, Gobelins; everyone got out and the conductor made his usual run-through of the bus. He discovered this under one of the first-class seats. Come on, pick it up."

Picard threw away an almost unsmoked cigarette and lit another. He was a restless, excitable person, but he knew his job.

Belot took the envelope. It was a white, business envelope with no lining or maker's name. In typescript it bore the following address:

M. Picard,
Chief of the Murder Squad,
Prefecture of Police,
Quai des Orfèvres,
Paris.

"Hmm . . . a meticulous person."

"And one who knows where to strike home," replied Picard.

Belot drew a sheet of paper from the envelope. Picard followed him with his eyes. They had worked together since their youth. They loved each other like brothers, and if his friend was now under his orders it was not his fault. Belot would have preferred to leave the police force rather than become tied to the office. Picard entrusted him with the most ticklish cases, consulted him regularly, and quoted him as an example to the new recruits.

The letter read:

My respects, Monsieur Picard, and my apologies for causing you an investigation which, I regret for you, will not be easy. Do I know myself who I am? In any case I am not very proud of the events of yesterday. I expect to do better tomorrow *for the others and for myself*.

(*Signed*) The Passenger on the U.

Belot, impressed, clicked his tongue.

"Here's a man who really knows how to write a letter. Slightly pretentious. . . ."

"A bit of a sphinx, too," agreed Picard.

"What is it you can't understand about it?"

"The whole thing."

"It's perfectly clear though! He regrets having murdered Tavernier. Probably not out of humanity, but because the crime was not stage A of his plans. Today he is telling the 'others' to be more reasonable than Tavernier was. What about, for what reason, I have no idea. Money, I imagine."

"Hmm," said Picard. "So according to you it all fits together. I am inclined to think we are dealing with a crackpot, like the lunatic who swore to do away with all the Paris concierges! Three victims on the first day. . . ."

"But the second day. . . ." said Belot. (He personally had received a knife thrust close to his jugular and his promotion to chief inspector.)

"That's the lucky break I'm hoping we'll get," said Picard. "Truflot!"

A small man sitting near the window raised his bald, domed head. "Send this to Records. We've also got to find the typewriter."

"That won't tell us anything," replied Belot. "A fellow who knows your name is bound to have taken the elementary precautions."

"But he likes taking risks. Fancy, there was not a *single person* there yesterday to grab him by the jacket. The police really get no help. . . ."

"I tell you," said Belot, "that this letter has a precise intention. He wants us to publish it. It would terrorise the people he is after, the 'others.' . . . And they'll fall over themselves to fit in with him."

"But it's an anonymous letter."

"Anonymous as regards the murderer, but *not as regards the victim.* It refers to Tavernier, so the 'others' must have something to do with Tavernier."

"And so you think we ought to publish it?"

"If the 'others' were to rush here to put us in the picture, yes. . . . But that's very far from certain. They may have reason to fear us *as well.* . . . No, it's up to me to identify them from the Taverniers' family papers. As for you. . . ."

"I have already detailed a man on each U bus, in case another one of them is used as a postbox."

"Better a postbox than a hearse." Belot stood up. "I'm going back to the Boulevard Gouvion-Saint-Cyr."

Picard leaned back in his chair.

"Did you notice anything else?"

"The Passenger on the U? For someone who is so meticulous about his style, this is rather odd. He might be a foreigner. This brings us back to Tavernier's trip to Brussels and elsewhere. Someone from Brussels? I must ask Mme Colet. She heard him utter a few words yesterday. She's quite a girl. . . ."

Truflot raised his head and winked at Picard. Belot shrugged his shoulders.

"I have no more time for her than for any other woman," he retorted. "All the same, I'm entitled to say she is full of surprises."

"And a pretty pair of eyes?"

"I will give you that piece of information at our next conference, Chief," said Belot, leaving the office.

The police officers remained silent, but the bus conductor spoke—or rather (Picard had asked him to remain silent) dropped hints. Since the Chief of the Murder Squad had received him personally, and since his fingerprints had been taken with care, it must mean that his find was worth it. The Press was agreed. It connected the event with the telephone call for Belot at the Boulevard Gouvion-Saint-Cyr. The following day all the newspapers devoted the greater part of their front pages to the news. *Le Grand Journal* reported:

FURTHER DEVELOPMENTS IN THE TAVERNIER MURDER. YESTERDAY IN A U LINE BUS—SIMILAR TO THE ONE ON WHICH THE MURDERER TRAVELLED WITH HIS VICTIM—AN ENVELOPE ADDRESSED TO THE POLICE WAS DISCOVERED. THE QUAI DES ORFÈVRES REMAINS SILENT AS TO THE CONTENTS. CROWDS OUTSIDE THE GASCOGNE AGENCY.

The headlines on the following day were even more spectacular.

3

The Mysteries of the U Line

The Quai des Orfèvres learnt of the disappearance of Maurice Verdon on the afternoon of Wednesday, October 5th, forty-eight hours after the murder of M. Tavernier and twenty-four hours after the discovery of the envelope. Up till that moment, Chief Inspector Belot had been employed as follows:

Tuesday evening: After he had left Picard he dined in a small restaurant (where the steak that evening for some reason tasted unpleasantly of writing paper) and then returned to the glimmering of candles, to the black shadows, the hushed whisperings and the family papers. The victim's family could not have been more solicitous. Logs of wood blazed in the boudoir fireplace (the nights had begun to turn cold). A plate of sandwiches and coffee were waiting for him near the desk. So much attention rather annoyed him. He wondered if, among the mourners in the drawing-room, there was not a man of over-average height, clean shaven, still young and rather smart—a foreigner perhaps and without whose existence M. Tavernier need not have been the object of crocodile tears. He wanted to check what each of these people was doing yesterday at the time of the murder and today at the time the envelope was delivered. If he had not discovered anything before Thursday, Mme Colet would have to attend the funeral.

"Oh, Inspector, ask me something else, please." Charming. Her husband was a decent fellow, but an imbecile.

Belot had sorted the papers into two piles, those that did not matter, and those about which he would have to find an explanation, signatures of more or less private letters, address books, expense accounts, bank slips and various receipts. The expense accounts showed that M. Tavernier was very economical, as his poor widow so charitably put it. "Birthday present, Jean-François (this was the elder of the two children aged fifteen and twelve) 5 francs; local charities, yearly contribution, 10 francs." Belot glanced at the expensive furniture of the boudoir, the log fire and the sandwiches, and said to himself that the Taverniers could not always have seen eye to eye. "It's the U I want to take, and I shall take the U." Was avarice at the root of the tragedy? Belot temporarily rejected this hypothesis. He had known men to give a present worth 5 francs to a son and a diamond costing 100,000 francs to a mistress. At least M. Tavernier took a first-class bus ticket. Undoubtedly the rush hour would oblige you to do this if you wanted to be a punctual director.

Paul Tavernier appeared from time to time at the drawing-room door. An odour of the mortuary compounded of lilies and cold invaded the boudoir as he did so. "Is there anything you want, Inspector? Is the fire all right? Do you want some more coffee? Do you work day and night?" Belot thanked him and postponed the answers until such time as he had fully worked out his analysis. Besides, he said to himself, who can say if I have *all* the victim's papers here. They are presented to me with the best grace in the world, but the fireplaces perhaps do not only serve for keeping police inspectors warm.

There was one question which he did not postpone.

"In M. Tavernier's will . . ." he began.

"My brother left no will, Inspector."

Paul Tavernier looked straight in front of him, but he kept his head slightly averted so that his glance always appeared distant. Belot observed him and was surprised by his calm. He felt a sense of discomfort which he tried to attribute to the wood fire and the mortuary smell. In fact he was nervous. He did not like the letter which Picard had received. Nor did he like cases where the next moves were announced by their own authors. He was convinced that this letter had a specific object, but this did not rule out Picard's theory. There is nothing more specific than the aims of an obsessed maniac. Picard should not have alluded to the "killer of concierges." Belot stroked the scar near his Adam's apple, and wondered what had happened to him. Probably dead months ago in his padded cell at Villejuif. He, too, could have been described as young, rather smart, clean shaven, slightly above average height. Was the resemblance to be carried further? Belot began to fear it. "If my present murderer is as mad as that other one, I shouldn't be here. Perhaps he intends to finish off all the directors of Automobile Agencies? A fine way of spending your time during Motor Show week. . . ." However, doesn't he seem to regret his crime? I'm talking rubbish, thought Belot. I think I'm sleepy.

One phrase haunted him. "I expect to do better tomorrow. . . ." If he was a madman, tomorrow would not mean some day, in the future. . . . Tomorrow would be tomorrow, tomorrow Wednesday, tomorrow the 5th October, tomorrow which might even be to-day. . . .

Belot consulted his watch. A quarter to twelve. He decided to return to the Prefecture by a U bus . . . at least as far as the Champs-Elysées.

He tapped on the drawing-room door, caught sight of Mme Tavernier asleep on a couch in the dark, and took his leave of the brother-in-law.

"I shall be back tomorrow," he said. "I have left all the papers here. I've listed the most interesting ones."

"Quite right, Inspector," replied Paul Tavernier.

On the stairs Belot repeated to himself: "Quite right! Of course I'm right. I have no need of his approval or his solicitude. Not one question, not one comment! Had he expected me not to find anything he would not have behaved differently." Madame Colet's voice echoed in his ears: "You've found nothing, Inspector."

Midnight struck as Belot reached the corner of the rue Laugier at the same time as a U bus. It was the last one of the day.

Tuesday/Wednesday night: On the platform the bus conductor and Clairval, one of the young policemen from the Murder Squad. In the first-class compartment two passengers—a couple whose backs alone could be seen.

"You must have wings, Chief," said the young policeman. "It's not five minutes since I phoned."

"Where did you phone, Clairval?"

Clairval looked at him astonished.

"I'm not in the picture. I'm here by chance," said Belot. "Tell me, I'm listening."

Clairval motioned with his chin to the couple.

"This is the fourth time in eight hours that they've taken this bus, and the other boys have had them, too. Better still, when they arrived just now at the terminus they didn't even get out. I think the fellow's having a doze, but the woman said to the conductor: 'Do you mind if we stay on the bus, I left my powder compact at a friend's.' Since M. Picard told us we should probably have to deal with a madman, I said to myself: 'This time, since it's the last trip, the conductor and I will prevent them leaving the bus until it gets to the garage.' I phoned H.Q. to send me some reinforcements."

He did not take his eyes off the backs of the couple.

Suddenly he burst out: "That little woman's got a nerve. Forgotten her powder compact! Look what she's doing."

"Good Lord," said the bus conductor.

Belot began to laugh. Then putting on a straight face he entered the compartment and sat down opposite the passengers. "Good evening, *madame!*"

"Good evening, Inspector," replied Mme Colet. She finished powdering her nose and glanced at her husband who was asleep with his hands on his stomach and his mouth wide open. "You must excuse him," she said, "he's so tired."

"He is excused," said Belot, "but I don't excuse you."

A look of innocent surprise was turned upon him. Grey-blue eyes, Belot said to himself. "Yes, you," he repeated, still frowning. "How many journeys have you forced poor M. Colet to make?"

"Twelve . . . no thirteen . . . yes, this is the thirteenth." And she added to reassure him: "We did have something to eat half way through."

"Are you superstitious, *madame?*" asked Belot.

"Oh, yes," she replied with a shiver of delight.

"I'm afraid this thirteenth trip won't bring you any luck."

She looked surprised again.

"When I've got exactly what I wanted."

"What did you want?"

She gave a little nod which seemed like a greeting. "To see you, Inspector."

"You were almost brought to me escorted by two policemen," replied Belot.

25

"I realise," said Mme Colet, "that that would have been better."

This time Belot could not hide his surprise.

"But . . ." he began.

The bus took a bend at full speed, flinging him against the window, and also flinging Mme Colet against her husband. M. Colet opened one eye, breathed heavily, and fell asleep again. Belot, recovering his balance, said with a trace of disappointment: "This afternoon I thought I had found a collaborator and now, on the contrary, you are making my work more difficult. Everyone is working on you."

"Who, Inspector?" asked Mme Colet. She went on with a smile: "I know, you're going to say once more 'professional secret.' But I don't need a reply. The gentleman on each platform, he is the one we have been distracting from his duty. . . . But suppose we had done it on purpose? To prove to you that it's easier in a bus to spot a policeman than a suspicious passenger. That it needs *thirteen* trips —and the thirteenth under what conditions, an empty compartment which we refused to leave—to run the risk of being taken to the police station when two trips in the same vehicle would allow *anyone* to spot the detective on the platform."

"But you are not anyone, Mme Colet," replied Belot, "and you seem particularly interested in this case. What made you catch the U bus today?"

Mme Colet lowered her eyes like a little girl confessing to a childish prank.

"When we left you after our visit to the Gascogne Motor Company, I thought that the murderer might have left a clue in the bus. We walked down the Champs-Elysées as far as the Rond-Point. I waited for this bus—three passed before the right one—and we took it."

"How did you recognise it?"

"By its number, of course—the 197—and by its conductor. Fortunately he didn't notice us. He was talking to the passengers on the platform and behind him I spotted a man reading a paper. He didn't seem to be reading it very attentively. We went and sat down. When the platform was empty the man and the conductor had a conversation. As soon as a passenger got on they ignored each other again. This performance put me on my guard. At the Levallois terminus, my husband and I went to the café opposite and we saw the man go back with the same bus. The next bus brought another man who did the same thing. I thought: 'What a clumsy piece of work!' "

She cast a swift glance at Belot. He looked at her without blinking. "I persuaded my husband to agree to my little manoeuvre by avoiding yesterday's conductor who would have ruined everything if he'd recognised us. I was counting on sleeping at the police station and sending for you."

"And the clue?"

She lowered her head once more.

"No clue."

"And in the other buses?"

"In the other buses?" she echoed in surprise. "Why in the other buses?" A gleam appeared in her grey-blue eyes. "Ah, so something was found in one of the other buses. . . . That's why you posted your men everywhere. You are much smarter than I thought."

"May she be right!" thought Belot.

"You see how dangerous it is to take the initiative," he said gently. The grey-blue eyes clouded.

"One more question," he went on. "Since this afternoon we have been wondering whether the murderer could have been a foreigner. A Belgian, for example?"

Mme Colet thought for a moment. "No . . ." she said, "yet he had an accent, that is quite certain." She repeated the words she had heard. "A very good morning . . ." She rolled the "r" a little. "A very good morning, M. Tavarnier. He said Tavarnier, and rolled his 'r's'. It was an accent, but a French accent."

"From the Berri, Burgundian?"

"Something like that. What a pity I did not pay more attention. I'm usually very inquisitive. I shall never forgive myself."

"Oh, you shouldn't worry," said Belot, "your observations have already been most valuable." He looked out into the street, and said: "We've just passed Montparnasse. Where do you live?"

"At the Porte Champerret." She turned her head towards her husband. "I'll let him sleep as far as the Gobelins and then we'll take a taxi."

Belot stood up. "Until tomorrow, then, *madame*. I shall have a lot of questions to ask you."

The second-class section was now almost full. A funny business, he thought to himself. I've forgotten to watch the route, and I've not been noticing who gets on or off! The young detective on the platform was almost bursting with an anxiety that had grown during this interminable conversation.

"You can forget it," Belot remarked to Clairval. "These people are working with me. Nothing more you can do but carry on to the depot and meet the boys you asked for. Too bad if they give you a rocket."

His cheeks on fire, Clairval muttered: "I'll catch it back at H.Q. . . ."

"No, no, I'll explain."

"Well," thought Belot, as he stood on the pavement, "all in all, I think I'll go to bed. This trip has done me a lot of good. I wonder why?"

Wednesday morning: At the conference on the Tavernier case Picard was in a foul temper. He waved his arms, scratched his forehead, rubbed his hands, picked up a ruler, tried to break it, put it back on the desk, questioned everyone at the top of his voice as if they were strangers. The unfolded dailies were on his table, with *Le Grand Journal* in the place of honour. *In a bus of the U Line . . . an envelope has been discovered. . . . The Quai des Orfèvres. . . .* Belot was seated and the team of detectives who had worked on the bus route the previous night was standing behind him. Picard's fury gave them the appearance of a band of robbers after a raid. Truflot was writing in a corner, as unruffled as though he were on a desert island.

"I've had my bellyful of the Press," Picard roared, banging his forehead viciously. "I'm sick to death of journalists. I'm going to give them something they will remember all their lives. And I'm thoroughly fed up with the U Line. I'm fed up with employees who can't hold their tongue, and of all you band of bunglers who get spotted by a ridiculous little female! I suppose she too is going to tell it all to the newspapers."

"No," said Belot.

"I don't feel so sure about that. She ruined my plan and has the impertinence to teach us a lesson into the bargain. That's too much."

"Your plan. . . ." Belot interrupted gently. "*Our* plan."

Of the whole squad Belot was the only one, among the chief inspectors, who stood up to Picard's violence. He knew he calmed him down by thwarting him. The matter was all the more delicate in front of subordinates, and he never forgot that he was one himself. In short, it was one more thankless job to be done.

"Our plan," he repeated. "We concocted it together. That 'ridiculous little female' has shown that it wasn't much good. Let's get it into our heads that we're not infallible. Besides, even if she did distract the attention of our men we mustn't forget that *she knows the murderer*. She could have been more use to us than anyone if he had boarded the bus when she was there."

The inspectors nodded and shuffled their feet. Picard did not appear to have heard. He went on shouting—but not quite so loudly.

"You don't think I'm going to get the whole squad out on the U Line? Look at the ones who were there yesterday! There are as many again this morning. Well, what do you suggest? That they should wear false beards?"

"Of course not," said Belot. "The conductors. . . ."

Picard exploded.

"Ah, they're a pretty lot, the conductors! Naturally if we could count on them, it would be fine. But the fellow the day before yesterday couldn't manage to arrest a murderer he had in his grasp, and the one yesterday let himself be pumped, even though I had warned him. He's a disgrace to his company!"

"You're right," said Belot. "The company is an honourable one. I am sure that it will give us all the support we need. And if 'The Passenger' has spotted our men he will think when he sees they're no longer there that we've lost heart."

"We'll try it," grumbled Picard.

He swept the newspapers aside violently and seized a sheet of paper and a bundle of telegrams which he handed to Belot.

"Here's the lab. report on the letter. Nothing, naturally. Typewriter: Imperial portable, four years old, the first owner dead, doesn't figure in the articles for probate. And here are the first results from London, Amsterdam and Brussels. Nothing here either, nor at Gascogne Motors nor at the hotels where Tavernier stayed. Well, I won't keep you. Try and make today more profitable than yesterday!"

Belot went to the Murder Squad offices, laid the report and the telegrams on his table and took a large album bound in red morocco from the drawer. "What a beautiful album, he thought. I'm sure Tavernier didn't buy it himself. . . ."

In the waiting room—three dilapidated leather armchairs, a huge table piled with old magazines, pictures of numerous detectives and policemen who had died on duty or on the field of battle—Mme Colet was waiting for Belot. "Strange," he thought, "I didn't notice what a pleasant scent she uses when we were out of doors."

"My husband begs to be excused," said Mme Colet, "or rather I must apologise for him. He was still asleep when I left. We folk from the provinces find Paris very tiring."

"Perhaps M. Colet is allergic to buses," replied Belot. He placed the album on Mme Colet's knees and sat down at her side. "M. Paul Tavernier assured me that his brother did not possess any others. Apparently he was never very keen on photography."

"It's an expensive hobby. . . ." said Mme Colet, opening the album.

Belot felt the little shock of surprise which he had felt several times before at Mme Colet's replies.

"You find it expensive?" he asked.

"Not me, I was speaking of M. Tavernier. I love photography, particularly when the object does not move. I took a beautiful picture of the Palace of the Popes at Avignon."

"But . . . M. Tavernier?"

She made a face like a grown-up whose patience is sorely taxed.

"Well, he was economical, very economical. His wife said so. *Le Grand Journal* published the fact in big type."

When I think, Belot made a mental note, that Picard considers her "a ridiculous little female!"

Naked babies on bearskins, youngsters leaning against pieces of Victorian furniture, first communicants, boys and girls, schoolboys, a nun, zouaves and cuirassiers, couples on their wedding day, middle class youth surrounded by grandparents and parents, judges in their robes, colonels in gala uniform and civilians in frock coats. Beneath each picture M. Tavernier had written a caption in red ink: my grandfather Tavernier, deceased; my brother Paul at college; my brother Vincent at college; myself at college; Finette at school (this was his wife); Finette's sister; our old friend Dr Jay, deceased; etc. Mme Colet examined the faces, then read the captions, each time giving a nod of approval which could have passed for a greeting.

From time to time she thought aloud: "A pretty mouth." (This was a grandmother.) "Oh, how alike they all are!" (This was my brother Paul.) "Poor wretch . . ." (This was the victim.) "She is good-looking very very good-looking." (This was Mme Tavernier.)

Suddenly, the photographs changed completely. They were no longer portraits taken in professional photographers' studios in the classic form for which the album had been designed. The second part contained amateur snapshots of all sizes, stuck close to each other without a margin except at the foot where Étienne Tavernier had continued to write his captions in red ink. Hideous pages which Mme Colet began to peruse with a shake of the head. She suddenly looked up.

"What do M. Tavernier's brothers do, Inspector?"

"The eldest is the managing director of a company."

"A big company?"

"Very big, yes."

"What about the other?"

"Young Vincent? A very talented engineer, it seems."

Mme Colet thought for a second.

"Do you know what I think? You're going to find me rather silly. Never mind. M. Tavernier's life is like his album. It's in two parts, and the second part is not as good as the first. It's all right to sell mass-produced cars for the sake of earning a lot of money, but it's not very brilliant when you're the son of a judge and you've been to a university. You're not even a tradesman selling something you've made yourself. Like my husband . . . whether one sells furniture or cars. . . . But Raymond does not come from an extraordinary family, he left school at the age of twelve! Besides, he provides our suppliers with ideas: we sell a folding bed which came entirely out of his own head. You see what I'm getting at? The brothers have been more successful in following the family traditions: managing director of a company and engineer. What stood in the way of the third? Greed? Lack," touching her forefinger to her forehead, "of brains? Lack of character? You think I'm silly, don't you . . . ?"

When the grey-blue eyes took on this shy gentleness, Belot felt paternal and would have liked to put his arms round Mme Colet "like one embraces a daughter." He confined himself to putting a hand on the album which was on her knees.

"Exactly!" she said, "to work!" She bent forward. "And what work!"

Belot had already removed his hand.

"I don't think you're at all silly," he replied. "More than that, I think you're very clever. You help me to see clearly."

Without raising her head, she replied: "I should help you better if I found the murderer. But how small they are!"

Belot took a magnifying glass from his pocket. Mme Colet laughed. "Just like Sherlock Holmes!"

"Ah, I've caught you out. I was certain that you read detective stories."

"Oh, Inspector," she demurred, shocked.

Then she was silent, motionless for a long time before each picture. Belot, patient, felt a confidence such as no witness had ever given him. Half an hour passed. Pictures taken at the seaside, groups in gardens and on barrack squares. Suddenly Mme Colet bent forward still further, quivering: "Is it possible . . . ?"

4

Continuation of 3

And, therefore, the continuation of Wednesday morning.

"Yes, yes," repeated Mme Colet, "it seems as though . . ."

She pointed out a face among twenty others: Soldiers in battle dress in a copse, in two rows with arms grounded. Caption: *Remiremont (Vosges), Summer manoeuvres 19***. A hand up to her mouth, Mme Colet whispered, "The third from the left in the front row. Much younger, of course. And Tavernier's not there."

She was flushed and bit her lip as though she had just opened a Christmas stocking and found a gift which surpassed her wildest dreams of it. Belot took the album and looked at the photo.

"It's a pretty ordinary face."

"Not at all. I recognise it. I'm certain I recognise it."

"Good." Belot rose to his feet.

"Wait a moment," she said. "I want to go on."

"You can, but in about ten minutes' time. I'll just take the album to Records. We'll remove the picture at once and while you're examining the rest they'll make copies and enlargements."

"Hurry up," said Mme Colet. "Now we have proof that it is not a foreigner!"

The rest of the album provided nothing of any interest. As they turned the last page a clerk brought Belot all the photographs he had asked for, adding: "Nothing in the records."

"Madame," said Belot, "before showing you these enlargements I should like you to meet my chief, my friend, Superintendent Picard. I think he should express his gratitude to you in person."

"I'm quite satisfied with yours, Inspector. But of course I'm very willing . . . a Chief-Superintendent. . . ."

The "Chief-Superintendent" was able to receive them.

"Well?" asked Picard, as they entered. He appeared to have calmed down a little.

"Everything's splendid . . . thanks to madame," Belot replied. "This is Madame Colet."

Picard stood up. "Sit down, *madame*. I am delighted to meet you. I have already heard a great deal about you."

"In my favour, I hope," replied Mme Colet coyly.

Picard frowned. He was on the point of losing his temper again.

"In your favour . . . and in the buses. Oh, I'm not reproaching you. We said so at our conference; you taught us a lesson; perhaps we deserved it."

Belot laid the prints down in front of Picard.

"Mme Colet has recognised the man in the photograph."

"From the records?"

"No, from the album which belonged to the victim."

"Are you sure, *madame?*"

Mme Colet left her chair, went calmly to the other side of the table, took up an enlargement and examined it.

"As sure as anyone can be, but much younger, as I said before."

"Naturally," said Picard.

"And also," she held the picture up to a better light. "It's funny. There's something different about the expression. . . ."

"Enlargements are always a bit hazy," said Belot.

"On the contrary," replied Mme Colet. "It is this expression which seems more clear cut. Oh, I hardly noticed it in the bus! But his eyes looked to me more dazed, a little vague. . . . I may have been wrong."

Picard had recovered his good humour. He snapped his fingers, glanced at Mme Colet's eyes, and asking: "Does this smoke disturb you?" he stuck a cigarette between his lips and forgot to light it. Then he examined the photo in his turn.

"Peculiarities—none. That's a pity. Anyhow, the reply 'as sure as anyone can be' pleases me. So even if this fellow isn't the murderer, his photo seems sufficient to you to permit us to restrict our investigations. Truflot! Send copies to everyone in the building, with a note: 'Twenty years older, expression probably more vague.'

Copies to the Sûreté and abroad, particularly London, Amsterdam and Brussels . . . and to all the Gascogne branches."

"I'll deliver them myself to the Champs-Elysées and the Motor Show," said Belot.

"Not forgetting those infernal conductors."

"Excellent," said Mme Colet.

Picard burst out laughing and Belot smiled.

"It only remains for me to slip over to the Taverniers," he said, "and consult the brother, who was not very keen yesterday morning for me to take away the album."

"One can almost make out the regimental number," said Mme Colet. She seemed now completely at ease. "What are *records?*" she asked Belot. "Someone said to you as he handed you the photos: 'Nothing in *records*,' and you, Superintendent, you also spoke of *records*."

Truflot, who was telephoning the chief's orders stared round at Mme Colet. Picard answered good-naturedly: "Nothing in the records means that we haven't yet had this client on our files. A pity, but it does not detract from the optimism which you have aroused."

"And is M. Tavernier on your files?" asked Mme Colet.

Picard looked offended.

"These files are for the criminals, not for the victims."

"Yes, I see," said Mme Colet. "But I think that in an affair as strange as this one should suspect everyone, even the dead man. If I had not *seen* the murderer, I should suspect the whole bus. If my husband had not remained by my side, I should have suspected him. And if M. Tavernier was killed, he had something to do with it." She blushed. "You must forgive me, I don't hold with the maniac theory."

Picard, astounded, shot at glance at Belot who looked back at him as much as to say: "You see what I mean?"

"Madame Colet," he said, swallowing hard, "it is our custom to collect information and not to give it. But M. Belot is right: a witness like you isn't to be found every day." He coughed to stifle a last vestige of hesitation. "So I'll tell you that M. Tavernier is not on our files either."

Wednesday midday: The candle flames rose straight in the icy air of the drawing-room, as if they were aware of being a symbol, and heedless of bringing the least aid to the living. The flame lit the flowers on the coffin and the white crucifix, leaving the rest to the darkness. "Darkness at noon," thought Belot, "it's a good definition of death." A corpse always appeared to him as an element of his profession, an object to study, a point of departure. The obsequies always disturbed him. But above all he felt a grudge against Paul Tavernier for receiving him here in this cellar-like obscurity to examine the photo of a criminal! Paul Tavernier had, it must be added, apologised for it. "My sister-in-law has only agreed to take a little food if I kept the vigil by our poor Étienne." An inadequate excuse. Without leaving poor Étienne, he could have opened the door of the boudoir and taken advantage of a strip of daylight. Standing by one of the candles, black as a notary of olden days, Paul Tavernier put on his horn-rimmed glasses and examined in turn the snapshot from the album and the enlargement. Had a breath of wind blown the flame in his direction it would have singed his hair. From time to time it fluttered like a brief sigh of death when Paul Tavernier peered through his spectacles at the enlargement of the photo. Then it became motionless once more, like the other candles and the two men—one who looked and one who waited. Paul Tavernier broke the silence.

"What did you say, Inspector, that my brother had written underneath . . . ?"

"Remiremont (Vosges) summer manoeuvres 19**."

He removed his glasses.

"The year fits," he said drily. "My brother did his military service at Epinal and it is quite possible that the summer manoeuvres took him to Remiremont. It is a detail which has slipped my memory. Our father had just died. Being the eldest and the only one of his three sons to have obtained his majority, I had to help our mother sort out a rather difficult estate. Poor Étienne obtained leave for the funeral, but then went back. Are you sure that this is a photo of the young men of his regiment? He is not in it in any case."

"Do you recognise anyone?"

Paul Tavernier put on his glasses again and looked at the enlargement once more. The flame flickered. Belot could not refrain from uttering the thought which had obsessed him since the beginning of the interview.

"You can't see properly, monsieur?"

"Yes, yes, perfectly well, Inspector!" Paul Tavernier replied swiftly. "But no, I don't recognise anyone. . . ."

"This man?"

"No more than the others, really, I doubt . . ."

"One thing of which there is no doubt," said Belot, "is that one of these soldiers, one *at least*, was a friend of your brother's. Otherwise why should this picture be in his album?"

"That's true," said Paul Tavernier.

"Did your brother have any friends whom you did not know?" Belot asked casually. "I seem to remember your sister-in-law saying you knew everything about him."

Paul Tavernier removed his glasses once more and answered loftily.

"By and large it's true, but a friend of that period . . . I repeat, Inspector, that I had other worries at the time."

Belot seemed to accept his reply. Staring at the flowers on the coffin he murmured as though thinking aloud: "And yet it would appear that your brother cannot have forgotten the friend in question so quickly that no one in your family heard anything about him."

Paul Tavernier pointed to a chair. "Sit down, Inspector." He sat down himself. "I don't follow you."

"Let me explain. The album is divided into two parts according to the type or rather the quality of the photos."

"Really? I didn't notice it."

"Now in the first part there are photos which are *later* than some of those in the second part. For example, the photo of the wedding. You told me that your brother got married several years after doing his military service. However, in the second part of the album we find close to the group which is bothering us, other scenes of his soldier's life in which he himself figures."

Paul Tavernier sought on the coffin for somewhere to put down the prints he was still holding. He realised the enormity of the gesture and held them out to Belot.

"I am still not with you, Inspector."

"I take it," Belot went on, "that your brother filled his album not *as and when* he got his photos, but at a period when he already possessed a certain number. In consequence when he pasted in the one of Remiremont, it was because he was still interested in it despite the years. . . ."

Paul Tavernier repressed a smile.

"My compliments, Inspector. And so I should have been familiar with it."

"Precisely."

"Well, I'm sorry, I don't know the man."

"Even if I were to tell you that he has a Berri or a Burgundian accent?"

Paul Tavernier gave a slight start.

"You already seem to know a lot about him!"

A candle flickered. He continued in a low voice:

"But it still doesn't help me."

There was a silence which he hastened to break.

"May I in turn ask you what is perhaps rather an impertinent question?"

"By all means," said Belot. (A question at last! he thought.) "About this photograph?"

"Yes," Paul Tavernier breathed slowly. "I suppose it was one of the passengers in the bus who identified it. How on earth in the turmoil caused by this incredible murder could he . . . ? and with a lapse of twenty years!"

"For fear of a mistake, would you suspect anyone else?"

Paul Tavernier shook his head vigorously.

"Alas, no! I have racked my brains night and day since the day before yesterday. . . ."

"Any more questions?"

"The morning papers speak of an envelope found in a bus of the U Line and addressed to the police. Obviously it has a close connection with the murder of my brother? This torments both my sister-in-law and myself."

He's calm enough for a tormented man! thought Belot. "Yes, monsieur," he replied. "But I have orders to remain silent on this matter, at least for the moment. It may be the work of a practical joker."

Tavernier bowed. "Well, I won't insist then."

You never do insist, thought Belot. You are really very discreet, and he wondered: suppose the letter threatened Mme Tavernier or a member of her family? Suppose it threatened this brother who

38

does not inspire me with much confidence, and whom the murderer is perhaps planning at this moment to lay in a coffin beneath a crucifix and flowers with candles round him like poor Étienne? He said aloud: "I shall merely add that until the day we discover the culprit it is best that M. Tavernier's family should remain on guard."

For the first time since the beginning of their conversation, Paul Tavernier peered intently at Belot. "I shall see to it, monsieur," he replied.

Wednesday afternoon: Mme Tavernier did not recognise the face on the photo any more than her brother-in-law had done. Belot left her a print so that she could show it to all her friends and relations. He announced that after due consideration he preferred to take away with him now the papers he had sorted out the night before. He added M. Tavernier's army pay book to the others.

At a quarter to two Belot finally left the Boulevard Gouvion-Saint-Cyr. After a quick lunch he went and showed his pictures to young Roux and the employees at the Gascogne showrooms, and to M. René Gascogne at the Gascogne stand at the Motor Show. Result: nil, zero, a blank. He was not unduly surprised. If anyone knows something, I am certain it is the brother, he thought. I'll find some way of making him talk.

He decided to return to the Prefecture. He now needed a larger blow-up of the photo which would reveal the regimental badge. . . . M. Tavernier's or someone else's regiment. After twenty years not all the officers or N.C.O.'s would have disappeared. It only needed one of them to have a good memory! But as he was about to enter the courtyard of the Quai des Orfèvres the first complication in the Tavernier case appeared in the shape of a tall, thin, shaky old man who said to him: "Excuse me, sir, is this the *Police Judiciare?*"

5

Continuation of 3 and 4

"Who do you want to see?" Belot asked.

"I don't know, sir, no one," groaned the old man, growing even more shaky. "I've just come from the Chaussée d'Antin Police Station. I was told to report here and that they would phone through to announce me. I did not want to come, sir, but they are probably expecting me."

"Is it serious, then?" asked Belot.

He took the old man's arm to help him walk more quickly. The old man shook him off in terror.

"Don't touch me. I have nothing to do with it, I swear to you. I'm terrified of the police. The lock up! Interrogations! Judicial errors!"

"But who has accused you of anything? I don't even know why you've come. There are the stairs . . . go up on your own. The duty officer up there will tell you what you want to know."

The panic-stricken old man protested. "No, sir, not on my own! With you, sir, with you!"

"All right then," said Belot. "Come with me."

"It's my boss who has disappeared," groaned the old man as they climbed the stairs. "What can have happened to him? It must be someone who was in the know! Think of it! With a mint pair of one-franc vermilions."

"Tut, tut," said Belot. "Calm yourself, calm yourself. I can see that you are very upset, but if you want the police to help you, you mustn't ramble on like this."

"Yes, sir, thank you, sir, oh dear, oh dear! You're very kind. You're not a policeman, are you?"

"Yes, I am. But I'm very kind all the same."

When they reached the floor of his department, he took him to the main office from which led two doors—Picard's on the left and on the right that of the High Commissioner, M. Malebranche.

"Here you are, I'll leave you here."

"No, sir, no!"

The old man appeared on the point of collapse. Helping him into a chair, Belot said to the clerk: "Apparently the Chaussée d'Antin has telephoned to announce this man's arrival."

"That's right," said the duty officer. "The Chief wants to see him as soon as he arrives."

"Well, he's all yours. I have no time to mollycoddle him. Get on with it."

He went to order his photos, returned to the office, sat down at his table and opened the package containing M. Tavernier's papers. Apart from the identity of the mysterious soldier, Belot was preoccupied with the victim's banking account. He was becoming more and more convinced that money must play a major role in the case. He also needed to know more about Paul Tavernier and the whole family. Another question suddenly crossed his mind—and he had waited forty-eight hours to ask himself it! What of the taxi which had been involved in a collision at the moment Tavernier was shot? Had this any connection with the crime, apart from being a miraculous piece of luck for the criminal? Was it possible that he had killed quite openly without taking the slightest precautions to cover his escape? Admittedly the opening of the Motor Show, the teeming crowd that day in the Champs-Elysées and the traffic jam gave him an excellent chance of vanishing into thin air, but the risks were still very great. They would be lessened considerably had the criminal with the help of one or several accomplices organised an accident like the one that had taken place.

Belot jotted down in his notebook:

1. Identity of the soldier.
2. Tavernier: a) bank account
                b) brother Paul
                c) the others
                d) How the victim normally spent his day.
3. Check: a) driver of the damaged taxi
                b) driver of the truck in collision.

"It's too much for me on my own," he thought. "I must ask for some help."

On his way to Picard's office he ran into the duty orderly.

"The chief's asking for you, M. Belot."

"What have you done with the jittery old bloke?"

"He's still there."

Good God! thought Belot. Could he have something to do with "The Passenger"? Could this be the follow-on to the letter?

When he entered the office the old man recognised him, looked up at him with a martyred air and muttered:

"Things aren't too bad. . . ."

"I don't know whether you will agree," said the Superintendent.

Belot noticed from the start that Picard was controlling himself to avoid increasing the old man's panic; but he was biting his nails and sniffing and his staring eyes boded no good. Belot sat down.

"Now," Picard said to the old man with an extraordinary smile of entreaty, "you're going to repeat your story very quietly, aren't you, without getting excited? Chief Inspector Belot is a very nice man."

The old man shivered before replying:

"That doesn't surprise me."

"You're lucky," said Picard. "Are you ready?" he asked, turning to Truflot.

Truflot nodded, delighted to look over a statement which he had taken down with much difficulty. Interspersed with groans, oh dear's and terrified glances, the second version was directed to Belot.

"Well, sir, you see my boss disappeared this morning! M. Verdon. M. Maurice Verdon, a stamp dealer, in the rue de Châteaudun, at the corner of the rue Taitbout. You must know it. He disappeared with more than a hundred thousand francs worth of goods on him.[1]

Belot realised that what he had taken for a jumble of words on the stairs had some meaning.

"Are you his only employee?"

The old man neighed: "Don't bring me into it, please sir! Don't bring me in!"

"All right," said Belot hurriedly.

[1] Francs of the Poincaré Government.

42

"Don't bring him into it and above all don't let's get excited. Don't let's get ex-ci-ted," said Picard, on the point of exploding. "Now, be a good fellow, Longspès, and tell us *as friends* what happened this morning."

"M. Verdon arrived at the office about ten o'clock as usual. 'Octave,' he said, 'I'm not staying. I'm going to see M. Musard and M. Archer. M. Musard has a few rarities to offer me and you know why I'm going to see M. Archer.' Just like that, sir, he said it. Just like that."

"Now, you must explain what it was all about," said Picard suavely, "and you must forgive M. Belot, he is no more a philatelist than I am. . . ."

"Pardon me," protested Belot, "if I had the money. . . ."

Picard gave him an approving glance. M. Longspès heaved a long sigh.

"Ah, so much the better, sir, so you'll understand at once! M. Verdon had received a marvellous item from London. A real marvel! A mint pair of the one-franc vermilion, quite unique. Used pairs have turned up, but never a mint pair! I have been forty years in the trade and this was the first time I saw a mint pair and was able to handle it. It was in perfect condition. Absolutely mint. The colour was very vivid and it had huge margins."

Belot began: "The issue of this one-franc vermilion was . . ."

"The 1849 Ceves issue. The first French set of stamps issued on January 1st, 1849."

"And its value?"

"Unused about 20,000 francs. This is the same price as a used pair, but you see a mint pair, which is unique, is naturally worth far more than two unused stamps, far more than twice 20,000 francs. It's quite simple. M. Verdon was going to sell this stamp to M. Archer this morning for 55,000 francs. This morning! The business was settled on the phone last night, dear, oh dear. . . ."

"Well done, M. Longspès, well done," said Picard, nodding his head energetically. "Now tell us quietly, some details of the other stamps that M. Verdon carried on him."

"Some Empire tête-bêche pairs, sir. They had also arrived from London. Since you are interested in stamps"—the old man was still addressing Belot—"you will know that M. Verdon specialises in France and the French colonies."

"So I've heard," replied Belot, without looking at Picard.

"He's not had his own business for very long. He learnt the trade with Ibert and Bélier. He started on his own two years ago and took me on. I was considered too old at Ibert's. But they would like to have kept him. What was I saying? Oh, yes, some Empire tête-bêche, 80 + 80 pink, value worth about fifteen thousand, the same carmine, about twenty-five thousand with a few other trifles . . . certainly more than a hundred thousand francs worth."

"Very, very well done, M. Longspès!" repeated Picard. And turning to Belot! "Very well done, isn't it?"

"Perfect," agreed Belot. "You told us that before seeing M. Archer . . ."

Longspès protested. "I didn't say it, it's the pure truth! From Musard's M. Verdon telephoned to M. Archer. Mind you, I warned him! What with all the things that happen every day, the thieves on one side and the police on the other, people never take enough precautions! M. Verdon should have gone direct to M. Archer's!"

"Do you suspect anyone?" asked Belot.

Longspès neighed once more.

"I was waiting for that. I was certain I should be accused of suspecting somebody!"

Picard cast a furious glance at Belot. "You must forgive him," he said in a filial voice. "Blow your nose, M. Longspès. Blow your nose, and go on please."

Longspès blew his nose.

"Yes, I will." He blew his nose again. "Yes, it's true, it clears the head. I don't know where I'd got to. Oh, yes. M. Verdon shouldn't have gone via Musard. But he wanted to see what Musard would offer, and at the same time, damn it, to show him the jewel."

"The jewel," echoed Belot, at a loss.

"Don't interrupt!" said Picard, rapping the table. "The jewel, the pair of—what's its name—one-franc vermilion. Well done, M. Longspès, go on!"

For a moment Belot, despite his exemplary patience, felt irritated. Picard would certainly not have forced him to listen to this interminable testimony had he not believed that it was somehow tied up with the Tavernier affair. But how? There were so many things which needed his attention elsewhere which were neither simple nor attractive.

"So my employer left," Longspès went on. "At one o'clock, I had lunch. M. Verdon allowed me to bring my food to the office because I live in the suburbs with my sister . . . but don't let's talk about me."

"No, no," said Picard.

"At one o'clock the telephone rang. It was M. Archer. 'Hello, I want to speak to M. Verdon.' 'M. Verdon isn't back yet, M. Archer,' I replied. He repeated in a surprised voice: 'M. Verdon not back!' 'Did he leave you a long time ago?' I asked. Then he replied, and this is when I began to be frightened: 'But he never came!' I asked his permission to sit down. He replied: 'Please do. I share you anxiety.' You can imagine after that I told him about M. Musard. He replied: 'I know, M. Verdon even telephoned here from Musard's, before I arrived.'"

"If it's not too much trouble, M. Longspès," said Picard, "please explain to M. Belot where these gentlemen were to meet."

"They were to meet at the Café de Marigny, you know? The philatelists café."

"Near the Stamp Mart," said Picard.

"I know," said Belot.

Picard persisted. "A stone's throw, therefore, from the Rond-Point of the Champs-Elysées."

"Aren't you going a bit fast?" asked Belot.

"You'll see. Now tell us the end of the story, M. Longspès."

"What end?" asked Longspès, whose voice had become more and more quavering. "Oh, yes, M. Verdon had telephoned therefore to M. Archer at the Café Marigny, and the proprietor told him that M. Archer had not yet arrived. M. Verdon had replied: 'All right, then I'll come along at my leisure.' The manager repeated this to M. Archer when he arrived, and this is what M. Archer told me on the phone. M. Archer waited half an hour, an hour, an hour and a half. Oh dear, merely telling the story. . . ."

"One more effort, Monsieur Longspès," beseeched Picard, "you've nearly finished. . . ."

"That's easily said, sir, I'm so frightened! Well, M. Archer then decided to telephone Musard. Musard said to him (this is what M. Archer repeated to me later): 'M. Verdon left five minutes after

45

his telephone call for the Café Marigny!' They had even joked, it seems, about the most convenient bus to take to the Rond-Point."

Belot looked at Picard who now had his eyes lowered.

The old man's voice grew more indistinct at each phrase.

"Musard replied that there were three, the D, the U and the U bis. He had even added with a laugh, 'Sir, you had better take the D, the U is not safe at the moment!' And M. Verdon replied: 'It's the U I want to take, and if it comes first I shall take the U.' *Mon Dieu, Mon Dieu!*"

"I'm not interrupting you, M. Longspès," said Belot. "I simply want to know—where is M. Musard's shop?"

"Boulevard de Courcelles, sir, near the Place des Ternes." The old man wriggled in his chair.

"That's it. . . . And so M. Archer telephoned M. Longspès," added Picard gently. "Learning that M. Longspès had not seen his boss again, he jumped into a taxi and arrived at the rue de Châteaudun."

Longspès sobbed and nodded his head.

"He put forward the suggestion that M. Verdon might have had an accident. He telephoned several hospitals and even phoned the Morgue. No trace of Verdon. He then took M. Longspès to the nearest police station, the one in the Chaussée d'Antin."

"I didn't want to go there, sir. No, I didn't want to go there!"

"The allusion to the U," Picard went on, "struck the men at the police station and the Superintendent himself telephoned me. M. Archer wanted to accompany M. Longspès here but he had a business lunch."

Belot was watching Picard with increasing surprise. "Perhaps M. Longspès could rest for a moment in my office?" he said.

As soon as Truflot had shown the unfortunate trembling old man out, Belot folded his arms.

"So, that's the whole story? A M. Verdon has been missing less than half a day and because before disappearing he joked about the U the local police feel entitled to put the wind up the head of the Murder Squad who immediately gets in a flap. As a result I lose an hour when I have enough work for four. *Bon Dieu*, the disappearance of M. Verdon is very interesting, I agree, and a hundred thousand francs even in postage stamps is always one hundred thousand francs, but everyone has his job to do and mine is the Tavernier case."

"That's not true," cried Picard. "Don't make me even more angry than that old clown has done already. Your case is *not* the Tavernier case! It's the U case! Which *begins* with Tavernier but *continues* with a letter! And follows on with a *second letter!*"

"What?"

"Quite so. And this time it was not left in a bus like the first one. Nothing so stupid! It was sent *through the post to the Chief at his private address!* Delivered this morning with the eleven o'clock mail! Have a look at it!"

Belot looked. The paper and the way the address was set out, were similar to the first envelope. This one was addressed to:

> M. Malebranche,
> Chief of the Police Judiciare,
> 63 Boulevard Saint-Germain,
> Paris.

It was postmarked: Late collection from No. 71 Post Office at the Place Victor-Hugo and bore only a postage-due stamp.

The letter was couched as follows:

> An envelope without a stamp! A riddle, Monsieur le Directeur, for your colleague Picard and yourself. You will soon know the answer.
>
> And I hope that the stamp will behave itself.
>
> > (*Signed*) The Passenger on the U.

"Now do you understand?" asked Picard.

"Yes," said Belot. "Has Longspès seen the photo of the soldier?"

"He has, no luck, of course. . . ."

6

The police investigate

In the course of the next hour a council of war was held in the Chief Superintendent's office. M. Malebranche had summoned Picard, Chief-Inspector Belot, Chief-Sergeant Gaillardet, and Sergeants Beauchamp and Vilain.

"I don't like this case any more than you do," remarked M. Malebranche. "It's assuming tiresome proportions, and what is more serious the murderer is making us look fools. A letter after Tavernier, and a letter before Verdon, both of which clearly reveal his cynical mentality. What sort of thug is he for M. Verdon not to put up any apparent resistance? No news of that bus, is there?"

"None. I telephoned," said Picard.

"What a pity that the conductors hadn't received the photo beforehand! Until proof to the contrary, I consider it our trump card. If the chap doesn't go to ground now, which would hardly seem in character with his impudence, we should catch him very soon. I'm relying not only on ourselves and our informers, but on the population of Paris. I think we should give the photo to the Press. 'The Passenger' has a taste for publicity and publicity will be his downfall. Any objections, gentlemen?"

M. Malebranche directed the question to Picard and Belot.

"The papers have made our lives a misery for the past two days," replied Picard.

"They'll have a chance to do something useful. One more thing, Belot. You can't handle this case on your own . . . this double case which tomorrow may have become a triple one. Take Gaillardet and make your own arrangements. You can also have Beauchamp and Vilain and as many men as you want. I'm poaching on your preserves, my dear Picard, but this case looks really grim. Speed is essential. I only hope that the new victim is not dead."

Belot put Beauchamp to work on the photograph and ordered Vilain to question the drivers of the taxi and the truck. He considered that it would be a mistake to pursue the Tavernier case alone and to leave the Verdon affair to Gaillardet. What he knew of the first case would perhaps allow him to discover more quickly than anyone else the link between them. On the other hand he would be glad of a second opinion on the Tavernier family, which would not disperse until after the funeral next day. Gaillardet fully approved of the suggestion and went off to the Boulevard Gouvion-Saint-Cyr where he was to announce the disappearance of M. Verdon. At the same time he would find out how M. Étienne Tavernier had been accustomed to spend his days.

In his office, where he had worked so pleasantly that morning with Mme Colet, Belot found an infuriated Longspès abusing Inspector Blondel, to whom Truflot had entrusted him.

"I am innocent, and this scoundrel accuses me of trying to escape? I don't want to escape, I want to go home, yes, I want to go home! Oh dear, oh dear, I am so frightened!"

Belot pacified him as best he could.

"I'm going to take you back to M. Verdon's office myself."

He beckoned to Blondel to accompany them.

"No," begged Longspès, "not him, not him!"

Nevertheless a quarter of an hour later the three men got out of a taxi at the corner of the rue de Châteaudun and the rue Taitbout. They were met by Inspector Assier, whom Picard had sent to watch the building after the old man had made his first statement. Despite protests from Longspès, Blondel stopped to talk to the concierge. Assier followed on Belot's heels.

M. Verdon had a well-appointed office on the second floor with two spacious rooms. Back in familiar surroundings, Longspès seemed to recover his calm somewhat. Nevertheless the mess tin with his lunch, still half eaten, on the sink in the tiny kitchen, drew a sob from him. He proudly pointed out his table, his files and albums of stamps. The rare items were kept in a safe. Longspès swore that he had no key and did not know the combination. The mint pair of one-franc vermilion and the Empire tête-bêche had been there the previous night.

Very cautiously Belot asked whether Longspès had noticed any signs of anxiety in his employer during the last two days.

"The day before yesterday, certainly not. But yesterday, yes, oh, yes! M. Verdon looked worried in spite of his newly acquired treasures. This was something unusual. He was always good-tempered, always ready to crack a joke."

M. Verdon arrived every morning about ten o'clock. (Longspès came at half past eight to clean and tidy the place.) Then he went to the salesrooms, to the Stamp Mart, or to see colleagues such as M. Musard, and clients such as M. Archer. He telephoned several times during the day and Longspès usually saw him again about six o'clock, before closing time. For his part, the old man sorted and classified the purchases, prepared the orders, received small clients and made a note of appointments with the important ones.

Belot spotted an address book.

"Our clients," said Longspès proudly.

After each name, the dealer had made a note of a country or a continent, showing to which part of the world his philatelic contacts were particularly attracted. Sometimes it was the whole world, signified by the single word: "General."

"What about his friends?" asked Belot.

"M. Verdon's private life does not concern me, sir," replied Longspès, huffily. "I only know M. Durand."

Belot's look of inquiry incensed him.

"Monsieur Durand," he repeated. "The United States specialist at Ibert and Bélier. M. Verdon's best friend. They are very close."

"Oh, yes, of course," said Belot. "What about the appointments, M. Longspès. Where did you record them?"

Longspès showed him a small diary bound in grey cloth. In it Belot found the handwritings of both clerk and master.

He examined the entries for the current week. On Monday, the day of the crime, M. Verdon had attended an auction room, the Frelault sale which, according to Longspès, had lasted the whole afternoon. On Tuesday, the appointments were spaced regularly from morning until evening. Wednesday—that very day—M. Verdon had made a note of his appointment with Archer and of another sale in the afternoon. The following days, further appointments, more and more spaced as was normal. Belot appropriated the address book and the diary, not without some protest from Longspès, then asked for M. Verdon's private address. It was in the rue Laffitte, no great distance away. Longspès had visited it two or three times the year before when his employer had 'flu. Since the death of his mother, M. Verdon had lived there alone. He was apparently a "confirmed bachelor." When Belot told him that he wanted to take him to the rue Laffitte, M. Longspès yelled that he wouldn't set foot there; that it would be a violation of privacy; that the police were worse than a disease and that he would lodge a complaint. Belot declared that in that case he would go without him, but that he would have to entrust the office to Inspector Assier, who would not stir from it as it was not out of the question that the enemy might attack.

"So you're turning me out?" shouted Longspès. "All right, I'll go and look for M. Verdon on my own."

"Where?"

The old man made a magnificent gesture embracing the whole world and replied: "Everywhere!"

Blondel had discovered nothing of interest from the concierge. For the very simple reasons that she was a personal enemy of Longspès but had a great respect for M. Verdon.

The two police officers went off therefore to the address in the rue Laffitte. It was a vast modern building, with a succession of courtyards and a maze of staircases.

"M. Verdon?" said the porter. "Staircase G on the fifth floor, the right hand corridor and the door ahead. No, I'm wrong: it's Staircase J." He reproached himself for forgetting because from time to time M. Verdon gave his little boy packets of stamps. Belot asked him a few details about the private life of the man who had disappeared.

"I can only tell you one thing," the porter replied emphatically. "He is a perfect gentleman."

He added that M. Verdon had lived in the building for eight or ten years. He himself had only been there for a year and a half. He recalled that Madame Verdon had died just before his arrival. He did not react at all to the photo.

"Well, let's go up," said Belot. "Here's my warrant."

As the porter walked on ahead Blondel whispered: "He couldn't possibly know everything that goes on in a great barracks like this which is obviously open night and day." If the stamp dealer received murderers or felt inclined to chase the girls, this chap certainly would not have noticed it!

The three men crowded into a narrow elevator which took them up to the fifth floor. A door which Blondel's skeleton key opened with ease. . . . . M. Verdon was a man of taste. He liked delicate furniture, and elegant eighteenth-century prints. Belot did not bother to see whether they were genuine. A well-filled bookcase with glass doors, a gramophone, records, a collection of pipes. . . . Papers in the drawers of a Louis XVI bureau.

"Take them out," Belot said to Blondel, "we have no time to examine them here."

Not a speck of dust to be seen in the first two rooms, which were silent as though asleep. The rooms of tidy bachelors, Belot thought, always give the impression of being unlived in. But in the third room, the bedroom, the bed was unmade. At five o'clock in the afternoon! Belot asked who looked after the flat. This time the porter made no mistake. "A pretty daily maid. She comes every morning."

"Well, she can't have been to work today," said Belot. "Blondel, you can clear up this mystery tomorrow."

"I'm always ready to get up early for a pretty girl," replied Blondel.

Neither M. Musard, not M. Archer, nor the director of Ibert and Bélier nor M. Philippe Durand was able to identify the photograph of the unknown man.

M. Musard sadly confirmed the pleasantries he had exchanged with M. Verdon about the U bus and praised his colleague warmly. He practically blamed himself for the disaster. But when Belot stressed the importance of his testimony, as he was the last person to have seen Verdon, M. Musard bridled. He was a ruddy-faced man and he now turned scarlet. He declared that he would not tolerate any insinuation that M. Verdon had not left him "safe and sound" and that he could later have met a hundred hooligans or a thousand murderers. Belot apologised, but not without asking whether anyone had witnessed Verdon's departure. One of the two assistants raised his hand. That's not very many, he thought.

M. Archer, very moved, recalled his anxious wait at the Café de Marigny. "He was such a punctual man, always so punctual!" He emphasised that M. Verdon was the greatest living expert on the stamps of France and the French Possessions. He praised his integrity, propriety and shrewdness. M. Archer had white hair, a magnificent house on the Avenue Montaigne and a passion for philately which his means fully allowed him to gratify. He put himself entirely at the disposal of the police.

"For that man," he said, "you can ask me anything you like. There is nobody I care more about."

Belot asked if they had any special reason for choosing the Café de Marigny as a meeting place.

"None, I like the atmosphere there and Verdon knows that I do."

The director of Ibert and Bélier asserted that their firm had never had such a talented employee. Since M. Verdon had gone into business on his own, they had continued to have the most amicable business relations with him. The junior partner, M. Philippe Durand, whom Longspès had called "the best friend," learnt the news with stupefaction. He was young, tall, bald and likeable.

"Verdon? Verdon kidnapped? On the U Line, like the recent crime? The man who reproached me one evening because I wanted to kill a mosquito? What sort of monster could have done such a deed?"

"It is to try and find out that I have come to see you," replied Belot. "I've been told that you were his best friend."

Durand nodded.

"His best pal, yes, I think so. Friend?"—He thought for a moment. —"A friend is a man you call by his Christian name, even when you address him politely. Verdon and I meet and joke and address each other as friends, but we are still Verdon and Durand to each other. Oh, Christian names would be all right by me but it isn't his way. Nothing secret or strange about him. No! A fellow who is fond of you but who can perfectly well do without you. With the ideas and the peculiarities of the confirmed bachelor, which incidentally are perhaps those of someone else—his mother for example. A mother is often more jealous than a wife and leaves a deeper mark on you. Madame Verdon wanted her son to herself, and she had her way. I met her through stamps. She too had a passion for them. She was almost friendly, but she did not hide from me that United States stamps did not interest her. The U.S.A. is my speciality. I got the idea and didn't go to the house again. Verdon and I always met outside. She died at the beginning of last year. He didn't want anyone at the funeral. And he is just the same as ever—gay, witty, full of life. Eating well, drinking hard, sometimes a bit of a rake, never too much! I'm sorry, all that's rather beside the point."

"No, on the contrary. Among the friends you went out with. . . ."

"We never went out except just the two of us, sometimes with girls," Durand blushed, "rarely the same ones. Every fortnight, every three weeks. . . . I don't think he went out anywhere else much. This year we made the time in between even longer, we met instead at midday. He went to bed early, and read a good deal."

Durand suddenly scowled. "*Bon Dieu!*" he exclaimed. "Why am I saying all this in the past tense? He isn't dead, is he?"

"I hope not," said Belot. "Did he ever talk to you about his family?"

"Never. I never imagined he had one apart from his mother. You would have thought that she had created him all by herself!"

Belot smiled. "When was the last time you saw him?"

"The day before yesterday at a big sale—the Frelault sale—which we attended together. He didn't buy much, but he stayed until the end. He was as cheerful as usual."

This eulogy did not prevent Belot, on his return to the Quai des Orfèvres, from telephoning the London dealer who had supplied the stamps which had disappeared with M. Verdon, to ask whether they had been paid for. "A long time ago," was the reply.

"None of this gets us very far," Belot muttered to himself. "There is no similarity between the two victims except their 'respectability.' Neither profession, mode of life, nor milieu—although one can care for cars and stamps at the same tme. And whereas a large family keeps watch over Tavernier's corpse, only strangers surround, so to speak, the disappearance of Verdon. On the one hand, presences around a presence, and on the other hand an absence around an absence. True no one knows so far that Verdon has disappeared. Shall we soon see a crowd of Verdons appear? Is the motive for the crime hidden in the papers we found at rue Laffitte? Has Gaillardet discovered at Boulevard Gouvion-Saint-Cyr that Tavernier and Verdon knew each other? Did Tavernier collect stamps? 'It would be too expensive,' Madame Colet would say."

"Investigate all the Verdons in Paris immediately," Belot ordered Blondel.

Sergeants Beauchamp and Vilain reappeared almost simultaneously, but Chief Sergeant Gaillardet kept them waiting. Their respective inquiries produced the following results:

Beauchamp: Identity of the unknown man.

The new enlargement revealed that the soldiers in the photo belonged to the . . . regiment of the line. This was not the regiment in which Tavernier had served, according to his pay book. The unknown man's regiment was stationed at Toul and not at Epinal. But the two regiments belonged to the same division, and in 19 . . the summer manoeuvres had brought them together in the neighbourhood of Remiremont. The War Office, which had given this information, had been asked to send the photo to Toul with a request for immediate inquiries to be made.

"If Mme Colet hasn't made a mistake," said Belot, "this is promising."

Vilain: Personal characters of the two drivers.

Louis Breton, 26, the truck driver, worked for five years in the Grands Moulins de la Seine, had never been involved in an accident until the day of the crime. His employers considered him an excellent driver. "I know," he himself had declared to Vilain "that one should always be in a position to pull up one's vehicle, but the taxi had just accelerated before putting on its brakes. I realise of course that it was an emergency. . . ."

More of an emergency than he had imagined. Indeed, the taxi driver, Fernand Camus, after waiting for his company repair van to tow away his damaged cab, had declared that he was going home to bed. He had not reappeared since. The company, thinking that he was ill, was about to send him its own doctor. It had given an address, in the rue Orfila, the same one the detectives had taken down from Camus's driving licence after the accident. At rue Orfila, there was no sign of Camus: he had left there four years ago.

"The fog begins to lift," said Belot. "Camus lied when he asserted that he had just dropped his fare before the murder. His cab was empty. I now see the murderer-to-be hiding in the back of the taxi, in the Boulevard Gouvion-Saint-Cyr, and lying in wait for Tavernier. Even if the latter had taken his car, the taxi would still have followed. Since he preferred to take the U, 'The Passenger' ordered Camus to follow the bus, changing into it in due course, and ordering his accomplice to cause an accident deliberately at the right moment. Possibly he did not yet realise that he would commit a murder, but this did not prevent him from taking precautions."

"Does the same apply for Verdon?" asked Vilain.

Belot shook his head. "No. We can presume that the U played a purely chance role in the Tavernier case. It was Tavernier who unwittingly chose the scene of his death. In the Verdon case things are not quite so clear. I think that this confounded route is no longer just the setting for a crime, but has become the murderer's *accomplice!* This sounds absurd, since we have no proof that M. Verdon did not take the D for example, but I can't help getting this hunch . . . this intuition."

Vilain, who was a fat man, replied diffidently: "The U Line. . . . Forgive me, but I can't see the connection. Do you mean to say that one of the conductors is an accomplice, or one of the ticket inspectors, or something?"

"I don't know what I mean," confessed Belot. "That is why my impression seems absurd to me as well. But I can well imagine the meeting! 'The Passenger' sits down next to Verdon, greets him as he greeted Tavernier. 'A very good morning to you, M. Verdon,' rolling his r's. And Verdon understands. . . ."

"Because in your view Verdon knew him just as Tavernier knew him?"

"After yesterday's letter—the one in the bus—it is difficult not to think so. 'I *expect to do better tomorrow.*' Had we published it Verdon would certainly have understood earlier. He would have complied with his wishes of which as yet we know nothing. As we did not publish it, 'The Passenger' had to set about things differently, and I'm in agreement with the Chief that he had no difficulty in getting his victim to go quietly. Verdon did not want to be shot at point-blank range."

"But would the murderer have had the nerve, a second time?"

"Perhaps not. But what mattered to him was that Verdon believed he would!"

"A second time and perhaps more! In his letter the murderer

56

does not speak of 'another,' but of 'the others.' His actual words were: 'I expect to do better tomorrow for *the others* and for myself.' We know now that he wasn't boasting and I'm scared stiff that he won't stop at a 'second' time. How do I know that this evening there won't be a third and tomorrow a fourth and that if Verdon hasn't been murdered actually in the bus it will have been done in some spot or other in Paris or in the suburbs, where we shall find his corpse one of these days. I can't wait to get the reply from Toul!"

Sergeant Gaillardet had arrived for the end of this conversation. "Have you finished worrying? Right! Now it's my turn."

Gaillardet: *The Taverniers' Timetable*

Mme Tavernier had quite simply fainted when she heard of the new crime on the U Line. Paul Tavernier had declared however that she did not know M. Verdon, and that he did not know him either; but his sister-in-law was at the end of her tether; she had been battling for two days to overcome her despair; she had been unable to bear the news that poor Étienne's murderer was still on the rampage. A little later, on regaining consciousness, Mme Tavernier confirmed her brother-in-law's statements.

Paul Tavernier had asked a mass of questions about Verdon. He appeared to be trying to establish or to confirm in his mind all the possible connections between the two cases. This curiosity had put Gaillardet on the alert but to no purpose. The dead man's son had indeed started a collection of stamps: from time to time he bought a cheap packet from the local stationers. It was nothing to go on.

A maid had then announced that Madame Tavernier was waiting for the gentlemen in her sitting-room. "Here was the opportunity," said Gaillardet, "to find out about Étienne's timetable."

Surrounded by members of her family, barely recovered from her collapse, "white as a sheet, but pretty as a peach," Mme Tavernier had talked. Her husband worked very hard at the agency. He left at half past eight in the morning, returned at a quarter to one, left again at a quarter to two and did not return for dinner until nine o'clock.

"We never went out in the evening," she added. "Besides, my poor Étienne did not care for the theatre or the cinema. I played the piano a little, he read his paper or played patience. We went to bed at eleven o'clock. Once a month he spent the weekend with very important clients who bought a number of the new Gascogne models. During these absences I occasionally went out, either with my mother and sister, or with Paul's family or Vincent's. We have hardly any friends. I also took with me my two children who live rather a dull life." Then she started to weep, as she said: "He was so cheerful on Sunday!"

Paul Tavernier had listened to her tale with the silent impassivity of a lawyer. Gaillardet had then discreetly questioned the persons present: Mme and Mlle Basset—Mme Tavernier's mother and sister; an old cousin, also a Basset; Mme Paul Tavernier, as formal and distant as her husband, and Mme Vincent Tavernier, the wife of the third brother who was absent. They had all seen the photo of the stranger but no one had volunteered anything of interest. But whereas the three Basset ladies, like Mme Tavernier herself, had expressed their distress in sincere and simple words, the two Tavernier sisters-in-law like the mysterious Paul, had shown themselves slyly contemptuous of the dead man. From the conversation it transpired that poor Étienne, a rather gloomy man by nature, had for some years now been in a state of deep depression. How many years? Mme Tavernier remembered exactly. Since the year their son, Jean-François, had taken his first communion . . . five years ago. Tavernier said he was worried about business.

"I've heard that mentioned already," said Belot. "What did you make of it?"

"Wait a moment," replied Gaillardet, "that's not all. On leaving them I went to the Champs-Elysées: I had a question to ask. What a crowd at the showroom! Those bastards don't miss out on their publicity! Above the Motor Show model, they have hung a photograph of the deceased draped in crêpe: "M. Étienne Tavernier, our late lamented director.' And you'll see the wreaths they'll pile on him tomorrow! Well, I spoke to the junior director."

"Young Roux."

"Yes. I asked him why M. Tavernier worked so late every day. He was amazed. 'So late? Why we always shut at seven o'clock and M. Tavernier left regularly between a quarter and half past six.' 'To go home?' He replied: 'I suppose so. M. Tavernier did not have to account to me for his movements but he usually told me of his appointments and he never referred to any when leaving of an evening.' I asked if the showrooms were open on Saturday afternoons. Yes. They were, and Tavernier went to work as usual for one Saturday a month. 'Why?' I asked. 'He used to visit relations of his in the country.' 'Not clients?' He laughed. 'Clients? What an odd idea! Our clients come to us!' 'Clients who might be friends. . . .' 'You must realise that in that case I should have known,' he replied. I asked: 'Were those family weekends a regular institution?' 'Yes they were, at least for the past five years.' I thanked him and came here as quickly as possible. Interesting, isn't it?"

"Very," replied Belot. "I am curious to see how Paul is going to deal with this contradiction."

"And Mme Tavernier!" replied Gaillardet. "It was Mme Tavernier who led me up the garden path."

"She was only repeating what Étienne had told her. He was not the first husband to tell his wife a fairy tale, or she the first wife to believe it."

Beauchamp sighed.

"Do you tell your wife fairy stories?" asked Gaillardet.

"No," replied Beauchamp. "It's her."

"And you don't believe them? There's the mistake. I believe everything my Hortense tells me!"

"The contradiction is even more interesting," said Belot, "since it may link Tavernier with Verdon. We know nothing about Verdon's activities after six o'clock in the evening! Everyone showers praise on Verdon, I agree, but . . . Could these gentlemen have met every day—either together or with 'The Passenger,'—plus one weekend a month?"

"A gang," mused Vilain.

"Why not?" said Gaillardet. "With the leader at present in the process of settling accounts."

Belot made a face. "It's a bit conspicuous. You don't usually settle accounts with such a wealth of publicity."

"Well, I don't know," replied Gaillardet, "Motor Show week! Unprecedented bargains! Perhaps there are others who have to be frightened. . . ."

The duty officer appeared with a note which he handed to Belot.

TAVERNIER CASE: PHOTO TO BE SENT TO GASCOGNE MOTORS: MAIN OFFICES AND BRANCHES IN PARIS (EXCEPT THE SHOWROOMS IN THE CHAMPS-ELYSÉES) AND THE SUBURBS. This photo has circulated everywhere from hand to hand, with no result.

Gaillardet yawned, looked at his watch and said: "Shall we go and see Picard?"

The Superintendent was not in his office. Truflot indicated the door of M. Malebranche's room.

"He's with the chief and the editor of *Le Grand Journal*. It seems there's something new."

7

Repercussions

Five minutes later the door opened and Picard appeared scowling.

"Truflot," he shouted, "get me . . ." He caught sight of Belot. "It's you I'm looking for. How are you getting on?"

"Slowly."

He made an angry gesture. "Come in."

Belot turned to Gaillardet: "Take Tavernier's bank book and leaf through it."

He followed Picard. M. J.-J. Rose, the Editor and Proprietor of *Le Grand Journal*, who was sitting opposite M. Malebranche, greeted him with a wave of the hand.

"Sit down, Belot," said M. Malebranche. "M. Rose has just brought me a letter, another one, the third, from 'The Passenger' on the U! This is getting too much. . . ."

M. Rose spoke with an affected tone of voice that was very unpleasant.

"Yes, it was delivered this afternoon to the porter of *Le Grand Journal*, who naturally can't remember who handed it in to him, they come in every few minutes. This one was marked 'Personal,' but with the exception of the subscriptions we are sent, all letters we receive are marked 'Personal.' You know of course that readers' letters come to *Le Grand Journal* by the ton. I have three secretaries busy from morning till night reading this 'personal' mail. The very few that are of any use to us are sent down to the editorial staff. Some of them are sent there without my even seeing them. There are hardly ten a month important enough to be sent through to my own secretaries."

"What about your friends, monsieur?"

"They know my home address. Or they use a code; my Christian name written out in full."

Malebranche and Belot smiled in spite of their preoccupation. Picard shrugged his shoulders.

"A code with the risk that someone might use it," he said, "without knowing it."

"No," replied Rose. "Because my initials are not J.-J. at all. My real name is Hippolyte."

Amidst laughter he took a digestive tablet from a small gold box.

"I have arranged," he went on proudly, "for all the letters left with the porter to be time-stamped, on the same principle as 'clocking in.' The machine, which I designed myself, and which is quite small, marks a serial number and reproduces a twenty-four hour clock on which the position of the hands indicates the exact time of the arrival. At midnight the date changes au-to-mati-ca-lly."

M. Malebranche handed an envelope to Belot.

"You see," explained M. Rose: "52847, that is the 52847th letter delivered to *Le Grand Journal* since the introduction of my gadget. The date, Wednesday October 5th, and the time, 15.25."

"There's a second dial," said Belot, "on which I can make out 17.53 hours."

"In red," M. Rose replied triumphantly. "That is the time when some secretary opened and read it. To which is added the number of the employee: 140. A chap called Basché."

"Hurry up and read it, Belot," said Malebranche. He went on talking to M. Rose and Picard in an undertone while Belot read:

"Dear Editor,

"Having twice written to the police, I am now writing to a newspaper, to *Le Grand Journal* which, as everyone knows, is the leading French paper just as Gascogne is the best make of cars (this comparison springs immediately to mind and I am sure will not displease you). I admire *Le Grand Journal*. It is worthy of its many readers. By a similar token it is worthy of my trust.

"The French police has been a great disappointment to me. Yesterday, using my usual vehicle, I sent a note of warning to the Chief of the Murder Squad, M. Picard, expecting it to be published in this morning's papers. It was not passed on to you. Without the amiable co-operation of an honest bus conductor you would have known absolutely nothing about it, a course of action as improper as it was ill-advised. It has obliged me to take certain measures which I prefer to divulge to you myself, in case the Quai des Orfèvres should maintain its silence.

"This morning—I have given the information to the Chief of the Police Judiciare, M. Malebranche—slightly before midday, a traveller on the U, M. Maurice Verdon, stamp dealer, was forced, thanks to my intervention, to disappear on my favourite section of the bus route: Porte de Champerret-Rond-Point. He put up no resistance, and is still alive. I am housing and feeding him. I do not know yet whether I shall have to dispose of him. . . .

"Why M. Verdon? You might just as well ask, why M. Tavernier? But the past can look after itself. It is the future which concerns us.

"Until Friday, the 7th October, the day after tomorrow, M. Verdon's comfort is assured. But I must think of my own. I am not really interested in rare stamps. They are difficult to get rid of. I need money immediately, that is to say within two days. Please acquaint M. Verdon's family and friends with the fact that a sum of five hundred thousand francs has become a necessity to me—necessary but sufficient.

"This money is to be left on tomorrow, Thursday evening, or more exactly during the night of Thursday to Friday, at the Gobelins depot where the U Line buses are garaged. The envelope containing five hundred well-used one thousand franc notes should be placed in the last bus of the last row—in the first-class compartment.

"These are my instructions. The man bringing the envelope should wait until the bus is driven forward by the cleaner to be washed under the full lighting. He will wait until the bus is washed and then place the envelope on the back seat. I advise him to go with the cleaner when he drives the vehicle back to its place. In business transactions unfortunately nobody is to be trusted.

"If everything goes well; if *no one* sets foot in this part of the depot until dawn, M. Verdon will be restored to his friends on Friday afternoon. But if the police should consider it their duty to spoil everything by their presence or trickery . . . then *so much the worse!*

"Two more points:

"(1) I have no accomplice in the Bus Company. I even suppose that the bearer of the envelope will come up against the strict company regulations which permit only employees to enter the depot. I appeal to the human feelings of those in authority to permit M. Verdon's friends to carry out their task unmolested.

"(2) An express letter from M. Verdon himself, addressed to his office in the rue de Châteaudun will confirm the terms of this letter. I should not like my proposal to be attributed to a practical joker or to a madman. *No more would he.*

"You are too great a journalist, sir, for me to apologise for having written to you at such length. The free contribution I offer you will enable you to increase your circulation tomorrow by several hundred thousand. Do not thank me, for we are both doing each other a good turn.

"Should you require any further information, you have only to mention it in your leader. I shall reply to you in time for the evening edition of *Le Grand Journal Soir.*

                    'The Passenger on the U.'"

Belot looked up. M. Malebranche turned to him.

"Well?" he asked.

Belot shrugged his shoulders.

"Neither a practical joker nor a madman. Does he think he's a genius? What have you decided to do, monsieur?"

"I'm publishing, we're agreed," said M. Rose, as if the question had been addressed to him. "This document, the express letter and the two earlier letters. I shall illustrate with the photo M. Malebranche has just been talking to me about and some other bits and pieces. I shall give the whole front page to the story!"

He added in his little finnicky voice: "It will be a bumper edition."

Picard made a gesture of resignation, which barely concealed his disapproval.

"What can you expect, *mon vieux* . . ." retorted M. Malebranche. "I don't mind our Passenger acquiring a bit of notoriety as long as it helps to hand him over to us immediately! He must be under lock and key before tomorrow night."

"What about the express letter?" asked Belot.

"Assier sent the concierge up with it," said Picard. "Here it is. Addressed to Longspès, and posted in the rue d'Amsterdam."

Belot recognised the writing, specimens of which he had seen at the rue de Châteaudun and the rue Laffitte.

"I suppose Longspès hasn't been told?"

"Oh, no. I sent Perraud to Bellevue to bring the old fossil in. We'll make him read it ourselves."

Belot thought to himself that Longspès at that moment would probably be half way across Paris and that Perraud would find no one in. But Longspès was not the one who mattered.

Poor Verdon's letter read as follows:—

"My dear Octave,

I have been told that you, and all those I am fond of, will soon know what has to be done for me in order for me to be set free. I know no more, but whatever it is, I beg you to see that everyone accepts it. I am not asking for a present. I am only asking for a loan. I will pay back everything! I am not afraid to die but I cannot endure what I am living through now.

M. Verdon."

"More trouble brewing," grumbled Picard, as he returned to his office with Belot. "First of all for the Bus Company. Make a note, Truflot, to get in touch with them at once. This ransom and the fancy set-up! I still say he's a madman. And all this publicity the chief is giving him! We shall look pretty foolish if some bumpkin catches him and we don't. Are you going to stand for that?"

"No, of course not," said Belot. "Let's get on with it."

He reported his visits to Verdon's office and flat, and to Musard and Archer; Vilain's check-up on the drivers; the fact that Camus was an accomplice; Gaillardet's visits to Mme Tavernier and to the Agents; the discrepancy in the accounts of Étienne Tavernier's timetable; and lastly the new information they had received thanks to the photo.

"Simple, isn't it?" groaned Picard. "And we've got to find the solution before tomorrow night! Who's looking for Camus?"

"Vilain's on to it," said Belot.

"What about Musard? Perhaps he had a rival's interest in Verdon's stamps. Did he look shifty to you?"

Belot pursed his lips in a non-committal way: "Shifty? No more than anybody else does in a temper. He doesn't add up to much."

"So it seems! Truflot, make some inquiries all the same about

Musard! Get Vilain to work on it and leave Camus to Malicorne —and then, Fred, while we wait for the reply from Toul about the photo, hurry up with Verdon's papers. The family, friends, everyone!"

"Just a minute," said Belot. "We can't possibly wait for the reply from Toul. Why not send Beauchamp there?"

"Truflot, get Beauchamp here at once."

"Are you going to send for Blondel, too?" added Belot.

Beauchamp, who had recently been promoted to sergeant, exhibited beneath his close-cropped hair a melancholy expression due, it was believed, to marital problems. He wrinkled his brow when anyone spoke to him as if he could not quite understand what he was being asked. He seldom spoke but he was a good worker.

"Hop into the first train for Toul," said Picard. "Tomorrow morning at the crack of dawn you must phone me with *full* and *precise* information about our man! I'll have your arrival announced by the War Office."

Belot looked at Beauchamp and said: "It won't be easy," in an encouraging tone of voice which meant, "It's therefore just the thing for you."

As Beauchamp left, Blondel appeared.

"Have you found out anything about Verdon's family?" asked Belot.

"Nothing," said Blondel. "I telephoned to three Verdons whose names are in the directory. They are not relations of his. I am going to make the rounds of all those who are not on the telephone next."

Picard fidgeted in his chair.

"But suppose he's only got married sisters! Off you go, Blondel."

"In any case," said Belot, as soon as they were alone again, "the morning papers will alert any possible members of his family. We shall still have a whole day to play with."

"You're an optimist," said Picard. "How far have you got with the Tavernier family? This discrepancy in the timetable—what do you make of it?"

"It's sending me back post haste to the Boulevard Gouvion-Saint-Cyr to get some explanations, a pleasant task in the final hours of a wake!"

"That's your worry. Truflot, get me Gaillardet. What was it you'd asked him to do? Ah, the bank account. I'll be neglecting my other cases if I don't watch out. This gentleman, 'The Passenger on the U' has practically mobilised the whole of the Murder Squad. I suppose you haven't a clue how we can get him tomorrow night at the depot?"

"Not so far," replied Belot. "But I'll go and take a look at the place. I hope we shall have got him before he gets there. I don't think I've done too badly in forty-eight hours," he added.

"Don't irritate me," replied Picard. "You're right. But for God's sake, don't irritate me."

Gaillardet announced as he entered. "Here's the account, Chief. A bank book begun three and a half years ago, nearly full. Very well kept and very accurate. For each withdrawal the number of the cheque on each counterfoil, the name of the payee and the details. There's nothing missing. The expenditure seems quite normal. When the cheque is drawn to 'self' or 'please pay cash' the detail is also given. On the receipt side it is even simpler. The first of every month, salary 8,000; ninety-six thousand francs a year. That's quite nice!"

"Ninety-six thousand?" echoed Belot in surprise.

"Yes, and he had quite a good credit balance over each year. Then there's the purchase of shares. I consulted Panigon. There's quite a big lump."

"Did you find the certificates?" Picard asked Belot.

"I found a receipt," said Belot. "Tavernier had deposited them with his bank. But what surprises me . . ." He turned to Gaillardet, "Were those the only entries you saw on the credit side—his salary?"

"And the share dividends, yes. Isn't that enough for you, ninety-six thousand francs?"

"Come, come," said Belot. "Tavernier not only got his salary— M. René Gascogne told me yesterday that *in addition* he earned a commission on all the sales in his branch . . . and in good years a bonus according to the company's profits."

Belot's irritation could be heard in his voice. Picard looked at him anxiously.

"What about the previous pass books?" he asked.

"I only found this one. I'll consult the bank tomorrow morning as soon as it opens."

"It's half past eight," said Gaillardet. "What about dinner?"

Picard gave a start.

"Half past eight? And it's my daughter's birthday! Truflot, get Madame Picard on the telephone. I must rush, I'll be back later."

"I'll have something to eat later," said Belot. "I really can't face arriving at the Taverniers after nine o'clock."

8

A *bad night*

Through the glazed door he could hear an angry cry of "For goodness sake!"

The "tuts" of indignation seemed to have set the candles flickering. A man burst out of the drawing-room. It was Vincent, the youngest of the Taverniers, the engineer whom Belot had seen the previous evening in a state of deep despair. He seemed totally unlike Paul or the dead man and appeared a very straightforward person. He went for Belot as if he was going to kill him.

"What do you want?" he asked. "Have you got the murderer yet?"

"No," began Belot, "I was just going to . . ."

"Going to what? Don't you realise what a nuisance you are being? We can't even gather round a coffin without the police coming and disturbing our grief a dozen times a day. Because you're not capable of arresting a criminal, you run amok with the victim's family, you plague my elder brother and my sister-in-law, you ask or make them ask the most treacherous questions. . . . Go away, sir, get out or I'll throw you downstairs! You can arrest me if you like, I couldn't care less!"

"M. Paul Tavernier. . . ."

"M. Paul Tavernier is asleep, my sister-in-law is weeping and as for me . . . I repeat, get out!"

Belot opened the door.

"You're wrong to judge us so harshly, M. Tavernier, but you at least . . ."

He left without completing the sentence. Tomorrow, he thought;

there'll still be time tomorrow. "The Passenger" will do nothing more until the time for the ransom to be paid expires.

The night was close and a storm was brewing. Outside the front door, Belot mopped his brow. "Odd," he said to himself, "yesterday up there sitting by the fire and today out in the street, these misgivings that I can't understand. . . . Could it be a madman after all?" Belot decided to go at once to the Gobelins Bus Depot to see what it would look like the following night if ill-luck willed it that no solutions appeared during the day. He had a quick meal and caught a U bus at a quarter past nine. He looked automatically for the Colets among the passengers. Mme Colet's smile would have done him good. Standing alone on the platform, he showed his card to the conductor.

"Anything new?"

"Nothing," said the conductor. "But we're keeping our eyes open, you bet." (From his pocket he took the photo of the mysterious soldier.) "I've got it here, you see. Is it true that someone has disappeared today?"

"Have you been told about it?"

"All of us! At the depot this afternoon. Pity we didn't get the picture earlier. But you know you can trust us. We'll do just as well as your detectives."

A passenger got in. The conductor scrutinised him carefully and although this face looked nothing like the photo, he did not talk to Belot any more.

A double iron gate opened on to a vast courtyard where the buses turned and reversed noisily to draw up in orderly rows like soldiers on parade at the far end beneath a high frosted glass roof. Just inside the door there was a small glass cabin which looked like a signal box. In the middle of the courtyard were the petrol pumps and a great open circle for washing the buses. . . . Very tall standard lamps cast a garish light on this entrance and the marshalling yard. The far end was in darkness.

A man in blue overalls came out of the cabin.

"I should like to see the foreman," said Belot, producing his warrant card.

"If you want the night foreman, that's me," replied the man.

"Pleased to meet you, Monsieur Belot. I'm Inspector Travers' cousin. My name is Champaine."

Belot smiled. "Your cousin's a splendid fellow, good to work with."

"I'm at your disposal. I've just telephoned the office. There were some reporters here just now. They told me something about a ransom in a U bus. Is it a joke?"

"Far from it." Belot gave him some details.

"But your murderer is completely crazy," said Champaine. "Nobody can enter here without being spotted, particularly after one o'clock in the morning. I lock the main gate and there's no other exit. It's dark, so you can't see it, but there isn't a single building over there with a window overlooking the depot. Come and have a look, Monsieur Belot."

They made their way across the courtyard beneath the light of the lamp standards. The cleaners turned away their hoses to avoid splashing them.

"We could have gone close to the wall instead of cutting across," said Champaine. "But it would have made no difference. You can be seen wherever you are."

Rows of buses with gaps here and there reached to the right of the garage proper, which was completely in shadow.

"This is where the U's go," said Champaine. "The empty places are for the buses which do not come in until one o'clock, or don't come back at all because they're in the workshop. We have to be able to see at once which are missing: for example, the third one in the last row—the one which interests you—hasn't got back yet, and neither have the two which go in front of it. They run until twelve, twelve-thirty."

Belot looked at the orderly row of buses in the darkness. Certainly, he said, a person could hide here and even play hide and seek.

The noise of the engines suddenly ceased in the courtyard. Nothing could be heard now except the jets from the cleaners' hoses and the sound of their voices. This false silence did not last for long. It merely increased the feeling of impending danger.

"Oh, no, Monsieur Belot," volunteered Champaine. "To hide here you would have had to cross the courtyard!"

"Or to have hidden in one of the returning buses."

"Oh, hell," said Champaine.

Belot thought aloud: "But in that case the conductor would have to be in the plot. As he would to get out again. Which might be possible on an evening when nobody suspected anything, but it wouldn't be tomorrow! Not when everyone has been warned! Besides, 'The Passenger' maintains that he has no accomplice in the Company."

"Perhaps he maintains whatever he likes?" suggested Champaine timidly.

Belot looked at his decent, anxious face.

"Of course! I've got to the point of letting myself be impressed by the audacity of this fellow, *I believe him*. Is there anyone you suspect?"

A bus had just reversed not far away into one of the empty spaces. The driver switched off the engine, jumped down from his seat and made his way across the courtyard without noticing them.

Champaine replied: "Anyone I suspect here? Not on your life!"

"Surely you can't vouch for *all* the drivers and conductors who pass through your depot?"

"There aren't any after half past twelve and I will vouch for my cleaners and my deputy—that makes seven chaps including myself, and I'll stake my life that they are all honest!"

"You'd better give me their names and addresses anyway. Any newcomers? Anyone standing in for a sick man?"

"No. We've always worked together here. We were on the trams before being on the buses and some of us, like myself, even remember the horse-drawn buses."

Belot sighed. "In that case I am unfortunately right to believe the murderer. He wants to act alone . . . and he wants us to let him! Do you know this man?"

Belot showed him the photograph. Champaine had already seen one in the hands of a conductor. He did not recognise the face.

When Belot put the photo back into his pocket, a thought entered his head which he kept to himself. Suppose the murderer had been acting on orders like the driver Camus? We have all believed that he wrote the letters himself. There is nothing to prove this. There may be a leader. . . . Between two buses the figure of Paul Tavernier seemed to hover. Belot could not suppress an angry gesture which surprised Champaine. I'm talking rubbish, like yesterday evening. Would he have murdered his brother and kidnapped Verdon?

Why not? There is nothing to prove or disprove it. These vehicles, these ridiculous vehicles! A dog would bark or groan and give me some clue, but these great stupid lumps! Let's admit, *he* had some good reason for choosing this incredible place, this setting, this problem fit for a thriller. The closed premises, the envelope stuffed with bank notes, the absolute impossibility of it disappearing. And could it disappear? No, no, it's nonsense! There's something behind all this which I can't put my finger on, something I must get to the bottom of.

"Sorry," he said, "I was thinking. I'll come back tomorrow in the daylight. How many U buses have you got here?"

"All of them. There are thirty in operation but they're not always the same ones, you know. When one of them is out of action it's replaced by any available vehicle. We just say where it's going, and stick on its letter U."

"I see," said Belot. "So that's no help at all . . . on the contrary in fact."

As they came back to the courtyard they saw a crowd of workmen had gathered round an employee. The cleaners had stopped their work to listen to him too.

"It's Mailly," said Champaine, "the conductor who found the envelope yesterday. He was summoned by the police this morning. I'd like to know what happened to him."

Belot recalled Picard's rage.

"I can tell you. He talked to the reporters when he shouldn't have done, and he got hauled over the coals."

"He's a decent fellow, though. . . . Don't you believe that he is?"

"I do," said Belot, without conviction.

"Oh dear," said Champaine sadly, "you're like my cousin, you don't trust anybody."

"That's what our profession demands, Monsieur Champaine."

"I didn't mean to offend you, Monsieur Belot! I know the work that you do in the Murder Squad. You risk your life. I'm not talking about you in the same breath as the cops nor with . . ."

"Come, come, no politics. Give me the list of your men and I'll see you tomorrow."

"Don't you want to see the men who have just finished?"

Belot shook his head.

"Nothing new will happen between now and tomorrow night, I'm quite sure."

Belot arrived at the Quai des Orfèvres at midnight. He had decided not to go home until he had gone through the Tavernier and Verdon papers. The corridor leading to his office seemed more full of echoes now that it was empty. From the far end the duty officer called out: "Monsieur Belot!"

He pointed with his thumb to Picard's open door. There was a sound of voices. . . . In the office stood an inspector of the Vice Squad, two men from the Bailiff's office and the chief himself. Truflot's absence spoke more eloquently of the late hour than any clock could have done. Picard seemed delighted.

"Good work here, Belot! These gentlemen have brought me some information on our Passenger. He frequents the Pigalle bars—cheap ones. He drinks like a fish and bets on the horses. (Picard consulted his notes.) His name is Oudart, Jean Oudart, forty years old, well dressed, often wearing the famous grey suit which he was wearing on Monday. He sports a grasshopper tie pin. That fits doesn't it?"

So, thought Belot, it was M. Colet who was right. He gave a little whistle of approval.

"It was the photograph which enabled us to track him down," Picard went on, "to the Hôtel Moderne in the rue Fontaine."

"Are we going to pick him up?" asked Belot.

Picard's mouth dropped and he made an expressive scoop of his hand.

"Vanished. *Since Monday*. Hasn't been seen anywhere, in any of the cafés or at the hotel."

"What sort of hotel is it?" asked Belot.

An inspector cut in with a grimace:

"Respectable. We've had no trouble there before. Small bedrooms but running water. When he saw the photo the manager thought it was a son of Oudart's which gave him a big surprise. And he even laughed at the uniform which he thought old-fashioned. When I explained matters to him he was positive. As for the dazed look, Oudart is under the table from morning to night."

"And not wine either," said the inspector from the Vice Squad with respect. "Nothing but whisky."

"Only," the first detective went on, "it seems he held his drink

74

well. The hotel proprietor told me: 'He's never drunk, just soaked.' He pays his bills promptly and has been there for three years. No visitors, no women, never goes away. The proprietor has been worried since yesterday morning fearing he must have had an accident. He had never thought for a moment that his client could be a murderer!"

Belot turned to the inspector who had mentioned the whisky.

"What about in the bars?"

"Good pals with everyone: the staff, the tarts, the bookies—yes, especially the bookies. Apparently spends money like water. He is not lucky, and excitable when he loses. But he drinks and then he calms down."

"How does he earn all this money?"

"Ah, that's the question," broke in Picard. "Oudart drinks day and night, and he never seems to have anything to do. On the police form he filled in on arriving at the Hôtel Moderne he gave his profession as checker. Checker of what? The proprietor said he imagined that he was a checker of weights and measures. I took the liberty of telling these gentlemen"—and Picard glared at the two inspectors from the Bailiff's office—"that their men should never have let such a form pass. In short, Oudart earns a mysterious living from mysterious sources."

After a moment the Vice Squad Inspector went on: "I visited the room. It wasn't my pigeon, but I thought it would help you." He said this almost curtly, as though in reply to Picard's reproach. Taking a notebook from his pocket he read: "Three suits, a dinner jacket, an overcoat, a raincoat, one pair of smart shoes and one pair of patent leather; linen with his initials on it, gloves—gloves that hadn't been worn—you know, flat and creased in the middle from being held in the hand, to give him an air. A fine pair of binoculars. A pile of copies of the racing newspaper Le Pesage heaped in one corner. Whisky, too. A notebook with figures and the names of horses but not a letter, nothing bearing his name. Eau de cologne and brilliantine, a packet of American cigarettes. . . . I'm afraid I jotted everything down as it came along."

He tore the page out of his notebook and laid it on the table.

"No need to apologise," said Picard. "If some day your services are no longer required at the Prefecture I'll take you on here." He scribbled a note and handed it to the inspector. "Before I let you go

I want you to do me a favour: give this note to the lab. Ask them to send someone as soon as they can to look for fingerprints—at once if possible. Can't be helped if the hotel proprietor grumbles at being waked up, the matter's urgent. Advise him to buy a copy of *Le Grand Journal* tomorrow morning. Well, that's it, thank you, gentlemen and goodnight!"

Picard winked at Belot and wrote two more notes, talking as he wrote:

"Telegram to Beauchamp at Toul. The name: Oudart Jean. This trip's not much use now, but it will at any rate give us confirmation. And secondly, circulate the name."

He called the duty officer, handed him the two notes and added: "Make it snappy!" Then he lay back in his chair and heaved a contented sigh.

"Your little Madame Colet did a good job," he said. "From now until tomorrow night, Monsieur Oudart would be better off betting on the races and forgetting all this talk of Gobelins depots and buses. Incidentally, talking of buses, the Company is appalled by the story of the ransom. They have sent us a plan of the garage. Vilain's inquiry into the stamp dealer Musard shows that his honesty is unquestionable. In any case things seem much clearer than they did an hour ago. Oudart is not a madman but an alcoholic. Same thing. He is constantly short of money. He can't get any the honest way, or else he has absconded with his colleagues'. After all, how do we know Tavernier and Verdon didn't gamble as well. Hence his reasons for killing, kidnapping and challenging. . . ."

Belot confined himself to remarking. "Do you really think so?"

Picard jumped up and grabbed him by the lapel of his jacket. "What does that mean?"

"I don't know, *mon vieux*," Belot replied wearily. "To begin with the fellow hasn't been arrested, and I smell something more complicated, and strange . . . I need time to think."

"What you really need is to go home to bed," grumbled Picard.

He returned to his chair and added almost timidly: "Do you really think so?"

Belot shrugged his shoulders.

"I hope not. It's true, I'm worn out, but I must go through these Tavernier and Verdon papers this evening. Well, good night. If I get any bright ideas I'll call you at home. Are you staying here for long?"

"As short a time as possible, but I've got other cases to deal with, you know. I'm going to phone the chief now."

"Are you giving it to the press?"

"Not on your life!"

At his headquarters Belot found Gaillardet sitting at his own table.

"I thought you'd be back," said the sergeant. "Two bloody hours I've been going through Verdon's papers! I haven't touched Tavernier's since you've already sorted them out."

"Well?"

"Nothing of interest. Some love letters with several different signatures: Nanette, Tototte, Cuddles . . . you know the type. They seem to be potty about the stamp dealer. No question of money, 'I love you, and I adore you.' Letters from his ma going back for years all done up in pink ribbon. Nothing from anyone else. Probably one of those chaps who tear up everything. . . . A few photos of women, including the mother. Insurance premiums, rent receipts. . . . As I couldn't find his bank book, I thought it must be at his office. I telephoned Clairval who has replaced Assier for the night: no personal accounts, but naturally some book-keeping. I'll go and have a look tomorrow."

"Did you compare the address book with Tavernier's?" asked Belot.

"They haven't a single name in common."

"No Jean Oudart in either of them?"

Gaillardet skimmed rapidly through the pages. "No. Why?"

Belot explained and went on: "Well, what's your feeling about Verdon?"

"An orderly man with a taste for the girls."

"No addresses on the letters?"

"Addresses on love letters! No envelopes either. Neither for their letters nor the mother's."

Belot spread Étienne Tavernier's letters on the table. Gaillardet handed him a note. "From Blondel. He's just been in."

Blondel had written: "Still nothing on the Verdon family. I'll try and see the cleaner tomorrow morning as arranged."

Gaillardet rose to his feet. "Goodnight," he said. "I have the feeling that tomorrow is not going to be funny."

Left alone Belot went on with the examination he had begun the night before at the Boulevard Gouvion-Saint-Cyr. Despite all the day's discoveries he found nothing new. Nothing which would shed light on the hours and weekends of absence nor the curious bank account. The names in the address books, the signatures of the letters remained silent. To make them talk would take a long inquiry . . . or the co-operation of the family. "That damned Paul," Belot muttered to himself.

When he got back he put the remains of the coffee on the stove. On bad evenings he drank it like an infusion to help him sleep. And although he tried to persuade himself otherwise, he knew that this was one of the bad ones.

9

Thursday, the 6th. From 6–8.30 a.m.
Le Grand Journal

To begin with it was raining.

Then the whole of the Paris Press carried lengthy reports on the double Tavernier-Verdon case, with the portrait of the murderer.

Le Grand Journal was in the lead. By an unprecedented tour-de-force M. J.-J. Rose had designed, printed and bill-posted during the night in all the metro stations throughout Paris, hundreds of posters—some of them enormous—showing a bus on the U Line speeding away from a question mark, with the caption: *The mysteries of the U Line. Today, October 6th, a murderer writes to Le Grand Journal.* Running through the streets, an army of newsvendors held the posters in front of them to ward off the rain. Sandwich men carried them on their backs and distributed a reduced version, postcard size. The city was in a fever within an hour. The small *Grand Journal* vans, normally sky blue, but today also covered with posters, kept the kiosks and the paper stalls supplied. The collective hallucination was so effective that each bus seemed to be a travelling advertisement for the articles in *Le Grand Journal.*

These articles were arranged on the front page round a reproduction of the poster and several photos, and surpassed even the fantastic promises of the question mark. To stress the unusual character of the news, Monsieur Rose, who was never seen at his newspaper office except at moments of national crisis or celebration, the visit of a sovereign, the declaration of war or the election of a President of the Republic, had deigned to write a few introductory lines. He greeted his new "contributor," at the same time wishing him a swift and exemplary punishment. "You have laid claim to my hospitality, monsieur. I give it to you. But make no mistake. In this house as, we feel sure, in the offices of our colleagues of the daily Press we are and always shall be on the side of law and order. We shall never allow a villain to play havoc with the citizens of Paris. Let me tell you, sir, that it is the ardent wish of everyone at *Le Grand Journal*, from the president to the youngest printer, from the editors to the compositors, the administrators to the accountants, that tomorrow, perhaps even today, the handcuffs of Justice will be around your murderer's wrist until such time as her blade falls on your neck."

The articles bore the names of the three principal reporters of *Le Grand Journal*, Messrs. Aumerle, Amand and Saint-Léger. They provided lyrical, quivering coverage from which the letters of "The Passenger" stood out in extra heavy type. M. Aumerle summed up the tragedy of the Rond-Point after the following opening: "Today, the day of M. Étienne Tavernier's funeral, the case of the U buses assumes proportions unique in the annals of crime." M. Amand, like a bolt from the blue, revealed the disappearance of M. Verdon. M. Saint-Léger had the honour of making known the relations between the murderer and the police; between the murderer and *Le Grand Journal*. He commented upon the demand for a ransom and asked in surprise: "Why the garage?" He had interviewed the board of the Bus Company. Everyone there was asking: "Yes, why the garage? Why pick on the U? Why this criminal connection with our route? Why these heinous crimes which cast suspicion on at least a hundred honest employees—conductors, drivers, ticket inspectors and depot personnel?" M. Saint-Léger finally approached the main question. "What will the Quai des Orfèvres do?" To spare the life of an unhappy captive would it meet the demands of a bandit?

These fine literary efforts were profusely illustrated. There was a portrait of the murderer. One of Étienne Tavernier. One of M. Verdon, very blurred and unrecognisable except for the spectacles and wavy hair, in the centre of a group (*Le Grand Journal* had discovered this photo at the Stamp Dealers' Association: souvenir of a congress held in Brussels last December). A picture of Camus the taxi driver. A facsimile of the express letter sent by M. Verdon to Longspès. A page of the typed letter from "The Passenger" addressed to M. Rose. The block of flats on the Boulevard Gouvion-Saint-Cyr, and the building in the rue de Châteaudun. The showrooms of Gascogne Motors in the Champs-Elysées. And—this must have caught Belot's eye—a smiling Mme Colet with the caption: "It is thanks to Mme Colet and her husband that the police know the face of the murderer."

Although the introduction bore the signature of M. J.-J. Rose, the epilogue was signed: *Le Grand Journal*. It could well have borne the title: Proclamation. "People of Paris! A single day separates us from the moment when M. Tavernier's murderer expects to obtain the ransom from his new victim. Should he fail you know his sinister intentions. In any event, his success would be a slap—whether cynical or base—in the face of society. Our police is at work, and works well, but can it work fast enough? We therefore appeal to you. We have shown you the photograph of the criminal. Keep your eyes open today! Do not be led astray by a vague likeness. *He* or no one. But if it be *he*, do not hesitate! You will be serving Justice and you will save an innocent man!"

The excitement caused in Paris by this sensational issue invaded the Prefecture. Everyone there, however, was already at work where he could be most useful. Since they had received the photo of the murderer—and some of them had his name, too—all the members of the municipal police, all the inspectors of the traffic police, the Vice Squad, men from the Warrants and Bailiff's offices had joined forces with the Murder Squad, and had combed the city and the suburbs unflaggingly, each in his special field. All informers had been cross-questioned. It was not the first time that such a huge drag net had produced nothing, especially in such a short space of time as one evening and one night. But never before, for the police, had the passing moments appeared so much in league with the criminal's accomplished crime and projected plans. Scanning *Le Grand Journal*, some in the metro or bus on the way to the Quai des Orfèvres, others travelling to their places of duty, every inspector of the *Police Judiciare* consulted his watch to check the time at his disposal before the hour of the ransom. The letters from "The Passenger," his originality and impudence had jerked them out of the usual dull daily round—sordid murders or crimes of passion, burglaries of varying degrees of boldness, embezzlements, fraud and blackmail. When they got to Police Headquarters they all thought that their "mates" looked odd or that the atmosphere "was stifling." The relationship between the "supers" did nothing to relieve the tension. Drama in high places. . . . From seven o'clock in the morning the Chief Commissioner had been pestered with telephone calls. A senator, two deputies, and several members of the Municipal Council had made the strongest protests about Le Grand Journal. What sort of behaviour was this on the part of the Prefecture? How could M. Rose have the audacity to claim that he did not want to cause a panic, while at the same time being the instrument of panic himself? He had taken it upon himself to publish an appeal, designed to turn every citizen of Paris into an informer. Had the police closed up shop?

The Prefect, who had not yet read the newspapers, replied that collaboration with the Press, particularly after the personal letter sent by "The Passenger" to Le Grand Journal, had appeared unavoidable. Experience showed that the publication of a single photograph always speeded up an inquiry. The reply had been: "A single photograph! Have a look at Le Grand Journal! Take a walk in the streets! You'll see then if M. Rose has contented himself with publishing a single photograph!" The Prefect had opened Le Grand Journal and had immediately blamed M. Malebranche for not having sent him a copy of this outrageous issue. M. Malebranche replied that he had received it at one o'clock in the morning, but the page bore no resemblance to his own copy. He had just telephoned to M. Rose. Aroused abruptly from his sleep, the newspaper magnate had declared that at two o'clock the page had appeared to him quite inadequate. The "Passenger" on the U had introduced gangsterism into France: new methods demanded new measures. What was more, M. Rose intended to ask the authorities to use the American method and to set a price on the criminal's head!

Result: a note signed by the Prefect himself and put on the notice boards. "I do not doubt that the services working to clear up the U Line case are determined to arrest the criminal before nightfall. I wish to follow in detail the activities of each branch and to be informed of the results as they come in. The head of each branch will therefore send a note to headquarters every hour and keep in direct touch with me."

"Every hour," grumbled Picard. "Why not every minute. Truflot, you'll deal with these notes every hour, I've got something better to do today. What does the Prefect imagine? That we want to go to sleep?"

Picard and Belot had been working since seven o'clock in the morning. They had spoken to M. Malebranche and had found out more about the mysterious Oudart. Belot was at the Hôtel Moderne at six o'clock. A visit to the deserted room brought nothing new, but the hotel proprietor, M. Trudon, had been very friendly. In spite of the fact that the police had visited him during the night he had given Belot a few details about his guest. It turned out that Jean Oudart, although given to drink and gambling and at times suspicious, gloomy and sour—he often remained for twenty-four hours locked in his room—was not a typical example of his class and that nothing about him during his three years' stay at the Moderne had made anyone suspect that he was capable of any criminal action.

But four years ago, he had taken part in a burglary. This was discovered thanks to the fingerprints. In the suburbs, at Asnières, a modest villa whose owners were away, had been burgled for silver and knick-knacks. Of the three men involved one had been picked up two years ago (he died in prison), the second who had been the "look-out" was given six months and the third had never been discovered, his comrades swearing that he did not exist although fingerprints proved the contrary. The "look-out" who served six months was none other than Camus, Fernand Camus, the taxi driver of the Tavernier murder.

"It confirms everything," said M. Malebranche.

"It confirms the identity of the fellow," rectified Belot. "But could Tavernier's murderer—" The question he had asked himself at the Gobelins Depot had kept him awake the whole night—"be only an accomplice?"

"Judging by the burglary," said Picard, "he would probably be the leader."

Belot protested.

"Can you see any connection between a petty burglary and the business of the U Line? Really, how? He may have been the leader at Asnières, but here . . ."

And M. Malebranche concluded: "Seeing that we haven't caught him yet, we should pursue our inquiries in other directions as well. If Belot is right we have very little time before this evening."

At the briefing, Picard allocated the main jobs for that morning.

"Sergeant Gaillardet will go to the bank in the rue Marbeuf where Tavernier had his current account, as soon as it opens. . . .

"Sergeant Vilain will go to the Bus Company and then to Tavernier's funeral.

"Inspector Blondel will go to the rue Laffitte (he had already left) to try and see M. Verdon's servant.

"Inspector Assier will return to his watch in the rue de Châteaudun.

"Inspector Avenant will relieve Inspector Perraud and look after Longspès."

("Where are they?" asked Avenant.

"I'll explain to you later," replied the chief. "It's quite a story.")

"Chief Inspector Belot will attend to the Tavernier family and the Verdon family—if the latter appears. He will also arrange the trap at the bus depot, in the disastrous event of our failing to pick up the murderer before night. He will join Sergeant Vilain at Tavernier's funeral."

After the briefing Picard said to Avenant: "Now, about Longspès: the express letter which arrived yesterday, you know, the letter from Verdon. It came direct to us and I sent Perraud to Bellevue to tell the old man he was to report here at once. To Bellevue. . . . Where was it, Truflot?"

"Villa Sans-Souci, Sentier des Voisinoux."

"Sans-Souci! A little bungalow, apparently, with a bit of garden. Perraud rang. A woman's voice answered: 'Who's there?' 'A message for M. Longspès.' 'What about?' 'From M. Verdon.' 'Take it to the rue de Châteaudun.' She certainly knew nothing as yet. 'Open up, please. I'm from the police,' said Perraud.

"Then he heard: 'The police? Please leave or I shall call for help.'"

"Was it his wife?" asked Avenant.

"And so much like him? Of course not. It was his sister, an old spinster even older than him. Perraud decided that if Longspès had not returned, he would wait. At about ten o'clock he noticed a figure approaching."

"M. Longspès?"

"At that moment a window opened and the old woman shouted to her brother: 'Look out, Octave, it's the police!' Before Perraud could make a move, Octave rushed into his garden and locked the gate; the front door opened and he was inside. Perraud decided not to leave. He spent the night there . . . in this rain! Seeing that he hadn't returned this morning, I telephoned to the Meudon Police

Station. They went there and Perraud was able to come on the line. Since the old termagant returned there hasn't been a light and not a sound. Perraud went back and must still be waiting. He didn't want to upset things and he was quite right, damn it. But if Longspès doesn't stir, we shall have to winkle him out. It was to him that Verdon appealed and we need him."

"I believed," said Belot, "that there was not much in common between Tavernier and Verdon. I was wrong. There is the attitude of their confidants towards us: Paul Tavernier is evasive and Longspès runs away from us. It is quite fantastic that they should be so afraid."

"Could there be someone at the Villa Sans-Souci who shouldn't be there?" suggested Avenant.

"That's difficult to believe," replied Picard, "when you know the old man. Had he been an accomplice of the murderer he would have known he was going to receive an express letter, and he would have done everything to avoid drawing attention to himself. Outside his own house he would have behaved differently with regard to Perraud. Thanks to the fuss, all he's gained is that Meudon has sent reinforcements and now his house will be kept under strict observation whether empty or full. Off you go—as soon as the phone rings, get ready to relieve your friend. He must be tired out and soaked to the skin."

"Well, let's get down to it, mon vieux," Picard said to Belot. He read aloud the obituary notice which had appeared in the morning papers.

"The funeral of M. Étienne Tavernier, director of the Champs-Elysées branch of Gascogne Motors, who died in tragic circumstances last Monday, will take place today, Thursday, at ten o'clock in the Church of Saint-Ferdinand-des-Ternes. No invitations will be sent. He will be buried in the family vault at St. Étienne (Loire)."

"Take a letter, Truflot! M. Paul Tavernier, care of Madame Étienne Tavernier. . . . He is bound to be with her and you will have it delivered immediately.

"Dear Sir, we apologise most sincerely for disturbing you once more, particularly this morning. But if, unfortunately, the law can do no more than avenge your brother, it must prevent the murderer from claiming a new victim. . . . How's that?"

"Fine," replied Belot.

"You will know of his sinister intentions from today's newspapers. It is vital that we see you as soon as possible. Would you be kind enough to come to my office, either before or after your distressing duties of this morning. I am, sir, your etc. . . . etc. . . ."

"Yes, that's fine," repeated Belot. "I don't want a repetition of last night's session with young Vincent. But Paul will say that since the burial is to take place at Saint-Étienne, he is obliged to accompany his brother's remains there."

A motor cyclist went off with the letter at eight o'clock and brought back the reply at eight-thirty. During that half hour Picard and Belot studied the plan of the Gobelins Depot.

"Gentlemen," wrote Paul Tavernier, *"since my brother is to be buried in our family vault at St.-Étienne, I considered it my filial duty together with my poor sister-in-law and her children, to accompany his body to its last resting place. Your summons indicates a more pressing duty. As soon as the religious ceremony is over I will, therefore, call at your office. Yours, etc., P.S. I am grateful that you have discontinued the visits of your detectives to the home of the deceased. I realise that these visits were necessary, but certain members of our family find them intolerable."*

"One up to you," said Picard. "The gentleman won't give in. Maybe your intuition is at fault. I get your idea of the murderer's accomplice, but before we can make any accusation we must have facts or at least a motive—*the* motive. What did you say?"

"Nothing. I'm waiting."

10

Thursday, the 6th. From 8.30 to 10 a.m.
From a certain Juliette to M. Archer via Longspès

He waited. The first to appear at Squad Headquarters was Blondel. It was eight-forty.

"Have you seen *Le Grand Journal?*" he asked.

Belot laughed. The idea that anyone could have *not* seen *Le Grand Journal!*

"And have you seen Verdon's daily?"

"Yes. I got to the rue Laffitte at seven o'clock. Everyone was reading *Le Grand Journal* in the porter's lodge, the porter, his wife and some of the tenants. They were all very upset and talked of making a collection. The porter's kid kept screaming, 'If they kill him I won't get any more stamps. I don't want them to kill him.'"

"Go on," said Belot.

"The flat was the same as yesterday except that the bed had been made. At half past seven the front door opened. A girl came in, pretty as a picture, smartly dressed. She was weeping bitterly. 'His girl-friend,' I thought to myself. 'Don't disturb yourself, sir,' she said. 'I am the cleaner.' That was a bit of a shock. She explained that this was not her usual time, but that she had just read *Le Grand Journal.* I consoled her as best I could and promised we'd return her master to her. She was only too willing to be reassured. Her name is Juliette Guillaume, aged 21. Verdon and she . . ." He completed the phrase with a gesture.

"Oh, really?" said Belot.

"Yes. Which doesn't prevent her from respecting him as much as she loves him. As for him, it appears to figure in his timetable as regularly as a meal. She arrives every evening at a quarter past six. Verdon is always there, back from his day's work."

"Did she give you any details?"

"No. But she started to cry again and kept repeating: '*Mon Dieu*, if only he comes back! If only he comes back!'"

"A wonderful recommendation. And—every day?"

"That's exactly what I asked. Yes. . . ."

Belot murmured, his eyes vacant. "Strange. . . ."

"Oh," said Blondel pointedly, "she's very, very attractive, Chief!"

Belot came out of his brown study.

"What's that?" He laughed. "No, I was thinking of something else. Well, go on."

"Regular as clockwork. At a quarter to seven Verdon went out for a walk and she set to work. It took her a good two hours for she also had to prepare the dinner. Afterwards she returned home, to her parents."

"Who must consider that she works late?"

"They are very fond of M. Verdon too. He pays her four francs an hour, although the normal rate is two francs fifty, or even two francs. Plus the 'perks.' Everything she had on was given her by him."

"And plus some pocket money? I suppose that the four francs an hour go to the parents?"

"She affirms that they don't. M. Verdon says that an honest girl must work for her living."

"Are you joking?" asked Belot staring at Blondel.

"She repeated it to me as though it were gospel truth."

"It is indeed. Did he take her out sometimes?"

"Never! When I asked her that she was shocked."

"Poor kid, and how long has this been going on?"

"Nearly six months. She has worked for Verdon for nearly a year, but it was only six months ago that he 'noticed' her, as she puts it. Before that she cleaned the place in the morning. The change in their relationship led to the change in her hours."

Belot returned to the detail which had set him thinking.

"Every day from a quarter past six to a quarter to seven? No, then its not impossible that Tavernier and Verdon . . . And Oudart . . . met. Tavernier left his office at a quarter past six. If the meeting took place in Verdon's neighbourhood that could fit."

The telephone rang. It was five minutes to nine.

"Hullo, Chief, this is Perraud. I am with M. Archer's porter at the Place des États-Unis. The crazy old fellow is here."

"Why at M. Archer's?"

"For the ransom. He's read *Le Grand Journal* and he's more excitable than ever."

"Avenant will relieve you."

"Couldn't you come yourself? It's too long to explain on the phone. Just for five minutes, Chief. I'll see that he doesn't leave before you arrive."

"All right, then, I'll come."

Belot went to notify Picard, and picked up Avenant on the way. He had taken Blondel along with him.

"Come with us down to the door. I still don't know the most important bits about the beautiful Juliette. Does she suspect anyone? A chap called Oudart, for example?"

"No one. Besides, nobody ever comes to the rue Laffitte when she is there. She finds Verdon smoking a pipe or reading a book. He buys her favourite records and puts them on as soon as she arrives. A peaceful existence! Never angry . . . always in a good temper."

"What about the evening of the crime?"

"Monday? She doesn't remember anything special, 'on the contrary.' But on Tuesday he seemed worried. She didn't dare to question him and, as she put it, 'it blew over very quickly.' Yesterday she was terribly scared: no Verdon, no little note—he always left one when he was away—and a drawer of the desk open and emptied. I explained that that was us."

"Didn't the concierge tell her?"

"She was too scared to go into the lodge for fear of hearing some bad news. Besides, 'you don't associate with such people when you enjoy your master's confidence.' It took *Le Grand Journal* this morning to send her flying to them."

"Nothing Monday, worried on Tuesday," Belot summed up, as the three men reached the ground floor. "That tallies with Longspès' remarks. Verdon only learned of the crime from the papers but then he felt a threat in the air. . . ."

It was still pouring rain as they stepped into the street. Belot hailed a taxi, and pushed Avenant inside. "That's all right, Blondel, and thanks."

Nine-twenty. Place des Etats-Unis, M. Archer's private house. Perraud, his clothes sending out clouds of steam stood by a blazing log fire in the porter's lodge, which was as luxuriously furnished as a drawing-room. Something of a dandy, his present state upset him desperately. Standing next to him, imposing as a major-domo, the porter served him with a cup of steaming coffee.

"Well?" asked Belot.

Perraud sighed.

"I'm damned glad to see you, Chief! I'm recovering. Longspès is upstairs. What a journey with him! *Mon Dieu!* I shall never forget it. You know how I spent the night at Bellevue? Right. At seven forty-five I heard the sound of keys and chains and a door opening . . . M. Longspès emerged at last. I was just beginning to think I should have to break into the place. He spotted me from a long way off—the men from Meudon were hidden round about—and he began to wave his arms as though he were chasing away mosquitoes.

" 'Be off with you, be off! I haven't done anything. Be off!' I followed on his heels—ran at his heels rather, trying to persuade him that I had come for his own sake and telling him we had received a letter for him from his boss. He replied: 'It's a trap, it's a trap, but you won't get me. I'm innocent!' He went on like this all along the avenue du Château. 'Look here,' I asked him: 'Where are you off to now? To the Prefecture, I hope.' 'To the Prefecture?' he replied. 'Not on your life! I'm going to the office.' "

"Make it short," said Belot. "Everyone is so long-winded this morning. . . ."

"The circus started at the station. Longspès spotted one of *Le Grand Journal* posters on a kiosk and a spread open copy of the paper. His finger landed straight on the facsimile of the express letter. He bent down and read: 'My dear Octave,' gave a cry, bought a copy—and so did I—and proceeded to take the crowd of travellers to witness, accusing the police of purloining private correspondence and abused me for having spent the night outside his front door instead of coming in. Soaked to the skin as I was, I could have killed him! The crowd looked hostile! They had nearly all got *Le Grand Journal.* We got into the train and we both began to read. The old man began to babble; tried to get out while the train was moving; slapped his old Adam's apple a number of times, shouting that he was a murderer and that he had let his boss down . . . his poor boss.

The old man is as strong as a horse, fantastic. I had a struggle to prevent him doing himself an injury. Everyone in the car was standing up which made him even more excited. He roared: 'Yes, it's me, disgusting old Longspès. I have let my benefactor, M. Verdon, be killed. I have got my name in the papers, and I deserve it, Oh dear, oh dear!' The passengers helped me to make him sit down and to hold his hands; all very proud to take part in the event of the day. If I may say so *Le Grand Journal* goes a bit far."

"You mayn't say so," said Belot. "Get on with it."

"I ran," said Perraud. "Ah, I'm forgetting my coffee!" He drank it. "At Montparnasse I halted a taxi, followed by a crowd of course. My 'pigeon' kept struggling. 'You won't take me to the Prefecture, I have to see about the ransom at once!' He burst into tears and begged me: 'Go to M. Archer's please, to the Place des Etats-Unis please.' I had never heard of M. Archer, but I wanted a bit of peace. Was I wrong?"

"No, on the contrary."

"In the taxi he tried to kiss my hand . . . but this did not prevent him checking the route we were taking. He told me who M. Archer was."

Perraud cast an admiring glance round the lodge.

"M. Longspès is with M. Archer," the porter broke in. "Monsieur asked that when M. Belot arrived he was to go up at once. If you would be good enough to follow me, sir."

Nine-twenty-five.

In the admirable library where Belot had been received the previous evening, a theatrical scene was in progress. Longspès, on his knees, had his skinny hands stretched out to a motionless, impassive Archer. *Le Grand Journal* lay on the floor.

"I implore you, Monsieur Archer," said the old man, "I entreat you. Monsieur Verdon will pay you back. He gives you his word. Remember he has always kept his promises. He found the Empire five francs with the error for you. He got you a complete sheet of the Bordeaux issue. He was bringing you the mint pair of the one-franc vermilion!"

Belot coughed. M. Archer turned round abruptly and hurried over to him.

"Good morning, Inspector. This affair is gaining disastrous proportions. Have you a clue yet?"

Alone now in the middle of the room, still on his knees, Longspès was weeping.

"Oh, please. Monsieur Archer, not disastrous if you agree. Everything could be over tomorrow, thanks to you. Monsieur Verdon will be free, thanks to you. You will go on working together. You will have your little stamp dealer back."

Poor ridiculous Longspès! Listening to him Belot felt a lump in his throat. He recalled a remark uttered the day before by this same Archer. "Ask anything you like of me for Verdon. There is no one closer to me." Today he was hostile, hard and exasperated.

"Our poor Octave is in a bad way," declared M. Archer.—He could have been a doctor giving a diagnosis on a dying man.—"Of course, it's quite understandable."

"It might be a good thing if you replied to him," said Belot curtly. M. Archer looked surprised.

"I should reply to him? But what is *your* reply? What do the police intend to do?"

Longspès let fall his long arms and huddled in on himself. "Oh dear, oh dear!" he groaned. Belot watched him. After a pause rendered intolerable by his sobs M. Archer continued: "Hasn't Verdon any family? It seems to me that the family should be approached rather than strangers. Half a million francs? Where do you expect me to find them?"

"Your hundred thousand francs," whispered Longspès, "your hundred thousand francs of yesterday."

This time M. Archer turned round abruptly. Both the same age, Belot thought, but what a difference!

"My hundred thousand francs of yesterday?"

"Yes. What you would have paid M. Verdon if he had delivered your stamps. . . . Lend them to him. . . ."

"How unfortunate," said M. Archer, turning to Belot. "I didn't have them on me yesterday morning. I intended to ask poor Verdon to give me a little time."

Belot did not reply because the only remark that sprang to his mind was too insulting.

"Come, M. Longspès," he said gently. "You'll find the money somewhere else."

Longspès raised puzzled eyes, then jumped to his feet. "Are the police going to yield to the blackmail of a criminal?" exclaimed M. Archer. "Have you no other alternatives? Is it possible?"

Belot shrugged his shoulders. "It can't be helped, monsieur, we are not always the strongest."

M. Archer ran a delicate hand through his white hair.

"In the circumstances, naturally, I want to play my part. . . . Five or ten thousand francs. . . ." He took out his notecase. . . . "Ten thousand francs. . . . Here you are."

He held out the notes to the inspector.

"Take them, Longspès," said Belot.

"I don't need a receipt, my good Octave," said Archer cordially. "I trust you."

Longspès grabbed the notes and stuffed them with trembling hands into his pocket.

"Come," said Belot, to him. And he forgot to take his leave of M. Archer.

On the stairs Longspès explained at great length. "Ten thousand francs . . . with my savings, that makes twenty . . . I don't know if M. Verdon has any family. I've no time to find out, but I'll go and see all the dealers and all our clients, and you people may perhaps give a trifle, there are so many of you in the police. Don't let us forget it's only a loan."

Belot repressed a smile.

"We'll see when you've finished your rounds."

"And then there are our stamps. If you let me into the office, I could sell them."

"If M. Verdon had wanted you to touch them, he would have said so in the letter. Go on as you've begun, M. Longspès, that's all I ask of you."

Perraud, steaming less than before, was adjusting his bow tie in front of the mirror. Avenant in his turn was enjoying a cup of coffee. The porter hung up the telephone receiver and said to Belot: "Monsieur Archer has just asked me to place the grey car at Monsieur Longspès' disposal."

"My friend Avenant will go with you," said Belot to Longspès. "Do you mind? He's a very nice chap."

Longspès looked at Perraud, gave a shudder, and then examined Avenant. "I'm sure he's a policeman, too."

"He's first and foremost a stamp collector. And talking about stamps . . ." He whispered into Avenant's ear: "Here are your orders. Let *everyone* think that we are accepting 'The Passenger's' conditions. Don't let Longspès out of your sight for a moment, and bring him back to headquarters by three o'clock at the latest."

"What did you say to him?" asked Longspès.

"That when we find M. Verdon we must get our hands on the mint pair of one-franc vermilion without fail. It's too beautiful an item for a bandit. By the way, do you know in which direction M. Verdon took his little evening walk before dinner?"

"More questions! No I don't know. And even if I did . . ."

Longspès suddenly looked so furious that Belot said quickly: "Never mind! You go off to bed, Perraud."

Ten minutes to ten. From a café Belot telephoned to Picard.

"Anything new?"

"There is indeed," replied Picard. "Beauchamp telephoned from Toul. It's incredible. Oudart's name is not Oudart but Devaux! Does that convey anything to you?"

"Nothing at all. Profession?"

"What?" said Picard, surprised. "Mechanic."

"Mechanic?—" A note of excitement crept into Belot's voice. "What training?"

"I've no idea. I'm having some research done at his recruiting office at Cosne, but I must say it was more to find out about his family and get his address than to ask about his training."

Belot persisted. "What rank? Was he ever an N.C.O.?"

"No."

"Any crime sheet?"

"No! Why the interrogation?"

"Hurrah!" Belot shouted into the receiver.

"Why?"

"I'll tell you later. Anything else?"

"I've just been seeing one of Verdon's cousins. Nothing out of the ordinary. He's here now."

"I must go to the church first. It's more essential than ever."

"All right. He'll wait for you."

11

Thursday, the 6th. 10–11 *a.m.*
Saint-Ferdinand and after

A sea of umbrellas flooded the crossroads near the church of Saint-Ferdinand-des-Ternes. For an hour the police had tried to stem it and push it back but the backwash, breaking against new waves, swept over, crushed, and engulfed the blue capes, spilt over on to the pavement, swallowing up taxis and cars and only separated to let the buses through—as though one of them although not a U might deposit here, at the victim's funeral, his extraordinary murderer. At three minutes to ten the whistles of a traffic policeman provoked reactions of unusual violence. A strip of road, however, became visible and silence fell abruptly as the bells began to toll. The hearse and the leading cars of the funeral procession approached Saint-Ferdinand.

Belot reached the square at five minutes past ten. It took him another five minutes to force his way through the crowd. "Excuse me," he said, "I'm a friend of M. Tavernier." People stared at him and a woman murmured: "No, he's fatter."

This is a triumph for *Le Grand Journal*, he thought. Let's hope we may profit by it! He crossed the cordon and entered the church just as the doors were closing. A man in black, standing behind a table collecting signatures, held out a pencil to him. He declined with a gesture. The service began. Someone tapped Belot on the shoulder. It was Vilain straight from the Bus Company. Belot raised his eyebrows. The sergeant made a grimace to indicate failure and whispered: "I've jotted it down for you on this slip of paper."

The church was full—the women on the left, the men on the right. Belot and Vilain walked along the aisle on the men's side to get a side view of the front rows and the rest full face. Paul Tavernier, sitting solemnly in his pew, looked more and more like a judge. Yes, a judge . . . thought Belot as he pointed him out to Vilain. He then looked at the rest of the congregation.

Belot's mind was working hard. Oudart's name was not Oudart. The police knew his true identity and his recruiting office would soon provide further details. But even now Belot was prepared to bet that he was right in taking him for an accomplice, a hireling, an accessory. Someone was directing him under the triple pressure of a dubious past—without which Devaux would not have changed his name—alcohol and gambling. There was a "Brain." This assertion drummed in his head with the droning of the prayers. In the past quarter of an hour he had worked out a new theory: first let us take Devaux independently from Oudart. Devaux the mechanic, a conscript twenty years ago, neither promoted nor punished. Could he write letters like those "The Passenger" had sent? In twenty years of course a man could cultivate his mind, could educate himself. That is precisely what I have been doing for the past twenty years, he thought. But that does not alter the fact that despite all my efforts I should be incapable of composing a letter like the one published in *Le Grand Journal*. It smacked of an upper-class education—or else of an exceptional personality. But you do not wait until the end of your military service to become exceptional. Your character is bound to show itself in the regiment. It would be damned odd if you did not acquire a corporal's stripes unless you are a rebel and then you get punished. The more exceptional you are the harsher the punishment. Now let us take Oudart—that is to say, Devaux twenty years later. The private who had never attracted attention either for good or for bad has progressed along the wrong path. We find him after sixteen years committing a petty burglary where moreover he idiotically leaves his fingerprints behind, just as he kept on the grasshopper on the day of the crime. Admittedly he got away with it on both occasions. But on the first occasion he had merely to keep quiet and rely on his pals. And the second—it was not his fault. Here he is today, a worthless idler, without a book in his room, a gambler, a drunkard—and a murderer. From Devaux to Oudart: a continual decline. From Devaux to "The Passenger," on the contrary, a remarkable ascent, and between Oudart and "The Passenger" an abyss! It was therefore Devaux-Oudart on the one hand and "The Passenger" on the other. The Brain.

Belot continued to scrutinise the congregation lost in the shadows. Was *he* among this crowd perhaps? Silent, outwardly composed, and dreaming of the evening? Belot knew where he wanted to look to give substance to his thoughts. He forced himself to dismiss the idea. In any case Vilain was watching and Picard was right: there was absolutely no proof and in a police investigation you cannot rely on intuition. He examined the faces one after the other—he knew nearly all of them in the front rows. Jean-François, the victim's son, Vincent Travernier, his younger brother, M. René Gascogne, young Roux, the relations and friends he had met at the Boulevard Gouvion-Saint-Cyr. And then a number of strangers with exceptions which were irritating because they were useless, such as M. Aumene, the reporter from *Le Grand Journal!* If *he* is there, Belot repeated to himself, the good Lord ought to perform a miracle! At a rap from the beadle's cane the congregation rose. In one of the rear pews a large man remained seated for a few seconds, then suddenly raised his head and got to his feet. M. Colet! So they had come! Belot cast a rapid glance over the faces of the women—further away and less distinct—decided that the church lighting was really inadequate, and finally distinguished Mme Colet. She was dressed in black and her attitude appeared to convey sincere emotion. Why not, he thought. She is a delicate, sensitive woman. . . . Which did not prevent her giving her photograph to *Le Grand Journal!* Now, seeing that she never does anything without weighing it up in her little head. . . . Another rap of the cane and the congregation sat down. M. Colet folded his arms over his stomach and closed his eyes. Mme Colet looked at her husband and then towards Belot. He gave her a slight nod. She smiled and then assumed the unhappy expression of an anxious woman. Obviously she doesn't consider that things have advanced much since yesterday morning. She doesn't know our results. She is on the hunt, but what clues does she have?

Ten-thirty and the service came to an end. The family lined up to receive condolences. Women, unrecognisable beneath their veils, a little girl, in the front the youngest boy and the men. Paul Travernier, more erect than ever, Vincent with a tear-stained face, and M. Gascogne who seemed really upset. Belot and Vilain slipped behind them, as unobtrusive as the undertakers. The congregation filed past, bowing to the family. Mme Colet rejoined her husband. They had a brief discussion, and the subject of it became clear to Belot when he saw them join the procession. "She's going a bit far," he muttered. She went even further when he heard her say to the Tavernier brothers. "I am Mme Colet, gentlemen, the witness from the U. Allow me to introduce my husband who was with me. We were the last people to see your unfortunate brother alive. Please accept all our sympathy. You know that you can count on us. We are staying at the Hôtel Royal, Place de la Porte-Champerret."

To everyone who shook his hand, Paul Tavernier replied: "Most kind." To Mme Colet he also replied: "Most kind."

But Belot saw his neck stiffen as though he was forcing himself not to turn his head and stare after the witness from the U bus. He took advantage of this nervousness, moved forward a few steps and said to Vilain loud enough to be overheard: "Now we know everything."

It was Vincent who turned round. He only saw the sergeant whom he did not know, and uttered an angry "Hush!" Vilain looked embarrassed, not without having noticed Paul give a start, almost a shudder, which he indicated to his chief with a raised eyebrow.

The Colets left. Belot followed. It was ten-forty.

The sea of umbrellas had drawn back to the other side of the avenue. Little groups of people stood in front of the church chatting among themselves.

"Good morning, Inspector," said Mme Colet.

"Good morning, Inspector," echoed a deferential M. Colet. "What horrible weather."

"My husband can't bear the rain," said Mme Colet. "He prefers the mistral. He shouldn't have come out this morning, but he wanted to pay his last respects. . . ."

M. Colet gave his wife an outraged look, then lowered his eyelids. "Yes, I wanted to."

"Haven't you an umbrella, Inspector? Come and have a drink. You must be terribly busy today, but just for a moment. . . ."

"Impossible, *madame*. I must get back. But I should have liked a few words with you."

Mme Colet tugged at her husband's arm. "Get a taxi, Raymond. We'll go with Monsieur Belot."

On the way she remarked: "How the case has changed since yesterday! But has it become simpler or more complicated?"

"I can hardly see in what way it has become any simpler," replied Belot.

"By the demand for a ransom from the stamp dealer's family. Before that everyone wondered why M. Tavernier had been killed. Now it looks as if he was killed because he would not give in to demands for money. Don't you think so?"

"I don't think anything, because I don't know anything. But your photo has worked wonders in Paris and at Toul. . . ."

"At Toul," echoed Mme Colet in amazement.

"Yes, with the . . . th regiment."

"The *what?*"

Then she burst out laughing. She had brilliant white teeth.

"Oh, I understand," she cried. "You said 'your' photo. I thought you were talking about mine! But you mean the other one, the one from the album? My photo and the regiment, Raymond! Isn't that funny?"

Uncomfortably perched on a folding seat, his expression blank, M. Colet did not laugh. He merely said: "Oh, yes."

"Forgive me," said Belot rather bitingly. "I forgot that 'your' photo also appeared elsewhere. It graced the front page of *Le Grand Journal*."

The grey-blue eyes smiled with satisfaction.

"It's a good one of me, isn't it? We have a real genius in Avignon. When you come to see us you'll find an enlargement in colour in his window. I offered it to *Le Grand Journal* and they accepted."

"What?" said Belot. "*You* offered it? You, yourself? It wasn't they who asked for it?"

"Good gracious, no! A Monsieur Aumerle came last night to the hotel. He told me about the Verdon case, 'The Passenger's' letter to M. Rose and *Le Grand Journal's* wish to publish a 'fabulous' issue. That was his exact expression. I asked him if they had your agreement. He replied that they had agreed with the head of the *Police Judiciare*—which was far better. I was on my guard all the same. This M. Aumerle asked me all sorts of questions. I apologised and said that I had nothing to say. I could have had but I preferred to keep my impressions to myself . . . and for you, Inspector. I only offered him my photo so that his journey would not have been in vain. He seemed a little . . . astonished. He wasn't sure if he would have room for it. I replied that he could do as he wished, but that a woman's face when she is neither too old nor too ugly never fails to please. And they published it. Isn't that funny, Raymond?"

This time M. Colet let out a sound half way between a sob and a sniff.

"The inspector's going to laugh at you, my lass! She is still such a child, Inspector!"

Belot replied: "I can't guess Madame Colet's reasons, but I am sure she has some."

Mme Colet gave him a look of gratitude.

"Yes, I have my reasons. But I'll whisper them to you because they don't concern my husband."

Belot bent forward, was aware more closely of her perfume.

"I don't want to scare him," she said softly. "I had this photo published *so that the murderer would not forget me*. Do you understand?"

"Is that why you came this morning?" he whispered back.

"Yes. I made a stupid little speech to the Tavernier brothers. But you must have heard it . . . You were standing just behind them. If 'The Passenger' is in league with the victim's family—and why not?—I want him to know that I exist and that I am a threat to him."

"Be careful, he may become a threat to you!"

"That's just what I want. He may be forced to come into the open. Besides, he's a threat to you, too."

"That's my profession."

"And I'm on holiday! Anyway, I have nothing to fear: I have my body guard." She jerked her chin in the direction of her husband. They laughed together.

"I hope your efforts will be unnecessary," replied Belot aloud, "and that we shall get our man today. We know his identity now. Let's see, you said something just now which caught my ear. . . . Oh, yes, you could have made a statement to *Le Grand Journal*, something you had kept for me?"

Mme Colet acquiesced by fluttering her eyelids.

"Yesterday as I left the Prefecture I was obsessed by the question of the accent. I thought back how it had needed a great effort on my part to remember it, but that my effort had been rewarded. Why shouldn't further efforts lead me to discover further details? After lunch in our room, I placed two chairs side by side. My husband and I sat down and the bus started. . . . Opposite us were M. Tavernier and a big fat woman. I said to Raymond, 'The lady's getting out.' Raymond, who always understands what I expect of him, began to repeat the discussion we were having. We were talking about a pretty little farm a few miles from Avignon which Raymond is very keen on buying. I would rather have a car, and I was maintaining that the farm without a car would be very tiresome. Raymond insisted that the bus service was quite good enough. We were at this point, when the lady got out and the man in grey took her place. M. Tavernier was reading his paper. He did not see the man sit down. At that moment I noticed the tie pin, that exceedingly vulgar grasshopper and the not unpleasant but rather undistinguished, ordinary face. I said to Raymond: 'How many buses are there a day?' Raymond replied: 'One every half hour.' I was just going to say, 'And you call that a good service,' when the man's knee touched mine. It was not done on purpose. He was turning towards Tavernier and at that moment said, 'A very good morning to you, M. Tavernier,' rolling his Burgundian r's and in a sarcastic tone, which now struck me. I looked at the newspaper. Then it was lowered, and I caught a side view glimpse of M. Tavernier, who said: 'Hullo!' A 'Hullo' of surprise, of amazement, yes amazement if not more. Then I looked at the man in grey and for a second he returned my gaze. It was at this moment that his eyes struck me—dull, vague and at the same time set, so strange. . . . But I must confess that I did not guess anything of the drama which was of course already being played out between these two strangers. The bus service was still occupying my mind. I finally answered Raymond. Then he dared to compare the timetable of this bus with the trains from Paris out to the suburbs. I laughed at him and mentioned Saint-Germain and Versailles . . . and at the word Versailles, I heard: 'It's not true.'—'Yes, it is true.' We repeated our cues and this exchange ten times. By the tenth, I was certain it was Tavernier who had said: "It's not true,' and the man in grey: 'Yes, it is true,' rolling the r of *true*. I'll spare you the rest of our discussion, but we reconstructed it word by word, we spent the whole afternoon at it. I was dead tired! The result, apart from the two little phrases I have just quoted, was that I felt again the tension between the two seats—and the tangible signs of this tension such as the knee of the man in grey which banged against mine several times. And then his dirty nails. I had noticed on Monday his ugly hands, but without any details. Quite well-trimmed nails, but filthy dirty. My goodness, I'm talking too much! You're laughing at me?"

"No."

"But you're disappointed? Wait till I give you my conclusions. Firstly, the murderer-to-be was far more on edge than his future victim. Secondly . . ."

Belot interrupted her.

"Excuse me; had M. Tavernier been sitting opposite you instead of the man in grey it would probably have been his knee which touched yours."

She gave a little ironical nod which Belot was beginning to know, and even to dread.

"But *he* was seated opposite me. The man in grey was opposite my husband."

"My apologies. And secondly . . ."

"Now you're going to think I'm really mad. But it seems to me that this man with his behaviour, his insignificant appearance, his nails and his grasshopper, *cannot* have written the letters published by *Le Grand Journal.*"

Belot gave a start and stared at her.

"*Madame,*" he said emphatically, "if our relationship permitted it, I would hug you for that. You can't imagine the pleasure you have given me! And now, do you suspect anybody?"

Mme Colet blushed at the praise.

"No, no one. What about you? Professional secret?"

"Professional indecision. . . . We'll discuss it later. You are too valuable a collaborator for us to keep anything from you."

Mme Colet, shy once more:

"Thank you, Inspector . . . but on the contrary, I'm ashamed I didn't notice all that right away. I have never been involved in an investigation, you see! I have never even done a crossword puzzle in my life!"

Belot looked at her. She looked at him out of the corner of her eye, bit her lip and her eyes twinkled once more.

"If I understand correctly," she said, in an innocent voice, "you find me valuable because I have reached the same conclusions as you have."

Belot remained serious.

"The same conclusions," he replied, "without the tremendous powers we have at our disposal."

"But it's quite easy, you know! You take two chairs. . . ."

". . . and the bus starts? These are miracles which only happen to children. Your husband is right, *madame!* Besides you may have discovered the truth—well, what I believe to be the truth—by completely false deductions. The state of nerves of the man in grey did not prevent his going off after his crime as calmly as a gentleman of leisure with a clear conscience."

"To all appearances!" replied Mme Colet. "And then you always have a clear conscience when you've done a job well."

Thursday, the 6th. 11 a.m. to midday
From Toul to M. Barbason

The corridor at Police H.Q. overflowed with an anxious and silent crowd. People of all sizes, all ages and of both sexes. Belot pushed his way through with some difficulty to Picard's office. It was so dark that the desk lamp had been lit.

"Did you see them?" asked the chief, with a sneer that would have made M. Rose tremble. "Hundreds of denunciations, and the telephone never stops ringing. I've given Truflot the job of receptionist. The best thing he's done so far is to have three women and an old man sent to St Anne's. We shan't forget *Le Grand Journal* in a hurry. I have a lot of things which concern you. Will you talk first, or shall I?"

"You."

"Right. Don't let's be too unfair to the newspapers. To begin with two men came in who recognised Oudart—betting types. Told us nothing more than we knew already. Then a hotel proprietor, a chap called—" Picard consulted his pad "—Frapin, Hôtel d'Azur, rue Pigalle. Oudart lived there for a year. There, too, profession: 'checker.' Left suddenly without any explanation but without leaving any debts, four years ago. Since Frapin keeps his books in order he was able to give me the exact date. Can you guess?"

"The date of the burglary at Asnières."

"Precisely. We are beginning to get the picture. Five years ago then, he put up at the Hôtel d'Azur, lived there for a year, took part in the Asnières burglary and disappeared. There is a gap of a year, after which he lived at the Hôtel Moderne until last Monday, in other words for three years. So far, so good. But look what happened twenty years earlier! Beauchamp telephoned from Toul. Here's a copy of what he said, you can read it later. I put a call through at once to Cosne and they promised to call me back before midday. There's been talk of a Burgundian accent, or something like that. This fits! But tell me why you were so keen just now to know his standard of education?"

Belot gave his reasons, adding the new details learned from Mme Colet and the reactions of Paul Tavernier at the church. Picard bit his nails as he listened.

"A Brain . . . maybe. After what you told me this morning I've been thinking. The chief also seems to share your point of view. It doesn't even complicate the investigation unduly. We've two pieces of luck today . . . possibly three . . . without counting the denunciations. The first and the best is the true identity of the murderer. Second, the impending visit of Paul Tavernier: he'll have to get what he knows off his chest eventually. Even more so since Gaillardet's discoveries about his brother's resources confirm your theories of yesterday evening, as you will see. The third, of course, if the two others produce nothing, is the garage."

"Yes," said Belot, "while we're on the subject . . ."

He described Longspès' visit to Archer and how, according to the plan Picard and he had worked out during the morning, the police as from now appeared to be agreeing to the demands of "The Passenger."

"I hope we shall have finished before then," said the chief, "but caution is indispensable. I've left it to you to talk to Verdon's cousin." Picard put on a Marseilles accent. "He's a bearded fellow called Barbason, it's quite a beard, too! He's waiting for you. Here's his statement. I've also received a visit from the friend, M. Philippe Durand, the junior director of Ibert and Bélier."

"Nice chap?" asked Belot.

"Seems to be. But the visit was useless. He's never heard of Oudart or Devaux. Says Verdon never gambled on the horses; not even at cards. That's all. What news from the Bus Company?"

From his pocket Belot drew out the paper which Vilain had given him at the church, and which he had just read as he climbed the stairs.

"Not much. The Company's very upset. Since this morning crowds round the U Line buses. One ticket collector refused to go on duty.

A noticeable drop in the number of travellers. They demand effective measures and naturally will help us as much as possible at the Gobelins Depot. They have never heard of anyone called Oudart. They are suing *Le Grand Journal* because of the bus which figures on the posters."

"Bravo," said Picard. "That'll teach Rose a lesson."

"Well, that's it. And now," replied Belot, "I'll go and see Gaillardet and the cousin. Is Gaillardet there?"

"No, he left you a note."

Belot picked up Beauchamp's report and Barbason's statement. As he reached the door Picard said, scowling at his nails, "I suppose you know I'm making inquiries about everyone? All those who are however remotely connected with this wretched business, from Musard to Archer. They are all being kept under observation and their telephones are tapped. So . . . This also includes the . . . Colets."

Belot turned round. Picard didn't give him time to speak.

"Listen to me. I know your methods. The moment anyone inspires confidence you gamble on him. That's what you call your intuition. Well, I do too. But this run of success may let you down with a bump one of these days. You yourself have discovered that there is a Brain somewhere, so I was sensible to collect information, wasn't I? Paris is in a state of ferment all because of a snapshot identified by a nice little woman. It's a serious matter!"

Belot's voice was calm: "And you didn't think of that until this morning? And if this identification turns out to be correct?"

"I thought of it this morning because the letter to Rose and *Le Grand Journal* keep waltzing round in my head. Perhaps also, to be fair, because your girl-friend was absolutely on the ball—and so easily. . . . I thought she was very impressive, and her husband very sleepy . . . they were having a very unusual holiday. Anyway, I telephoned Avignon."—Picard sniffed and looked at his watch. "We're wasting time. Well, I learned that the police superintendent at Avignon buys his furniture from the Colets. An excellent establishment with a first-class reputation. The hallmark of honesty."

"What does that prove?" asked Belot.

"Eh?" Picard was astonished. "I thought you'd be pleased, and now it's you . . . ?"

"So he sells furniture to a police superintendent—a fine guarantee!" said Belot. "There are purveyors to crowned heads who have committed crimes and thefts."

Picard shook his head.

"You are pulling my leg. But be careful, all the same, especially when there's a woman."

Belot opened the door.

"Felix," he said, "you're quite right. We're wasting our time."

On his table he found the draft report from Gaillardet who had written in the margin: "I am off to the rue de Châteaudun with Panigon (an inspector who specialised in accountancy, stock exchange transactions, etc.) to examine the stamp dealer's accounts. If you need me, telephone."

But before going any further Belot wanted to know how Beauchamp had fared with his inquiry at Toul.

6th October, 9.38 a.m. Call from Beauchamp at Toul. To begin with: the result of my inquiries. They contradict yours. The person's name is not Oudart, but Devaux, Jean-Marie-Lucien (here followed the information which Picard had already passed on to Belot).

"Arrived tonight at one o'clock. Went immediately to the barracks who sent someone with me to the . . . th regiment. We woke up the N.C.O.s who were here in 19 . . . , all of whom lived in barracks. No one recognised the photograph. Before going to bed I went to the gendarmerie because an idea occurred to me. Soldiers love being photographed. The captain of the gendarmerie came with me this morning. We began with the most popular photographer—Rond, rue Gambetta. A bit of luck! He always chooses handsome fellows and he had photographed our man. Since he keeps careful records he discovered the ticket and the name within five minutes. I rushed back to the barracks. The registers gave me the details. There was *nothing* in the name of Jean Oudart. I shall be back at about five o'clock."

A nice piece of work, thought Belot. Beauchamp, whom he had promoted to sergeant, gave him nothing but satisfaction. Now we must find M. Devaux . . . and if possible before nightfall.

He took up Gaillardet's note.

At nine o'clock I went to the Banque Parisienne de Crédit, rue Marbeuf. I was shown Étienne Tavernier's account. Corresponds exactly to the dead man's bank book. 8,000 francs a month always paid in *in cash*. But this has only been the case for *the last five years*. Before that Tavernier deposited sums much bigger than 8,000 francs, never the same, and *in cheques*.

The bank also holds the share certificates mentioned in the statement. I learned that three years ago Tavernier rented a private safe. He gave no power of attorney to anyone to open it (nor for that matter to inspect his account). It must be opened as soon as possible. What did he put into it if not share certificates?

I then went to Gascogne Motors in the Champs-Elysées, which is quite near the bank. Found none of the directors there because of the funeral. A salesman told me that all financial questions, involving either sales or salaries, were handled by head office: a cashier spends the last day of each month going round all the branches with an envelope for each employee from the director. I asked whether they were paid in cash. I was told: "By crossed cheque for sums above 2,000 francs."

Seeing the discrepancy I went to the head office, on the Quai de Grenelle. The head accountant was also at the funeral, but his assistant was there and I saw M. Henri Gascogne. As Chief Inspector Belot said, ever since Tavernier managed the Champs-Elysées branch, his income has always included commissions and bonuses. His earnings for the past two years were 172,000 francs and 229,600 francs! Paid to him by cheque, but *for the last five years* T. asked for the cheque to be left open. Moreover, he came every month to collect it in person. I was shown the receipts from which I took the figures above.

I went to the bank used by Gascogne Motors, the Comptoir Français, Boulevard des Italiens, where I found that the cheques had always been cashed by Tavernier the day he received them.

The question is: where did this money go? Did he deposit it in the strong box, being such a miser?

Belot then leafed through M. Barbason's statement before going into the waiting-room. It was eleven-twenty-five.

The first thing he noticed about M. Barbason was his beard. This plump little man with sparkling eyes and capacious overcoat, sported a mighty beard—so black that it might have been dyed—waxed and split into two wings by a perfect parting which fell from his lips like a plummet. It looked like a diabolical flower or a bewitched bat, which M. Barbason kept, as Socrates kept bees. One forgot its true nature, all the more since his hair did not match it at all. His hair was dull, short cut, almost shaven, revealing the shape of the skull, with no other pretensions than to lie flat behind the temples and in front of the ears where it was suddenly transformed into this bird, this flower, just as one may see a twisted yew tree in the park blossom forth in the sunshine.

"M. . . . Barbason, I presume?"

M. Barbason pointed to his hairy decoration.

"As you see, monsieur, the trade mark of the house. Whom have I the honour . . . ?"

A strong southern accent completed the picture. Belot introduced himself. M. Barbason quickly pulled off his kid glove and extended a plump, rather moist hand.

"Thank you for having waited for me," said Belot, "I appreciate your impatience. . . ."

"Oh, I have complete confidence in my staff," replied M. Barbason, who had not understood. "But it's my wife . . . I should not like to leave her too long on her own. When she read of the tragedy in the newspapers she fainted and since then she hasn't stopped weeping. As I said to her: 'Be patient, your cousins's not dead yet!'"

He rolled his eyes and shook his head violently as if trying to shake off the bat.

"We'll be quick," said Belot. Offering his visitor a chair he sat down and scanned the statement.

"I see that you have a restaurant in the rue de Châteaudun."

"Restaurant keeper," replied M. Barbason. "That's my legal title. I can say without any false modesty that I serve the best food in Paris. Specialities: duck, capon and sole Barbason. The name of my place is 'Chez Barbason, caterer, business lunches.'" He pointed once more to his chin. "It was my wife's idea that I should let it grow and tend it carefully—for the publicity."

Belot raised his eyebrows. M. Barbason, suddenly nervous, explained: "You understand, Inspector, a play on words . . . Barbason . . . barber . . . beard . . . ?"

And he added at once: "I'm not telling you this for a joke. I am giving you facts." He heaved an enormous sigh. "What can have happened to the poor cousin?—Why does it matter to you if I own a restaurant?"

"I want to know if M. Verdon ever took his meals at your place, and with whom."

M. Barbason looked suspicious.

"If Maurice *took* his meals. . . . Do you really want to know, or do you know already?" He did not wait for the reply. "It's not the sort of story I should have repeated on a day like today . . . the poor fellow."

He raised his forefinger to the cleft in his beard and ran the nail delicately down it, as a sign of concentration.

"After his mother's death, Maurice ate nearly all his meals at my place, *Chez Barbason*. The whole of last year. He had his own little table and he brought his book with him. Naturally I gave him a special price. Firstly, because my wife and he are of the same blood and secondly because he had occasion to mix with the best society, because of his stamps. And I freely admit he sent me some of them."

"Did he come with them?"

"Oh, no! He bowed to them; sometimes he was invited to join their table; he always refused. 'You see, Bébé (the family always calls me Bébé because my name is Bastien; so Bastien Barbason . . . B.B. Quite amusing, no?). You see, Bébé,' he said to me, 'that gentleman is a great collector. If I accepted his invitation it would look as though I had recommended you on purpose!' The poor fellow was always very tactful. Only, there was this affair with a woman. . . . Shall I tell you?"

"Yes, please."

"At my place I have a head waiter, junior waiters, wine waiter, everything. . . . But the rest of my staff are girls."

He smiled with regal modesty. "Pretty girls, eh! The clients are not likely to lose their appetites when they see them weaving among the tables. At first Maurice did not seem to notice them, but one day he began to look at one of them—Suzanne, a tall, dark-haired girl with flashing eyes. You know the type." M. Barbason's eyes lit up. "He said things to her which made her laugh each time she passed. I paid no attention but my wife, who sits at the cash desk, called me over and said to me: 'Where does Maurice think he is, in a workman's café?' This distressed me. I went over and had a quiet word with him. He promised he would not repeat the behaviour. That evening my wife said to me: 'He's off again!' We had words and he did not come any more. My wife was very upset. I had to give Suzanne the sack."

"Was this a long time ago?"

"Last spring. Oh! we continued on good cousinly terms. I have children and Maurice never forgot their birthdays: candy or stamps. He's a fine fellow, you know, apart from this little episode. It seems he's a big dealer. I take it stamp catalogues do better than cookery books!"

"Provided you have funds to buy yourself. Is M. Verdon rich?"

"No . . . I wouldn't say rich. He's comfortably off. He inherited a small sum after his mother's death."

"I see from your statement that you don't suspect anyone?"

M. Barbason raised his right hand.

"No one. To attack a man like Maurice, after that unfortunate gentleman in the bus. It's a complete mystery to me."

"You didn't know M. Tavernier? Nor your cousin either?"

"I don't know about my cousin. I certainly didn't. He may have come to lunch *Chez Barbason*, like everyone else in Paris. His photo doesn't mean a thing to me. Nor does the picture of the murderer either."

"Does the name Oudart, Jean Oudart, mean anything to you?"

"No. Is he the murderer?"

"Yes. What about Devaux? Jean Devaux?"

"No."

"Are you M. Verdon's only relation?"

"Yes, Inspector. The poor chap always said: 'In our family it's always been one son, from father to son.' His mother was an Etrange."

"A what . . . ?" replied Belot.

"A Mademoiselle Etrange, the Etranges, the coal merchants. They're a limited company now, a bunch of thieves who robbed us and in which there's not a single Etrange left. His mother and my late mother-in-law were sisters. That's all. So when this murderer appeals to the family to try and raise 500,000 francs, where does he expect them to come from? If I had them—" M. Barbason's voice was solemn—"and if the police of my country couldn't do anything in such a situation, I would hand them over, Inspector! According to the newspaper it's only an advance, a loan! But I haven't got the money."

"So business isn't too good?" Belot inquired sympathetically.

M. Barbason stared at the inside of one of his gloves as though hoping to find a fortune there.

"There's great competition. . . ." He raised his head defiantly. "Even if business was flourishing I shouldn't have 500,000 francs in ready cash to play with."

"What about the Etrange side of the family?"

"There's only my wife."

"And on your side?"

"Oh, forgive me," said M. Barbason, "I'm the cousin but my family is nothing. . . . It's just my family. To be frank they haven't a sou either."

"In fact you can't see anyone who could come to the aid of the poor man. . . ."

Barbason shook his head sadly.

"My wife will go off her head."

Belot paused for a moment. "You can go home and give her a piece of good news, monsieur. We shall get the 500,000 francs."

"Eh?"

M. Barbason bounded in his chair, which groaned under his weight. His eyes lit up as they had done when he mentioned the waitress, Suzanne. Belot smiled briefly and went on.

"Only we need you. It will be you, representing your family, who will be supposed to have raised this sum and who will take it to-night to the bus depot . . . unless we have arrested the criminal beforehand. You will now telephone *Le Grand Journal* at once and inform them of your decision. The news must appear in the evening edition. I must also ask you, after this telephone call, to return home and see *no one* until you receive fresh instructions. *Le Grand Journal* will send their reporters. Have them told that neither you nor Mme Barbason are receiving visitors. Don't even show yourself in the restaurant . . . neither at lunch nor at dinner.

Your customers will forgive you when they learn of the bond which unites you to the hero of the day."

M. Barbason had listened to M. Belot without a single interruption. His eyes had narrowed and suddenly gave his face a cunning look. When Belot had finished he winked his right eye.

"So it's a trap. You're pretending to give way, and the moment the murderer comes to pick up the ransom, you'll pounce."

"No," replied Belot slowly, repeating the phrase he had used to M. Archer. "Alas, we are not always the strongest."

"But," asked M. Barbason, growing excited once more, "who's putting up the money? Collectors?"

"I can't tell you any more, and it is essential that the money appears to come from you. This can't do you any harm. It is never a disadvantage to appear rich."

"And above all to be a good cousin!" added M. Barbason. "Inspector, in the name of the family I thank you. My wife will be delighted."

"Do you mind waiting for me a moment?" asked Belot. He went into the outer office and found Clairval.

"Haven't you gone to bed? You were up all night."

"I had a good nap in Verdon's office," replied Clairval. "It would be a fine thing to go to bed on a day like this."

"Agreed," replied Belot, and gave him some details about M. Barbason.

"You are to stick on his heels as soon as you see him come out of the telephone box. He is to go home and see *no one*. If he receives anyone or leaves the house again let me know immediately. Try and get the lowdown on his wife."

As M. Barbason left the Quai des Orfèvres after telephoning to *Le Grand Journal,* the clock struck midday. At the twelfth stroke, as in any self-respecting melodrama, a tall, dignified man dressed in black said to the officer on duty at Police Headquarters: "Will you please announce me at once. I am sure that I am expected. I am Paul Tavernier."

13

Thursday, the 6th. Midday to 2 p.m.
M. Paul Tavernier

Belot had just gone in to Picard. At the name of the visitor they exchanged a glance of "Here we go," like the two backs of a good team just as the game starts. Picard said to the duty officer: "Keep him in the waiting-room until I've seen Sergeant Vilain, he can't be far behind. And get me Truflot. Let him put someone else on to the denouncers! Come on, get cracking!"

"Shall I stay?" asked Belot.

"What do you think? Sit down over there."

Picard pointed to one of the two chairs at the table, which had its back to the window. The telephone buzzed; Picard picked up the receiver, listened and replied: "Of course!—It's Vilain," he said to Belot, "he's coming up. Shall we play it tough?"

"I should almost prefer the full treatment. . . ."

"Not really!"

He stood up, went over to the window and drummed on the rain-drenched pane, whistling. He broke off to declare: "With this downpour we might avoid the buses tonight, we wouldn't be the worse for that. . . ."

Returning to his seat he switched off the table lamp, plunging the office in the gloomy darkness of the storm. Truflot appeared, Picard relit the lamp and changed its position.

"A baker's boy thinks he saw the murderer on Monday at about 2.30," said Truflot. "In other words half an hour after the crime, in the rue de Valois, with his collar turned up. He seemed to be watching for something or somebody."

"Who do we know in that district?" asked Picard.

"No one," replied Belot.

"Metro Station: Palais-Royal," observed Truflot. "The Rond-Point line."

"Oh dear," sighed Picard, "another inquiry. . . ."

"Ligaire can attend to it."

"Get ready, *mon vieux*, I'm going to call in brother Tavernier." There was a knock at the door. It was Vilain.

"Nothing to report," he said. "On leaving the church the coffin was put into the motor hearse; Vincent Tavernier and two other gentlemen rode in it. Paul put his sister-in-law and the children in the first car with two ladies."

"Probably Madame Tavernier's mother and sister," said Belot.

"His own wife travelled in the following car with Mme Vincent, etc. They made off in the direction of Saint-Étienne. He himself hailed a taxi, went home and did not emerge again until he came here. . . . In his car, a Gascogne, which he drove himself."

"Has the house only one exit?" asked Belot.

"The main door leads on to the Quai d'Orsay and the back door on to the rue Malar. They can both be kept under observation at the same time, although the quay is pretty deserted in this filthy weather. I used a car."

"Well," said Picard, "now you can go and have lunch until your client comes out. Provided . . ."

"He does come out!" replied Vilain.

He laughed jovially and disappeared. Picard rubbed his forehead.

"The full treatment, Truflot."

"Very good, sir."

Picard switched off the lamp once more and rang for the duty officer. Belot and he stood up.

Paul Tavernier bowed in the doorway and then, raising himself to his full height, tried to make out the three figures in the room in the artificial gloom. He recognised Belot and gave him a little additional greeting. "Allow me in person to express once more all my condolences," Picard began ceremoniously.

Paul Tavernier replied as he had done at the church: "Most kind."

He accepted the seat offered him next to the chair in which Belot had sat down again, so that the chief inspector and the semi-suspect seemed to be paying a joint visit to the head of the squad.

Picard switched on the lamp. The beam fell directly into the visitor's eyes. Paul Tavernier gave a start and tried to push back his chair, which would not move. He put a hand up to his eyes but when he withdrew it seemed ready to accept the embarrassing light. Picard observed the severe features, the black eyes under the thick eyebrows, the deep lines on the forehead, the greying hair and the whole robust, cold face which recalled that of the victim, as the finished sculpture recalls the vague sketch. Belot also observed him. "This is somewhat different from candlelight," he thought. With a violence that was difficult to contain he added to himself: "If this man doesn't know everything—or practically everything—I'll hand in my resignation!"

"Have you read *Le Grand Journal?*" Picard asked affably. Paul Tavernier nodded. "You know, then, that time presses. I must also inform you at once that we do not hope to escape from the demands of 'The Passenger' tonight."

A glimmer of surprise flashed in the eyes of the visitor.

"But . . ." he began.

He bit his lips, and in that haughty voice which Belot found unbearable he said, "You mean that it's 'The Passenger' who escapes you."

Picard in the shadow clenched his fists until his bones cracked, but he replied suavely with the ritual phrase: "Alas, monsieur, we are not always the strongest. Perhaps we do not always get all the help and co-operation to which we are entitled."

"Oh, really," replied Paul Tavernier with courteous indifference. Truflot's shrill voice suddenly broke in: "M. Tavernier!"

He turned sharply towards the elongated skull which was outlined in silhouette against the white square of the window. The shrill voice went on: "Your name, Christian names, date and place of birth, profession and address, if you please."

The visitor's eyes opened wide under the lamp. He was undoubtedly ignorant of the formalities of making a statement. Why don't you say that you think you're being accused, thought Belot. Why don't you protest? Paul Tavernier made no protest. He closed his eyes and replied to Truflot's questions. Then the interrogation began.

His hands bathed in the edge of the bright light, clutching a short ruler, Picard summed up the case. According to the reports of Belot and Gaillardet he recalled that Paul Tavernier suspected no one; that he had not recognised the photo of the murderer, although the latter figured in the victim's album; that he had discovered or could imagine no motive which would provide any explanation for the murder (Paul Tavernier confirmed this in silence); that he had nevertheless asked *no* questions, evinced *no* surprise at *no* instant during these three days *except* when it was a question of Verdon. Gaillardet's report stressed this curiosity with regard to a stranger who had merely disappeared, whereas the others reported complete resignation regarding a brother who had been murdered. How did this come about? The mystery of his behaviour was put forward without the least acrimony, it seemed to await and even to hope for the most natural explanation.

Paul Tavernier shot a glance at Belot, smiled disdainfully and said in his slow voice:

"The atmosphere here is one of suspicion, I see. My congratulations, gentlemen, but your implications could have very serious consequences."

". . . very serious consequences," repeated Truflot, like a schoolboy finishing a dictation.

Paul Tavernier gave a start.

"Well, there's an answer for you," cried Picard with gruff cordiality. The ruler passed into one hand and began to beat on the table with short regular taps. Belot remained motionless. Paul Tavernier waited two or three interminable minutes.

"The answer is quite simple," he said at last. "On the one hand there are facts and on the other people. Totally ignorant of the reasons which might have led to the death of poor Étienne, I thought that the disappearance of this M. Verdon was going to put us on to the right path. I asked questions. All the more voluntarily, and now we come to people"—he turned towards the shadow of Belot—"in that I was faced by Sergeant Gaillardet, a frank, cordial and direct man." He paused, and stared at the ruler. "To my great regret I cannot say the same for M. Belot."

"Perhaps you would like to explain that," said Belot quietly.

"With pleasure. From the very start you showed yourself suspicious and reticent. You were convinced that I knew more than I was willing to say. You laid traps for me, you had me followed and you've had me brought here."

The voice had raised a tone and betrayed a trace of anger. Truflot repeated: ". . . had me brought here."

The visitor could not take his eyes off the ruler.

To everyone's surprise Belot fidgeted in his chair. "But I am most distressed," he said quickly—the ruler remained poised in the air and silence fell on the room, while the witness's eyes now freed, tried to make out the inspector's face—"most distressed. Composure always surprises us. I did in fact wonder whether you were not hiding . . . certain things. . . . And I admit that I asked my chief to see you. . . ."

He stuttered. With neck stretched forward and eyes half closed to avoid the dazzling lamp, his forehead wrinkled by this vain and exhausting effort, Paul Tavernier did not conceal his mistrust. Whereupon the ruler began to strike the desk again. At the same time Picard's face came forward into the light. It wore the most disconcerting smile.

"Please accept my colleagues' excuses, and mine too"—the face returned into the shadow. "We were to a certain extent deceived by your poor sister-in-law. She assured us that the victim never had any secrets from you . . . and I'm sure you would agree that there were secrets in his life?"

Perhaps because the lamp and the obsessive noise of the ruler would not allow him to relax, perhaps because this new politeness on the part of the police hardly appeared to him as genuine, Paul Tavernier's face remained set. All the same, he agreed. After the disappearance of M. Verdon no one could believe indeed that it was merely the gesture of a madman. Nevertheless he repeated that he knew ab-so-lutely nothing.

"Let's try and find out together!" suggested Picard. "What sort of a man was your brother?"

Paul Tavernier lowered his eyes. A veil of weariness descended upon his features.

"You must forgive me, Superintendent, emotion and sleepless nights have told on my nerves. That ruler . . ."

"Oh, but of course!"

Picard dropped the instrument of torture. Paul Tavernier gave a sigh of relief. His eyes flickered between the lamp and the blurred

118

figure. Since he obtained nothing further, he raised his head like a man ashamed of his weakness.

"It is difficult to analyse someone who is so close, particularly when you are of different temperaments. Étienne was a shy, introverted man. Our father always used to say that he could recognise nothing of himself in the boy. Our father was a man of admirable character, Superintendent, and he left behind him at Saint-Étienne the memory of an exceptional judge. He taught us to respect honour, the family, our status and our name. My mother was a Louant from Pelouze. She always showed herself the worthy consort of a man of such integrity. Yes, from birth we had two unique models. My father brought us up strictly, and he was right. 'Caesar's family must be above suspicion,' he used to say. He considered that everywhere, at college, or during the holidays, we ought to set an example. When I or my young brother, Vincent, were not top of the class he punished us as though we had been bottom of it!"

Paul Tavernier spoke arrogantly and aggressively. He no longer seemed to be blinded by the lamp. Picard had now bent forward with his hands joined beneath his chin. He listened without interrupting and thought, as Belot did, that this filial praise made a strange reply—but useful. He asked, however, for one detail.

". . . And was your brother Étienne never top?"

Paul Tavernier, who was resting his eyes—if not his mind—on the now good-natured features of Picard, looked at him with surprise. His voice was even more hostile as he replied: "That's true. He was not very bright . . . in fact very mediocre at school. And his punishments only served to make him more timorous and afraid. He was crazy about games. He wanted to be an airman, a tennis champion, and goodness knows what. Childishness, since he could never even hold a racket properly. All this distressed our parents. They had intended us for higher education. I graduated third from the Polytechnic. Vincent, after my father's death, was one of the best pupils at the state school of civil engineering. Étienne . . ."

A grimace intended to be sad but which was merely contemptuous, ended the phrase. Belot recalled Mme Colet's remarks while looking at the album. He also recalled an indication from Gaillardet's report: the equally contemptuous attitude of the Tavernier sisters-in-law towards "poor" Étienne.

"But your unfortunate brother made a success of his life, all the same?"

"That's true," Paul Tavernier replied curtly. "I must admit that I never thought he would. When he joined the firm of Gascogne—"

He broke off. Picard disappeared once more.

"When he entered Gascogne's. Go on, monsieur. On that subject we have some information which needs confirmation."

This information covered eighteen years of work in a few words. Étienne had started as a salesman in the Passy branch. He had become under-manager, then under-manager in the Champs-Elysées branch and finally director.

Paul Tavernier seemed to overcome an obstacle before replying. "I merely wanted to allude to this! When my brother, on leaving the regiment, joined the firm of Gascogne as a junior employee" —he uttered these words like a supreme insult—"rejecting the teaching and example of our father . . . of our father who had just died . . . my mother and I, faced with an accomplished fact, were so overwhelmed that Mother decided to cut off his allowance. I was unable and unwilling to oppose this indispensable sanction. I thought that my brother would give up everything for his monthly allowance. But no, this time he showed himself to be a man. Two years later our mother, who was seriously ill, wrote to him. He went to Saint-Étienne at the same time as myself. We met in the train. He told me that he had just been appointed under-manager of his business: he was only twenty-four. We spoke together. Our mother passed away a few days later. I thought that if I married him off suitably I could restore a lustre he should never have lost. Since childhood we had known the Bassett family, which was worthy in all respects of our own family. One of the two girls did not hide her feelings for my brother. He had never dared to notice it, particularly since she possessed a very substantial dowry. I arranged this marriage."

Paul Tavernier expressed himself like an officer taken prisoner, who boasts of his exploits to his captors.

"Did the marriage appear to have been a happy one?"

"No one could have been happier, Superintendent. My sister-in-law's grief affords the best proof."

"In these circumstances how do you explain. . . ."

A sharp knock at the door interrupted the sentence. The duty sergeant entered and laid a slip of paper in front of Picard. He read it. For some moments complete silence reigned. All that could be heard was the rain falling on a gutter and the distant noise of the city. Paul Tavernier rubbed his hair, his temples and his eyebrows. He was obviously trying to take advantage of the pause to collect his strength, and to prepare for the next round, for the interrupted sentence foreshadowed that the enemy was going over to the attack. But in what manner? That lamp. . . .

You're getting tired, thought Belot. We shall get you in a minute.

Picard wrote a swift note, handed it to the sergeant with his familiar gesture which meant "get on with it!" Then he wrote a few words in the margin of the slip of paper, handed it to Belot and turned once more to his visitor.

Belot read:

"6/10, 12.25 p.m. The Tavernier case. Communication from the Gendarmerie of Cosne (Nièvre).

We visited the Mobilisation Centre concerning the said Devaux, Jean-Marie-Lucien. Your information agrees with the particulars in his pay book. We have taken the successive addresses of the said person. (Five, all in Paris; the latest, in the rue Poncelet, was preceded by a date fifteen years old. Picard had just written in the margin: *Circulated to all parties.*) Devaux then gave as his domicile: Aboard the *Filipin*, Phocaean Navigation Company. He remained on the books of this company for ten years, then disappeared and the Gendarmerie's inquiries have been in vain. (Picard had written: *Despatched immediately to the Company.*) We then visited the hamlet of Villechaud, the man's birthplace. His parents live in a small shack on the bank of the river. The father is well known to us. He is seventy, a fisherman, a poacher and a drunkard. We found him dead drunk. The mother assured us in tears that her husband had got drunk because they had been shown the photograph of their son in the newspaper that morning. They recognised him, all the more because she claims they have not seen him since his military service. Despite our insistence she swore that she knew nothing about him, either in the past or in the present. They had only received a few postcards years ago from the colonies. She insists that the police are mistaken and that although he has been a bad son he cannot be a murderer. (Picard had written in the margin: *Insufficient, have notified Nevers.*)

From the age of twelve until his military service, Devaux was an apprentice mechanic and worked at the Colas Garage in Cosne. Apparently quite able, but someone always had to be behind him when a job failed to interest him.

We are sending you by post the typed text of the present report."

In the meantime the interrogation continued. Picard was once more in the shadow.

"If this marriage proved as happy as you say," he went on, and his voice was suddenly sharper, "how do you explain the fact that your brother concealed from his wife certain everyday details of his life?"

Paul Tavernier's cheeks flushed as if an invisible hand had struck them.

"I don't understand you, monsieur."

"So you don't understand me, monsieur? Yet it's very simple: your brother never got home before nine o'clock in the evening. He left his office *regularly* between a quarter past six and half past six. Once a month he went to spend the week-end with rich clients. For the benefit of Gascogne Motors he visited relations in the provinces. *Relations,* monsieur! I hate to accuse a dead man, but your brother lied to someone. To whom?"

Paul Tavernier sought visibly for a withering protest. All he could manage was: "Superintendent . . ." and his voice rang false.

"If he was not lying," Picard went on ruthlessly, "you are the only one who can prove it to us. Since he did not visit clients—Gascogne Motors would have known of it—and since he did not visit Mme Tavernier's family—Mme Tavernier would have known of it—it must have been *your* family he visited? *Your* family?"

Paul Tavernier bowed his head and closed his eyes.

"Of course . . . he was lying. We have no relations left in the provinces."

"Did he go to see Verdon?" Picard asked abruptly.

The eyelids half-opened in a look of astonishment.

"Verdon?"

This possibility had clearly never crossed his mind.

"Did he go to see Oudart?"

The face remained immobile. But the whites of his eyes became bloodshot and the veins of his neck stood out. Just as he had repeated Verdon, Paul Tavernier repeated:

"Oudart?"

Less experienced observers might have been taken in. A feigned reaction had just copied a real reaction. But the man covered up nobly. He frowned and asked: "Who is Oudart?"

"What are your relations with the firm of Gascogne?" was the reply.

He answered briskly. "I have none."

This was a mistake. He should not have seized with such enthusiasm upon such a different question. The witness without a secret does not willingly accept the jugglery of an interrogation. He will persist and protest. Paul Tavernier realised his mistake. He tried to repair it but Picard gave him no time.

"What about Mme Tavernier? Did Mme Tavernier have any dealings with the firm of Gascogne?"

"None either, I don't think."

"Which explains that your brother's . . . fairy stories ran no risk of being discovered by her. For there are others! Do you know what he earned latterly?"

"No."

Paul Tavernier seemed to have made up his mind either to be silent or to reply "no."

"No?" echoed Picard ironically. "You are the elder brother, the friend, the counsellor and marriage-maker, you are in the forefront during the days of mourning, and yet you don't know such a commonplace detail as your brother's salary?"

Paul Tavernier was silent. Less flushed and less tense he now stared at the lamp itself almost without effort, and appeared to be dreaming.

"Very well," said Picard. "This afternoon, at half past two, you will be good enough to go to the bank of the deceased and open his strong box in the presence of one of my inspectors. I am sorry that Mme Tavernier is away. She will understand."

Paul Tavernier nodded his assent and then turned his gaze on Picard.

"Is that all?"

A wild hope shone in his eyes. A sound on his left dispelled it forthwith. Belot had got to his feet. He walked round the table and stood by the side of Picard. Paul Tavernier looked savage. This double adversary now joined together to concentrate on the attack roused him to obvious rage, which he had difficulty in controlling.

"When you came in," said Belot, "you began a sentence about 'The Passenger.' Would you be good enough to finish it."

"What sentence? How do you expect me to remember? You have a way here of mixing up everything."

The shadow of Belot bent down to Picard.

"Truflot," ordered the chief, "let us have the gentleman's first hesitation!" There was a sound of pages being turned over. Paul Tavernier did not stir. The shrill voice of Truflot: "Here we are: I must also inform you at once that we do not expect to escape the demands of 'The Passenger' tonight. The gentleman replied: 'But . . .' Then he stopped, and he went on: 'You mean it's "The Passenger" who escapes you!'"

"*But* what?" asked the quiet voice of Belot.

Paul Tavernier was mute.

"*But* what?" Belot repeated.

"We cannot permit this silence, sir," said Picard. "I warn you that I shall keep you here until you have answered all our questions satisfactorily. Your behaviour is mysterious enough for me to make some painful decisions."

"*But* what?" repeated Belot.

Paul Tavernier exploded. "Keep me here as long as you like! Treat me as a suspect! Put me in jail. Drag me down in the mud! Ruin my name, my honour and my family . . . !"

He put his head in his hands.

"I shall reply for you," said Belot, still just as calm. "M. Picard's declaration struck you because just now in the church during the service you heard someone behind you say . . ."

Paul Tavernier's fingers grew taut in his hair.

"Now we know everything," added Belot.

The visitor raised his head. The light dazzled him once more. His mouth twisted in a ghastly grin. He murmured: "It was a trap."

"So you heard me," replied Belot.

"Did your brother gamble on horses?" Picard followed on.

Tavernier shook his head and said in a dull voice: "No."

"Oudart gambled on the horses," said Belot.

"Did he?" said Picard, feigning surprise. "So Oudart gambled on horses."

"That's right, isn't it, M. Tavernier?"

Since his outburst Paul Tavernier seemed exhausted and incapable of putting up any resistance. "I don't know who is Oudart."

"*What about Devaux?*"

Picard had sprung this name like a whiplash, and Paul Tavernier reacted like an animal. He sat up in his chair with lips drawn back and haggard eyes, but no sound came from his mouth. Picard declared brutally. "M. Tavernier, you know Devaux just as you know Oudart. Admit it. Admit it!"

He picked up his ruler and began to rap the table so vigorously this time that it seemed that the storm had burst in a downpour of hail in the study itself. Paul Tavernier lifted his hands towards his ears, but forced them to grip the collar of his overcoat.

"I-don't-know-him," he said in a low voice.

"So you don't know *him*. The use of the singular has betrayed you. You know that Devaux and Oudart are one and the same person and that this person . . ."

Picard broke off. Paul Tavernier collected himself and tried to assume his normal aspect of dignity, haughtiness and contempt. "I know nothing," he said.

"And you're not interested enough to let me finish the sentence—a sentence which will enlighten you on this Oudart and this Devaux about whom we are pestering you? Admit that you know him, monsieur! Admit that you know who murdered your brother. Admit it, monsieur!"

Paul Tavernier admitted nothing. For nearly an hour Picard and Belot gave him the full treatment, increasing every second the torture of their alternate questions. He continued to reply: "I don't know."

"Why had your brother been unhappy for years?"

"I don't know."

"Was your brother a miser?"

"I don't know."

"Why was he so gay last Sunday?"

"I don't know."

When asked how he had spent his time on the day of the crime he was up in arms for the last time. "You want to drive me to the limit of my wits by insulting me," he said. "What does it matter what I did that day since you know the murderer!" He finally had to give in. At two o'clock he had been to his office, which he left later to go to the Motor Show. There he had learnt of the murder. He had then hurried to the Boulevard Gouvion-Saint-Cyr. That was all.

He now stopped answering "I don't know," and replied "no," or shook his head. Sometimes his replies didn't make sense. Either he did not realise it or he did not care. The veins stood out on his temples. Each wrinkle, each fold in his face had become filled with sweat.

At ten minutes to two, Picard pushed back his chair declaring that he had finished . . . at least for today. He informed Paul Tavernier that he would probably have to question him again, and requested him therefore not to leave Paris. He then asked him to sign his statement. Paul Tavernier replied in a low voice that he would only sign it after having read it.

Truflot came forward with the pages in his hand. Picard rang for the duty officer.

"When the gentleman has finished reading you will see him out."

To Paul Tavernier he said: "Our respects, monsieur."

Picard and Belot went into the next room.

14

Thursday, the 6th. 2 p.m. to 7 p.m.
Police get up to tricks

At two o'clock, with all the lights on, Picard and Belot were finishing a dreary meal of sandwiches and beer on a corner of the office desk; Truflot, having finished his, had gone back to his table. Seated near them M. Malebranche was reading over once again all the reports of the case which had now been augmented by Paul Tavernier's statement.

"I couldn't have him locked up, nevertheless, because of his facial expressions. The swine," grumbled Picard.

"He's not the 'Brain,'" said M. Malebranche.

"I don't think so either," said Belot. "But *he knows!*"

"You were a bit tough with him all the same," muttered Malebranche. "Tired out emotionally and physically. . . ."

"A bit tough!" repeated Picard. "Not tough enough, you mean! Do you really believe that if he had a clear conscience this son of a judge wouldn't have defended himself? With his 'family' and his 'honour,' he would have threatened to sue, to send for his lawyer, to appeal to the Prefect, the Minister, the Pope! Read again his ridiculous little attempt at resistance in the first pages . . . and that's all there was! Belot's right. He *knows*."

"Agreed, but what does he know? Does he know 'the leader,' or only the tool, Devaux-Oudart? The idea of a gang becomes more and more attractive."

Belot finished his beer and wiped his mouth.

"We shan't be able to avoid the party this evening," he said.

The three men consulted their watches. M. Malebranche said weakly, "We may be in for a fine surprise."

At five minutes past two Belot saw Panigom and Gaillardet. They had checked M. Verdon's accounts and found them to be impeccable.

At ten minutes past two, studying the plan of the Gobelins Garage with Vitet, the managing director of the *Compagnie des Autobus*, Vedel, the architect of this Company, and the night foreman, Champaine, Belot began to work out his plans for the evening. Since dawn the garage had been kept under discreet observation, an easy matter thanks to the number of inquisitive onlookers. But Belot had not been back there. "The Passenger" had to be made to believe that he was master of the field.

M. Vitet brought with him a negative piece of news: Devaux had never been employed by the Company. Which obviously did not prevent him from having one or several accomplices in the place, working for him or for his master.

Private cars or buses, Belot thought to himself, its all the same world.

At a quarter past two Avenant telephoned that Longspès had given him the slip. In M. Archer's car they had made a tour of the stamp dealers. The director of Ibert and Bélier, Musard and Philippe Durand had emptied their wallets. Others had limited themselves to half-opening theirs. All of them had wanted to help save Verdon. The rounds were going to end with a sum which naturally bore no relation to the demands of "The Passenger." At each stage Longspès had grown more sombre and more excitable: Avenant had thought it a good idea to make him eat some lunch. He had chosen a peaceful little restaurant, while M. Archer's chauffeur returned to the Place des États-Unis with orders to pick them up an hour later. They had got to the coffee. The old man seemed more or less normal. He was initiating his companion into the charms of philately and then said that he needed to retire for a moment. As chance would have it the toilets were near the entrance, out of sight. But Avenant kept an eye on the stand where Longspès' overcoat and hat were hanging, and it was raining cats and dogs.

"Even so, the old fool had gone off bareheaded. God knew where!"

"Oh, I know too," said Picard. "Telephone all the stamp dealers you've not yet visited. Let the first one who receives a visit from Longspès keep him there and call us immediately. Report back here and you can leave again once we have information."

Picard then telephone to the Meudon Police Station.

"Are you still keeping the Villa Sans-Souci under observation? Good! If Longspès returns home, bring him in of his own free will or by force."

At half past two in the vaults of the Banque Parisienne de Crédit, rue Marbeuf, in the presence of the manager and a notary public, Gaillardet met Paul Tavernier. The dead man's bunch of keys—Mme Tavernier had entrusted it to the police—supplied the necessary key, but it needed a good twenty minutes for a specialist to discover the combination: 6-9-14. The strong box was half full of slim little packets, all of the same size, placed in regular piles and wrapped up in newspaper. A hand-written note bore the words: "As I have written in my will, the contents of this strong box are the property of my wife, Mme Étienne Tavernier, née Basset, and *of her alone*. Étienne Tavernier." Each packet contained twenty 1,000-franc notes, and there were thirty-five in all.

Gaillardet had an affidavit drawn up and affixed seals. He took away with him the hand-written note. Paul Tavernier did not utter a word throughout the whole proceedings.

The allusion to the will, however, contradicted one of his first allegations: he had assured Belot on Tuesday evening that his brother had not left one. Had he himself destroyed it in the fireplace of the boudoir at the Boulevard Gouvion-Saint-Cyr? Furthermore the note confirmed Étienne's attachment to his wife *against* someone. Who? Picard studied the numbers of the combination: 6-9-14. A date? More likely letters: F-I-N. Either an allusion to Mme Tavernier's nickname, Finette, or, with macabre intention, a precaution—like the note—against the day when this strong box would be opened in the way that had just been done. . . .

At two forty-five a small, plump, keen-eyed little woman, well-dressed but rather dishevelled asked to see Picard. It was Mme Barbason. (Clairval had telephoned twenty minutes earlier that she had just left her home.) She had obviously wept a great deal and had a handkerchief in her hand. She wanted to know if it was true that the ransom would be paid that evening to "The Passenger," and whether M. Barbason—she called her husband M. Barbason—had not lied to her, "to cheer her up." On the other hand she was loath to let a bandit ruin her cousin, since M. Verdon would have to repay this considerable loan. She felt it her duty, therefore, to put the police on its guard and to tell them to: "Look for the woman!" She was certain that M. Barbason had not given this a thought because, like all men, he never noticed anything. She was not so naïve. "Look for the woman!" Her cousin, Maurice, was a man of great charm. She knew it better than anyone else. "A relation sees most of the game. But like all men—" Mme Barbason liked to generalise—"his successes flattered him and he was easily taken in by one or another. Often by girls who were not of his class. Yes, *cherchez la femme!*"

Picard asked which one he had to look for. She did not know. For some time Maurice had been sulking with his family and they saw less of him. She admitted that she herself had been the cause of this little disagreement. On several occasions she had tried to open his eyes for his own good. She recommended marriage. He replied: "Find me the right bird." As though that was so easy! And Maurice continued to "be chosen," instead of choosing. There was certainly some creature. . . . Catch her before tonight and everything will be settled!

At ten minutes to three Inspector Ligaire, sent by Truflot to the rue de Valois (where the murderer had been seen on Monday half an hour after his crime), brought back from a certain Café Biard a valuable piece of information. This café was on the corner as you went in to the street; Devaux-Oudart had telephoned from there. He had drawn attention to himself as he left the booth because he had drunk two whiskies at the counter, gulping them down as though they were water. The waiter could not remember his face, but remembered his upturned collar, his glazed eyes and shaky hand.

Unfortunately it was a public box with automatic dialling and the call could not be traced. As for the loitering of the man in the street, no one, no tradesman or concierge had been struck by it.

At three o'clock the Gendarmerie of Sarlat (Dordogne) telephoned a piece of vital information. That morning they had received the photo of the murderer for circulation in the Gascogne works. A few of the old workers who had been employed twenty years earlier in Paris—the Sarlat factory did not yet exist then—had recognised Devaux. Some of them had worked with him as driver-mechanics on test cars, and sometimes on delivery of cars to the dealers. Devaux had just left the regiment. In the general opinion he was a "tough kid" with a sense of humour, skilful, reckless but lazy and inclined to show off. He was sacked at the end of a few months.

Ten minutes later a telephone call from M. René Gascogne, notified by the works manager, confirmed the information, after a search through the personnel records. Picard asked who had been employed first: Devaux or Étienne Tavernier. It was Devaux. He then asked if by chance Tavernier had not been employed on the recommendation of Devaux. M. Gascogne referred him to the manager of the Passy Agents who already held that position at that time.

The Passy manager had no recollection of the temporary delivery man, but he recalled quite clearly that Tavernier had applied on his own. "The son of a magistrate. . . ."

At three twenty-five Vitet, Vedel and the head foreman, Champaine, were shown in to M. Malebranche's office by Belot, where they were joined by Picard. The architect demonstrated once more the impossibility of entering the garage except by the gates. Belot produced his final plans. They met with general approval, the details were finalised and the party split up full of hope.

At three-thirty the inspectors, who had been checking Devaux's former lodgings, the last of which in the rue Poncelet dated from fifteen years before, returned empty-handed. Of all the landlords, porters, tenants and neighbours of these buildings some had disappeared and the others remembered nothing.

On the other hand detailed information was provided by the Phocaean Shipping Company. This was to be expected since Devaux had left the Company only five years before after having worked with it for ten years without a break. Employed as a mechanic, originally in the cargo vessels *Filipin* and *Trinité*, of the Indo-China-Far-East Line and then ashore in the Saigon workshops, with a good record, until the day when the disappearance of spare parts had attracted attention. Although it had been impossible to catch him red-handed, his guilt was beyond doubt and it was touch and go whether the Saigon Company would not hand him over to the authorities. Put on a boat for Marseilles, Devaux had been sacked without asking for his balance of pay. He had been told: "Look out, we shall keep an eye on you!"

The Company had sent his record to Picard.

At four o'clock, their raincoats dripping with rain as if they had fallen into the Seine, Inspector Malicorne and two of his men brought in to Picard the driver, Fernand Camus, in handcuffs. An informer had reported his presence in a Saint-Maur *bistrot* in which the said Camus had lived for some years and where, since Monday evening, seated at the back of the café behind a frosted glass partition he had not left the proprietor's table not even bothering to shave and turning pale each time the door opened. When the inspectors came in he fled through the back shop. A chase followed through the streets of Saint-Maur. Camus showed surprising speed for his age and corpulence. "It was miles before we caught him," said Malicorne, who was always inclined to exaggerate.

The owner of the *bistrot* accompanied the police officers. He was a sorry sight. He, too, was in handcuffs.

Camus apologised profusely for having fled. Such ridiculous behaviour showed that he had lost his head. The whole story of the crime, "The Passenger" and the ransom had driven him crazy and he was very ready to "come clean." The name Devaux meant nothing to him. The name of Oudart aroused his admiration: "I must say the cops are on the ball." He admitted without difficulty that the third rogue in the Asnières burglary had been Oudart. The two others had not denounced him for obvious reasons of honour. But today this did not apply; things had gone too far!

On all the facts leading up to "the accident," Camus confirmed the theory which Belot had put forward the evening before. Oudart, whom he saw from time to time with pleasure because it always earned him an expensive apéritif, had spoken to him the week before of an easy and *honest* job (for since the burglary Camus

132

naturally only accepted honest work). It was a question of a former mate to whom Oudart had lent money when they were in the army; the mate had become a millionaire; in spite of this he refused to pay the debt back and even refused to see his creditor. In short, he was a swine. Naturally, since then the newspapers had enlightened Camus. But at that time he couldn't know, he had been trusting. So Oudart wanted to stick on to the chap's heels for just half a day only: he undertook to be paid back that evening. He had hired Camus and his taxi for that unfortunate Monday by promising him a tip—large enough to buy a car of his own. On Monday they had taken up their position on the Boulevard Gouvion-Saint-Cyr. They had waited for Tavernier to come out. They had followed him to the U bus stop. Oudart then decided to take the same bus a few stops further on. Camus had followed behind to pick up his passenger again when the latter chose to get out.

About the "accident" itself he protested with the greatest vehemence. Nothing had ever been planned between Oudart and himself for the very good reason that Oudart had *never* mentioned murder. Camus had seen Tavernier fall and this had upset him so much that he had put his foot down on the accelerator instead of on the brake. He had recovered himself immediately, of course—and the truck ran into him. Nothing planned . . . pure chance! Picard remarked that a chance so favourable to the murderer risked costing Camus very dear. Camus looked at his handcuffs and said sadly: "Could be."

To the question: "Did Oudart appear to you to be in his normal state?" he replied: "Absolutely. Full of drink, as usual."

At a quarter to five Inspector Nevers, who had been to Cosne and then to Villechaud on Picard's orders, telephoned the results of his inquiries.

They confirmed those of the Gendarmerie. Devaux's mother had been speaking the truth when she maintained that she had not seen her son for twenty years. The whole village corroborated this. But what the gendarmes had failed to report, perhaps wrongly, was that there was another child—a daughter, Marie, a year older than the criminal and who like him had left the village many years before. The women of Villechaud who today were between forty and forty-five remembered her as a trollop. Some of them used an even stronger word. The men leered, some of them with embarrassment, but all of them agreed that she had gone to Paris to "hit the high spots." The mother, who had not been the first to mention her daughter, declared that she worked in a shop there. Nor had the daughter abandoned her parents as the son had. She had been back to see them from time to time, staying two or three days. And if they wanted proof that she was not hitting the high spots she was always glad to accept a five-franc piece. But when the inspector had asked the date of her last visit the mother had hesitated quite a bit before replying: "Years ago . . . Five years . . ." and she had added at once: "I am sure she's dead, otherwise she would at least have sent me a card." She agreed that the son had forgotten his parents, but Marie—no, "she was a good girl."

The detective had asked to see the letters or the postcards from the two children. The mother had not kept any. It seemed more likely that she had kept all of them until that morning in view of the warm ashes in the hearth, which she did not explain. No photographs . . . she had forgotten the addresses of both son and daughter. The inspector would have arrested this mother, who was a little too slick for his taste, without a qualm, but he was certain that even in hell she would not say any more.

At five o'clock the duty officer laid three copies of *Le Grand Journal Soir* on Picard's table. Splashed across the front page in enormous type was the announcement: "M. Verdon's family having asked the police to abandon the search, will this evening pay 'The Passenger' on the U, the sum of 500,000 francs demanded by him." The telephone call from M. Barbason to *Le Grand Journal* filled the centre of the page accompanied by a rather reticent commentary, for the restaurant keeper had refused to see anyone. On the other hand "The Passenger," despite the promises in his letter, had not replied to the requests for an explanation published in the morning edition of *Le Grand Journal*. Was it to be concluded that he had learned of Barbason's decision *before it was made public*? If this were so, in which group of close friends or family was he lurking? A hypothesis so serious that *Le Grand Journal Soir* refused categorically to entertain it: it merely printed it in big type.

The leading article recorded with subdued bitterness the triumph of evil over good, for "The Passenger" was not only the kidnapper of

M. Verdon, his hands were scarlet with the blood of M. Tavernier! Restrained by the emotion—and the financial strength—of a family more sensitive than heroic, was the hand of Justice to spare the criminal because he had committed two crimes instead of one? *O tempora o mores! Le Grand Journal Soir* generally so strictly conformist, almost ranged itself with the opposition Press.

At five minutes past five, Sergeant Beauchamp returned from Toul. He immediately joined Belot and Gaillardet who for the past hour had been working out the team for the garage that evening.

At half past five, when they were expressing surprise that no news had been received of Longspès, M. Barbason telephoned Picard.

Longspès had just paid him a visit—if one could call his crazy intrusion a visit. Bareheaded, his long white locks in disarray and glued to his temples, his suit wringing wet, he had pushed past the maid, rushed into the flat, flung himself upon Barbason and had pummelled his hands and half broken his arms with wild cries of "Thank you!" "Thank you!" mingled with sobs. He had related that since the morning he had been trying to collect the sum needed for the ransom: the results were pathetic. To make matters worse the police had followed him to rob him of this money; he had given them the slip; he was being careful not to fall into their clutches by going anywhere where they might find him; but he had just read *Le Grand Journal Soir* and learned of the abandonment of the search, of "the family's decision." He was out of his mind with joy.

M. Barbason had then asked him for the money he had collected. This request though natural enough completely transfigured the old madman. He had shouted in a voice of thunder: "So you haven't got the money—not if you need mine! You're in the swindle! You're working with the police! You want to kill my boss! You're a murderer!" Then he disappeared, as if by magic, leaving behind only a pool of water on the carpet.

At six o'clock a conference took place in M. Malebranche's office. Picard addressed it with a sheet of notes in his hand.

"We now know nearly all about the life of the criminal, and some of his relations with the victim. He was born at Villechaud forty years ago and seems to have inherited the drinking habits of his poacher father. From the age of twelve to twenty, he worked in the Colas Garage at Cosne. Military Service at Toul, during the summer manoeuvres made friends with Étienne Tavernier. Joined Gascogne Motors as a mechanic and probably suggested to his mate that he should also join the firm. Étienne was crazy about sport. He must have been dazzled by the stories of this specialist: 'A witty kid, a dare-devil and a show off.' But since he, Étienne, was an armchair sportsman there was no question of his driving test cars. He was only good for an office job—in which he later was to make a fortune. One of Devaux's jobs was to deliver cars to the different showrooms. He must have learned at the Passy Agents that they had a job vacant. Meanwhile he got the sack because he was lazy. We then have a gap of about three years during which time he lived in Paris. We can presume he worked in various garages; he did nothing to draw attention to himself. He felt an urge to travel: there follows the Phocaean Shipping Company, cargo-ships, Indo-China and the Far East. Then he decided to settle down and was given a job in Saigon. He became involved in some shady transactions. Through drink or bad company? In any case he was threatened with prosecution, brought back to France and sacked. He himself has given us proof of his guilt: the moment he leaves the Company Devaux disappears for ever and Oudart enters the scene. The dates fit. Dismissed from the Company: Marseilles, January. The appearance of Oudart: Paris, Hôtel d'Azur, February. This alias not only proves his former lapses but also that the fellow had no intention of mending his ways. A year later there is the Asnières burglary. A petty affair. What interests us is that as soon as he returned to Paris, his former comrade, Étienne Tavernier, becomes depressed. Here, too, the dates agree. We learn from Mme Tavernier herself that her husband's mood changed during the year their son took his first communion five years ago. This is Oudart's year. *Five years ago* constantly appears in our reports. *Five years ago* Tavernier changed his mode of life, altering his way of receiving his salary and of depositing it in his bank. *Five years ago* he declared that he was obliged to stay late every evening at his office and to spend one week-end a month with clients. The first point is that part of his money went in an unknown direction. The second that he himself followed suit. For a moment we thought that he must have joined the gang to which Devaux supposedly belongs. I now think he was only its victim. How did they put pressure on him? Was it a woman —Devaux's sister?"

"I was expecting that," said M. Malebranche.

"A tart who however never was arrested. We don't know anything about her yet, except that she stopped seeing her parents *five years ago*. Five years again! Her mother insists that she must be dead. I've looked into the murders and disappearances of the past five years and unsolved cases of which she might have been the victim. . . . Nothing. Nor on the civil register, either. I imagine she is still alive and her brother's associate. I think that the note in the strong box in which Tavernier declares expressly: 'The entire contents of this box belong to my wife and to her alone,' was a kind of reaction with regard to another woman who might have considered that she, too, had some rights."

"Fair enough," said Belot.

"The actual location of this strong box shows that he was protecting himself from someone. It looks as though Tavernier, after two years of absolute submission during which he handed over everything he earned over and above his fixed salary, organised himself and hid part of his resources from the enemy. He wanted to ensure his wife's future and through her that of his family (for there is no shadow of doubt that Mme Tavernier loves their two children). The first letters of the affectionate nickname he gave her served for the combination. And if he was content to leave a note inside instead of a will which might explain everything, it was probably so that his wife could find this will at home in an accessible place—for example, in the drawer of a piece of furniture. . . ."

"Yes," said Belot, "and it wasn't she who found it."

"So much for Tavernier. Now let's deal with Verdon. During the twenty-six hours since we heard of his kidnapping, nothing—apart from the aggressor—allows us to link these two cases. We only know that he appeared anxious after the crime. He is a few years younger than Tavernier and Devaux, so they did not meet in the army. . . . No mutual friends, no common activities. No apparent mystery in his life. It's true that because he's a bachelor and lives alone since the death of his mother, it is difficult to cross-check for him.

At any rate he has an excellent reputation, which does not give us the right to accuse him of complicity either. Still better than an impeccable reputation, he inspires affection and devotion. Remember the statement of his friend, Durand. And Longspès! No, like Tavernier, Verdon fell into a trap."

"Suppose it was set by the same Marie Devaux?" suggested M. Malebranche.

"Then we should have the missing link. Verdon's cousin begged us to 'look for the woman.' She is obviously in love with her cousin and her request might be a sign of obsession. But she seemed sensitive, a good observer and very much superior to her husband, Barbason. We know that Verdon liked little intrigues, harmless enough ones, if we are to believe his friend, Durand. He even appears faithful to his daily help. This does not exclude the possibility of a more serious affair, which perhaps ended six months ago—this is the date when he flirts with his cousin's waitress and when he falls back on the daily cleaner—but whose consequences could have led to his being kidnapped."

"Marie Devaux is older than her brother," said Belot.

"A year older. I can guess what worries you. She is six years older than Verdon. Well, what of it? If their affair started a long time ago she might, on the contrary, have used her experience to get the young man under her thumb. We see it done every day. Whatever the truth, one thing is certain—and we must come back to this— Verdon appeared anxious the day after the crime. Whereas Tavernier, twenty-four hours before being shot was in exceptionally high spirits, as though *he had been delivered from his torment,* Verdon sees in the murder a warning, a sign. . . ."

Picard was just finishing when the Prefect appeared in person. He had read *Le Grand Journal Soir* and did not conceal his ill temper. He listened without a word to the explanations and plans and when they had finished he merely replied: "I wish you luck, gentlemen!" in a voice which left in no doubt what would happen in the event of a setback.

Belot sent off Blondel to Barbason with a thick envelope sealed with red wax and specific orders. He then stood up abruptly and said: "I'm like the Prefect: I'm getting irritated. In three days we have assembled a magnificent dossier on the murderer which leads to a telephone call made from the rue de Valois half an hour after the crime. Since that moment, half past two on Monday, M. Devaux has disappeared, flown, evaporated into space. To whom was this telephone call made? If we knew we should know everything! And where is he hiding? At Paul's?"

M. Malebranche gave a scandalised "Oh!"

"I can't help it," Belot went on. "Paul Tavernier obsesses me. He lies every time he breathes. . . . Never mind, I'm off to see him!"

At seven o'clock Belot rang the bell of Paul Tavernier's flat. Opposite the building he had seen Sergeant Vilain sitting in a taxi, the rain drumming on its roof. Paul had not stirred since his return from Police Headquarters.

He himself opened the door. Was he expecting someone? Was he looking from a window at the passers-by on the Quai d'Orsay? Had he dismissed the servants? In this luxury building, sumptuous in quite a different way from the apartments of the Boulevard Gouvion-Saint-Cyr, this manner of answering the door suggested the holidays, the family at the seaside, the husband alone in Paris between weekends. But the family was only away accompanying a corpse, and this lone man himself seemed to belong to the next world.

He displayed no emotion other than a kind of dull bewilderment. Belot having announced that he wanted to search the flat, he replied in a toneless voice: "Have you a warrant?"

"No."

And he stood aside as though Belot had replied: "Yes."

Examination of eight rooms, plus those of the two servants, produced nothing. In the pantry Belot found a cook and a chambermaid. He did not ask them a single question. Nor did he question Paul Tavernier although the name of Marie Devaux was on his lips. He knew that he would receive no reply and he did not want to prolong an illegal search more than he need.

As he passed Vilain again he said: "I'll have you relieved."

"Don't bother. I'm not sleepy."

"Well, goodnight!"

"And the same to you!" cried Vilain from the bottom of his heart.

15

The night of the 6th/7th October,
Commonly called "the night of the ransom"

It had poured since dawn. In the evening the rain finally ceased, and crowds of people began to invade the Gobelins. The crowd did not think there was anything tragic in the situation, nor feel any guilt for its curiosity. It simply wondered how much spectators would get to see today. People envisaged trouble from the police and so took precautions. They were surprised to be allowed to get as far as the wall of the depot, disturbed, almost disappointed at being greeted by good-tempered policemen repeating: "You won't see anything! Move on!" Those posted at the main gate said in fatherly tones: "Don't stay there, you'll get run over!" The buses certainly returned at ferocious speed. Someone said: "They've been given orders." A conductor coming out of the garage replied: "What orders? Orders to want a bit of a nap?" Many after a few colourful wisecracks at the expense of the police, wandered off to the cinema, a café or to bed. The artful and the oafs did not budge: they formed a small crowd which the police left in peace, following the orders they had been given and perhaps because men from the Murder Squad were dispersed discreetly amongst them.

From time to time one of the inquisitive stood on tiptoe to examine from a distance the courtyard and the big washing bay where nobody had started work yet—a brightly lit void. Every quarter of an hour or so a bus noisily carried out a final turning and backing before being engulfed in the black depths. The driver and conductor reappeared directly, stopped at the glass cabin and had a conversation with an invisible interlocutor which could not be heard outside. The man on tiptoe imparted the fruits of his observations to his neighbours.

In this quiet street, which might have been in the provinces— three cafés had closed at eight o'clock at the request of the Prefecture —a smell of damp earth, as mysterious as the rest, recalled the countryside after rain. It was a cool evening. Pipes were lit. A woman who had remarked aloud that she was the only one of her sex in the gathering, attracted a volley of pleasantries which in no way alarmed her. Slightly before ten o'clock a diversion was caused by the arrival of two men in plain clothes, soon followed by two others and then a fifth. One by one they went into the glass cabin and reappeared in overalls. This was the team of washers. Everything happened in fact exactly as on any other evening. At the usual time Champaine and his assistant had relieved the day shift. At ten o'clock the first bus was brought out to be given a bath. Apart from the presence of the police at the gateway you would never have suspected anything unusual.

Half past ten . . . eleven o'clock . . . half past eleven. The theatregoers provided a new and mixed public. At the same time the newspaper vans arrived with their news sheets. A gay and noisy pack of journalists disappeared into the houses opposite the depot. They had paid very high prices for windows on the top floor with a clear view of the courtyard and the glass roof at the back. For they knew that the main gate would be shut as usual at half past twelve.

The three last buses of the U Line, which were to occupy the end of each of the three rows of vehicles, came in at twelve midnight, twelve-fifteen and twelve-thirty. The first in naturally took its place in the back row, the second in front of it and the third in front of the two others. It was the first bus—today No. 28—which had been selected by "The Passenger" as the receptacle for the ransom. Following its normal timetable the No. 28 had left the Levallois terminus at eleven-thirty. It was empty. Throughout the day nearly seventy-five per cent of the normal passengers had boycotted the U Line. By nightfall the figure had risen to 100 per cent. The pedestrians pointed to the empty, brightly lit interiors in which the imaginative could distinguish the outlines of the victim and the man in grey. Out of contempt for public cowardice the conductors stood reading newspapers on the platform, and the drivers no longer even drew up at the compulsory stops.

Although it was boycotted like its brothers, No. 28 was carrying out its last journey without any interruption to routine. Everything was normal until on the Boulevard Saint-Germain near the rue Bellechasse, the engine started making disturbing noises. The conductor made his way up the bus, opened the small glass window which allowed him to talk to the driver and uttered these strange words:

"Is it here?"

Bent forward as though anxiously listening to his engine, the driver replied: "Yes." Anyone observing them from a distance would have seen nothing strange in their behaviour.

The monster gave two or three jolts and conked out. The driver leapt down from his seat and opened the bonnet. He was joined by his mate. Cars slowed down and passers-by stopped: "A U bus broken down on this night of all nights!" But no one dared approach. The conductor looked up and down the street.

"Go and telephone from that café," he said.

The driver obeyed. When he got back he announced loudly: "Not for half an hour. Just our bloody luck!"

This half an hour allowed the two following buses to overtake the one which had broken down. The first one was told to notify the depot. The second, to the amazement of the crowd, contained two passengers—two men sitting in the first-class compartment. They were seen to get up and rush towards the back platform where one of them exclaimed:

"So that one there will be the last!"

They immediately got out and took up position near the open bonnet.

"We're from *Le Grand Journal*. Can we give you a hand? It'll make such a good story."

The driver merely replied: "Hands off!"

"At least tell us what happened."

"That!" replied the driver maliciously. He was a man with greying hair and an imperturbable face. With his mate he formed "a perfect team" (*Le Grand Journal* of Friday).

After half an hour a small truck hurled out of the rue de Solferino. It took the corner on two wheels, charged up behind the bus, only coming to rest a couple of inches away with a screech of brakes. The man at the wheel had a placid rather sleepy face and his companion sported a big moustache. They were both wearing mechanic's blue overalls with the Company's cap.

The man with the moustache said to the two men of the 28: "Hi, Douhet! Hi, Brigaille!"

And they replied: "Hallo, there! You can't be in much of a hurry to get to bed!"

The driver of the small truck who was also the mechanic's mate, replied:

"And I suppose you find this a good moment to choose? Unless it's another of 'The Passenger's' tricks."

The driver, Brigaille, amiably remarked to the reporters: "Look out! I know these men. They look harmless enough but if you get in their way they'll bash your face in."

Then he climbed back into his seat. The man with the moustache dived into the engine, after which he lay down under the bus asking his assistant from time to time to pass him a tool. The assistant whistled with eyes closed. The spectators began to get bored. But who would think of leaving when something dramatic might happen at any moment? Reappearing from the bowels of the earth, the man with the moustache said to Brigaille: "Try her!"

The engine fired, but very shakily.

"Try and get home like that," he said. "Keep it slow, of course."

Brigaille protested. If the expert couldn't do better than that he had better take the bus home himself. That was the rule. The expert shrugged his shoulders, climbed up into the driving seat and Brigaille sat next to him. He ordered his mate: "Follow us!"

"All aboard!" shouted the reporters.

"No, gentlemen," said the conductor.

He drew the chain across the platform and hung out the notice. "Bus Full." The bus drove off at snail's pace, followed by the truck and a taxi into which the journalists had clambered. It was like a circus procession behind an invisible corpse.

Brigaille said to the man with the moustache: "Everything all right?"

"Fine," he replied.

Between midnight and a quarter past Champaine had shown surprise and then anxiety at the lateness of the 28. The crowd had seen him leave his cabin, come out of the main gate twice and peer down the street. The explanation brought by the quarter past twelve bus apparently allayed his fears. He halted the vehicle in a corner of the courtyard, and did the same with the one which arrived next: a washer would park them after the 28 had got back.

In this way the regular places in the garage would not be changed despite the breakdown, and "The Passenger"—since everyone obeyed his orders—could reproach no one. This at least was how Champaine expressed himself to the crews of the two buses as he wished them goodnight. He then returned to the street to watch for the 28. The remarks he exchanged with the crews were heard by the crowd because he spoke in a loud voice. It was in this way that they discovered the reason for his restlessness. Some of the reporters came down from their dovecotes and Champaine was kind enough to repeat his speech. Everyone was on the alert for the sound of an engine coming from outside the depot.

"I can hear something," said one of the policemen.

It was a taxi, bringing M. Barbason—a taxi well known to the Prefecture. M. Barbason got out, looked suspiciously at the silent groups of civilians and uniformed police. Champaine introduced himself. M. Barbason replied with an accent broadened by emotion: "I am the cousin."

With his right hand he tapped the briefcase held tightly under his left arm, adding:

"I've brought it!"

Champaine led him to the cabin. The taxi left and the police took up a watchful attitude. A murmur rose from the ill-lit ground to the dark sky (the journalists were no longer the only ones leaning out of windows): Wealth had just appeared. Five hundred thousand francs! Villas, gardens, jewels, motor cycles, enough happiness for several families, and all that was being offered to a criminal! For a moment the whole street shared the feelings of *Le Grand Journal*. It would be a thousand times better that M. Verdon should perish and that morality should be preserved.

The end of the first act was not long delayed. At five minutes to one, the 28 and its escort reached the garage. Champaine emerged

144

once more. On the driving seat the man with a moustache said softly to Brigaille: "You take the wheel as soon as we get through the gate, and continue at a snail's pace until you reach the middle of the courtyard."

Brigaille nodded. As soon as he was through the entrance the man with the moustache braked, leapt down and said: "She's all yours!"

Some journalists tried to approach but the police intervened.

The street then witnessed a surprising spectacle. The breakdown truck, which had now also entered the courtyard, passed the 28, sped towards the washers and pulled up short with a screech of brakes in front of them. Its driver, the assistant mechanic, shouted: "Hi, you bunch of cowards!"

The washers burst out laughing.

"It's Valée! You old bastard! Hi, Valée! Hi there, mate! Come down and we'll soon fix you up."

Valée did not get down. The truck zig-zagged to the end of the courtyard like a drunken vehicle, made a sudden half-turn, went into reverse and was swallowed up in the dark corridor which was ready to receive the three buses, disappeared from view only to reappear a moment later and shoot back to the gateway. The washers were still laughing. The man with the mustache shook hands with Champaine and climbed in quickly beside his assistant.

The truck left the garage. As the two employees of the 28 left at the same time, Champaine closed the doors of the gateway behind them.

The people in the street wondered what the police would do. They simply withdrew. They left behind them *one* policeman who did not even remain in front of the entrance. Most of the crowd decided to go home. All that remained were a few fanatics and a few down and outs—just enough to prevent the anonymous representatives of the Murder Squad from remaining alone. Visible only to the gallery spectators the second act opened in the following manner.

The 28, which its driver had left in the middle of the courtyard, was washed according to regulations. As soon as the job was finished one of the washers sounded the horn. M. Barbason and Champaine came out of the glass cabin side by side. M. Barbason carried a fair-sized white package in his right hand: binoculars revealed that this was a very thick envelope. He climbed into the bus and when he got out again his right hand was empty.

Champaine then took the wheel and M. Barbason got in at his side. Beneath the eyes of the silent washers, the 28 moved forward slowly with great difficulty; then in reverse it disappeared beneath the frosted glass roof. The washers seemed turned to stone. When the sound of the engine suddenly died, a great silence descended on the depot and rose to the windows where the onlookers were holding their breath.

M. Barbason and Champaine reappeared one behind the other. Beneath the beard with its blue glints, the cousin's cheekbones were pale. Champaine motioned to the washers. Some of them rushed for the twelve-fifteen and others for the twelve-thirty bus. These vehicles had to be cleaned and parked as quickly as possible. Champaine and M. Barbason stood motionless and silent some distance apart.

At this moment the spectators made out a curious figure approaching swiftly from the end of the street. It was waving its arms, leaping in little bounds from one paving-stone to the other. It was like a puppet worked by a nervous manipulator. On reaching the wall it leapt forward. It was a tall, thin, bareheaded old man in a black shiny suit which seemed to cling to his body. He reached the gate, wavered, snorted and began to bang vigorously on the iron. The policeman who was walking up and down ran over to him.

"Is this the Gobelins Depot?" cried the old man. "Open up at once! Have them open up! I'm bringing the ransom. Not the 500,000 francs, but all I could scrape together. I'm M. Verdon's clerk—I'm Longspès. I'm the one he wrote to. I'm in the newspaper and I'm bringing the money!"

There were noises at the windows. The journalists scuttled down the stairs. Longspès continued to drum on the door.

The policeman replied:

"But . . . his family is there!"

"It's not true!" roared Longspès. "It's not his family. It's the murderer!"

A thrill of eager and terrified pleasure ran through the spectators.

The policeman, beside himself, joined Longspès in hammering on the door. The journalists from the gallery saw Champaine cock an ear and make swiftly for the door. But he did not open it, and confined himself to asking: "Who is it?"

"It's Longspès," roared the old man. "It's me, it's the ransom! O dear! O dear! They're fooling you. The police are fooling you. M. Verdon's family is fooling you. They want him killed. Open up!"

The policeman considered the time ripe to add some explanation to these curses. He said in a loud voice: "This gentleman insists that the person in there is not one of the family, he is the murderer!"

Champaine's voice rapped out: "The person in here is a member of M. Verdon's family. I have orders to let no one in, not even the police . . . not even my directors. I shall not open."

Longspès' reply was so prompt that none of those around had the time to interfere. He stepped back a few paces and flung himself with lowered head against the iron door. A cry went up from the crowd. The old man spun round and the policeman caught him in his arms. They expected to see him with a bleeding gash in his forehead. But there was no visible sign of damage, except—an ominous sign—that he was smiling beatifically. The policeman called for help. A reporter and a gloomy faced spectator—he was the living image of Sergeant Beauchamp—immediately volunteered. The policeman chose the spectator. "You look the stronger," he said. And held up by the two men the puppet with the broken strings was led away without resistance.

Order was gradually restored. On the other side of the wall, Champaine had joined M. Barbason. They had conferred, Barbason had shrugged his shoulders. Throughout the episode the washers had gone on with their job. The two buses were now ready. Champaine parked them as he had parked the 28. M. Barbason accompanied each vehicle on foot. The ceremony over, the two men were seen to make their way to the cabin and disappear just as a taxi, presumably called by telephone, drew up outside the gate. Champaine half opened one of the doors, shook hands formally with M. Barbason and closed the door again as soon as the taxi had driven off. He returned to the washers. He was obviously going to stay with them until dawn. A strange comedy, of which the last act was in principle to be played in the wings. At one of the windows a voice recited:

"If everything goes well: if *no one* sets foot in this part of the depot until dawn, M. Verdon will be restored to his friends on Friday afternoon. But if the police should consider it their duty to spoil everything by their presence or trickery . . . then *so much the worse!*"

The moment the 28 had been parked at the back of the garage and the noise of the engine had died, even before Champaine and M. Barbason had left their seats, a shadow had jumped silently into the vehicle. Bent double it made its way to the first class. A diffused light, the fringe edge from the distant lamps, outlined the seats in black, on one of them lay the thick envelope containing the ransom. The shadow seized it, turned it over, felt the five seals with his finger. Then he crouched on the floor and used the time to reflect while he waited.

Things had gone off very well. Of course they had been obliged to appeal to several outsiders. How many? The director of the company, M. Vitet, one; the architect, M. Vedel, two; Champaine, three; the conductor and driver of the 28, four and five; the assistant mechanic, six (a splendid fellow, Valée!). Six. It was a lot, but there had been no alternative. Unless the director of the Company could be taken for an accomplice or an imbecile the reputation of the five others stood so high with him that it was impossible to suspect them. In the operation itself the half dozen had been reduced to four. It was to be hoped that apart from them no one suspected anything, despite the number of individuals involved.

Seated like a Buddha on the floor of the 28, his ear strained to the slightest sound and eyes alert, Belot sought to assure himself that he had made no mistakes.

First of all, by delaying the arrival in the Boulevard Saint-Germain of the repair truck, the last two buses had been forced to overtake this one and their teams to leave the garage without learning anything of the breakdown except the official version. Otherwise, they might have been surprised—firstly, that there were two breakdown men when at night only one went out as a rule, and secondly, that the mechanic with the moustache, a figure as familiar as Valée, had undergone certain almost miraculous changes as regards the shape of his cheeks and the colour of his eyes.

At the depot the manoeuvre had called for the greatest delicacy.

Careful investigation had stressed the reliability of the night foreman and the five washers: but they had nevertheless to be kept out of the secret. It had therefore been necessary to organize an apparently futile and idiotic backing of the truck right into the garage, idiotic perhaps—but essential if a clandestine passenger had to be dropped from it. The providential reputation of Valée as a joker had carried it off to general applause.

In the same way it was Champaine and not one of the washers who had just parked the 28. Beneath his expert feet a perfectly sound engine had continued to groan just as it had when driven by Brigaille or the man with the moustache.

Belot recapitulated.

At the central workshop Brigaille's telephone call had been answered by a night foreman who replied: "At once!" (Brigaille's translation: "not for half an hour"). He had informed Valée. Valée had left with the truck. In one of those deserted streets which are as well known to the police as to night prowlers, two men were waiting for him. One dressed as a mechanic of the Company with a moustache: Gaillardet. The other looking like any casual passer-by and who was going to turn into a phantom, a shadow. Gaillardet next to Valée, he in the truck—all three had waited for zero hour. Then at breakneck speed the plan had been put into practice.

Under the tarpaulin hood of the truck, Belot could see nothing. He continued nonetheless to follow in his mind's eye each of the details he had planned minute by minute. The stop on the Boulevard Saint-Germain, Gaillardet with his head in the engine then sliding under the bus, hidden as much as possible: disguises are distrusted at headquarters. For the same reason on reaching the depot, the shadow knew that Gaillardet would be met by Champaine alone to learn from him whether anything abnormal had happened so far.

Champaine had promised he would meticulously search the vehicles already in place before the arrival of the washers: on top, inside and underneath, as well as those which returned later. If he had discovered anything at all he would have notified Gaillardet who would have blown his whistle twice. Gaillardet had not whistled, so there could be no one at the back of the garage. Once out of the truck, Belot in the darkness had in his turn examined each vehicle. He had discovered nothing either. And now sitting on the floor of the

28 with the white envelope on a level with his eyes he repeated: "So far it looks good! Yes, it looks good to me!"

Two o'clock . . . three o'clock in the morning. In the street a new policeman had long since replaced the one who had taken Longspès away. He had joined the vacant group in the pavement, led the conversation, spoke a little about the rain and a great deal about his career, breaking off to exclaim: "What an obstinate lot you are! To think that you could be tucked up in your beds instead of out here!" Collars were turned up and someone's teeth chattered. Another yawned. A reporter, bored to death at his window, had just come down with the idea: I'll write a piece on these idiots. As he took stock of them one after the other his eyes fell on a feminine face which did not seem unfamiliar. Charming, mouselike features, grey-blue eyes, astonishingly wakeful for this time in the morning, a trim figure, standing next to a large man who was asleep on his feet. "In this turnip patch," the reporter thought to himself, "a rose keeps watch beside its prop." The rose noticed this attention and nodded with a little smile. Of course we know each other, he decided.

He approached, took off his hat and said in a low voice, so as not to wake the "prop": "Excuse me, madame. . . ."

"That's all right, monsieur," replied the young woman, "it's only natural. You recognise me without knowing who I am. I don't recognise you for the very good reason that I have never seen you before. But you have looked at everyone so openly, with such little discretion, that you are certainly neither a police inspector, nor 'The Passenger on the U.' What is left then? A reporter!"

He turned away to blush. "I've got it," he cried. "You're Mme Colet! We published . . ."

"Ssh!" she raised her eyes towards her husband. "I think he's asleep. I advised him so much not to come. . . ."

Some of the crowd round the couple had heard the reporter's exclamation. They cocked an ear. On the other hand a short man, wearing beige gloves, with a rather bushy but well-tended black beard, moved off saying to his neighbours: "The policeman is right. I'm going to bed. Good night, gentlemen!"

And he walked away unhurriedly.

Belot's anxiety increased as the hours passed. Once more he examined the bench with the envelope. Nothing suspicious, no faking; to collect the ransom "The Passenger" had to appear, or Devaux or someone else. Nobody appeared. The luminous dial of his wristwatch showed a quarter to five. Was there a leak despite all the security precautions? Would it not have been better to arrest—provisionally—the crew of the 28 and the driver of the truck? But assuming them to be accomplices this would have alerted "The Passenger" as much as a report. Besides, Belot was loath to entertain any such suspicion. Had one of his inspectors mingling with the crowd outside the gate given himself away? It was difficult to believe. The team was first-class. Had the elusive Longspès—Belot had heard nothing of his latest demonstration—committed some new piece of stupidity? Had M. Barbason guessed that the envelope contained nothing but blank paper—and who knew exactly what part M. Barbason was playing? No one, thought Belot: It was not enough just to "think." What of the breakdown on the Boulevard Saint-Germain? It was unusual, of course, on a night like this but what breakdown is not unusual? Belot had too often met with chance in his career. Why shouldn't the 28 break down on the night of the ransom? But why should it? replied the enemy. Belot was getting annoyed with himself. It was a stupid plan, he thought. Although it was too late he tried to conceive it differently, but did not succeed. *But was the problem there?* Suppose the mistake lay not in some detail of his plan, but in the plan itself, in its whole conception, in its principle? "The Passenger" the day before had given notice of a certain course of action. Belot had established on the spot that such action was impossible. Champaine and the Company architect had confirmed that it was impossible. The police had, nonetheless, organised themselves to deal with this action as if it were possible! While taking precautions to keep the wall and the gate under observation from the street—it would need a ladder to negotiate the one and a tank to break down the other—they had given credence to the unbelievable: a being descending from the sky, passing through windows, winged, invisible, a superman, a magician! It was crazy. It was all crazy! "The Passenger" had demanded used 1,000-franc notes. Their numbers would betray them just as much as new notes. He had demanded five hundred of these notes, a sum absolutely out of proportion to the liquid assets of Verdon and his relations. Yet "The Passenger" had not attacked Verdon by chance. No, there was *something else*. A mysterious intention which Belot had suspected since his first visit to the depot and which he still could not put his finger on. He felt that lump in the pit of his stomach which the most hardened sailors feel during a storm.

"I wish you success, gentlemen!" The hint of punishment in the Prefect's threat did not affect Belot; he saw in it a scornful mistrust —which he was beginning to share. "While I'm playing the giddy goat here, 'The Passenger' is at work . . . *where?*"

At half past five hurried footsteps broke the fateful stillness which surrounded him. He drew his revolver. It was Champaine, red in the face and dumbfounded.

"M. Belot, M. Picard wants you on the telephone. M. Verdon has been killed!"

Belot leapt out of the bus, leaving the envelope on the seat. He dashed across the courtyard.

Picard, who had slept at headquarters said briefly: "'The Passenger' has just telephoned *Le Grand Journal*. He declared that since the agreement had not been kept he was keeping his promise. He had disposed of Verdon!"

"The proof?"

"A package deposited in a public call-box at the Gare Saint-Lazare. I've sent a man there."

"Are you sure it's not a trap? I'll call you back in a moment."

Belot ran back at full speed to the back of the garage. The envelope was still on the seat. Belot broke the seals. It was *his* envelope all right. There was no reason why Verdon should not be dead.

16

The bearded man with the beige gloves

Paris learnt of this new crime with disgust. So far it had built up a not unattractive picture of "The Passenger." He was seen as a lone wolf holding in check one of the most powerful police forces in the world, paying for his liberty with unusual daring, a brilliant organiser of kidnappings, a redoubtable and graceful writer of letters. Had the case not been born of murder, "The Passenger" would have taken his place among the most fascinating rascals of history and legend. Even the murder, in which he had risked his life and which appeared to be a settling of accounts, gave food for thought. M. Tavernier, of whom nothing was known, inspired but slight pity. The letter to Le Grand Journal of course had contained a terrifying threat. But the public had already made up its mind that "The Passenger" would gain his ends, that nothing could resist him and that no more blood would flow. It was Le Grand Journal, despite its righteous outbursts, which had created this collective illusion. It had been strengthened by Le Grand Journal Soir. The second victim inspired no more sympathy than the first, he was a rich man. A dealer in luxury goods, a speculator who bought his stamps at the issue price and waited for them to rise in value. A man therefore who could afford to wait. The proof? He was asked for half a million and the family immediately opened its coffers and said "Here you are."

But on Friday when the special editions of all the dailies—the Prefecture had not wished the case to remain the prerogative of M. Rose—published the story of the new crime in all its details, "The Passenger" lost his popularity more rapidly than he had acquired it.

To kill a defenceless man, a prisoner, in confinement, no doubt in fetters, was a revolting action. Paris learnt at the same time that the police had not really thrown in their hand but had laid a trap. And "The Passenger," powerful enough to learn of this (so he did not work alone?) had not been able to get round it! Unable to collect the envelope (the papers did not say that it only contained blank paper) he had carried out the horrible "Either . . . or" of his threat. Now he was boasting about it! No one dreamed any longer of considering him an audacious and witty outlaw. He was a coward, a thug, a butcher.

In the call-box at the Gare Saint-Lazare the police had found an old cardboard box bearing the name of a well-known store, containing a navy blue suit, tan shoes, a blue tie, a blue shirt with the initials M.V. and an undershirt. The undershirt was covered with long streaks of blood. A typed letter cynically confirmed the communication received by *Le Grand Journal*:

> I warned you. It is unwise to flout me.
> Here are a few spare parts of the late M. Verdon. I have no intention of keeping "the remains." But their transport needs care and I do not want to keep you waiting for a token of my displeasure.
> Take care, ladies and gentlemen, things are no longer running smoothly.

"The Passenger" had not signed the letter but it had been typed on the same machine as the preceding ones. Moreover, in the infirmary at the Police Headquarters where Longspès had been taken, the old man recognised his employer's clothes with agonised screams. No keys or wallet, however, no one-franc vermilion, no Empire *tête-bêche*.

At first the police, in spite of everything, were sceptical. As a general rule until they have a corpse—in default of a murderer— they are doubtful about a murder. They have not forgotten the double murder, Joseph-sold-by-his-brothers; they distrust bloodstained tunics just as they suspect the evidence with which the wives of Potiphar support their accusation.

However, criminology having improved since the case of Joseph, it had to be admitted that the blood which stained M. Verdon's undershirt did not come from a goat.

The letter itself provided no clue. Picard and Belot were struck by the odious expression "spare parts" and by the last words: "things are no longer running smoothly." It smacked of a motor car. . . .

Of all the actors in the case, great or small, whom Picard looked upon a priori as suspects, only the Colets had spent the night out. M. Barbason had returned home after the ceremony at the garage; Longspès had been well guarded with cold water compresses on his head; Musard and his wife had gone to the cinema; M. Archer had dined with friends; Paul Tavernier had not left his flat. The telephone tapping service had reported at 10 p.m. on the previous night that he had just telephoned the home of one of his colleagues: "I haven't been feeling well the whole afternoon, with all the emotion of the funeral. But I shall be in the office tomorrow morning."

At the Gare Saint-Lazare, after many inquiries, Belot discovered two young employees who had passed a man near the call-box at about twenty minutes past five. This was the time at which *Le Grand Journal*, having received the announcement of the crime, had telephoned the police. The men had not paid any attention to this encounter; they only remembered a black beard, for one had said to the other: "The first one we've seen today. Fifteen to me!"

At half past seven Belot received Mme Colet at his office. She had circles under her eyes and looked apprehensive. She was still in the dark as to what had happened as the special editions would not appear for another hour.

"How tired you look," she said. "Haven't you slept?"

Belot ran his hands over his unshaven cheeks. "As much as you have."

"You know where I was?" She gave a sigh of relief. "I was sure that you *could* not have given in. When I read *Le Grand Journal Soir*, I said to Raymond: 'It's not possible, M. Belot can't have accepted. He's just pretending. The garage will be watched and "The Passenger" won't get away with it!' I thought we might see something. We saw nothing and I could not resist coming this morning, so here I am. . . . Well? How strange you seem! Did he take the ransom?"

Belot related the comedy at the depot, and the criminal's reaction. Mme Colet gave a shudder of horror.

"He's a monster! A monster who seems to have accomplices everywhere. Perhaps one of them was outside the gate. But, surely your detectives would have spotted him?"

"I suppose so."

"Who told you I was there?" she asked with a knowing smile. "The man with a beard?"

Belot's stupefaction hit her like a blow. "The man with a beard," he stammered. "What man with a beard?"

She described the man with the black beard who had stood for hours not far away from her. "Very erect, in spite of being short, well dressed, with beige gloves; he looked like a headmaster, or the chief clerk in a lawyer's office." She had noticed his attitude of casual spectator, nodding amiably when one of his neighbours addressed him, but almost never replying. Two things had struck her apart from the beard ("I do not know if you are like me," she said, "a beard always comes as a surprise to me"). She could not make out his eyes: He wore a felt hat pulled down so low he must have been blinded by it! Secondly, and most important, she had frightened him.

"That's what I thought to start with. A reporter had spoken to me using my name. At this the man went off, without hurrying, but he went. He said something to his neighbours which I could not hear because of the reporter. I thought to myself, well, evidently I don't attract everyone! And then I pulled myself together: ninny! I thought, of course, he's one of the police! He's giving you proof that they are there and that they are keeping everyone under observation . . . even your own poor little person!"

She looked at Belot anxiously: "Who was it, Inspector?"

He bent his head.

"Unless it is an extraordinary coincidence, it was the man who went to the Gare Saint-Lazare with Verdon's clothes."

Mme Colet's face showed genuine distress. Her voice trembled with anger.

"Why didn't you trust me? If I had been warned I would have tipped off one of your men and he would have followed him. None of them moved. . . ."

"Trust had nothing to do with it, madame. I had no idea that you intended spending a sleepless night. Had I known it, I should have dissuaded you from doing so. You are exposing yourself and your husband and you will end by calling down upon yourself the worst unpleasantnesses."

She replied with her little nod.

"I'm sorry but we are not children. And provided we don't get in your way. . . ."

"You don't get in my way," acknowledged Belot, "but since you suspected him why didn't you follow him yourself?"

Mme Colet shrugged her shoulders sadly.

"Yes, *madame*, you who are so subtle, so sensitive, you made a mistake! Not a complete one though, because your first impression was right."

"Do you really believe he went off to kill M. Verdon? In no hurry, like someone just out for a walk?" She shuddered again. "In any case it wasn't the man at the Rond-Point."

"A beard can be false."

She frowned, forgot her distress and her face once again took on the expression of a preoccupied little girl.

"I hadn't thought of that. But it wasn't only the beard! His figure. Oh! Yes, he was shorter and slimmer. His general bearing, his appearance of extraordinary calm. The beige gloves. The other man's huge coarse hands couldn't have got into those gloves. His walk. Oh, if only I'd heard his voice! But it wasn't the same man. It wasn't the same!"

He remained absorbed and silent. She stood up, and he saw her to the staircase.

At once he went off to question the men who had been posted outside the gates. They had noted the presence of the bearded man. He had arrived between half past eleven and midnight together with many other people, and had remained until three o'clock in the morning. They had taken him for a well-to-do resident of the district, one of those sensation mongers to be found under the most middle-class exterior. His beard was like a million other beards, and was no competitor to Barbason's, for example. As for the felt hat pulled down over his eyes, it was a hat like any other. If all the comings and goings had had to be under suspicion a hundred men would not have been enough.

Nevertheless, a number of voluntary testimonies provided later by a few early morning travellers confirmed Mme Colet's description. They had seen the man with the black beard and beige gloves at the Gare Saint-Lazare. Some had seen him with the sinister cardboard box and a tan leather suitcase, others with the suitcase alone. He sauntered along, with no sign of haste. The young shorthand-typist who had received the message from the call-box had taken it down automatically. It was fortunate that her profession had become second nature, otherwise panic-stricken at the first words, her pencil would have slipped from her fingers.

"Hallo! 'The Passenger on the U' speaking."

" . . ."

"Yes. The police have not fulfilled their commitments for the Gobelins Depot as arranged. Can you hear me?"

" . . ."

"I always keep my promises. *So I have done away with M. Verdon.* I am leaving a small bundle of relics for the family—or *Le Grand Journal* or the police, whichever you wish—at the Gare Saint-Lazare. Good morning!"

The girl could give no details of the voice, except that he spoke through his nose. He had expressed himself calmly without shouting. On repeating the words she began to cry. She had to be taken home.

As an exception that morning, "The Passenger" conference took place in M. Malebranche's office. Relieved of duties which, for some of them, had lasted twenty-four hours on end, the detectives looked weary and anxious. A note from the Prefect who had been reassured by the tone of the Press had come as an agreeable surprise. It recognised the setback without acrimony, stressed the unusual character of the adversary and substituted for reprimand the promise of a reward. Everyone breathed a sigh of relief, but no one smiled. Picard fiddled with his ruler; Belot addressed them in a bleak voice.

"Now that it has been proved that Mme Colet's bearded man and the man at the Gare Saint-Lazare are one and the same person, I maintain that this man is also 'The Passenger.' Perhaps he didn't kill Verdon with his own hands; perhaps he left him in the care of Devaux and, on his return from the Gobelins Garage, ordered the other man to kill him. Possibly he confines himself to the initial planning. Don't ask me to prove what I'm putting forward, but I'm convinced this time that it's not a matter of an accomplice. The man with the beard is the Brain."

"I agree," said M. Malebranche.

"And so? With his description circulated everywhere, he need only make the effort of taking off his beard to disappear. He has resumed his daily life among his associates, is probably discussing the new crime with them, feigns revulsion, fear! In the meanwhile he is probably meditating God knows what new ignominy. 'Take care, ladies and gentlemen!' For the first time he addresses both sexes. Has he decided that the next victim shall be a woman?" Belot thought of Mme Colet and controlled his anger. Picard did not disguise his. "No doubt what usually betrays criminals of this nature is that they never know when to stop. Like gamblers. But after how many deaths?"

"You've only one hope," said M. Malebranche: "the corpse. The murderer must get rid of it. Have all the trunks in the left luggage offices searched, the river, everything!"

"He's brazen enough," said Belot, "to organise an ordinary funeral."

M. Malebranche added: ". . . And the undertakers. And pay a visit also to the shops which supply wigs and beards. But your real task, unfortunately, remains unchanged. Since we still have only one serious customer, Devaux alias Oudart, he's the man we want."

17

Two bloodstained victims are not enough!
A new disappearance

Despite the injunctions of M. Malebranche the day passed without providing a single trace of murderer No. 1. On the other hand it provided the most exciting details on the subject of his sister.

On Monday, September 26th—a week before the death of Étienne Tavernier—the passport office had received two application forms in the name of Devaux. The first referred to DEVAUX, Marie, Anne, French, born on August 24th 18** at Villechaud (Cosne), no profession, living rue du Ranelagh, Paris, XVIe; the second: DEVAUX, Jacques, French, born in Paris, VIIIe on November 19th 19** (making him a little less than seventeen), student, same address. Both applicants wished to go to Spain. The passports had been delivered on Thursday, the 29th.

On the same day two first-class seats had been reserved in the same name at the Gare d'Orsay on the Paris-Madrid Express for the following Saturday and, according to the ticket collector, the seats were occupied when the train left.

The photographs with the passport applications showed a rather handsome, common-looking woman with thick features and dark eyes, who bore little resemblance to her brother; and a youth who was the living image of his mother, though it was impossible to tell whether he was intelligent or stupid.

While Picard telegraphed to Madrid, Belot hurried to the rue du Ranelagh. An old, small one-storied house in a tiny garden. All the windows were closed, the garden gate also. A board was up: "To be let furnished. Keys with Bouchard & Co., Boulevard Malesherbes." The concierges of the two neighbouring buildings confirmed the owner had gone, saying:

"Yes, Madame Valence left a week ago."

"Madame Valence? You mean Madame Devaux?"

"Devaux? Who's she?"

Belot did not insist. A splitting headache had begun to throb behind his temples and to give him an obsessive desire to sleep. "And Mme Valence left with her son?"

"Her son? She never had a son? Oh, you mean that boy? It's true he does look like her. Well, well . . ."

At Bouchard's, the estate agents, Belot was received by M. Bouchard in person, whom he had known for years. He, too, had never heard the name Devaux. Mme Marie Valence had rented the "villa" in the rue du Ranelagh five years before. (Five years again . . .) She gave herself out to be a widow living alone. She had never mentioned a child and had been so keen to rent the villa that of her own accord she had offered four quarters rent in advance.

"A nice bit of business!" said Belot. "So you concluded that you would have no need to take up references?"

"Exactly. And I was quite right. I saw her furniture when she moved in: very good quality and brand new. She asked my advice about her insurance and all manner of things. In short, for five years we have been on excellent terms."

"Wasn't Mme Bouchard jealous?"

Bouchard burst out laughing, but looked rather self-satisfied.

"I don't say that if I'd wanted to. . . . Particularly as she wasn't at all bad looking. . . . But I never mix business with pleasure. Well, on Monday, a week ago, she came to tell me that one of her uncles had died in Spain and had left her an unexpected bit of money in that country. She had decided, therefore, to leave at once since she had no ties in Paris. She wanted to dispose of the rest of her lease and offered me part of her furniture, in compensation because she could only take with her her personal belongings. She had inherited a castle."

"Yes, a castle in Spain—we've heard that one before!"

"Naturally, I agreed to sublet, and took the furniture, paying for it, incidentally. With the shortage of flats today I made a profit. The villa is already let and the agreement is being signed this morning. An hour later you would have found the board gone."

"I'm going back there," said Belot, "and I want you to come with me."

On the way he informed Bouchard of the relationship which linked Mme Devaux-Valence to M. Devaux-Oudart, to the unfortunate Tavernier and Verdon, and to "The Passenger on the U." Bouchard sweated profusely.

"If my new client hears of this, he won't sign!"

Under his haggard gaze a team of specialists took fingerprints, unhooked pictures, ripped up carpets, tapped the walls, shoved around furniture from which all the drawers were removed, subjecting the villa to a barbarous but fruitless examination. Through the cotton wool haze of his headache, Belot wandered from one room to another trying to discover the important clue, the ultimate explanation, the key to everything. Nothing! Those spots where, in normal circumstances, the dust accumulates despite the most careful cleaning, where the finding of an envelope, a button, a match, provide stimulating if generally useless clues, were as clean and tidy as in the centre of the drawing-room. Marie Devaux, alias Marie Valence, had pulled off a double coup: while ensuring that Bouchard retained kindly memories of her she had left none which might have helped Belot. What had happened in this peaceful, feminine house among this rose lacquered furniture, under this tall lampshade, among the silk cushions and muslin curtains, in front of these crystal glasses and decanters which today stood empty?

Belot imagined mysterious confabulations. The Devaux woman lying on the sofa in diaphanous and scant attire revealing a milk-white skin and, grouped round the table, the brother with the glazed eyes, the bearded man with the beige gloves, grim-faced Paul Tavernier plus the two victims, Étienne with his anxious air and Verdon with his tortoiseshell spectacles. In his mind's eye the drawing-room grew larger until it became immense. Here were M. Archer, Musard, the director of Ibert and Bélier, Philippe Durand; here was Longspès, the third Tavernier brother, the two Gascognes, young Roux from the Champs-Elysées showrooms, old Rose from Le Grand Journal. Here was Mme Tavernier (face to face with Marie Devaux!), her mother and sister and her children. The Barbasons, Camus and the men from the bus, Messrs Vitet and Vedel, Douchet and Brigaille, Champaine and Valée. Here was M. Colet, here . . . Belot pressed

162

his thumbs into his eyes to throw off the effects of a headache now threatening him with hallucinations. "Who *really* used to come here?"

In a neighbouring porter's lodge the concierges of the district had assembled in conference. When Belot came in, a thin woman who was holding forth stopped short. He asked their permission to sit down. Everybody knew already that he was directing the inquiry and his courtesy touched their hearts. One of them explained:

"Mme Dispenser was telling us about her mistress."

Mme Dispenser was only waiting for this introduction to start talking again. Yes, she was the former maid of Mme Valance's. Last Friday she had been hastily dismissed, but she wasn't complaining because she'd been given a month's wages. As for the idea that Mme Valence might have had something to do with this horrible story of the U Line, no! All the five years she'd served the lady they'd never had a cross word. "I've never seen anything fishy in the house, and I've got my eyes about me!" M. Terrasse's visits? Nobody had any right to criticise them, Mme Valence was a widow and free. "I'd like you to show me women who are free and who don't change their men in five years!" M. Terrasse came every evening and stayed an hour or two hours; Mme Dispenser had to keep to the kitchen. He didn't want to be seen, that was his affair. That didn't prevent him from giving her handsome presents through Mme Valence. He left his car in the rue Raynouard? The roads belong to everyone! No sound when he was there, no scenes, no anger.

"You really never saw him?" asked Belot.

Mme Dispenser looked at him out of the corner of her eye: was he mocking or was he stupid?

"The inspector is joking."

He drew from his pocket the photo of Étienne Tavernier.

"Oh!" she cried. "That's him."

"Didn't you see this photo in the newspaper on Tuesday?"

"What do you mean? Was M. Terrasse the first gentleman who was killed? But that wasn't the name!"

"No," said Belot wearily, "that wasn't the name."

After Devaux-Oudart, Devaux-Valence, there was now Tavernier-Terrasse. Things were becoming clearer in a way which did not improve his headache. Belot thought bitterly: later on we shall find Verdon calling himself Toiture. He handed Mme Dispenser his collection of photographs: first Verdon, then "Mme Valence's" brother, and then M. Terrasse's brother. She recognised none of them. Moreover, although Mme Valence sometimes went out she never had anyone in except the house agent, Bouchard, who "probably had some ideas in his head."

"And what about the son?" The other women looked suddenly attentive. Only Mme Dispenser winked. Madame often mentioned a godson in the country. "I am his godmother and M. Terrasse is his godfather," she said. And each time she sighed. Mme Dispenser had drawn her own conclusions. "A son, of course, but for reasons best known to them they had to hide him. Perhaps M. Terrasse was married? In any case I kept the secret to myself, didn't I?" This was so true that one of the agreeing voices murmured: "Sly puss!"

"And where was this son?" "Now you're asking!" Mme Dispenser could only say one thing. Once a month Mme Valence went away from Saturday afternoon to Sunday evening. M. Terrasse certainly accompanied her, although he never came to fetch her.

Thus one by one the small question marks gradually disappeared, while the big ones grew larger. The poster which poisoned Paris yesterday morning burst like a luminous sign in Belot's exhausted head. If only he could sleep for a couple of hours. No, he must find out where they kept the son.

It was at his own headquarters that Belot collected the next piece of information. Blondel brought details from the town hall of the XVIIIe *arondissement*, of Jacques Devaux's birth certificate: "father unknown, mother Marie-Anne Devaux, spinster, living in the rue Francoeur."

Blondel had been to the rue Francoeur. The old concierge remembered Marie and her boy. "A decent sort, flighty, with lots of 'friends' —not all at the same time though!—and a good mother. She fed him herself. When he was two she put him in an institution near Mantes—an orphanage. One wonders how she made him pass for an orphan, with all the fathers he had!"

It only took a few hours to discover not only the orphanage where little Jacques had for ten years of his life shared the miserable existence of more than three hundred children, without learning anything but hunger and cold, but also the vocational school at Vendôme to which he was afterwards sent with an excellent wardrobe and a monthly visit from his mother—here she did not conceal the relationship—accompanied by the godfather. Five years ago. . . .

The director of the school gave all the required details to Belot over the telephone. Jacques had indeed left the week before, after staying there for five years without a break, even during the summer! His mother had decided that having learnt nothing at the orphanage he had to catch up. He stayed on at school during the holidays, as well as the nine other months of the year. An indifferent pupil, a character without charm, a bad comrade, indifferent to the family visits, interested only in the presents they occasioned. The headmaster knew the mother. He was of the opinion that she was frivolous and "nothing out of the ordinary." He had caught sight of the godfather several times, but since the latter seemed to prefer to remain in the background they had done nothing more than raise their hats at each other.

By comparing reports and dates, M. Malebranche, Picard and Belot drew their conclusions. During their military service or immediately after it, Devaux had introduced Étienne Tavernier to his sister. Étienne became Marie's lover—or one of her lovers. She had a child. He refused to recognise it and left her to marry Mlle Bassett. When Devaux returned from the colonies he forced his former comrade to look after the boy, using irresistible pressure, the most effective doubtless being some proof of paternity. None of this, however, justified the actual tragedy nor the departure on the eve of it of Marie and her son. Was it to be supposed that Étienne had come to an agreement with Marie, hence his gaiety on the Sunday, and that Devaux, kept in the dark, had on the other hand became exasperated to the point of committing a crime? Might he not have seen his main source of income disappearing with his sister?

But where did "The Passenger" fit into this puzzle? Picard telegraphed once more to Madrid and sent for Paul Tavernier.

Everyone at the Quai des Orfèvres knows the meaning of the expression: "to age by ten years." No one could have been a better illustration of this than Paul Tavernier. Apart from the cold fire which occasionally flashed from his eyes Picard and Belot would have taken him for an old man. With bent head, and fists which though clenched still trembled, he listened to the story of Marie Devaux-Valence. But when Picard stated that Étienne was the father of

Jacques Devaux, he stood up, drew himself up to his full height and raising his hand said, "I give you my word of honour that that is untrue."

"Will you explain yourself?"

He sat down again.

"Yes. I admit that Étienne spoke to me of this episode. . . . It was a long time ago . . . when we became reconciled. That is why the name of Devaux made me jump yesterday when you sprang it on me. It was a relationship with the sister of an old army friend, without the slightest importance. After a few months this woman of loose morals had left him for another man, and he was delighted. You say that the boy was born on the 19th November 19**. Now I remember perfectly well this detail of his confession. Étienne and this girl had parted at the very beginning of January—ten and a half months earlier! And if my testimony does not convince you, how do you explain that she didn't immediately appeal to him when he was still free? He did not get married until the following year. She thinks of it, you tell me, more than ten years later. That is simply because Étienne had grown rich. So she then arranged a blackmail which was to lead a poor, weak-minded fellow to his doom. . . ."

In his effort to be convincing Paul Tavernier had strained every muscle. He fell back exhausted. Picard asked another question.

"Can you explain to us why your brother took the name of Terrasse?"

"Did he take that name?"

Picard did not detain him any longer.

"If your headache still allows you to think," he said to Belot, "what do you make of it?"

"That despite the fact that he now looks like an old man, Paul Tavernier is still very clever. He only talked about the sister, he did not say a word about the brother. He confessed to knowing about this affair, but only the first episode. He forgets that he reacted yesterday to the name of Oudart, as well as to Devaux. All this aside, his outcry convinced me. First of all of his sincerity: Étienne may have deceived him on most points. And then quite simply convinced one, by his reasoning, which is good and which is even better in that Devaux did not leave France when his nephew was born: he did not sail until two years later. Étienne's character only changed when Devaux-Oudart reappeared five years ago. It should have changed twelve years earlier had the paternity been certain and verifiable. Paul is right. The blackmail was organised by Marie and her brother on the latter's return. At whose instigation? Of 'The Passenger.' It is he who planned the affair and spun the web in which Étienne allowed himself to be caught. It is he who sent the woman and the boy abroad, and forced his pal to murder their victim, the day things did not work out any more."

Picard chewed his pencil.

"Now that we know Marie a little better," he said, "I can't see her any longer as the link between Tavernier and Verdon. That worries me."

"We don't know everything yet. Verdon perhaps did not go to the rue du Ranelagh, but Marie went out! Again, we can consider another possibility. Suppose Devaux met 'The Passenger' in Saigon? Suppose Verdon therefore got his Indo-Chinese stamps from one or the other. . . ."

"That is the last straw! Starting inquiries in Saigon!" Picard flung down his pencil in a rage. "Send a telegram, Truflot. . . ."

"Excuse me," said Truflot, looking up. "You asked just now the reason why Étienne Tavernier took the name of Terrasse. The Taverniers come from Saint-Étienne. Now there are two stations at Saint Étienne—Châteaucreux and La Terrasse."

This type of discovery always enchanted Picard.

"You are fantastic, *mon vieux!*"

"Unless, of course," Truflot went on, "he took that name by chance. . . ."

"Now he really *is* being fantastic," said Belot to Picard. "And what about Valence, for someone who is fleeing to Spain?"

Naturally the bearded man could not be found. Verdon's colleagues and friends telephoned, expressed distress and fulminated against the odious criminal. M. Barbason appeared, and his loud lamentations tortured Belot's already painful eardrums. His wife had fainted three times that morning. He had caught some of the tenants in his block of flats eyeing his beard "with hostility." He was at loggerheads with the undertakers—as if he could pay for any kind of ceremony without the corpse of his unfortunate cousin! He hadn't had a moment yet to mourn. But that was not the trouble. He had come to lodge a complaint against Longspès. He maintained that the scandal caused by that wretched old man outside the depot was the cause of everything.

Belot implored him to calm down: Longspès was being kept under observation; if the inquiry demanded it he would be prosecuted; the Barbasons must have confidence in the police. M. Barbason's only reply was a hollow laugh, against which Belot had not the energy to protest.

Early in the afternoon Mme Colet reappeared. Her face looked even more drawn than it had done that morning.

"You're not any better," she said to Belot. "And I've got such a headache. . . ."

He mustered a smile.

"We make a good pair," he said, but refrained from adding that he felt better when Mme Colet was there. But she was not smiling.

"Why are you having me followed? Your inspector is about as discreet as a sheepdog! He wears a bow tie and I detest them!"

"He'll be heartbroken," said Belot. "I'll introduce him to you presently, his name is Perraud. He's not keeping you under observation, he's protecting you. And he has no orders to keep out of sight, on the contrary. Remember this morning's letter: 'Take care, ladies and gentlemen!'"

Mme Colet opened her handbag.

"'The Passenger' himself has reminded me. . . ."

She produced a large sheet of paper on which were pasted words cut out of newsprint.

> You persist in interfering in what does not concern you. You are wrong. I repeat, therefore, to you personally: take care!
>
> "The Passenger"

On the envelope in one clipping "To Mme Colet."

"I know where he got that," she said, "from the caption in yesterday's *Grand Journal*, under my photo."

"And you complain about our protection!" Belot closed his eyes and pressed the eyelids together. "My head's going to burst. When did you receive this note?"

"I didn't receive it. I found it at the hotel this morning on my return from here. The hall was empty. I caught sight of an envelope on the table nearest the door. I looked . . . It gave me such a shock! I didn't breathe a word about it to my husband, he was asleep. I made my inquiries but, you know, although our hotel is called The Royal, it is only a small one. No page boy, a commissionaire part time and the door always open. Obviously 'The Passenger' or his accomplice had no difficulty."

She laughed unconvincingly.

"Why didn't you telephone me? Why didn't you come earlier?" Belot examined the letter once more, concentrating his remaining strength on it. "Why isn't it typed this time?"

She seemed pleased with this remark.

"I wondered the same thing! If it's only a joke? I thought. That is why I didn't come." Her voice dropped. "And then after all, I preferred. . . ."

Belot placed a hand gently on her arm.

"Don't worry. Let's go and see Perraud. Everything will be all right."

She gave him an unclouded smile.

"I still want to help you," she said.

It was a quarter of an hour after the departure of Mme Colet and her guardian angel that the news of the third disappearance rocked Police Headquarters like an earthquake. The Superintendent of the XVI *arrondissement* telephoned that a guest at the Villas Kléber, Viscount Guy de Laeken, had just been kidnapped in his turn by "The Passenger on the U."

"Get there at once!" Picard roared to Belot. "At once! *nom de dieu!*"

"I'm coming with you," said M. Malebranche.

Belot staggered. He muttered in a thick voice: "You must forgive me, Chief. You'll have to go with someone else. 'The Passenger' can kidnap whom he likes—The President of the Republic, if he feels inclined. I must get some sleep!"

Part Two

THE OTHERS

1

Gwendolyn's despair

Every American who stays in Paris knows the Villas Kléber. On the even numbers side of the avenue, not far from the Arc de Triomphe, their five small grey stone façades closely joined together look far older than the tall buildings surrounding them. Hotel history has it that each of them in the old days was surrounded by a pretty garden full of flowers. One day some terrible modern blocks approached all five of them like gangsters and told them to pack up as quickly as possible. The five villas put up a heroic resistance, but because they were afraid of the great brutes who settled all round them, they decided to live together and make a united front along the avenue, with the five gardens hidden behind them and thus transformed into a real park. And the terrible modern blocks never dared to touch these noble little villas. This ridiculous story invented in New York and entitled *The Five Old Ladies of the Ville Lumière* has been read by all American travellers in a brochure which can be found in the lounges of every big hotel, every boat and every travel agency in the world. "Where are you staying in Paris?"—"At the Old Ladies." "For a long and really French visit, the Arc de Triomphe and the Old Ladies." The Old Ladies, like the legend, belong to a big American hotel group. They were built in recent years and beneath their modest and outdated exterior they conceal unostentatious but impeccable comfort. A boarding house for millionaires. . . .

A visitor that day would have wondered what madman or crook had recommended the place to him. In the entrance hall guests crowded round the porter, at the reception desk anxious voices were raised, interrupted by bells ringing and nervous "hallos!" Maids and valets ran along the corridors, exchanging whispers as they passed each other. Outside Room 17, a silent group with ears cocked listened to the lamentations coming through the double doors. In the bedroom on either side of the bed two serious gentlemen, one young, one old, held two wrists and watch in hand observed the two pulses of a single heart. Bending over a distraught face a nurse applied an icepack; another in the bathroom was sterilising a syringe. The curtains were drawn across both windows and the only light in the room came from a small bedside lamp. No one spoke except the patient. She did not speak, she raved. In excellent French with a very strong American accent.

"Oh, Guy! Oh, darling! My darling! More if you like. . . . Everything if you like! But come back quickly to Gwen! To your poor, unhappy Gwen! Why did they bang you on the head? My own poor head hurts so much for you! You have the money, you bandit, you murderer, so let him go! Hangman that you are, with your mask. To kill him like the others? No! No! . . . ! My little Guy, my adorable little Guy! We'll leave at once! You agree, don't you? You won't hold out against your Gwen any longer. You naughty darling! Porter, two tickets for Truro, Massachusetts. Yes, the direct boat to Boston, not to New York, Boston! Oh, Daddy, this is Guy. He is my husband. He couldn't resist after the kidnapping! Why are you wearing a mask, Daddy? Why are you holding a hammer? Oh, my head! My head! Guy . . . !"

Miss Gwendolyn Abbott suddenly sat up in bed. She tore her wrists away from the doctor's hands and flung the icepack across the room. Her horselike features were distorted by fear.

"Hurry up," said the younger of the doctors.

The nurse with the syringe ran forward. While the patient was held down, she bared a long skinny thigh, rubbed it with alcohol and plunged in the needle.

"Well, well," said the white-haired doctor, "don't worry, Gwen!"

Through the door which communicated with Room 18, a fat man in a morning coat whispered:

"The police."

"I'll go," said the young doctor.

From the bedside table he took an envelope and two sheets of paper, one of which had been crumpled and uncrumpled. In Room

18 he emerged once more into daylight. The man in the morning coat did the introductions.

"This is M. Malebranche, head of the Police Judiciaire, who has taken the trouble to come in person. And one of his detective inspectors."

"Sergeant Gaillardet," volunteered M. Malebranche.

The doctor introduced himself. "Doctor Cohuau, resident doctor at the Old . . . I mean, the Villas Kléber."

"French, I suppose?"

"Like everyone else here, except the guests."

"M. Villeneuve has explained the matter," continued M. Malebranche, gesturing towards the man in the morning coat who was the manager of the Old Ladies. "But since it was you, Doctor, who thought fit to notify us I shall be pleased to hear what you have to say."

Both he and the doctor sat down: M. Villeneuve and Gaillardet remained standing. In the other room Miss Abbott's groans had ceased.

"I will first sum up," said M. Malebranche, "what M. Villeneuve has told me. At eleven o'clock this morning Miss Gwendolyn Abbott received an express letter. In a distraught voice she immediately telephoned to the porter to call a taxi at once. She gave the driver the address of her bank, the American Bank in the Place Vendôme. This woman, who is usually so calm, seemed completely out of her mind. She returned about half past twelve, still in a great state of agitation and asked you—" M. Malebranche turned to the manager—"to prepare her bill and the bill of M. de Laeken, her neighbour and friend, who had been absent since dawn. She told the porter to reserve a seat for her on the Havre Express tonight. She sent for her trunks and suitcases, and refused to go into the dining-room. With the help of the chambermaid she began to pack. Suddenly, about half past one, she had a fainting fit. Correct?"

"Word for word," replied M. Villeneuve, full of admiration.

"It was then they sent for me," continued the doctor. "As it happened I had lunching with me the Embassy doctor, Dr Brayer, a great friend of the Abbott family. We rushed here together. We found that Miss Abbott had regained consciousness and had been put to bed by our nurses, although she was struggling."

"Your nurses?"

Dr Cohuau replied without a smile:

"When tourists such as those who stay at the Villas want an aspirin tablet, they like to have it administered by a qualified nurse. We have two here."

M. Malebranche nodded, to show that he understood. The doctor went on: "Newspapers were lying all over the floor. Miss Abbott did not recognise us. She shouted that they were trying to prevent her from leaving and that she had a vital appointment at Le Havre this very day, one on which her life depended. In her hand she clutched a sheet of paper which we tried in vain to take from her. We gave her an injection of pantopon which calmed her slightly, very slightly. Miss Abbott has an extraordinarily tough constitution. She has the slow and flabby exterior that one normally associates with a fragile physique, and the height and thinness that often go with poor health, yet she has the health of an athlete. There's no other word for it: of an athlete. She assimilated the pantopon as though it were distilled water. This in itself is proof enough that the news she had just received must have been serious! We have just given her a second injection with a triple dose. The first had at least one result in that we were able to take the paper from her." The doctor handed the crumpled sheet to M. Malebranche. "We felt it our duty to read it, and having done so I persuaded my colleague that our Hippocratic oath did not apply in view of the gravity of the facts."

M. Malebranche had already recognised the typeface of the typewriter.

Friday morning, 8.30 a.m.

Mademoiselle:

Undoubtedly you read the newspapers, so I have no need to tell you who I am. Nevertheless, should you not have yet read the special morning editions, I suggest that you look at them before reading this letter. It will give weight to it.

At dawn today your friend, Vicomte Guy de Laeken ventured on my U Line. He is now my guest. Less comfortably lodged perhaps than with you—at the Old Ladies—and if he is superstitious perhaps haunted by more ghosts, one of which is of quite recent date. But I assure you he lacks for nothing. For lunch he will have his boiled potatoes. You see that I am looking after him for you! I shall not spice his dishes except in the unthinkable event of your failing to take an interest in his diet. . . .

You hold his fate in your hands: 80,000 dollars. I repeat, eighty thousand dollars. A trifle to you, the daughter of an American tycoon. A nice little nest egg for me and my charitable works.

Eight 10,000 dollar bills. They will not take up much room. I will arrange to exchange them myself. Do not make a note of the numbers . . . neither you nor your bank. It will be better so.

You will slip them into a carefully sealed envelope—let us beware of intermediaries—and go yourself and deposit it at the Venus Agency, in the rue Thorel. The Venus Agency specialises in lovers' correspondence. It's for your love that you'll be bringing the notes, isn't it?

You will address the envelope to: M. Richard Verdon. Be careful, not Maurice!—Richard. I have in my possession an identity card which with a scratch or two I have been able to alter very easily. It will be rash I admit to use this card, when the name of Verdon is on everyone's lips in Paris. But there is no reason why a M. Richard Verdon should not receive a love letter on the same day as a M. Maurice Verdon has been the victim of an unfortunate accident. You would have to denounce him. You wouldn't do that to the viscount!

If the envelope is deposited at the Venus Agency today before midday, M. de Laeken will be at Le Havre this night, or tomorrow morning at the latest, at the Hotel Transatlantique. He wishes you to leave this evening and to wait for him there.

Everything leads me to suppose that he will finally accede to your wishes. In fact, he will marry you. I shall receive the dowry and all three of us will be content.

Not a word to the Press. It has disappointed me even more than the police. Let this affair remain our secret, our dear secret!

Accept, Mademoiselle, my devoted and sincere respects.

The Passenger on the U.

M. Malebranche held out the letter to Gaillardet.

"Read it, inform your men below and do the necessary immediately."

"Here is the envelope," said the doctor.

M. Malebranche examined the postmark.

"Sent from No. 65 Post Office, Avenue de la République. Where is the rue Thorel?"

Gaillardet took a street plan from his pocket.

"It begins at the rue Beauregard and ends at the Boulevard Bonne-Nouvelle."

"In the same district, then."

The doctor handed M. Malebranche the second paper which was periwinkle blue.

"In addition we found this little note on Miss Abbott's bedside table."

A tall, ornate script written with a thick nib. . . .

My dear, I'm leaving you very early this morning. Do not worry. I hope to be back for lunch.

G."

"In her delirium," said the doctor, "Miss Abbott certainly alluded to it for she repeated several times. 'Yes, I was worried.'"

Gaillardet left the room. M. Malebranche looked at M. Villeneuve who, since the beginning of the conversation, had stood politely to one side. He pointed to a chair and said with an amiable smile:

"Now we can have a little chat."

The doctor obtained permission to return to his patient.

As soon as M. Villeneuve sat down, M. Malebranche asked: "Would you please tell me all you know about M. de Laeken."

"Not very much. He came here at the beginning of July—that is four months ago—at the same time as Miss Abbott, who had never been one of our guests either. We know her, of course, she is the only daughter of one of the twenty richest men in the United States. But up till then she had always preferred luxury hotels and she used to stay at the Victor-Hugo. It is from there that both of them came to us. M. de Laeken belongs to a distinguished Belgian family. A very reserved man, far less cordial than our usual American clientele, and always as smart as paint. Wears a monocle. He's a type we are not very accustomed to, but he's a real aristocrat."

M. Malebranche looked round the room. A few books on the mantelpiece, and newspapers on a stool . . . *The Times, Le Grand Journal, La Nation Belge,* and the *New York Herald.* On the table a marble inkstand, a pad of periwinkle blue paper which clashed with the delicious vieux-rose wallpaper, and a large framed photograph.

M. Malebranche's eyes came to rest on it.

"Miss Abbott," said the manager in an undertone.

M. Malebranche pursed his lips briefly. He looked at the communicating door.

"I shall not ask you any questions about their relationship," he said.

"Nevertheless, I must tell you that M. de Laeken paid his bills. To be more precise, before coming here Miss Abbott informed me that she wanted to help with her friend's expenses. But since, according to her, he would never have agreed to this arrangement had he known of it, she asked me to quote M. de Laeken a price far below our normal rate and said she would pay the difference. We naturally agreed to her proposal."

"Has M. de Laeken an occupation?"

"I have no idea. He was out every day. Miss Abbott also went out a lot, perhaps they met somewhere. Another point which distinguished them from our other guests: they hardly took any meals at the Villas, until quite recently."

"Ah, since when?"

M. Villeneuve picked up a telephone and asked to be put through to the desk.

"I can let you know that at once."

The door opened almost immediately, but it was Gaillardet who appeared, looking furious. Behind him the hall porter, a majestic giant in his black frock coat embroidered with gold keys, tried to look inconspicuous. Gaillardet growled: "*Le Grand Journal* is downstairs."

The same irritation showed on the faces of M. Malebranche and M. Villeneuve.

"It wasn't my fault," said the porter. "It was Number 9. Several of the guests heard mademoiselle shouting. Others heard the telephone conversation from the desk to the police station, although I hardly opened my mouth. But Number 9 ran to the switchboard and called his agency. What could I do? The switchboard and the desk. . . ."

"The switchboard, the desk and you yourself will all be responsible for the scandal, if there is one," retorted M. Villeneuve.

"Not to mention the complications you are causing the police," added M. Malebranche. "You can go!"

The porter left like a whipped retriever. Gaillardet handed back to M. Malebranche the letter from "The Passenger." He announced: "Blondel and Ligaire have left for the American Bank and the Venus Agency. I have telephoned the chief. He has notified Le Havre, Brussels and the frontier posts."

M. Malebranche returned to the painful subject of the Press.

179

"Who is Number 9?"

"Mr Quentin J. Foucquet," replied M. Villeneuve, "Chairman of the I.P., the International Press Service."

"I know them," M. Malebranche nodded gloomily.

"He gives out he's having a rest in Paris. In actual fact he's all over the place. The U Line case intrigues him enormously. He telephones from morning to night to his agency. It is this agency which bought *Le Grand Journal* articles and 'The Passenger's' letters for America."

M. Malebranche shrugged his shoulders.

"He won't get hold of this one," he said, pointing to the smoothed paper. "But it would be quite useless to ask him to keep silent. When Foucquet has smelt blood somewhere in the world he is in his element and he will end up one day by committing a murder himself. And since he's thick as thieves with Rose, it must be he who passed him the tip. . . ."

"In any case," said Gaillardet, "I have forbidden them to come upstairs."

"But how much do they know already?"

"Only that a M. de Laeken has disappeared, kidnapped by 'The Passenger.' There will be nothing else in the five o'clock edition."

"Nor in the later ones," declared M. Malebranche. "Let's carry on. Come in!"

There had been a knock at the door. A slim, good-looking head waiter handed a note to the manager.

"This is what you wanted to know," said M. Villeneuve. "Miss Abbott and M. de Laeken have taken all their meals at the Villas since midday on Tuesday."

M. Malebranche summed up:

"The day after the first crime. The day on which M. Verdon showed signs of stress. The murder of Étienne Tavernier has an instantaneous effect on the existence of the future victims."

"If I may give evidence . . ." said the head waiter. "When on duty I get a chance of overhearing odd pieces of conversation. On Tuesday M. le Vicomte mentioned the murder. I remember this quite well because he said: 'This business could have repercussions.' And Miss Abbott asked him: 'Why do you say that?' And M. le Vicomte replied: 'Oh, nothing, no reason!' But he looked very strange. He knows something, I said to myself. And then I went back to my waiters. But yesterday when I heard of the kidnapping of the stamp dealer, the ransom and the buses, I remembered the remark and during lunch I kept an eye on their table. They did not talk about anything special, but Miss Abbott looked very worried and M. le Vicomte said to her: 'Let's be gay, Gwen. Let's be gay!' But he seemed rather to be forcing himself to it. Yesterday evening it was the same. But M. de Laeken, who is on a very strict diet, took the whole menu: the lobster, the steak, two helpings of soufflé potatoes and he even ordered as an extra a rum omelette after the ice cream. Miss Abbott said to him: 'Isn't that a bit too much, Guy?' and M. le Vicomte replied: 'We must make the most of it!' He drank on his own a whole bottle of champagne and half a bottle of Côtes-du-Rhône. He began to speak of Brussels and of his childhood. Miss Abbott said: 'Be quiet, Guy, anyone would think that you were expecting trouble.' And he replied: 'No, Gwen, certainly not, my dear Gwen.' That's all."

The head waiter lowered his eyes.

"You are an excellent observer, my friend," declared M. Malebranche. "Thank you." The head waiter bowed and left.

"I don't suppose Miss Abbott is in a condition to see me. But I must speak to her. Would you find out, please."

M. Villeneuve tiptoed across to the communicating door. His head and shoulders disappeared and there was an exchange of whispers. Then he turned and stood aside to let Dr Brayer pass.

Dr Brayer was a typical old Anglo-Saxon: white silky hair, brick-red face, small laughing blue eyes. He extended a cordial hand to M. Malebranche.

"Glad to meet you, I am a great admirer of the French police. I'm sorry, Miss Abbott is resting. In fact she's alseep. When she wakes up we'll see about it. Can I help you?"

Dr Brayer rolled out his phrases vigorously with a nasal accent which delighted M. Malebranche. He selected a comfortable arm-chair and took a blue packet out of his pocket.

"Have a cigarette? I only smoke French Gauloises. . . . Forgive me, 'French Gauloises' is ridiculous. What a business, eh? This incredible 'Passenger!' I'm sorry for you."

"We have another worry, Doctor," said M. Villeneuve. "M. Foucquet has notified the Press."

The doctor frowned, but his face soon brightened.

"Can't be helped, my dear Villeneuve. Royalty has no private life. The misfortunes of the well-to-do are the distraction of the poor. That is as it should be."

"But the distraction in this case may cost the newly kidnapped man dear!" retorted M. Malebranche.

"Really?" replied the doctor, who did not seem impressed by this theory. He thought for a moment. "But why? The kidnapper has the ransom and you haven't caught the kidnapper. It's a very different story from your business last night. Naturally, I realise that poor de Laeken is in rather a horrible situation."

"You are an old friend of Miss Abbott's?"

M. Villeneuve withdrew discreetly. Gaillardet was rummaging in the cupboards.

"A very old friend. Her father and I were undergraduates together at Harvard. We hadn't a single thing in common, and that delighted both of us. He wanted to make guns and I wanted to look after the sick. He wanted a wife and a daughter and I wanted peace and quiet. He wanted to live and die in Massachusetts and I wanted to live and die anywhere in the world except Massachusetts.

"God granted us both our wishes . . . as regards the living, at any rate, and it's thirty-eight years since I last saw Oliver. Just the age of his daughter." Dr Brayer looked at the photo. "A fine girl. She's not a classic beauty, of course, not even a non-classic one. She takes after her father, whereas her mother really was a beauty. The sad thing about Gwendolyn is her height. An ugly, little bit of a woman is still a little bit of a woman, whereas a tall ugly woman is always an ugly woman. With my six feet one inch I'm still not quite as tall as she is. I think this is the cause of her shyness and peevishness. She travels to amuse herself, and spends her life between Florence and your capital—Florence because of the climate and Paris because of the dressmakers. These may not be all the reasons there are for living in Florence and Paris, but they are hers. She lives alone. She *lived* alone. Naturally she could have married fifty times. You can always find buyers for good shares, even if the certificates are not very well printed. But I must say this for my female compatriots, they are not ashamed of spinsterhood, which is ridiculed by European women. They want Love! At least to experience it even if they don't inspire it. Naturally Gwen must have had an affair or two in the course of her travels, she's a very healthy woman. But nothing more."

Dr Brayer lit another cigarette. He went on unhurriedly: "I love chattering and you're in a hurry. Let's come to recent history. Gwen was bowled over when she met the Viscount. I won't enlarge on her passion. Policemen and doctors have plenty of opportunity to study its effects on nerves and morals. Gwen's peevishness turned to melancholy. She never honoured me with her confidence, but her deep sighs, her constant need to evoke the beloved, to praise him and grow sentimental about his whims soon showed me to what extent she had fallen for him. I saw him once. We met one evening in this house. About five foot eight inches, my dear sir! Very respectable, very much the aristocrat of the old school, with a monocle, a lot of brilliantine and a charming Brussels accent. Very reserved and dignified, too, perhaps because he suffers with his stomach. But five foot eight inches beside Gwen, who moreover was wearing the longest possible evening dress! It was really distressing. I never interfere in other people's affairs. My profession is enough for me. I did, however, out of friendship for my old friend, Oliver, draw Gwen's attention to this symbolic disproportion. For the appearance of human beings can be symbolic; physical harmony implies harmony of character and soul. I refer you on this subject to your famous compatriot, the poisoner Voisin, and her *Treatise of Physionomy based on six unshakable pillars*, the first pillar being the sympathy between the mind and the body. Gwen replied that minds don't care a fig about bodies and that if it had only been up to her she would have been called Mme de Laeken months ago. But it was he who temporarily refused marriage because she was too rich. She explained this word 'temporarily.' De Laeken is suing the family of this name in Belgium which, apparently, has usurped it from him. As soon as he wins the case, Gwen and he would get married."

M. Malebranche took notes.

"Do you need me any more, Chief?" asked Gaillardet. "I'm going downstairs."

As he left the room he ran into Belot.

"Ah, so you've come to life again already!" cried M. Malebranche.

Belot shrugged his shoulders. His face was still very sallow and weary.

"I was too tired to sleep."

"Doctor," said M. Malebranche, "let me introduce you to Chief Inspector Belot who bears the whole weight of U Line case on his shoulders."

Brayer examined Belot keenly.

"I'm sorry for your shoulders. You are like those strong men of the circus. . . . I adore the circus . . . who bear the weight of a dozen people. . . . Arabs. Then, Atlas was an Arab. Are you an Arab? No? Well then, be careful of your liver. It's no laughing matter, you may have jaundice. Would you like to bet me that Miss Abbott will be no cure for it?"

"You don't know who Miss Abbott is," Malebranche said to Belot.

"I do," replied Belot. "I stopped downstairs. I also know who the Viscount de Laeken is, or rather who he isn't! I telephoned the Belgian Embassy. They say that no member of the Laeken family resides in France other than for short visits, that in any case, they have their own house in Paris."

M. Malebranche repeated what Dr Brayer had just told him about the claims of the Laeken living at the Old Ladies.

"Interesting," said Belot. "The Embassy didn't mention a word of it. How long has Miss Abbott known him?"

"I've no idea, my dear chap," replied the doctor. "Gwen has been back in Paris for a year and she came on her own. Six months, perhaps."

"And for six months M. de Laeken has been preparing a lawsuit without anyone knowing about it?"

Dr Brayer slapped the arm of his chair.

"Well done, Inspector. I also had the idea that this usurpation story might be a fabrication to deceive Gwendolyn. But I can't see the object since *she* is ready to marry him and *he* is the one who resists this very profitable union."

"We're beginning to get used to mysteries," said Belot with a sigh. "We've never had such a harvest!"

M. Malebranche handed him "The Passenger's" letter. While he read it the doctor went on: "In short, for months now our little doves have been cooing together. I don't know who is the banker in the nest, and I don't mind. In love what is yours is mine. Oliver will make a few extra bombs. But 80,000 dollars, will mean quite a sizable cannon. As a result of which, says the letter, the carrier pigeon immediately agrees to get married. No more question of susceptibility, of a lawsuit. Or is this merely an invention on the part of 'The Passenger'?"

A cry came through the wall. Dr Brayer got up deliberately, taking a last voluptuous puff at his cigarette.

"What a constitution! With my triple dose anyone else would have slept for a hundred years. Just listen to that! That is how we make 'em on the other side of the Atlantic."

Miss Abbott was shouting as if out of her mind. She was calling for her watch, talked of the boat and her departure. Leaving the door open, the doctor rejoined his colleague. Malebranche and Belot heard him asking in French: "Do you recognise me, Gwendolyn?"

"Oh, Dr Brayer," she cried, "my dear old friend. Do hurry and give instructions. I've got to go at once. Guy is at Le Havre, you know. He's waiting for me, we're leaving for Cape Cod!"

"But Gwen, you're not well. You can't travel. We'll send a telegram to the Hotel Transatlant. . . ."

He broke off abruptly. There was a silence during which M. Malebranche and Belot stood up in spite of themselves. A strangled, unrecognisable voice whispered: "What did you say? The Hotel Transatlantique? How do you know? My letters! The letter from Guy and from the murderer! *Where are they?* You've taken them! You've read them! The secret which nobody, nobody. . . . You read it! And you read it, too, Dr Cohuau, and you, nurses?"

Two terrified replies: "No, mademoiselle, not us!"

The voice recovered its erstwhile violence.

"And you passed it on. You've talked. Wretches that you are! You've dared. . . ."

There was a sound of a struggle. Suddenly Gwendolyn Abbott appeared in the doorway—a huge, bony figure, swathed in a dressing gown like a cyclamen-coloured shroud. She blinked blindly at Malebranche and Belot. A hand raised in their direction pointed its forefinger like a weapon.

"And I suppose you're from the police?"

She leapt forward. They hurled themselves at the door on to the corridor, opened it, banged it behind them and seized the handle. Their double effort was hardly enough to keep it closed. On the other side the doctors rushed forward and there was a further struggle. Malebranche and Belot exchanged meaningful glances.

"I left my hat inside the cage," murmured Belot.

2

Exchange of feminine confidences

Sickness and tears reduced Miss Abbott's holy anger into despair. Shivering in her bed she kept repeating softly: "He will kill him! He will kill him!"

"He won't kill him at all," said Dr Brayer firmly. "Naturally we have warned the police, but they won't act until your friend has reached Le Havre and is under their protection."

Miss Abbott, who was extremely shortsighted, blinked her eyes to try and read the doctor's face.

"How can you tell?"

"An intelligent police force can't act in any other way!"

She gave a sob.

"And the Press?"

"It has only been given the barest facts. And furthermore I'm going to see to this myself."

He left. From one corner of the room Dr Cohuau kept his eye on the patient. The nurses had sat down. The silence was now in harmony with the obscurity; Miss Abbott's sighs and the little gleam from the bedside lamp completed the effect. But when footsteps were heard crossing the room of the man who had disappeared, she called out:

"Guy! Is that you . . . Guy?"

"No," said Dr Brayer, "it's Frankie back again. I'm bringing you the papers. Only *Le Grand Journal Soir* mentions the story and then only in a few lines. Listen."

"I'll read it for myself. My glasses, nurse!"

She put on a pair of thick tortoiseshell-rimmed glasses. On the front page five out of seven columns of purple prose reported the morning news of the murder of M. Verdon. Nothing about Guy except one headline: Another disappearance! (see stop press news).

Miss Abbott turned to the stop press. "The mysteries of the U. Another disappearance! Reliable sources inform us that 'The Passenger' claimed another victim only a few hours after his second murder. A distinguished Belgian staying in Paris in a hotel in the Étoile district popular with our American friends, the Viscount Guy de Laeken, has been kidnapped by the sinister malefactor. Having ceased using this newspaper as his confidant—on which we can only congratulate ourselves—we shall publish the outcome of our present inquiries in out later editions."

"You see, Doctor Brayer!" said Miss Abbott in despair. "They will give details."

"Not a bit of it. I've just met the inspector whom you chased away so energetically. He swore to me that they'll learn nothing more. Delightful chap, that inspector, most obliging. Do you want me to bring him in now?"

She went back to the front page of the newspaper. "Are you crazy? Leave me alone. It's so hard to read. . . ." Her attention was caught by the photograph of a young woman whom she thought she remembered having seen on some occasion, when could that have been? It seemed centuries ago—yesterday morning; Guy had still been there. . . . Under the photograph was a name: "Madame Colet." This name was also prominent in one of the headlines which were scattered among the five columns of newsprint. "Madame Colet, too, a target for the murderer." She read the threatening message which this lady had herself passed on to *Le Grand Journal*. What a villain! Never, even in America, let alone Europe, had there been such a brute. She dropped the paper, gazed at the ceiling, and said:

"I must go. Straight away. . . ."

But she knew that her legs wouldn't carry her. In fact, if anything untoward happened to Guy, it would be her fault, hers! Nobody would have ever heard of the letter if she had not fainted like a baby. Sickness shook her frame. Dr Brayer gently removed her spectacles.

"She'll finish by having jaundice, old fellow," he whispered in Dr Cohuau's ear. "It needed Love to bring Miss Abbott face to face with illness. Isn't that touching? Have you a hard heart or are you the disinterested practitioner?"

"My dear Dr Brayer," asked the unfortunate heiress, in a plaintive voice, "Wire to Le Havre . . . you're right, I haven't the strength."

"Well done, Gwen! Dictate."

"No, I want to write it!"

She wrote: "Regret unwell cannot leave yet stop Please return Paris darling if you can manage journey stop So worried your health and longing see you again your Gwen."

The old doctor asked, "Do you want me to dictate it over the telephone?"

She cried, "No! No! The operator!"

"Right, I'll stop at a post office on the way home."

"Oh, Dr Brayer!" she said, in a ridiculously childish voice, "bring me the little receipt of the telegram. . . ."

"It's a fine thing to see someone as confident as that," said the American doctor to his colleague as he was leaving the room.

A bell boy brought up the receipt. Dr Cohuau had left. One of the nurses had gone down for her lunch. The other one, Mlle Thérèse, too far away from the light, was straining her eyes to read the paper. Miss Abbott, who seemed to be dozing, sometimes gave a little cry, or murmured to herself. When this happened, Thérèse lifted her head, then back she went to her paper. A smell of ether and eau de Cologne filled the room. The minutes passed like hours.

Suddenly someone scratched at the door leading on to the corridor. Mlle Thérèse went and half opened it. There was a little woman there dressed in grey with beautiful grey-blue eyes, who whispered: "Is this right for Miss Gwendolyn Abbott?"

The nurse recognised her, had indeed just seen her picture in the paper. "Warned by the Murderer!" What a thing to happen! But duty first.

"Yes, madam," she said, with tremendous politeness, "but unfortunately the doctors do not allow visitors. And mademoiselle is asleep."

The little woman replied very quietly, "I understand." She added, shouting: "I don't want to wake her!"

From the bed, a tired voice called, "What's the matter, nurse?"

The nurse ran up, her eyes bright with excitement.

"Mademoiselle, it's the woman who's in the papers. She would like to see you."

"Who?"

Miss Abbott raised herself abruptly on her elbows. The little woman, closing the door behind her, came forward and said shyly,

"I am so sorry, mademoiselle, I didn't know you were so ill. I don't suppose my name will mean anything to you. I'm Madame Colet."

"My lorgnette, nurse!" ordered Miss Abbott. "No, not my glasses, my lorgnette! Madame Colet? Are you the one who is being threatened by this horrible wretch, madame?" She stuck her lorgnette on her nose: "Yes, it's you, all right!"

She tried to take a deep breath, pointed to a chair near the bed, and asked anxiously: "You look so worried, madame. Do you know anything about . . . ?"

She did not finish and resumed her inspection with flagrant distrust.

"How did you get here?" she asked. "How do you know . . . ?"

Helplessness, fear and supplication fought together in Mme Colet's expression.

"I, *too*, mademoiselle, am afraid for the one I love," she replied.

The nurse had returned to her chair in the shadow, and was listening avidly. Miss Abbott shivered.

Mme Colet repeated gently, "I am afraid I am not a Parisian and I have no one here I can confide in. I read in an evening paper about M. de Laeken's disappearance. I guessed that he must live at the Villas Kléber. I thought perhaps he had a wife and family. I came here without thinking. I asked downstairs if M. de Laeken was married and I was told: 'No, he's engaged and his *fiancée*'s upstairs, and very upset!'"

Miss Abbott let fall her lorgnette, sniffed and mustered a smile.

"*Fiancée*," she echoed. "Yes, and very very upset, that's true. More upset than if I myself were in the clutches of the fiend."

"Like me," said Mme Colet. "I'm afraid for Raymond, for my husband. . . ."

The creases deepened in Miss Abbott's forehead.

"Has he been uneasy recently . . . since the first crime?"

"You know perhaps that we were witnesses. But Raymond only began to be uneasy on Tuesday."

"Like Guy . . ."

"It's no good asking him questions or begging him to trust me. He remains silent and every day his anxiety gets worse. I can see it. I'm going off my head. . . ."

"Like me," said Miss Abbott passionately. "Exactly like me. Oh, madame . . ." She extended a long hand which imprisoned Mme Colet's tightly. "But," she added, suspicious once more, "why did you give the threatening letter to the newspapers?"

Mme Colet looked grieved. "I didn't give anything at all. My confidence was betrayed."

"Like mine!"

"You can't trust anyone," said Mme Colet, sadly.

"That's true," replied Miss Abbott, "no one."

She fell silent. Mme Colet did not seem to draw any conclusion from this silence, she didn't even pay any attention to it, and her words fell over each other.

"I wanted to lock him up before leaving, and to take away our bedroom key! To know that he was *my* prisoner! I didn't dare! They never allow us to watch over them . . . it's not done. I hope I'm not tiring you, mademoiselle. This visit has done me good. For four days I've been torturing myself, hiding from everyone what I wanted to cry from the housetops. Raymond, of course, tries to maintain his usual calm but you can't deceive a loving heart."

"How long have you been married, madame?"

"Oh, I'm already an old married woman. For ten years, and I'm thirty. We must be the same age?"

"Nurse," ordered Miss Abbott, "go into the bathroom. I'll call you if I need you."

Mlle Thérèse tried to protest. "The doctors . . ."

"It's not the doctors who pay!"

As soon as they were alone:

"Nearly the same age, madame . . . but it was only this year that I met the one man in my life."

"I think that's better," declared Mme Colet. "I was lucky but it's usually a mistake to get married too young. You take the first-comer, you lack experience, and you build nothing lasting. It is so much wiser to wait. Besides, you love so much more strongly when you are thirty."

Miss Abbott burst into sobs.

"What will happen to him? I paid all the money the monster asked for, but with the newspapers and the police he will . . . will he . . . what will he . . . ?"

"I'm sure he won't," Mme Colet replied emphatically. "He's only interested in money. You'll see him again."

"He," "him," they mixed up kidnapper and victim, but understood each other. Miss Abbott sniffed, a trifle comforted.

"I don't know what happened. I, who am always so solid, so well balanced—he told me that's why he loves me—I suddenly . . . went to pieces. I did what was necessary at the bank and at that horrible agency, but afterwards I had a fainting fit and became delirious . . . and now I can't walk. He'll be very angry with me. Yes, he will, I know him. He is extraordinarily attentive, he is adorable, but he likes a woman to be strong. I am ashamed."

Mme Colet protested. "In such a tragedy. . . ."

"Even in a tragedy! Since Monday's murder he kept saying: 'Whatever happens, Gwen, I'm relying on your self-control, on your marvellous self-control.' 'What for, Guy?' I asked him, and he merely said: 'Hush!' and went back to his work. He was suddenly in such a hurry to finish it."

Silence.

"Like Raymond," said Mme Colet. "He, too, has suddenly gone back to his work, although we are on holiday. We make furniture in Avignon—and he keeps on saying: 'I want everything to be put in order at once so that you will have money.' I correct him: 'so that we shall have money.' He replies: 'Yes, yes, of course!' like someone who does not believe what he says. . . ."

Mme Colet raised her handkerchief to her lips.

"He wanted the lawyer to have all the documents for his case," said Miss Abbott, "because in Belgium there are some wicked people who have taken his name and his fortune. He explained to me that that often happens in Europe with aristocratic families. The whole of this week he has been typing out documents and his genealogical tree. He looked so relieved last night when he had finished. 'I'll go and lodge it tomorrow morning,' he said to me. This morning . . ."

She sobbed.

"It's perhaps there that we must look for an explanation?"

"No! I asked him yesterday and he assured me that this was not so. The Laekens of Brussels do not know that he is going to sue them. Not even the lawyer knew. Guy was to speak to him today for the first time. A very good lawyer—I don't know his name—but very good and very famous."

"What a mystery . . ." sighed Mme Colet. "When I think that my Raymond may be mixed up in this. I remember the moment we first met. I still had pigtails down my back. He was already set up in business. . . . I met him one Sunday at the Grand Théâtre. He was with one of my cousins. . . . Oh, that first meeting!"

"I was on a boat coming back from England. I had spent Christmas and the New Year in London with some friends. I was miserable and lonely and it was very cold. I intended simply to cross Paris and get to Florence as quickly as possible. I was on deck, the weather was rough and I had dropped my lorgnette. I'm very short-sighted, you know, and I was completely lost. He came up and looked for it for me but could not find it. But he suddenly said to me: 'You're standing in a draught, *madame*.' Such a voice! And it was so funny that a stranger should be as considerate as that. We went on talking. I had never met a man like him before. He did not know who my father was and he pitied Americans because they have no aristocracy. I agree. And he was so poetic about the 'polar sun' and the 'grey foaming sea.' I couldn't see a thing but it was much better to listen to him than to see. At Calais he dealt with my luggage and secured our seats in the train. I could have taken my glasses out of my bag but during our conversation he had said that glasses make a woman ugly. He did not even like my lorgnette. So you can understand. . . ."

"Of course I understand," replied Mme Colet, with all her heart. "At the theatre Raymond said to my cousin: 'Pity she wears pig-tails . . . she could look like a grown-up girl.' I spent the night in front of the mirror putting up my hair."

"We lunched together in the dining car. He, too, had spent Christmas in London but he lived on his own in Paris. He talked to me about Belguim and Brussels, as he did last night (she began to cry). It all ended as it had begun. It's too awful!"

"No, no, you mustn't think about unhappy things, mademoiselle, they won't happen. Keep on remembering the good times. All this week I've been delving in my memories and saying: it can't all be over, it isn't possible!"

Miss Abbott seized the small proffered hand once more.

"You are right, *madame*, it can't all be over. . . . All these weeks, all these months that we have lived together. He took me in a taxi, you know, for at that time I had a suite at the Hôtel Victor-Hugo. He lived in a boarding house in Auteuil. He sent me flowers and came to see me. He was unhappy at the idea that I was to leave for Florence. I did not go. He found time to come and see me each day. Each morning there was a telephone call: Good morning, Gwen, have you slept well? He sent me flowers and all sorts of little gifts. And he learned English. I wanted him to come and live at the Victor-Hugo because he got so tired, and has such a bad stomach, but he replied: 'I can't afford it.' He was very strict—sometimes rather cruel—about money matters: 'You are too rich, Gwen!' he used to say. And I replied: 'It's not my fault, Guy.' He accepted small presents: a tie, a fountain pen, a signet ring with his coat of arms, or stamps because he was making a collection of Belgian stamps—poor Verdon was one of his dealers—but never anything important. Nor did he want me to meet his friends for the same reason. So I suggested leaving the Victor-Hugo myself so that we could both come here. It's very cheap and he accepted." She glanced trembling at the communicating door.

"But how is it possible," cried Mme Colet, "how can a sensible man in full command of his faculties and cautious into the bargain, how can he get caught like that? 'The Passenger' seems to fascinate people as a snake fascinates birds. Your fiancé simply left without saying a word? Forgive me, I don't want to remind you of those unhappy moments, but I am thinking about Raymond and wondering if there isn't *some sign* which would indicate to me that he is off to . . . to deliver himself up to the monster."

She shivered. Miss Abbott shook her long head.

"He left me a note, a note which those hideous doctors gave to the police. I found it beside me this morning as soon as I woke. He told me that he had to leave me very early, that he hoped to be back for lunch and that I was not to worry. I had heard him coming and going during the night. I don't know whether I was dreaming but I think he went out. I went to bed very early last night. He thought I looked ill and insisted that I should rest. I thought that he was restless because he had indigestion and that he was going for a walk in the park. He did not stick to his diet at all at dinner. It was extraordinary. He ate everything—very indigestible things—and he drank, and said: 'We must make the best of everything, Gwen, we must make the best of everything!' I tried to persuade myself that he was pleased because he had finished typing his lawsuit. But I was very afraid."

Mme Colet gave a mournful smile.

"How like Raymond he is! Raymond, too, poor fellow, suffers from his stomach. I always have to watch what he eats. And he, too, is masterful. He is strong and protects me. Let me show him to you. . . ."

She took a small notecase out of her bag, and from the notecase drew a photo. Through her lorgnette Miss Abbott saw two tiny shapes against a background of apple trees. "I haven't a photograph of both of us," she said, returning the picture, "but I have one of him."

From under the bolster she took a huge leather handbag into which she piously inserted her long fingers. Surprise, anxiety and distress succeeded each other on her features. Dispensing with all coquetry this time she quickly put on her glasses, scattering on the bed a cheque book, bank notes, keys and a passport, and rummaged with both hands in the empty case.

"It's gone!" she murmured. "Oh, no! I looked at it last night before going to sleep. It has a special case. Nurse!" Mlle Thérèse came running. "Have you touched this bag?"

Mlle Thérèse flushed with indignation.

"Oh, mademoiselle!"

"Someone has touched this bag! Your colleague has touched it. The doctors have touched it!"

"No, mademoiselle, nobody has!"

"I'm surrounded by treachery," replied Miss Abbott vehemently. "Forgive me, madame, I must say goodbye. I shall see you later. Nurse, telephone Dr Brayer immediately."

Dr Brayer replied to Miss Abbott.

"My dear Gwen, we gave the police the letter from the kidnapper and the letter from your friend. *That's all*, do you hear? Absolutely all! If you are certain that you put this precious object back in its place and you can't find it, it must be because some one has taken it since last night, but it wasn't one of us."

3

A quarter of an hour was enough

The day of Friday, October 7th, already enriched by two important news items—the murder of M. Verdon and the kidnapping of the Viscount de Laeken—and which was to end with a *coup de théâtre*, also gave the police the long awaited pleasure of "swooping"—but slightly too late.

Let us first sum up the reports of Inspectors Ligaire and Blondel, from the American Bank and the Venus Agency respectively.

Miss Abbott had arrived at the American Bank at about a quarter to twelve. Shown in at once to the manager's office she had demanded 80,000 dollars in cash. Her reason—a sudden departure. She displayed an unwonted impatience. Even more odd and ingenuous into the bargain, she had asked for 10,000 dollar bills whose numbers were not to be taken. These rather rare notes always have a special docket. But the manager was accustomed to the whims of his clients and Miss Abbott had unlimited credit. Payment was made within five minutes, just the time to sign the receipt and she had left. . . .

In the rue Thorel not far from the boulevards, between two brothels, the Venus Agency looked as austere as a religious bookshop. The books displayed in the window dispelled the illusion. Mlle Hermine was the saleswoman. In a small glass box, not unlike that of a tobacconist, and on which was painted in black letters the words *Agency*, Mlle Isaure received and distributed letters. Some people maintained that the inner shop had access to the two neighbouring houses. Neither the appearance nor the behaviour of the girls ruled out this possibility.

The rules of the agency were very simple. You could be a registered client; you were given a number and paid a certain sum each time you were handed a letter. If you were a casual client, since the agency was a serious one, you had to produce some proof, true or false, of identification, and you paid double.

Miss Abbott had burst into the Venus Agency at five minutes past midday. She had displayed obvious distress as she handed in her envelope. Was she too late? After casting a glance at the address Mlle Isaure assured her that she had not yet seen anyone of that name.

Blondel asked with mock severity—for Mlle Isaure had very pretty eyelashes—"Didn't this lady's emotion strike you any more than that . . . ?"

Despite their embarrassment at being visited by the police the girls burst out laughing: "If we were to notice every time some great booby comes and whines here. . . ."

"But didn't the name strike you either?"

"The name? Why?"

Blondel raised his eyes to heaven.

"Don't you read the newspapers?"

"Thank you!" replied Mlle Hermine, who also had very pretty eyelashes. "We've something better to do."

Duty made Blondel impervious to this. He continued his interrogation. Before two o'clock a boy of about fifteen had come to collect the envelope. He had shown his employer's identity card, paid and left. What did he look like? Just a young kid, that was all. From midday to two o'clock Mlle Isaure was too busy to scrutinise her customers.

A fifteen-year-old boy in Paris. . . . Leaving the rue Thorel the inspector glanced at the two streams of traffic on the boulevard which flowed by endlessly. It's like trying to find a certain wrench in all the tool boxes of all the cars in the whole of Paris, he thought. He rang up the Villas Kléber.

Belot had made it his headquarters. He had not given up hope of seeing the mad American woman and wanted to remain on the spot. M. Malebranche had returned to the Prefecture. On parting Belot had said to him: "Do you remember, Chief, a remark you made the day before yesterday? 'This double case which tomorrow

196

may be a triple one.' Bravo! You're not expecting it to be a quadruple one, are you?"

M. Malebranche had replied: "It's a catastrophe."

In telephonic communication with Picard, Belot had learned some facts of varicd importance:

(a) The statement of a taxi driver who at three o'clock in the morning in the Gobelins district had taken a fare with a beard to the Place du Châtelet. The man had made off in the direction of the quays. A search was being made in this direction to see if he had taken another taxi.

(b) The name of the viscount figured in the books of several stamp dealers, including Verdon—with the mention "Belgium"—and the address of the Villas Kléber replacing an earlier one, a boarding house in Auteuil to which Picard had sent one of his men. Longspès was being questioned, the mail at the rue du Châteaudun examined, and the safe was to be opened.

(c) On the other hand, there was no mention of the man who had just disappeared in Étienne Tavernier's address book.

Blondel's report on the Venus Agency completed Belot's exasperation. Despite his persistent neuralgia he compiled from memory a list of all the places where "The Passenger" and his accomplices had undoubtedly been present.

(1) MONDAY: In Camus's taxi (*Devaux*);
(2) In the 197 bus of the U Line in the Champs-Elysées (*Devaux*);
(3) In a café in the rue de Valois (*Devaux*);
(4) TUESDAY: In the 805 bus of the U Line (*Letter to Picard*);
(5) NIGHT OF TUESDAY/WEDNESDAY: Post Office in the Place Victor-Hugo (*Express letter to M. Malebranche*);
(6) WEDNESDAY: at *Le Grand Journal* (*Letter to M. Rose*);
(7) Post Office in the rue d'Amsterdam (*Express letter to Longspès*);
(8) NIGHT OF THURSDAY/FRIDAY: Outside the Gobelins Garage (*the bearded man*);
(9) In a taxi from the garage to the Place du Châtelet (*the bearded man*);
(10) TODAY, FRIDAY: At the Gare Saint-Lazare (*the bearded man*);

(11) Post Office in the Avenue de la République (*express letter to Miss Abbott*);
(12) At the Hôtel Royal, Place de la Porte-Champeret (*threats to Mme Colet*);
(13) At the Venus Agency, rue Thorel (*the young boy*).

"We could add the two meetings between Verdon and Laeken in buses on the U Line," Belot said to Gaillardet, "but they could have taken place somewhere else, even at 'The Passenger's' house, who might only have mentioned the buses for the sake of publicity. Let us stick then to these thirteen points. They are sufficient proof that the 'gang' rambles about as and where it pleases."

"Mind you," said Gaillardet, "the boy from Venus is probably an unwitting accomplice. His employer sent him there. . . ."

"With an identity card in the name of Richard Verdon? If he thought that quite normal the boy must be a congenital idiot."

Belot was wrong. The boy was not a congenital idiot. Gaillardet was wrong. The boy's employer was not "The Passenger." Their conversation was interrupted by a new message from Picard requesting Belot to report immediately to the Hôtel de la République, Place de la République, to pick up a sensational piece of evidence. "The Passenger" had spent the day there, and he had just left. Fifteen minutes earlier.

A short bearded man, *this time with a fair beard,* had arrived that morning at about eight o'clock with a small suitcase in a grey canvas cover. He had asked for a room with bathroom and had been given No. 25 on the second floor. He had registered in the name of Richard *Berdon,* born in Paris, coming from Carpentras and going to Saint-Quentin. He had ordered a copious breakfast. He went out twice—about 8.45 for a good quarter of an hour, and at 1.30 after lunching at the hotel. On his return at 5.15 he announced that he would not be staying, making the excuse that a Parisian friend had offered to put him up. He had gone upstairs to his room, paid the bill and left with his suitcase. At no moment did his behaviour appear the slightest bit unusual.

Two young page boys watched the departure of the taxi which was swallowed up in the traffic on the square. The taller one, thin and red-headed, had a cunning, prematurely worn-looking face. The other looked in his uniform like a timid and studious hospital orderly.

"For a long stay," said the timid one. "Half a day . . . !"

The red-head asked: "What makes you think he was coming here for a long stay?"

"He told me so, he told me. . . ."

The sentence remained unfinished, and the timid one blushed. A new thought made him blush even deeper. Without looking at his comrade he murmured: "I know one. . . .

"One what?"

"A place where they sell books. I've seen it."

The red-head looked at him scornfully.

"So what? It's not enough to have seen it. I bought one last night. It's hot stuff, I tell you. *Lulu on Holiday*. It's a sequel to *Lulu at School*. And much better!"

He ran his tongue over his lips. The younger one begged: "Will you lend it to me?"

"No, I've told you a dozen times. I don't lend I only swop. It would be too easy, see! You don't dare, and you save your pennies. When our little sissy stops being a chicken, O.K.!"

The boy blushed once more.

"I went in."

"Liar!"

"It's in the rue Thorel, a shop painted brown between two . . . two what you call 'ems . . ." He went on eagerly: "With a box on which is painted *Agency* and books . . . and two girls. . . ."

"Come here!"

They disappeared into the luggage entrance. Hiding behind the lift the red-head ordered: "Let's have a look!"

The other hung his head.

"I didn't buy anything. I hadn't got time."

The red-head burst out sarcastically:

"You had the cheek to go in without buying? Are you making a fool of me? I'm tough but I wouldn't dare to go into a joint like that without buying." Suspiciously: "What were you doing there, Robert? An errand? For the hotel or for a client?"

Robert turned away. "It's a secret. I gave my word."

The red-head grabbed him by the wrist. "Is that so!" He looked into Robert's anxious eyes. "You like making a fool of me! When did you do this errand? You couldn't have had time in duty hours."

Robert tried to free himself, but the red-head twisted his arm.

"You're hurting me!"

"You went in your lunch hour, didn't you? You know it's forbidden!"

Robert plucked up courage to say: "But you do it!"

"Ah, so you're going to tell on *me* now. Besides, I'm not stopping you doing it. I forbid you to hide it from me and keep all the money to yourself. Come on, I'm listening!"

"I promised."

The twisting of the arm became intolerable, and Robert groaned.

"Make yourself at home," said a deep voice behind them. It was the porter. "I've been looking for you outside and here you are fighting like a couple of street urchins."

"It's Robert, monsieur, who doesn't obey the rules," said the red-head. "He did an errand during the lunch hour for a client."

The porter looked at Robert severely.

"Is that true, eh?" Silence. "So you won't answer? Where did you go? A good boy like you." Silence. "Do you want me to fire you on the spot?"

Robert looked terrified. "Oh, no, monsieur!"

"Who did you run the errand for?"

"For M. Verdon," he murmured.

"Berdon," corrected the porter. "Verdon is the new victim on the U."

"Yes, he explained. . . . It was a mistake on his card."

"What are you blathering about? What card?"

"His identity card."

The porter was appalled: "You saw his card? With *Verdon* written on it? What is all this about?" Robert began to tremble. "Come with me!"

They went to the reception desk, followed at some distance by the red-head. The porter asked the name of the client who had just left. "Berdon. Richard Berdon." Robert was trembling:

"I don't know, monsieur. It was Verdon on it."

The manager was notified. He was a nervous man whom the name of Verdon and the sudden departure of the client terrified. He telephoned to Police Headquarters. The inspector asked him to telephone at once to the Prefecture. The Prefecture justified his fears:

The identity card did belong to the unfortunate stamp dealer; it had been falsified by the murderer, and all the evidence suggested that the murderer himself had used it. He had left fifteen minutes earlier? The manager heard a string of curses at the end of the line, uttered by Picard himself.

Until the arrival of an inspector, poor Robert in the manager's office told the following story:

About nine o'clock, after his first brief excursion, the man with the fair beard caught sight of him in the hall and asked him to come up to his room. He had come to Paris, he said, to recover some letters addressed to a lady that she was to return to him. "But, you understand, I cannot meet this lady again. She is to send them to me to an office not far from here. If I go myself she might be lying in wait for me and will start to ruin my life again. I need a go-between whom I can trust. You look honest and discreet. Have you a moment off during the day? What time? From one to two? Couldn't be better. Get out of uniform. I'll pick you up in a taxi on the other side of the square and we'll go together." And things had happened just as he had said. He stopped the taxi on the boulevard near the rue Thorel and gave his identity card to Robert. "You've only got to show it saying that you've come from your employer. And here's the necessary money. There's a joke on the card: A V instead of a B, but it doesn't matter. I've asked the lady to put the same on the envelope. Be quick now."

"You little wretch," groaned the manager. "Didn't you realise that it was impossible to have a joke *about an initial?*"

No, he hadn't realised, he didn't know . . . besides, the client seemed such a decent sort. Quick as he was getting back, Robert had glanced at the card and the envelope: Richard Verdon. He'd thought of the gentleman whose murder had been announced that morning. He had read the paper. But to have the same name as a victim is not to have the same name as a murderer! M. Berdon—Verdon was delighted. "Now I've got them, and she won't get me!" He took Robert to where he had picked him up, gave him fifty francs and shook him by the hand. "Not a word to anybody," he said. "Affairs with women are sacred. Besides, I'm going to spend at least a week in the hotel and each time I want something I shall ask you. You can make some money!"

Robert was in the depths of despair. The manager paced up and down repeating: "We shall be bankrupt. 'The Passenger' here! We are ruined. . . ."

Belot heard Robert's statement which he considered to be entirely trustworthy. Then, after visiting Room 25 where "The Passenger" had not left the slightest trace, he telephoned Picard and left the Hôtel de la République to return to the "Old Ladies."

Seven o'clock. It was dark and the boulevards were brightly lit. The taxi stopped, drove on and stopped again. "I should have taken the underground as I did earlier," Belot muttered to himself. "But I'm too done in." The slowness of the journey gave him time to meditate and his headache made him bitter. Victory seemed further away than ever. The man was certainly clever. He had created a perfect circle with cunning and disconcerting ease.

Dr Brayer loves the circus, he will enjoy this! A real farce. The clown comes into the arena, meets the "funny man" who does not recognise him, takes him with him up to a huge bank note on which is written 80,000 dollars, makes him take it, only to take it back again at once, thanks him effusively and goes off. He has turned the tables and the public begins to roar with laughter. And when the copper arrives with his big cardboard revolver, the laughter becomes delirious. Only a circus copper's job is to be funny. But not mine. We do not work in the same kind of arena. . . .

Belot lowered both windows and inhaled the fresh air.

To use ingenuous accomplices, incapable of the least suspicion . . . that is perfection. I wonder if "The Passenger" didn't use Devaux-Oudart for the Tavernier crime, as he has just made use of this boy? Devaux only got away by a miracle, and "The Passenger" is no fool. He would not have launched him on that sort of adventure if Devaux had known the real facts about him. Were we to arrest this drunkard he would probably not be able to tell us anything! In fact, Devaux could be to "The Passenger" what the driver Camus was to Devaux? That doesn't help much.

The fresh air, however, altered the trend of Belot's reflections.

Don't let's exaggerate. "The Passenger" may be clever but he has shown the cloven hoof. The opposite to Devaux. Devaux hides himself and goes to ground, whereas he has taken to circulating freely. We know now that he is short and slender, that he has brown eyes and a straight nose. That is a beginning. Strange that in the case of a bearded man all that people notice is the beard! The first time, it alone must have been false. It was at the hotel that everything was a disguise; beard, eyebrows and hair. While on the subject of beards, he's using up his resources quickly! Dark and fair the same day. What about tomorrow? Could he be considering that his exploits were completed?

The night air was delicious.

Besides, he had taken a great risk today. This business of the identity card, this Berdon-Verdon. If the argument between the two page boys had taken place before he left. . . . This was unlikely of course. So long as young Robert thought the client was staying for some time he had good reason to be silent. All the same . . . he would have been picked up by now! I should like to know why he didn't leave the hotel earlier. After having got the money he could have said to the boy: "Thank you very much, you can go home on foot!" and have disappeared in the taxi.

Belot said to the driver: "Stop at a druggist's. I must get some aspirin."

4

The first discovery

At the "Old Ladies," in M. Villeneuve's office which had been com-
mandeered by the police, Belot found Inspector Perraud with Gaillardet: Perraud who had been ordered to keep an eye on Mme Colet.

"Where is she?" he asked anxiously.

The two men, looking pleased with themselves, pointed to the
ceiling. Belot sank into an armchair. "She had read *Le Grand
Journal Soir*," said Perraud, "and had telephoned the chief who gave
her the address. She got round him too, that's certain."

"We chatted . . ." began Gaillardet.

"She learnt what she wanted to learn. . . ." said Belot.

"I wasn't going to suspect her when my superiors . . ."

"Dry up, Sergeant! What then?"

"She said quite casually: 'All right, I'll go upstairs.' And she's
been up there for three-quarters of an hour. Apart from that nothing,
but there's a glorious smell of cooking. D'you think we could have
dinner here like millionaires?"

"You turn my stomach," said Belot. "And Monsieur Colet?"

"He stayed at home," replied Perraud. "She promised me he
wouldn't go out."

Belot told them the story of the Hôtel de la République and just
as he finished Mme Colet came in. She smiled at him.

"How's the headache?" he asked, offering her the bottle of aspirin
tablets.

She made a grimace.

"Without water or sugar. . . ."

204

Perraud and Gaillardet rushed out. Alone with Belot, she asked: "You're not surprised to find me here, Inspector?"

"The contrary would have surprised me."

"You agree? When I learned the details of this new affair from M. Picard, when I knew that this time a woman was involved, I felt sure that 'The Passenger' was carrying out his threat: 'Take care, ladies and gentlemen!' "

"But we thought that this woman was you."

She turned scarlet. "Naturally," she said quickly. "All the more reason. . . ."

Perraud and Gaillardet reappeared. One was carrying a glass of water and the other a sugar bowl. She welcomed them with a great show of gratitude. While waiting for the two tablets to dissolve she said: "Poor woman, I think my visit did her good. She received me very amiably."

"Wasn't she suspicious of you?" asked Gaillardet. "Everyone here declares she is as suspicious as a barn owl. Usually a suspicious woman is even more distrustful of other women than of men."

Mme Colet stopped stirring and looked at Gaillardet with deference.

"You are a psychologist, Monsieur Gaillardet. But Miss Abbott and I happened to have plenty of grounds for understanding each other. Oh, she didn't tell me anything certainly that you don't know already. If I had come to be useful to you I should have little to be proud of. . . . There was one thing, however, at the end. . . ."

She emptied her glass at one gulp with an "Ugh!"

"We're listening," said Belot.

It was the story of the photo, which astonished her audience. Belot asked her if anything else had aroused her curiosity. Yes; the lawsuit of the real Laeken against the phoney Laekens.

"Miss Abbott assured me that this case could have no bearing on his disappearance, for neither the Laekens of Brussels nor the lawyer were aware of her friend's intentions. The lawyer! Doesn't that seem to you rather peculiar? A 'very famous' lawyer whose name she doesn't know! What an eccentric this M. de Laeken must be. He loves a woman, he loves her *very much* since he won't marry her until he is as rich as she is, and he hides things from her? He lives for his lawsuit, typing documents from morning till night and . . ."

"He types. . . ." interrupted Gaillardet. "You mean to say that he uses a typewriter?"

"What else do you suppose he types on?" asked Belot.

"I didn't see a typewriter upstairs," persisted Gaillardet, "and yet I looked over the bedroom and the cupboards. No, there was one locked and without a key."

"Go and open it," ordered Belot. "Go on, madame. So you thought you hadn't learned anything useful! Try and remember everything."

Mme Colet put her face in her hands.

"Very well, then. I knocked at the door and a nurse opened. . . ."

She repeated word for word without an omission or mistake the confidences made to her by Miss Abbott, though leaving out her own which she replaced each time by a moment's pause. Belot took notes. When she had finished he read them back to her, stressing a few of the words.

"Well," he said, impatiently, "where's Gaillardet got to?"

Gaillardet returned, looking very cheerful.

"No typewriter—neither in the cupboard, which is completely empty, nor anywhere else. I turned out everything. Nothing! I got hold of the little nurse and she searched in our crazy friend's room. Nothing!"

"What about his papers?"

"Nothing. A few clothes and some linen, that's all!"

"You must have found some stamps, a collection of stamps?"

"God help us . . . excuse me, madame. . . . I tell you there's nothing!"

"Ah," cried Mme Colet, her eyes shining. "I understand why the photo's missing."

The three men exchanged glances. She looked at them one after the other and thought that they really loved their profession.

"The floor staff!" exclaimed Belot.

Perraud went to fetch them—a valet and a chambermaid. They confirmed that the gentleman in No. 18 often used a typewriter and that the previous day they had heard him at it practically all day. They had never seen the machine. The gentleman kept it in the cupboard which was always locked. And what else was in that cupboard, they had no idea.

Belot then questioned the porter. Miss Abbott thought that M. de

Laeken had taken a walk that night in the park. Had he gone out? The porter, still offended by the criticism he had received, declared that this was impossible to check. Each guest at the "Old Ladies" had a key. This was one of the features of the place because it made them feel more at home. Naturally there were people on duty—the telephone girl, the wine waiter, a chambermaid, etc., but no one on permanent duty in the hall.

"Very imprudent for a millionaire's hotel," said Gaillardet.

"To begin with," the porter replied almost haughtily, "all the rooms on the ground floor have a safe. Besides, if someone had evil intentions he could always come in as a guest."

Belot approved. "You couldn't be nearer the truth. I'm going home. Goodbye, madame! Once more I'm grateful to you! Gaillardet, you stay here. Telephone to the lab. to rush some men round here to take fingerprints."

He felt the elation of a gun dog which among all the odours of the soil suddenly picks up the acrid scent of his prey. Or the joy of the helmsman when his ship rides a huge wave which could have smashed it. Neither Devaux-Oudart, nor Paul Tavernier had ever made him feel like this—only irritation and frustration. They had gathered round them a galaxy of question marks. The bogus Vicomte de Laeken was a different matter. Here was—doubtless because there are convictions which only the truth inspires—here was—and I bet we'll find a dozen cross-checks, yes, here was "The Passenger!"

Belot told Picard everything. He told him how sure he was, supplied the first proofs and asked for the latest results of the inquiry, which were beyond his wildest hopes.

"To begin with, the Auteuil boarding house in the rue Jouvenet," said Picard. "Your Belgian moved in there during January."

Belot had spread out in front of him the notes dictated by Mme Colet. He replied:

"My Belgian made his American girl-friend believe that he was already living there before the trip to London.

"At the boarding house he declared that he had just come from England, where he had spent several years.

"To the girl he declared that he lived in Paris and that he had simply been to spend Christmas with some English friends.

"The Belgian Embassy was very voluble when I told them the

story of the lawsuit. A secretary gave me all the lowdown on the Laeken family from which I gathered one would have to be quite mad to embark on such a campaign.

"So our man only embarked on it in words, exclusively for the benefit of his girl-friend.

"The secretary asked me the name of the lawyer."

Belot was jubilant.

"No name! A lawyer without a name, a lawyer who knew nothing, who was to learn everything this very morning! What a series of coincidences, don't you think? To disappear with all the documents *and the machine on which they had been typed!* And which perhaps didn't only type them, eh? And he'd accepted a signet ring. We must find the shop which engraved it. We shall get a laugh! You realise that it's him? The chap who used the U, who wanted to use the garage, who worked out his scheme with a fantastic care for detail."

"Don't get so excited. I shall begin to think you're me. You haven't arrested him by any chance?"

Belot recovered his calm.

"Go on."

"The Embassy has asked therefore, for a description of the phoney Laeken."

"It's too late for them to go and look for his photo under the American's pillow! Besides, he must be about as Belgian as you or me. The telephone box at Saint-Lazare and the Hôtel de la République prove that. A comedian who wears his accent with the same ease as his false beard."

"Well now, there you seem to be taking a bit of a long shot," said Picard. "You have a way of working out things to suit yourself. If he were a real Belgian it would explain the odd phrase or two in his letters: 'the French Police,' and so on. A Belgian might have met Tavernier in Belgium or in London—if it's true that he lived in London. As for the gentleman with the dark-fair beard, he could be an accomplice, like Devaux."

"An accomplice, the visitor at the Hôtel de la République, the author of my perfect circle? Not on your life! If he went off with the 80,000 dollars in *his* pocket, he is 'The Passenger' and 'The Passenger' is Laeken! I see the chief has given you back the two letters written to the American woman. Read the express letter again. All the details it contains could of course have been wheedled out of his victim by 'The Passenger' but do you think that an unfortunate prisoner would have thought of boiled potatoes? Particularly as last night the Viscount indulged in a decidedly ample repast: his diet is, therefore, not his sole preoccupation. No, this time there is no accomplice, and no victim, the American woman excepted. In fact he had on hand three jobs, all three of which were to be put into effect this week. The first two failed, and the third would have succeeded even better if Miss Abbott had not had a fainting fit. He advised her so strongly to keep cool. I see his point. If she had kept her head no one would have known a thing at present. And tomorrow morning at Le Havre she would have found something or other which would have still got her to take the boat. . . ."

"Or would have forced her to take it," said Picard. He bit his nails. "It's possible. We'll find that 'something or other' when the time comes."

"It's not so sure—however little *Le Grand Journal Soir* has published about it, 'The Passenger' knows that his precious secret is no longer one for us. Oh, he can still give us plenty of trouble! All the same, I feel much better."

"What d'you think happened last night?"

"He insisted that his Gwendolyn should go to bed early. He went out between eleven o'clock and midnight. Wearing his black beard he went to the Gobelins Depot. His plan? That's still the greatest mystery to me. Was it Longspès' outburst which put him on his guard? No, since he stayed until three o'clock in the morning. It was Mme Colet, the name of Mme Colet. So he left, took a taxi to the Châtelet, a second, perhaps a third, and returned to the Villas Kléber without being noticed by anyone. Each guest has his own key and I imagine that if he agreed to live there it was far more for facilities of this nature than for love of our American friend. He wrote the farewell note which he left beside the next bed, collected all his papers—or what remained of them, for some had probably already been removed—and took them away together with the typewriter. He went to the place where he was holding Verdon prisoner, killed him or had him killed by Devaux or someone else, packed the clothes in a cardboard box, typed the accompanying message, typed the express letter to Miss Abbott, which he was to send this morning, took the box and a suitcase and went off to the Gare Saint-Lazare. Why not the box in the suitcase? Because he needed some luggage at the Hôtel de la République and being a prudent man he wanted it to be full of belongings in the normal way."

"Hmmm!" grunted Picard. "That's all very plausible, but I have evidence which makes me think that he went to the Villas *after* his crime. He took one of the first métros at Les Ternes, the Villiers Line—that's to say Saint-Lazare. The man who punches the tickets noticed him: black beard, beige gloves, cardboard box and tan suitcase. I imagine that he did not dare to board the train at the Étoile and that he carried on to the next station."

Belot seemed sceptical.

"He couldn't have increased the risk he was running to the point of journeying with the box and the suitcase from the scene of the crime to the Villas Kléber, and from the Villas to Les Ternes. I am more inclined to think that your ticket collector has given us a new clue and that Verdon's corpse must be somewhere near there . . . like . . . who was it?—Musard, the stamp dealer? On the Boulevard de Coucelles, just before the Place des Ternes."

"That's so. But Musard is under observation and there is nothing to report."

"Who was on last night?"

"Bourré, the new man. A serious fellow, you said so yourself."

"I hope I wasn't mistaken. Will you go and see, Truflot?"

The two friends were silent for a moment.

"With regard to the stamp dealers," Picard went on, "I have details of their dealings with the Viscount. He wrote the same letter to all of them in April, asking for their catalogues and informing them that he was interested in the stamps of Belgium and the Belgian Congo. Here is the one that was addressed to Verdon. Periwinkle blue paper and the same writing as on the love letter. We compared it with those to his colleagues: they are all the same. He wrote a standard circular letter. Why, then, didn't he use the typewriter?"

"Because he kept that for other purposes!"

"The orders were given by Miss Abbott for and in the name of the Viscount—with her money, probably. There are orders worth thousands of francs. With Verdon, too, but particularly with Ibert and Bélier, specialists in Belgium, according to Philippe Durand."

"And 'The Passenger' wrote to *Le Grand Journal* that stamps didn't interest him! Motor cars probably didn't interest him either, and he did Tavernier in . . . oh dear, my headache's coming on again."

Picard consulted his watch.

"We're going to have dinner again at an impossible hour. Off you go, Truflot. Let's hope that you'll get some sleep tonight, and us also! I'm taking you with me, Fred. We're going to recelebrate my daughter's birthday, as Wednesday was such a failure. Ah, the latest bit of news: Verdon's safe: stamps agreeing with the inventory kept by Longspès."

Belot folded up his precious notes. Without Mme Colet, he thought, we should be floundering again. . . . But why her sudden reticences? When she is directly under fire from the criminal?

An excellent meal . . . Mme Picard's good humour, Ginette's satirical comments on the 5th Form at the Victor-Duruy Lycée, and then with the promise of an imminent return home to bed . . . the telephone burst in like a curse. Picard swore and disappeared. They heard him reply curtly, then exclaim, then call out: "Fred!"

"What a profession!" said Ginette.

In the bedroom Picard had already taken off the second receiver and was holding it out to Belot.

"Listen to this," he gasped: "Repeat it, will you please. Just listen to this!"

5

Coup de théâtre

It is hard to imagine any greater contrast than that between the Villas Kléber and Maison Cercu. On the one hand wealth, a gilded paradise, every fantasy and caprice, the silence of carpets and the sparkle of diamonds in their jewel cases; on the other, abysmal poverty, foul, revolting, lice-ridden squalor. There by the Arc de Triomphe the noble trees, the smooth surfaced roads of imperial avenues. Here by the cemetery of Montrouge, the care-worn streets, the depressing alleys, a cul-de-sac with cobblestones.

Cercu claimed to be a philanthropist. "With a hall like this I could have made a ballroom," he said. It is certain that bipeds standing up and clinging together in twos could be got into the place in greater numbers than the bodies which slumped there every night in search of sleep. "Dancing would put up the sales of lemonade." The tramps drank plenty in any case. To reach the doss house you only had to go through a tall iron gate and follow a stinking alley where there were more puddles of urine than pools of rain: it does not rain every day. The hall was entered through a side door, but the serious customers went morning and evening through the café with a stop at the bar. By doing so they not only got a drink of wine which was rough on the throat, but they were safe from the risks of the "inspection." From time to time a sanitary inspector appeared early in the night. He made his way to the evil smelling dormitory and looked in with a jaundiced eye. Every time Cercu declared. "On my word of honour there is the regulation air space." "Air space!" replied the inspector. "Chuck half of them out, and if I catch you again I'll close the place down." Cercu then chose the "uninteresting parties," the "tight fisted" and the penniless—in short, those who did not buy drinks. They got up bewildered and muttering, but submissive. A notice warned them: "In the event of justifiable expulsion the money paid for the night will be retained by the house." In the winter the others, the favourites and the elect, those who had the right to stay to the end, expostulated against this cruelty: it means so many stoves less. As for the inspector's threat, it was never carried out, no one knew why, nor complained.

"Good or bad, they're all layabouts," said Cercu. He himself worked. Every night between eight and ten he extorted from his tenants the price of a night's accommodation. He kicked the sleepy and the slow; barred those who had no money, threatened everyone with the police; roared out the elementary laws of cleanliness and the fines to be incurred if they were broken. Uneasily, the newcomer would examine his mattress and was reassured. However filthy he was, there was no danger of his making it any dirtier. As for the regulars who were already inert, they let themselves be lulled to sleep by Cercu's roars as a prelude to blissful oblivion.

Cercu's work then consisted in extinguishing one of the two bulbs which lit up the hovel, and in closing the alley gate. That was all. The twice nightly rounds—smoking forbidden!—were carried out by his son who at dawn would open the gate and wake up the clients by slapping them with a rag, which he called doing the chores. "I can't go in there in the morning," said Cercu. "I would lose my appetite." A customer one day asked him where he could get a wash. He was thrown out on the spot because Cercu would not stand for insolence. Had he not just installed a pail at the end of the alley? What more did they want? Cercu admitted that in this episode the regulars behaved very well and that they all had approved his action. He slept fourteen hours a day: since he had lost his wife he was catching up. (The son prepared the midday meal and also the supper.) In the afternoon he drank, counted his pennies and grumbled that there were so few. "With all I do," he said, "I am sure to go to heaven."

We shall not describe the nights in the dormitory, the mutterings in dreams, the warm blast from the drains which all these panting mouths breathed: on this Friday night of October 7th, we shall spend less than an hour there. Nor shall we try and find out who frequents this hell. Let us merely note one detail. Miraculously blackened with soot, as the room had no means of heating, the walls were covered to waist-height with ritual graffiti, all with a flavour of rancour and despair, all of them of the greatest banality.

Cercu had bawled his daily invective, had just switched off one of the two bulbs, and was about to step over the bodies which blocked the alley gate, when in the doorway he suddenly saw an alarming apparition.

It was a man. He was dressed only in a pair of underpants and socks. But he did not seem naked. Bruises, dust and congealed blood stained his unshaven cheeks and his hairy chest. One eye was half-closed and the other vacant. He shivered from head to foot—either from cold or terror.

What immediately struck Cercu's eye was the good quality of the pants and socks and the paleness of the skin wherever it was visible. "This," he said to himself, "is a well-to-do chap who has been chucked out of the window. Probably caught in the act."

The man was staggering. Neither he nor the doss house keeper had uttered a sound, but the whole dormitory had woken up, warned by that sixth sense of paupers who at any hour of the day or night are on the alert for the unusual, in other words, for danger. All the sleepers looked at the man and the man saw nothing.

Suddenly he collapsed. He fell across an old drunkard, one of the most famous beggars of Montrouge, who roared with pain. Cercu rushed over to him.

"You swine," he cried. "Can't any of you bastards give me a helping hand?"

Four or five clients slowly got up. He shouted once more: "Switch on the light!"

The beggar struggled beneath the dead weight of the stranger.

"He's going to cover me with blood. Get him off me." And someone said in a hoarse voice: "Wait a bit. Be human. . . . Perhaps he's croaked."

"What?" cried Cercu. "I'll beat up the next person who talks such rubbish. I'll smash his teeth in!"

He bent over the man and turned him over roughly. This brought forth a groan. The old beggar heaved a sigh of relief.

"Better give him a glass of brandy," said the hoarse voice.

For the first time a murmur of approval ran through the room.

"You don't imagine he's going to buy you a round?" shouted Cercu, "with what he's got in his pockets! A glass of brandy, indeed . . . !"

From the haversack which served him as a pillow the old beggar brought out a bottle, rubbed his greasy palm on the neck and raised the head of the man who had fainted.

"Here, drink this," he said.

The red wine met with closed teeth and trickled down the heaving chest. The beggar quickly took away the bottle.

"If he shivers," said his other neighbour, "it proves he's still alive."

Now half the inmates of the dormitory were on their feet in a semi-circle, still silent but impatient to learn.

"Perhaps you'd better call a doctor," said the hoarse voice.

A young man who was a little less dirty than the rest of the company—or who had not been dirty for so long—called from the back of the dormitory: "I'm not a doctor, but all the same . . ."

He came over and examined the wounded man. The glass door of the bar opened violently, and young Cercu shouted from the threshold: "What's the trouble—nightmares?"

"Bring a jug of water," ordered his father, "and a cloth."

"Not too good," said the young man-who-was-not-a-doctor. "Aie!"

He had pricked himself as he felt the stranger's abdomen. A piece of paper had been pinned to his pants like a bill on a parcel of laundry. The paper bore a single typed sentence. The young man read out: "*I've no further use for this idiot. I'm returning him to you.*"

"Returning him to me?" said Cercu in amazement.

The young man continued calmly: "Signed, '*The Passenger on the U.*'"

An extraordinary phenomenon then occurred. Within a second everyone was back on his mattress. Only the young man and the proprietor still knelt by the stranger. The son, bringing a jug of water and the cloth, asked regretfully: "Is it all over?"

The hoarse voice began to laugh. Cercu yelled: "Shut your mouth, you idiot!" without knowing whom he was answering. "The Passenger on the U!" In this quiet spot at the end of this blind alley which asked no favour of anyone! Streaming with cold water, the wounded man moved his lips and the lid of his sound eye. In an urgent voice Cercu said into his ear: "Get up, monsieur, you must leave. You must return home!"

"Where am I?" murmured the injured man. Then seizing Cercu's arm he gave a cry: "The police!"

"Don't be afraid," replied Cercu, "they're not here."

Hoarse Voice laughed once more and said: "He's not afraid of them. He wants you to send for them."

"Yes," hiccupped the wounded man, "at once. Call them, monsieur, please! And the car . . ."

Cercu's amazement increased at every moment.

"You came by car?"

"Tell them that I'm . . . They must know. . . . Ah, it hurts. . . ."

He raised a hand to his nose, which was bleeding, and the other to his left arm, which had a long slash along it.

"I'll pay anything you ask," he said.

"Bring a glass of brandy, at once . . . and your overcoat," Cercu said to his son. "Who are you, you poor chap?"

Although everyone appeared to be asleep, the silence of the doss house became as hollow as an abyss. The victim flung back his head. "Verdon," he said. "M. Verdon, the stamp dealer from the rue de Châteaudun. . . . They know certainly. . . . Be quick!"

Cercu pressed: "Wouldn't you like us to take you home first? You would be far better off. We are poor people here and there's no real comfort."

Hoarse Voice jeered.

"No," said the injured man, "I couldn't. . . . I will pay you for your trouble, monsieur."

The younger Cercu had thrown his coat over the unhappy man and handed him the glass of brandy.

"Very well," said Cercu, with resignation, "you . . . you'll tell them the truth, eh? That we've had nothing to do with it."

"After what I've been through. . . ." muttered M. Verdon. "You have been good to me."

Cercu got to his feet.

"Well, then, I'll telephone. Don't worry, it's only five minutes from here."

A score of the inmates stood up. One of them said: "We'll come back later."

"Not on your life," said Cercu, "you're all witnesses."

He locked and bolted the entrance to the alley, put the key in his pocket, then going out through the café he also locked the glass door.

Within half an hour a coach-load of policemen, the Montrouge Superintendent's car, two motor cyclists from the Prefecture, the doctor's car, a taxi carrying Picard and Belot and M. Malebranche's car, had all pulled up at the entrance to the cul-de-sac. The news had soon got round. A police raid at Cercu's! The local residents, who hated him crowded round the vehicles to see him taken away.

The younger Cercu played host at the door of the café, the father at the bedside of the wounded man, around which a space had been made. An outrageously white pillow, a relic of the late Mme Cercu, supporting his aching head, a scarlet eiderdown had replaced the overcoat. After some deliberation Cercu had allowed his patrons who were uneasy on the count of illegal overcrowding, to slip away; this left only one man per mattress. After great efforts the windows had been opened. "Thank you, thank you!" repeated M. Verdon. "I will repay you."

"I have always been a philanthropist," replied Cercu, "but I thank you in advance." Privately he was convinced that he had acted with deplorable irresponsibility. This fellow will never be able to pay me enough: they'll close the joint!

In actual fact no one paid the slightest attention to the appalling surroundings. By the time Picard and Belot appeared, slightly ahead of M. Malebranche, the doctor was completing his examination and the superintendent was listening to Cercu. With wrinkled forehead and his mouth bleeding, M. Verdon tried to smile, but he was still trembling.

"I don't think there's anything broken," the doctor said to him, opening his bag. "We'll take an X-ray. I'll put on some dressings and then we'll send for an ambulance."

"Thank you, Doctor. . . . Thank you, gentlemen. So it's all over." His one good eye filled with tears.

"So you are M. Verdon," said Picard, bending over the unfortunate man.

"Yes, Verdon, Maurice Verdon. Stamp . . ."

"Save your breath," said Picard. "We know."

M. Malebranche entered the dormitory as Picard was giving his name. Introductions were exchanged. The superintendent reported the statement of the proprietor. The piece of paper which had been pinned to the underpants was passed round. The doctor wrapped the battered face in bandages. On their mattresses the inmates seemed deep in unruffled slumber. Two policemen—a third had just gone to order an ambulance—stood motionless, waiting for orders.

"It's all going quite well," Cercu thought to himself.

"We don't want to tire you," M. Malebranche said to the injured man, "but you can imagine the mass of questions we are longing to ask you. You are the victim of the most audacious criminal we have ever known. I ask you not to mention any name here, but do you know him?"

Verdon tried to shake his head.

"I don't think so. . . . No, I don't think so. . . ."

He winced and groaned.

"Take it easy," said the doctor.

"Yes," said M. Verdon, "I should like. . . . But I don't understand! The money . . . were they given it? And my home? Did they break into my home? . . . Excuse me . . . it hurts. . . ."

"No," said M. Malebranche, "they weren't given anything, and they didn't break in." He turned to Picard and Belot. "We can't really. . . ."

Picard muttered: "He need only tell us where he's been held prisoner. Near here, probably."

"But," said Belot, "the bird . . . or the birds, since he uses the plural . . . must have flown with their victim."

"Never mind!" countered Picard. "If we go on arriving too late we shall end up by arriving in time!"

M. Malebranche bent over the injured man and asked him the question. Under the bandages which now covered his lips, M. Verdon replied in a faint voice.

"I don't know, I don't know. They took me in a car and threw me out . . . at full speed! Oh, do look after me, do protect me . . . !"

"Don't insist, gentlemen," said the doctor. "He's not well enough to talk. We'll take him to Broussais and give him a thorough examination."

The ambulance men bore M. Verdon away on their stretcher. Before following them, M. Malebranche said to Cercu: "Absolute silence, eh? From your clients as well as from you! If there's the slightest leakage to the Press we shall hold you responsible."

Cercu held out his hand. "My word of honour, your worship!"

Picard and Belot looked round. "Do you ever get a visit from the sanitary inspector here?" Picard asked.

"I'm in order," asserted Cercu. "We're not overcrowded."

"No . . . n . . . n . . . o. . . ."

The visitors and the police disappeared. There was the sound of cars starting, the spluttering of motor bicycles, and then the din died away. . . . The only traces of this coup de théâtre—a pillow stained with blood and a scarlet eiderdown which in the midst of this bleak poverty looked like the bed of a Beggar King whom death had overtaken. Cercu picked them up and said to his son: "Shut the windows," adding: "They quite liked the place. . . ."

The jeering of Hoarse Voice made him wheel round abruptly, scarlet in the face, more scarlet than the eiderdown.

"Nom de dieu," he roared, "you've been getting on my nerves for a whole hour. Now who is it, eh? Who is it? I tell you there'll be trouble!"

He cast a thunderous glance round the dormitory. Everyone was asleep.

6

At the Broussais Hospital
Anatomy of a kidnapping

Two doctors in white overalls—the house surgeon who had received M. Verdon and the radiologist—finally appeared in the glossily painted waiting-room where for half an hour Malebranche, Picard and Belot had been asking themselves fruitless questions.

"Nothing broken," said the radiologist. "The worst damage is to the face. Blows with a fist and a violent fall."

"Can he speak?" asked Picard.

"We can't keep him quiet. He has obviously received a severe shock. Besides, he is asking for you."

"Have you any objection?" asked M. Malebranche.

"I would rather he rested," said the house surgeon. "We've turned him this way and that and bandaged him and I have given him a sedative. But if you must see him. . . ."

"I must!" cried Picard.

The radiologist withdrew after promising a report. The other led the small group down corridors, a staircase and more corridors. The muffled sound of their footsteps hardly disturbed the silence. Here and there a lamp glowed.

Two inspectors were speaking in undertones outside the room to which M. Verdon had been taken. M. Malebranche said to the house surgeon: "Stay with us, Doctor, and we'll leave when you say so."

A blue light from a wall fixture lit up the bed. A nurse came forward and said: "Just above normal."

"Some chairs, please," said the doctor.

The new bandage was even more voluminous than the one which had been applied in the doss house. All that could be seen of the patient were his ears, the top of his forehead, hair, nostrils and mouth. A single eye gleamed strangely in this white inert mass.

"It was kind of you to have been so patient, gentlemen," said the survivor. "I am so anxious to know. . . ."

"It is we who have to thank you," said M. Malebranche. "Your testimony is crucial. You are the king pin in a case such as I have never before experienced in my twenty-five years in the police."

The single eye registered surprise and terror.

"Yes, you already spoke just now of a criminal so. . . . It was not because . . . of what I have endured." His voice sank. "I'm afraid." It sank even lower. "I'm still afraid."

He was trembling. M. Malebranche assured him that he had nothing further to fear, that he would be guarded even here. And he added:

"No, the case isn't confined to your . . . private worries. It began with a murder."

"The director of the motor company."

"You knew him?"

"Not at all!"

The police exchanged glances of disappointment.

"No," replied M. Verdon, "but I thought as much. I thought as much. . . ."

He put a hand up to his head.

"Don't get excited," said the doctor.

M. Verdon groaned. "I must know! I know nothing! Everything is spinning in my head, it's terrible."

"It would be better if you talked first," said M. Malebranche, "we'll give you all the facts later."

The nurse brought in two chairs and then two more. M. Malebranche sat down on the right of the bed with the doctor opposite him. Picard and Belot installed themselves a little further off; in spite of the shadow they were in, they took out their notebooks and pencils. The nurse disappeared. And M. Verdon spoke. He was obviously trying to master his pain, to be clear-cut and useful, but at the same time he continued to stress the enormity of his adventure.

"Even now in this room," he said, "with these bandages and face to face with you, I still think I must have been dreaming, gentlemen. A schoolboy's nightmare after reading a thriller. Such things don't happen, I keep on telling myself. They *can't* happen."

It was obvious, too, that he liked talking and that he was something of a speechifier. To hold such an audience as this enthralled probably gave him a satisfaction which made up for his previous fears.

"On Wednesday, as I do every morning, I called in first at my office and then went to see my colleague, Musard, in the Boulevard de Courcelles. He had told me he had some new stock in; for my part I wanted to show him a very fine item before delivering it to one of my best customers, M. Archer. I had an appointment with this customer at the Café de Marigny at about half past eleven. At a quarter to eleven I telephoned to make sure: M. Archer had not yet arrived. So instead of taking a taxi I decided to go by bus. On the U Line, the famous U! Musard and I even cracked a joke on the subject. It was a joke in bad taste I admit. I have been well punished for it. . . .

"Just as I reached the bus stop at the Place des Ternes, someone touched me on the shoulder and said to me with a Belgian accent: 'Aren't you M. Verdon?' I turned round and saw a very well dressed gentleman, wearing a monocle. 'I am M. de Laeken,' he said."

Picard murmured from the shadow: "Splendid!"

M. Verdon tried to raise the white mass of his head. He almost shouted. "What?"

"Go on," said M. Malebranche.

The wounded man gasped for breath.

"Come, come, it's not possible! During those three days, during my martyrdom, I, too, kept on thinking: 'it can only be him!' But I answered myself that something . . . something inconceivable had happened. And that he had nothing to do with it."

"And yet you didn't know him?"

"Didn't know one of my customers? one of my best customers? I had never seen him, it's true; he made all his purchases by correspondence, and sometimes through a secretary. A strange way of doing business, monsieur, I agree. Usually the stamp collector living in Paris comes round in person, takes pleasure in coming round. But a Viscount, living at the Villas Kléber, an enthusiast who knew how to choose, who never bargained, and who paid on delivery. Could it be him? Have you arrested him?"

"Not yet," replied M. Malebranche. "Go on, please."

"He said to me: 'I saw you on Monday at the Frelault sale'—very important sale, gentlemen—(the one that Philippe Durand had mentioned to Belot) 'and I wanted to talk to you but there were too many people.' Why not gentlemen? I was even flattered. I thought: there's nothing like a man of the world! And he added: 'If you are not in too much of a hurry we could have a word about a project. . . .' I thought: I'll take a taxi. At that moment he brought a cigarette case out of his pocket."

His one eye flashed.

"I haven't thought about it ever since. I had never felt uneasy like that before. But remembering also that I might have refused, I thought, no, it's impossible! And besides, you can sense a narcotic. I have read books on criminology, I know that drugged tobacco is easy to spot. Some new invention?"

"Go on," said M. Malebranche gently.

"Well, I took a cigarette, and so did he. He lit them from his lighter and we began to walk up and down. His project. . . . But why bother about that twaddle! My head began to swim. Each time I swallowed my saliva I felt that my eardrums were bursting. I tried to speak but my tongue was too big for my mouth. I don't know what I did, I must have clung to his arm. I heard his voice which seemed to come from the end of the world say, 'Aren't you feeling well, M. Verdon?' No, I wasn't feeling well! I couldn't keep my eyes open. I heard him shout: 'Taxi!' and then: 'My friend's not feeling very well. Rue Laffitte, quickly, please!' This was my office address. I still managed to think: 'He's very nice. . . .' I'm thirsty."

The house surgeon gave him a drink.

"Taxi, not bus," muttered Picard between his teeth. "Despite the statements in the letter to M. Rose."

"Of course," said Belot.

M. Verdon breathed heavily after his drink. He gave a painful laugh.

"That was the end of the first episode, gentlemen. I woke up on a floor vomiting. I called for Longspès, my clerk. I wondered: Why am I on the floor? Where is Longspès? And M. de Laeken? Why did I faint? I looked around me. It was dark. An electric bulb on the ceiling was alight. I did not recognise the globe the bulb was in, nor the furniture nor anything else. I got up and went over to the window. I could distingush the daylight through the chinks of the shutters. I opened the window, and the shutters were closed with a padlock. A padlock! And it was daytime, there was no doubt about it. I could see a little garden and some walls. I must be on a first floor. I wanted to know the time. My watch had gone. I felt in my pockets, particularly in the one where I kept my notecase, in which were the stamps. The notecase had gone. So had my keys and my fountain pen. Nothing left—not even a handkerchief. I rushed over to the door but it, too, was locked.

"I am not easily frightened, gentlemen, but I began to scream. To scream for help, naturally, but above all because I did not know what had happened to me. I screamed louder and louder. Loud enough to arouse the whole of Paris. Can you imagine, with the window open? Nothing stirred. Neither in the garden, nor in the house. I thought I had gone off my head. And then I was sick again, on a mat in front of the window."

He shivered.

"Could you describe the furniture to us?" asked M. Malebranche.

"It would be better not to interrupt him," said the doctor, "I'm afraid. . . ."

"The furniture? By heart! In every detail! Having spent two and a half days alone with it. Middle class!"

"Go on," said M. Malebranche.

"Well, I tried to reason. By the shadows in the garden I realised that it must be about midday, and that only a short time had passed since I was taken ill. I thought that M. de Laeken and I had been victims of a kidnapping, that it was he whom they were after and that I had been taken into the bargain, that he must be shut up in another room of the house. But why didn't he reply to my shouts? Had they slipped a single drugged cigarette into his case which he had offered me instead of smoking it himself? Had he put up a fight, had he been gagged, or perhaps killed? Thriller stuff! I dismissed it. I had a very good motive for developing another theory—a letter received at home the night before, an anonymous letter in a feminine handwriting, which read: 'Take care, someone wishes you ill.' I chucked it in the wastepaper basket. No one could wish me ill, gentlemen. I have never been on anything but good terms with all my acquaintances. Some woman perhaps, as happens to all of us? But I have never known any but very sweet women. In any case you can well imagine I remembered this letter! I was the one who had been attacked and M. de Laeken had suffered the repercussions.

"Then I thought: the stamps. I was carrying stamps on me worth a good hundred thousand francs. And in my office, I had others of course worth considerably more. My pocketbook and my keys had been stolen. They would break into the rue Laffitte and take everything they wanted. Gangsters who had picked me up so easily could certainly blow a safe. They'll keep me just as long as it takes them to sell the stamps. And how can one expect to recover stamps?"

M. Verdon asked for another drink. The doctor took his pulse.

"All this still seemed to me incredible. But having racked my brains, having found a serious reason, I felt relieved. I have always been a thoughtful man, gentlemen, with my wits about me, one might say a philosopher. I reasoned: loss of money is not fatal. I said to myself: you've certainly had a fine joke played on you. I examined my prison. I found a novel on a chest of drawers and leafed through it. I even began to be hungry. Suppose they had decided to let me die there?

"After I don't know how many hours the light suddenly went out. I heard a key being turned in the lock. Someone came in and flung himself on me. . . ."

The good eyelid closed and he stiffened.

"I was on the ground once more. An enormous shape was standing over me. I was in too much pain and the chinks in the shutters did not let in enough light for me to be able to make out his face. In any case it was not M. de Laeken, for this man had no accent."

No one stirred.

"He spoke like a tough. 'I've put a sheet of paper, an envelope and your pen on the table,' he said. 'Write to your clerk: you will add a request to your family and your friends. If you don't want to be tortured and done in, insist that they obey.' 'What do you want?' I asked. He laughed and replied: 'Money!' I begged him to explain. I offered my best assets, my finest stamps. I swore to him that my family and my friends were even less well off than myself. He knew that already. Obviously he knew everything about me because he spoke of my clerk. His only reply was a kick in the stomach. Then he left, saying: 'Now you can yell to your heart's content.'

"And I did yell, gentlemen. With all due respect to you, I kept on yelling. I kept thinking it's impossible. There must be neighbours and tradespeople. There must be a street somewhere near. Not the slightest echo. It was only then that I thought of the country. For some reason I had thought I was in the suburbs. But now the thought of the country made me lose all hope . . . I wrote."

"Yes," said M. Malebranche.

The injured man looked feverishly pleased.

"Ah, so you knew it? So much the better. You can't imagine how alone in the world I felt. I wondered: how can I get in touch with the police? I thought I was going to die without anyone knowing anything about it. Money? Who would give any money to save me? I have no illusions about human beings, gentlemen. Since my mother died my family has consisted only of a female cousin, whose husband keeps a restaurant. I expected nothing from them. My only friend was old Longspès—a pauper."

"And M. Philippe Durand," Picard murmured from the background.

"Yes, that's true, but he has no money."

He continued in a lower tone: "Nevertheless, I wrote. The light had gone on again and everything was set out on the table. When I had finished I banged on the door and shouted: 'I've finished.' And the comedy with the lights began again, followed by a punch which knocked me half across the room.

"This was obviously some form of tactics. The tactics of a bully, of a coward. In exchange for my letter I received a slice of cold veal, a chunk of bread and a glass of water. I tried to eat, but I did not drink because I was afraid of another drug. Can you imagine that wait, gentlemen? Night had fallen and it started to rain. The light was still on. At one moment I had an attack of diarrhoea. There was a slop-pail in one corner. I thought to myself, I must really be dealing with experts.

"The whole of the next day—yesterday, gentlemen—I was knocked down only once because the man visited me only once. That was to bring me the same food as on the night before. He did not say a word. I spent hours at the window looking through the shutters at the rain. I can't tell you everything that went through my head. If things go on like this, I thought, I shall kill myself. And I drank the glass of water hoping with all my heart that it was poison."

M. Verdon paused for breath.

"I must hurry for I am beginning to get tired. And yet what I had suffered so far was nothing compared with what awaited me. Not in the way of brutality, no—except for the razor—but in terror. The following night—last night in fact—the man reappeared, this time he was not alone. He had brought with him another shorter man who smelt as though he had just come from the barber after having his hair cut. I hid behind the chest of drawers, trembling like a frightened dog. Well, this time I was spared. The brute simply leapt on me and stuffed a hat on my head, it may have been mine, and pulled it down over my eyes. I find that comical now, but at that moment I can assure you it was not funny.

"He said to me: 'If you try and take it off I'll kill you.' Then they must have put on the light. The other expressed himself better. He said: 'M. Verdon, if you obey me quickly you will soon be free. Otherwise there is a risk that you will share the fate of the poor man who perished three days ago. . . . Get undressed, un-dress your-self!' he repeated. I took off my jacket and waistcoat. I was thrust into a chair. 'Now your shoes,' he ordered. 'Keep on your socks. Your trousers! Your trou-sers! Now your tie! And your shirt! And your undershirt!'"

M. Verdon was obviously reliving the scene, even his voice had changed. The doctor took his pulse again.

"'You can keep your pants.'" Then the man said: 'Now—don't move! I'm going to hurt you for a moment. I have a razor in my hand. Don't move!'

"I was shivering, gentlemen. Shivering. . . . He then ordered the other: 'Hold the undershirt under his arm. No, not like that! Like that!' And I felt a cut on the left arm. A stab of pain. I heard: 'That's it!' Like a doctor. Like a dentist. I didn't understand. I still don't understand.

"He stained your undershirt with blood," explained M. Malebranche, "to make us think he had killed you."

"You don't mean it?" said M. Verdon, astounded. "I tell you, it's all crazy! They left. When the key had turned in the lock I pulled off my hat. I could see what I looked like, in my ridiculous garb, with a long gash that was still bleeding. At that moment, I know I nearly lost my reason. I am terrified of blood. And not even a handkerchief. I took a sash from the double curtains and made myself a bandage. Then I wrapped myself in the tablecloth and started to wait once more . . . to wait this time for death. The punches I had received the day before now seemed unimportant in comparison with this, which was organised, threatening and terrible.

"And today passed. My cut had stopped bleeding. I fell asleep in an armchair. I was all in. The brute gave me some more bread and meat and a glass of water. He did not bother to hit me this time. He half opened the door, slipped his hand through and put the food on a little table. I wondered whether they had got their money. I tried to account for the scene of the night before: my clothes being torn off, the razor slash and above all the allusion to a crime three days earlier. Three days earlier, of course, was Monday. I remembered the murder in the Champs-Elysées, and what I had read in the newspapers, the envelope found in the U bus, and my joke with Musard. But that could not have any bearing upon this. . . ."

"We'll discuss it again tomorrow," said M. Malebranche. "You have exhausted yourself quite enough this evening."

"I want to finish," said M. Verdon, panting. "Then you will know as much as I do. He returned later, probably with his leader. They gave me a terrible beating up. With the hat which served to blindfold me and a cloak over my shoulders they frog-marched me down the stairs, into the garden . . . the gravel under my socks . . . and into a car. 'Where are you taking me?' I asked. 'Shut up!' was the reply. The car drove and drove. Suddenly I was lifted from the seat. My cloak and hat were torn off so violently that I thought my head was coming off. I was shoved . . . that is all . . . I felt as if I had smashed my face on the ground. And yet I did not lose consciousness. I had enough strength left to stagger to my feet. I shouted. . . . No, I couldn't have shouted. . . . I whispered: Help! Help! I was stark naked. I could make out an alleyway and a light. . . . The doss house. . . ."

His solitary eye filled with tears, which soaked into the bandage.

"When did the aggressor actually pin the piece of paper to your pants?"

"What paper?"

Picard handed it to M. Malebranche, who in turn handed it to the injured man. "I've no further use for this idiot. I'm returning him to you. The Passenger on the U."

"What a cad," said M. Verdon. "The U! So there is some connection? And you say this was pinned to my pants? Probably in the car. I didn't feel anything that time. . . ."

"It is nearly midnight," said the doctor.

"We'll come back tomorrow," said M. Malebranche, rising to his feet. "So you didn't know M. Tavernier?"

Picard and Belot also stood up.

"Tavernier?" cried M. Verdon. "I have been trying to remember the name for the past two days."

"And Devaux?"

"Devaux? No."

"And Oudart?"

"No."

"Have you ever bought any stamps in Saigon?"

"Never."

He asked for some explanation. The house surgeon said that if he wasn't sensible he would not be able to go home next day.

"But I don't want to go home," he cried. "If old Longspès can put me up in his little villa, that's where I'd like to go. I don't want to be alone."

"We'll tell him," said M. Malebranche.

"And you'll tell my friend, Philippe Durand, gentlemen, please, and Mlle Guillaume, Juliette Guillaume . . . who . . . looks after my house and who is a real friend. Won't you?"

"What about your cousins, M. Verdon?" asked Belot.

A note of ill temper crept into the sick man's voice:

"I'm afraid they'd tire me. . . . My cousin talks a lot, and his wife. . . ."

He did not finish the sentence.

"We must apologise"—interrupted Malebranche—"for breaking open your safe."

"Since someone has stolen the key I should have had to do it myself. Was anything taken? In any case they've got my vermilions and my tête-bêche. . . ."

"One last word: who knew on Wednesday morning that you intended going to see M. Musard?"

"Musard himself . . . and my clerk, Longspès . . . and M. Archer. Those three are above suspicion, aren't they?"

"Let us hope so."

"Do you think we should look for the taxi?" Picard asked Belot, once they were in the corridor with the police inspectors, who were awaiting their orders.

"The one that the viscount hailed in the Place des Ternes? Of course not! He's a 'friend,' of course . . . like Camus for Devaux. He must have helped to drop Verdon just now as well."

"So Devaux must be the strong arm man and Laeken the 'Brain.'"

Picard told one of the detectives to keep guard on the room and despatched the other to search around Cercu's doss house at the spot where M. Verdon could have been thrown from the car.

"I think he'll have a peaceful night," said the house surgeon. "If I need one of you, whom should I send for?"

"Me," said Belot, giving him his telephone number.

As the three policemen made for the exit, M. Malebranche declared that there was nothing more to be done that evening, and he added: "It's a really crazy story."

"So you're coming round to the idea!" said Picard.

"In any other circumstances," said Belot, "it would seem invented from one end to the other, but with 'The Passenger' anything seems possible. If he's crazy, he's also infernally clever."

Picard slapped his forehead. "Nom de dieu! If 'The Passenger' did not kill Verdon after his defeat at the garage. . . ."

Belot turned to him. With glittering eyes he continued the sentence . . . "if he was content to simulate the murder, it means that as far as he's concerned the ransom business was only a prelude . . . ?"

The three men had come to a standstill. Although the heavy silence of the hospital forced them to speak in low tones their whispers took on a note of excitement.

"If he returned Verdon," said M. Malebranche, "it was because today he's got what he really wanted."

"The American woman . . ." said Picard.

"That's it," said Belot suddenly furious. "The final comment on the garage! The deal there was impossible *and he knew it!* We all fell for it like idiots. I felt it. He made fools of us!"

"It was not us he was interested in," said M. Malcbranche, "he wanted to terrify the American woman."

"Of course!" said Picard. "We have all served as his accomplices—from Verdon to *Le Grand Journal* and its ridiculous publicity! The whole of Paris has served as his accomplice. When he really wanted to get hold of money he did perfectly well without the Press, without us and without everybody. A simple express letter to his lady love, and he told her to keep quiet."

"And if she had not had a fainting fit," said M. Malebranche, "we should still know nothing at all at this moment."

"He asked the impossible," said Belot, "to ensure the more-than-possible, the certain!"

"But why pick on Verdon to set the trap?" asked Picard.

"And why not?" asked Belot. "Someone he knew and who hardly knew him. It was a good choice."

"A subordinate in any case," said M. Malebranche. "There is a more serious objection. If Laeken is 'The Passenger,' as everything goes to show—his fingerprints are not in our records did you know? —why should he have staged such a tremendous set-up? If it was to fire his mistress's imagination, he could have done that far more simply."

The enthusiasm of the conversation was damped.

"And above all," added Belot, "why simulate a crime when one has committed a real one?"

"Let's go to bed," said Malebranche.

7

The Villa Sans-Souci

The ringing of a bell woke Belot from a deep sleep haunted by nightmares. As he had done every morning since his early childhood when he went to the primary school in the rue des Poisonniers, he brought himself up to date while his hand reached out to turn off the alarm.

"Saturday. The sixth day of the Tavernier-Verdon-'Passenger' case. Still nothing."

It was not the alarm clock. It was the telephone.

"M. Belot? It's the Broussais Hospital. . . . The house surgeon. I'm sorry to disturb you so early. M. Verdon has been in an anxious state and keeps saying that he wants to make an urgent statement to the police."

"I'm on my way," said Belot.

M. Verdon was indeed agitated. An idea had struck him during the night with regard to the piece of paper pinned to his pants.

"I've no further use for this idiot. . . . Let's forget about the idiot part," he said to Belot, "although I view this judgment with great reservations. 'The Passenger' had no further need of me because he had not obtained the ransom he wanted. So it was all playacting. Like the blood he took from my arm. Well, sir, I've discovered the reason. Suppose he wanted to impress someone other than me? A colleague, perhaps. . . . A *really* rich man from whom he'd *really* get big money? There is only one detail that worries me: I don't understand why the ruffian let me go. That considerably diminishes the value of his blackmail."

"It was because the attack had already taken place," said Belot.

The lone eye stared. Belot gave him an account of the Miss Abbott affair. M. Verdon displayed further agitation.

"We must go and see this lady together. If we inform her of the part played by her friend we may get some information of the greatest value. I must see her!"

"I was going to suggest it," said Belot.

"Can I get up?"

"Out of the question," said the doctor.

"Well, let's meet here!"

"Or even better at Longspès' place, since you've given me permission."

He then described in detail the room in which he had been imprisoned. But as for finding the house. . . .

At the prison infirmary Longspès, learning of the miraculous return of his employer, sobbed on the shoulder of the attendant who had to dress him because he was trembling so much. He was taken to the Broussais Hospital. It was an indescribable scene. He positively neighed with happiness, kissed M. Verdon's hands and placed sad fingers gently on the huge bandage. He spread out on the bed all the money he had managed to collect for the ransom and whispered: "Beware of the police!"

"My good old Octave! My best friend!" said the injured man. "Will you let them take me to Bellevue?"

"Where else? At once!"

Inspector Malicorne, who had come with him, declared: "I'll order an ambulance."

Longspès examined him out of the corner of his eye.

"Thank you so much," said Verdon.

"You have a fine bruise on your forehead," the house surgeon said to Longspès.

"That's my business," replied the old man.

"There is only one person who can go and see Miss Abbott," said Belot to M. Malebranche and Picard, "without creating in her mind some connection with us: Mme Colet. She even has her doubts about Dr Brayer. And she must feel she can trust Verdon."

"Agreed."

Belot telephoned to the Hôtel Royal. Mme Colet and her faithful Perraud arrived half an hour later. When she heard that the stamp dealer was still alive, she exclaimed: "Fancy that!" and seemed absorbed in her thoughts.

"Nothing new since last night?" asked Belot.

". . . Nothing."

He was conscious of the slight hesitation. Her reticence since receiving the threatening letter had begun to irritate him.

"You're hiding things from me again."

Her only reply was a shy smile. "Such a desire to take her in my arms like a child is quite abnormal," thought Belot. He explained what he wanted her to do: to take Miss Abbott to Longspès' house at Bellevue. She agreed.

In her bed Miss Abbott, who had been awake all night, whimpered without pause: "He doesn't answer my telegram. Why doesn't Guy answer my telegram?"

"It's still too early, Gwen," Dr Brayer replied patiently.

"It's you who have ruined everything, with your wretched patience!"

When Mme Colet was announced as the bearer of great news, the unhappy woman brightened like the dawn.

She had seen him!

She had not seen him but she knew that M. Verdon was not dead, "which changed everything," and she was going to call on him.

"I'll come too!" cried Miss Abbott. "It won't be too tiring in a car. We shall learn something at last!"

"I'll come with you," said Dr Brayer.

"As far as the door but no further. You're too indiscreet. This lady is the only person I trust. Besides, before going I'll telephone Le Havre. . . ."

M. Verdon's ambulance arrived about ten o'clock at the villa Sans-Souci. Longspès, Inspector Malicorne and a nurse were with him. Longspès was polite to Malicorne. He now knew that his employer himself had asked for police protection.

Mlle Longspès welcomed them with tears pouring down her cheeks. Smaller than the old madman and far less skinny, she had adopted his loves and his hates and was his absolute twin in all her demonstrations of emotion. She opened her brother's room, immediately changed the sheets without help having told the nurse: "You can go. I am a qualified nurse."

The nurse, therefore, left with the ambulance. Seated one on each side of the bed the two Longspès smiled at the one visible eye of the poor invalid and held his hands. Malicorne had withdrawn to the parlour.

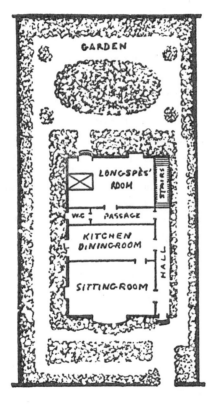

At the villa Sans-Souci Mlle Longspès lived on the second floor which consisted of two rooms. She would have given the other— the guest room (which no one had ever occupied)—to M. Verdon had they been able to get the stretcher up the stairs. Longspès lived on the ground floor. Fearing thieves as much as the police, he considered that a man ought to keep watch or to sleep at the most dangerous spot of his house. Locked, bolted and chained, the French windows of this room and those of the entrance hall were both impassable day and night. Through them M. Verdon could admire from his bed the charming garden, with its gay autumn tints, which Longspès himself cultivated.

"A paradise," he sighed, "after that infernal garden behind the shutters."

Belot appeared at two o'clock. He found the injured man reading the newspapers of the last few days. The morning papers contained nothing new and divided their attention between Laeken's disappearance, and his, Verdon's, own death.

Belot announced that Miss Abbott was due to arrive with one of her friends. "I would like," he said, "to hear your conversation without being seen." Unfortunately, the bedroom did not lead into any other room. He was forced to hide in an uncomfortable cupboard under the stairs opposite the bed. He stuck a chair among Longspès' few bits of clothing. The door was left ajar.

Shown in by the brother and sister, Miss Abbott appeared, her lorgnette raised, leaning on Mme Colet's arm. She had telephoned to the Transatlantic Hotel at Le Havre: no one was waiting for her there. At the sight of the enormous bandage, she burst out sobbing.

"Did the kidnapper do that? Is he as vicious as that with everyone?"

She collapsed in an armchair. M. Verdon mumbled a few comforting words while he studied Mme Colet, who stood with downcast eyes next to the American woman.

"Excuse me, madame," he said at last. "I have a feeling that I have met you before."

Mme Colet pointed to the newspapers on the bed.

"I am Mme Colet."

"Oh!" cried M. Verdon, "'The Passenger' has threatened you, too, hasn't he?"

"Yes," she said with a wry little smile. "You are the past and my husband and I risk being the future. . . ."

"What about Guy?" protested Miss Abbott indignantly. "Doesn't M. de Laeken count for anything?"

"His is a special case," said M. Verdon.

She gave a cry. "Is he dead?"

"No, mademoiselle . . . it's more complicated than that."

And, as had been agreed on with Belot, M. Verdon in a low voice repeated the tale of his kidnapping. Mme Colet drank in his words.

Her lorgnette at the ready Miss Abbott began to tremble.

"What are you saying, that it was M. de Laeken who kidnapped you?" She gave another loud scream. "Do you know what you are? You are a poor nitwit. Your misfortunes have driven you out of your mind. To accuse the most generous, charming, noble man in the world. . . . Confess that you are crazy or I'll sue you for defamation. Guy, rob a stamp dealer? Why not rob me? Come on, Madame Colet, I don't know why you have brought me to this house. Perhaps M. de Laeken is going to kidnap you, too? That's too funny!"

She stood up. Tears of rage ran down her horsey features.

"I didn't mean anything of the sort," said M. Verdon in a loud voice. "Sit down!"

She obeyed. Mme Colet looked at him with an air of approval which signified: "You at least know how to speak to a woman." Her glance caught M. Verdon staring at the cupboard door.

"I would not dream of accusing M. de Laeken of anything at all," he went on. "'The Passenger' used him as he would have used you, or this lady, with extraordinary cunning, and before striking him himself. . . ."

Miss Abbott was still weeping, but now with grief. The situation was saved. M. Verdon heaved a sigh and continued: "If you rack your brains perhaps we shall see things more clearly. The ruffian asked you for money but he has not yet returned your friend to you."

"That's true . . . oh it's true. . . ."

Mme Colet stood up.

"You're not leaving us, I hope?" asked M. Verdon.

"You must excuse me," she said. "I have a headache. I shall go for a little walk. My presence here isn't really necessary."

"But you will return?" he asked eagerly.

"Of course!"

On her way past the parlour she saw something which must suddenly have cured her headache, for instead of continuing she went in.

As if in a waiting-room, strangers to each other, Longspès and a pretty young girl, sat one at each end of the room. Longspès looking very cross, kept his eyes fixed straight ahead, his long gnarled fingers drumming on his knees. He did not seem to notice Mme Colet's entrance. He was talking aloud to himself.

"If this goes on the villa will be a regular market-place. M. Verdon sees anyone that comes along. He believes everything he's told. And here's another of them. There have never been so many women here. What with police and women, all that's missing now is the murderer! M. Durand is the only person I would like to have seen and he has to have 'flu. It will all turn out badly . . . it's bound to."

"Another of them," thought Mme Colet, "must be me. But all this speech is aimed at that poor, charming creature." The young stranger was well aware of this. She tried to preserve her calm and to appear relaxed; but her flushed cheeks and the way she fiddled with her bag betrayed her nervousness. She had shot an appealing look at Mme Colet, then dropped her eyes again. She was dressed tastefully but not expensively. She perched on the edge of the armchair like a person who had no knowledge of society and was ill at ease with it.

"You're wrong to get angry, M. Longspès," said Mme Colet engagingly. "Don't you trust your employer?"

She thought he was going to kill her. Rising to his feet and already in a frenzy he roared: "No confidence? Me? In the only. . . . In the . . . In my benefactor?"

"Well," she replied, without batting an eyelid, "why are you so worried? If we are here, it is because he wished it."

Longspès let out a deep sigh. The wrinkled corners of his mouth puckered like a child about to cry. "Who does he look like?" thought Mme Colet.

"Since the wretched day M. Verdon disappeared," said the old man, "I don't know how I live or what to think. Such a thing had never happened to me before!"

"Fortunately," said Mme Colet. "And just see how things have turned out well."

He shook his head sadly.

"It's not over yet. . . ."

"I know who he looks like," she thought suddenly. "Built on the same lines, the same devotion, the same distrusts, the same obsessions. He's like Miss Abbott!"

"I agree the police are rather terrible," she replied, "just like firemen who replace fires by floods." Longspès nodded eagerly at the analogy. "But why do you speak so badly of women, M. Longspès?"

The old madman recovered his ill temper. He cast a sour look in the direction of the stranger, replied simply: "I don't like them," and fled from the room to avoid having to explain himself.

8

"There is no connection"

From the window Mme Colet could see her husband and Dr Brayer. They were waiting for her and the American woman, walking up and down the lane not far from the car which Miss Abbott had hired for the occasion. The stalwart doctor seemed almost a weakling beside his companion. He talked and M. Colet remained silent. In the garden, Perraud was chatting with Malicorne. The Colets had introduced him as a friend; during the trip he had sat next to the chauffeur.

As soon as Longspès had disappeared Mme Colet exclaimed:

"Well, that puts us in our place! I suppose he bears us a grudge because we don't often collect stamps."

The girl did not smile. "He's terrible," she said. "I thought he would be more gentle."

"You had never seen him before?"

"No," she replied briefly, then stood up suddenly and ran to Mme Colet.

"Tell me, madame," she asked with a catch in her throat, "how is M. Verdon? He's alive, it's unbelievable, it's marvellous, but how is he? The police notified me. I came at once. I was told that there were people with him, that I had to wait. Oh, I don't mind waiting, but why did M. Longspès refuse to speak to me? I'm still so anxious, madame. Has he been injured: Did they hurt him?"

She gave free rein to her passion. Mme Colet took her hands, led her back to the armchair, sat down beside her, and gave her detailed and reassuring news. The young girl wept and trembled with joy.

"Might I ask who you are?" Mme Colet asked at last.

The girl replied, with a radiant face: "His daily maid, madame."

Mme Colet raised her eyebrows but too fleetingly for her to notice it. The girl only wanted to talk just as she had on the morning when Blondel had consoled her when she had thought Verdon was dead. She did in fact apologise for it:

"I should control myself, madame, shouldn't I? I'm so happy. He's so kind! He might not have asked me to come, with all these people he has to see. But here I am."

"You love him very much," said Mme Colet softly.

Juliette replied that it was not love, it was admiration. Mme Colet guessed at the natural basis of this admiration. Juliette spoke of her job in the rue Laffitte as a bride would have done of her honeymoon on the Italian Lakes. Mme Colet listened with a tender smile and nodded from time to time. But Belot would have detected in her eyes that strange little light which appeared at moments of crisis. Twice the sound of voices, snatches of conversation, made Juliette jump. Each time she swiftly took her powder case from her bag.

"So long as M. Verdon doesn't see that I've been crying. He doesn't like me to cry, even with joy. What would I look like!"

The second time the noise of voices grew into the sound of footsteps. Juliette and her confidante saw Longspès with Miss Abbott passing in the corridor. Mme Colet stood up.

"Do you know that lady?" she asked.

"No."

Longspès reappeared: M. Verdon was asking for Mme Colet.

"Make my excuses to him, M. Longspès," she replied. "I must leave with Miss Abbott and my husband. Besides, this young lady mustn't be kept waiting any longer, it wouldn't be kind. Tell M. Verdon—whisper it in his ear—that I will come back tomorrow *when the cupboard door is closed.*"

The whole company took the same places in the car that they had occupied on the outward journey. Miss Abbott and Mme Colet sat in the back. On the folding seats M. Colet and Dr Brayer. Perraud next to the chauffeur. The American looked round her like a blind, unhappy owl.

"Why did you leave the room, madame?" she asked Mme Colet. "Couldn't that man have told us something important?"

Mme Colet replied that she had retired out of discretion.

"And what did he tell you, Gwen?" asked Dr Brayer.

"Nothing, alas! nothing at all. . . . He was very amiable, but what could the poor man know? And how frightened I am for you, madame!"

Mme Colet pointed to Perraud's back.

"With our friend here I don't think we have anything to fear. He never leaves us. . . ."

Dr Brayer, whom the police had not informed of their discoveries and who still believed Laeken to be a victim and not a culprit, continued to examine the theories he had poured out at M. Colet for the past hour. The latter watched his wife through half-closed eyes. She seemed absentminded. Her charming little mouselike face seemed to be in pain and yet to be unaware of its suffering.

When the car dropped the Colets and Perraud in front of the Hôtel Royal, Mme Colet said to the detective: "We needn't keep you. We'll be staying quietly in tonight as we did yesterday."

"Very well. See you tomorrow, then. Let's hope that we shall have some luck tonight."

As they climbed the stairs, M. Colet said: "Don't you feel well, my dear? You hardly opened your mouth in the car. Still got a headache?"

"Yes, I have."

Up in the bedroom she said: "I think I'll write to Mother." M. Colet looked at the bed.

"May I lie down?"

He fell asleep. She sat for a long time without moving with the table and paper in front of her, and a frown on her face. Then she began:

Dear M. Belot,

We are just back from Bellevue and I think I ought to write to you. It's not easy. It's never easy to confess that one has lied. I can't yet explain why, but I haven't the right either to hide something from you which is perhaps very important. When you asked me this morning if anything new had happened, I replied: nothing. I should have said, yes. I paid a visit last night. You mustn't scold

M. Perraud, he didn't know. On returning from the Villas Kléber I promised him that we would not go out again. It was half true, because my husband stayed in the hotel.

I saw the Taverniers. I went first to M. Paul Tavernier's. He was at the Boulevard Gouvion-Saint-Cyr with his sister-in-law, who had just returned from Saint-Étienne. I went to the Boulevard Gouvion-Saint-Cyr. I was received first by Mme Tavernier on her own, very brave despite her grief and her tiring journey. M. Paul appeared almost immediately. He no longer looked disdainful, as he did at the church, but he seemed more distrustful than ever. The way he looked me up and down was terrible. I talked all the same. You believe he knows something, don't you? I have suspected it ever since the morning we looked through the album together; in M. Picard's office, you said: "All that remains is to consult the brother, who was not very keen on my taking away the album."

I have not forgotten. (That is why I went to the funeral, you know. At the church the eyes of that man, his flushed cheeks . . .) So I told them my little troubles as I had told them to Miss Abbott. The threatening letter—they had just read it in the evening paper— and to what extent I was anxious for my husband's safety, particularly after the new disappearance. Don't worry, I did not say anything in this connection except what was in the paper. I was very touched by Madame Tavernier. A woman as unhappy as she is and suffering from such an irreparable grief could well have been indifferent to the perhaps perfectly foolish anxieties of another woman. On the contrary she shared them, she offered to put us up since we have no friends in Paris. This suggestion made the brother-in-law even gloomier. And yet listen to what happened at the end. When the conversation had ended—it had been fruitless—Mme Tavernier wanted to show me out. Paul said: "No, I'll go." In the hall, looking very distressed he said to me in a low voice: "Madame, you look very worried. . . . If I ask you to give your word of honour not to talk about us, can I rely upon you . . . ?" I said, "Yes." He looked me straight in the eyes and said: "There is no connection." "What, monsieur?" I asked. He replied with violence: "Everything, madame, everything!" And he added: "Good evening."

I didn't understand. And I promise you that I thought it was the smallest little lie this morning when I replied "Nothing!" I thought that I should not betray my word of honour for such an insignificant remark! But now after today's drama, after the visit to Bellevue, after all that I heard, all I begin to glimpse, it is no longer the same! It is essential that I tell you. . . .

The pen which had sped over the paper until these words, suddenly came to a stop. Mme Colet reflected once more in the silence which was broken only by the breathing of the sleeping man.

She tore up the letter. Then on half a sheet of paper, she wrote: "Don't worry, my love, I shall be away for an hour." She put on her hat again and went out.

In Picard's office Belot was finishing a report of no interest.

". . . All this chit-chat, all Verdon's efforts to make Miss Abbott talk about Laeken came to nothing. I'm as stiff as hell from being in that cupboard, and that's the sum total."

Picard sniffed and repeated: "The sum total is a dead loss. . . ."

Since dawn they had both been in a filthy temper: Belot even more than Picard. They could not get rid of the thought that "The Passenger" had made a fool of them at the Gobelins. The whole intricate plan, the besieged garage, the breakdown on the Boulevard Saint-Germain, the truck, the envelope, the reporters, the excitement in Paris, the attention of the whole of France and the world! And not only at the Gobelins. At Saint-Lazare with a murder which had only been a hoax. True, Verdon had been beaten up, but he was alive. Had there not been the corpse of Étienne Tavernier—a real genuine corpse and a real murderer—there would be nothing left for him but to resign, and to disappear with his shame.

Picard rustled the papers on the table in exasperation. He recited: "From Spain. Marie Devaux and her son have indeed been in Madrid in a respectable hotel since last Sunday, the eve of the murder. She knows no Spanish, doesn't read the papers and learned of Tavernier's death from the police. Her amazement and despair were certainly genuine. She declared that he was a great friend, an intimate friend *but nothing more!* On learning the name of the murderer she had seemed horrified and had then called her brother an incorrigible drunkard and gambler fit for a lunatic asylum. She did not know, she said, that he had taken up again with Tavernier —her brother—since his return from Indo-China. She had not seen him for years, each visit being to ask for money. She had even taken the name of Valence so that he could not trace her. And since she thought he was still in touch with their parents she thought it wiser not to see them either. This all makes sense. When asked what she lived on, she replied that 'her son's father' helped her. She refused to say who the father was. When asked whether it was M. Tavernier she protested vigorously. Why did Tavernier call himself Terrasse when he went to see her? She replied that she had no idea; perhaps because his wife was jealous; she respected him too much to ask him questions of that kind. Why had she left France? For a holiday and to visit Spain. A sudden whim if you like; she was sick of Paris, and above all she wanted to be with her son more often and to show him a bit of the world. Why had she spoken to her landlord of a legacy and a Spanish uncle? To avoid that gentleman's attentions. Yes, it all makes sense. She was being kept under observation."

From Le Havre, as might be expected, nothing. Miss Abbott's telegram waited in vain for the viscount.

From Paris. First, they've picked up the taxi driver who took the man with the fair beard to the Hôtel de la République. And at the same time the tan suitcase with the grey cover, and *in it the famous typewriter.*

Belot caught his breath:

"He took twenty-four hours to discover that a suitcase had been left in his taxi?"

"No, but he had left it in his Company's lost property office. They were waiting for the owner."

"And the papers are full of it," said Belot, overcome. "Where did the taxi take the fellow?"

"To the Samaritaine."

"Twenty or thirty exits! In any case that confirms my theory: dark beard and fair beard the same day, and that evening he jettisons his precious machine because he considers the operation to be over."

"Go easy. He still has the method he used on Mme Colet: words cut out of a newspaper. But what we must not lose sight of I think is that he *had* to abandon the suitcase the way he did. So he couldn't hide it anywhere?"

"Correct," said Belot. "Nor the machine either. Yesterday I imagined the suitcase normally filled in case it was seen by prying eyes in the hotel: I was wrong. From the Gare Saint-Lazare, *before* the Gare Saint-Lazare, he lugged it with him! Then the place where Verdon was? Where Devaux was—or perhaps still is, if it is Devaux?"

"Let me go on. The wigmakers—a blank. The viscount's visiting cards: ordered *through the post*, like the periwinkle blue notepaper, from a shop on the Boulevard Malesherbes and delivered to the Auteuil boarding house where our fake Laeken lived first. The signet ring—another blank: it can't have been made in Paris.

"Now for the taxi driver, Camus. A watertight alibi. He hasn't moved from the Saint-Maur café since Monday. So he did not drive the car which picked up Verdon and Laeken in the Place des Ternes. As for the one which took Verdon yesterday to Cercu's—we've held it since last night.

"Now: Paul Tavernier. Beauchamp has made discreet inquiries at his office. The telephone girl remembers quite well that at about half past two on the day of the crime someone asked for M. Tavernier, saying, 'It's a personal call.' She had therefore put him through. Paul left a little later and said to her as he passed: 'Someone else who mistakes me for my brother!'

"If he was speaking the truth, this proves that half an hour after the crime he had no inkling that anything was wrong. If he was lying, this telephone call could be the one which Devaux made from the Café Biard in the rue de Valois. . . .

"As for Musard and Archer—nothing at all suspicious. Finally, nothing in the area around Cercu's doss house. There you are old chap! What have you decided about the protection for Bellevue?"

"Oh!" replied Belot, "I'm leaving Malicorne there simply to please Verdon. For this case is over. It's over for 'The Passenger' if not for us. . . . He's off with the American woman's lovely bank notes, plus the vermilion tête-bêche or tête-pas-bêche stamps which he pinched from his intermediate victim!"

In his office, his elbows on the table, his hands to his ears, fingers under his hair pressed to his skull, eyes staring into the blue, Belot silently cursed himself violently in the Picard manner:

"That'll teach you, you silly fathead, that'll teach you! Instead of following your intuition you had to reason, and you reasoned like a clot! Because all the time you had sensed the truth about the U Line! You said right from the beginning that you considered it just chance in the case of Tavernier and an accessory after that. And when you visited the garage for the first time, and you were fooling about on the floor of your bus, you idiot, you felt that all that didn't make sense, that there was *something else*. Do you understand now?

"What do I understand? That 'The Passenger' in order to get

80,000 dollars out of an American woman, kidnapped a stamp dealer, made everyone believe he was dead, and turned the world upside down. That being the woman's lover he could have gone about it with more discretion, more intimacy! But that's a detail. What counts is that it is *obvious* the Verdon affair was the prelude, the pretext for the Abbott affair. But heavens above, wasn't the Tavernier affair quite enough for a prelude and a pretext?

"Be careful, Belot! Are you using your reason now or are you just letting yourself go? If you start to reason again you will put your foot in it. Let yourself go, old man, let yourself go. What's stopping you? The murder of Tavernier? Yes, because after it things all fit together. It is this murder which upsets everything, which fogs your brain, haunts you and hypnotises you. The less links you find between this case and the other the more you look for them, and the more exasperated you become. Why look for them? Who has persuaded you there are any, *except 'The Passenger' himself?* And who has really made a fool of you? Stop reasoning, Belot, and let yourself go. . . . What do you feel? That you have been made a fool of all down the line, all down the line of the U? And that there are no other connections except those which 'The Passenger' has wanted you to think existed.

"Of course! That's the point from which I must start to look afresh at everything and to understand everything. It's just that *there is no connection! There is no connection at all!*"

Chapter without a number

The shoe and the dead leaf

. . . The rain stopped and the morrow was as fine as a May day. The Parisians put on a festive look: bare heads, light clothes and shoulders squared. Women, pigeons and sparrows fluttered in all directions, like unexpected flowers. There were street singers at the crossroads, magical bargains on the stalls and children playing truant from school. All the cars gleaming in the sunlight seemed to be leaving for the country. Had the buses been on strike, happiness would have been complete. On a bench in a little public garden Belot and Mme Colet sat side by side. Belot was looking straight ahead and Mme Colet was looking at Belot.

"You're discouraged, Inspector," she said.

He raised his head in surprise.

"Discouraged? Disappointed, madame. I am never discouraged."

It was her turn to be surprised.

"What, never? There must be some investigations which lead nowhere."

"They always lead somewhere. If it's to a dead end, you turn about. If it's to, how shall I say, into a fog. . . . Then you wait for it to lift."

"And you always succeed."

"We have to."

"But you have not always succeeded?"

"No. But I've not yet retired. New cases do not make you forget the old ones." And he added with a sort of gravity or pride: "Besides, I am not alone. What one of us begins another can finish."

With the tip of her shoe Mme Colet touched a dead leaf. "It's strange," she said, "I should never have thought that the police. . . ."

She did not finish the sentence. Belot smiled.

"It's true. We're not very popular. I'm not in a position to judge that. But when you hear us criticised, ask yourself if a mother whose child has been stolen isn't happy to get it back again, or if a widow does not wish her husband's murderer to be caught."

Mme Colet asked with a slight catch in her throat: "It's your squad which does all that isn't it?"

"Yes."

And she added with a note of respect: "I'm not talking about it."

"And I," replied Belot with some heat, "am talking of nothing else! I only talk about what I know."

Mme Colet began to laugh.

"Oh, Monsieur Belot, this is the first time I've ever seen you get angry! So you really are a human being. You have weaknesses? What a disappointment!"

He glanced at her nervously. The grey-blue eyes reassured him. Then Mme Colet's shoe returned to the dead leaf.

"I have never met a man like you."

"I have never met a woman like you," replied Belot in all sincerity.

"That's not quite true," she continued, as though she had not heard his answer. "You remind me—although of course you are younger—of an old officer I knew as a little girl, a colonel who had been in the jungle somewhere or other, on some extraordinary campaigns. Every 14th July he put on his uniform, with a great mass of decorations. . . ."

Belot stared at her shoe and at the dead leaf.

"Uniform and decorations apart it's a bit the same," he murmured. "My particular jungle is not far away but the savages in it are not always very gentle!"

Automatically he stroked the scar on his neck. Although she had not noticed the gesture, Mme Colet turned to him in dismay.

"*Mon Dieu!*" she said.

She stared at Belot's right leg, and her eyelids beat rapidly. But she frowned and said calmly:

"All the same he left a leg there. Try not to resemble him as far as that. . . ."

"I'll try."

The shoe, the dead leaf. . . .

"How unhappy the wife of an army officer or a policeman must be," Mme Colet said slowly. "And even so, the officer isn't fighting every day. But you! She must wonder every evening in what state her husband will come home to her, *if* he's coming home. . . . It's frightful."

"We mustn't exaggerate. A furniture dealer can also smash his fingers with a hammer, a housewife can burn herself while she's doing her washing. What about a pilot? Or an electrician? And a peasant with his scythe? And the factory worker with all the machines which are always waiting for the moment when he'll take his mind off the job?"

Belot coughed, ashamed of his eloquence.

"Oh, well . . ." said Mme Colet, shrugging her shoulders, "those are only accidents."

"They are injuries," he corrected, "like ours. And they are certainly more frequent than ours."

She shook her head in disagreement.

"For the wife who waits at home, if her husband is a factory worker, a peasant or a furniture dealer he does not have danger as a profession."

She repeated:

"But you!"

"Oh, my wife never gives the matter a thought!"

"Eh!" cried Mme Colet. "You're married?"

"No, I am not."

"I don't suppose you're interested in women."

"Well," confessed Belot, "you have to have a lot of time to attend to them. I haven't the time, that's all."

"That's evading the issue," retorted Mme Colet. "Time! As though that mattered. Love laughs at time as well as everything else."

In her extraordinarily childish face her eyes shone even brighter as she asked: "What do you think of love, Inspector?"

Belot began to laugh.

"Love, madame? It is a feeling one sometimes experiences, but which one cannot talk about!"

She turned her head away and looked down at the dead leaf.

"Really," she murmured, "I should have thought the contrary."

The shoe pushed the leaf into the gravel. Belot suddenly felt a strange melancholy. He felt that it was getting late, that his un-accustomed rest would shortly come to an end and that the winter was drawing near despite the deceptively bright sky.

"We have only been talking about me," he said reproachfully.

"Do you think so . . . ?" said Mme Colet. "Yes," she went on, "but a provincial middle-class woman has nothing to tell! The best of husbands, unfortunately no children, a family which occupies ten houses in Avignon, a quiet life, holidays in Paris . . . usually less exciting than the present one."

"Do you regret it?"

"I'm not very fond of blood. I shouldn't have been sorry to have met you in different circumstances."

"Of course."

With a swift twist of the ankle she brought the leaf back to the foot of the bench.

"You must come to Avignon," she said brightly.

"I'm afraid the provinces come under the National Police."

She burst out laughing. "But not for a murder! To see us!"

"It's a long way off. Do you know that this short break in this garden is the first rest I've taken for months, perhaps for years?"

She looked at him gravely, and then said softly: "And I'm afraid it is already time to go." She looked at her watch. "Oh, yes, Raymond will be wondering where I've got to."

She stood up. Belot bent down to the dead leaf, was still for a moment, then he stood up.

As they went through the gate of the little garden she said: "Thank you for having given up some of your time to me. It will be a pleasant memory."

He coughed to clear his throat and replied simply: "Very pleasant."

9

M. Colet's turn?

Sunday. Dawn. Belot had worked all night. He had gone over all the files and all the evidence. Alone, and later with Picard, who had not left the Prefecture either. Then with Picard and M. Malebranche, whom they had awakened at about two o'clock in the morning. Another sleepless night, but how marvellous is the night which brings the light! Indeed, the conclusion was so fantastic and so preposterous that M. Malebranche at first refused to believe it. A team from the fingerprint department despatched somewhere in the city returned at about six o'clock with the absolute proof.

"Take it gently, all the same," he said.

Belot had already sent three men in advance as an observation party. He would follow them later. He seemed to have recovered his calm. In the wash-room he had just had a careful shave. He had however cut himself under one ear.

Eight o'clock. He telephoned London and Brussels, and to Musard and Archer. Now, under the eyes of M. Malebranche and Picard, he was getting ready to leave with a Gaillardet speechless with amazement.

The telephone rang. Picard answered it.

"Perraud . . . ? *What?*"

Forgetting all questions of rank Belot tore the receiver out of his hand.

"Belot here. What is it?"

He listened. His face showed incredulity and then anger. He retorted at last: "And all your fault? I'm coming!"

Seizing his hat, he grunted to the others: "Colet has disappeared and Mme Colet too. Come along," he added to Gaillardet.

In the small hall of the Hôtel Royal they found Perraud and the proprietor, in pyjamas, both of them in a state of great consternation. Perraud did not utter a word; he held out a letter. On the envelope: M. Perraud. On a half sheet of paper inside:

"My husband has disappeared. I'm going to look for him. I am quite out of my mind. Forgive me, I think I know where I can go for information. Don't do anything for the moment. Charlotte C."

"That was a good hour ago," explained the proprietor. "She came into the pantry where I was preparing the breakfast trays. She was terribly upset. 'I've got to go out at once!' she said. 'Will you please give this note to the gentleman who has been here regularly and who will be coming back.'" He pointed to Perraud. "This gentleman, of course."

"And she didn't tell you that her husband had disappeared?" asked Belot.

"No, she told me nothing more than I've just told you. She went off towards the taxi rank on the other side of the square."

"I dashed there," said Perraud, whose voice was unrecognisable. "None of the drivers was there at that moment."

"Let's go upstairs," said Belot.

In the bedroom an unmade double bed and normal disorder. The room pervaded by Mme Colet's scent.

"I don't understand," Belot said to the proprietor. "Did Mme Colet go out last night? Was it on her return that she realised her husband had disappeared?"

The proprietor protested once more. "Oh, no! She could always have gone out because the door can always be opened from inside. But to get in again she would have had to wake me, since my night porter left me only this week."

Perraud, pointing to the bed, suggested: "She must have woken up and found her husband was no longer there."

"And then," interrupted Gaillardet, maliciously, "instead of informing us she takes the time to write a letter and to put it in an envelope, to take it to this gentleman and then go off like that? With a piece of advice to the police: 'don't do anything for the moment!'"

"In any case," said Belot, "M. Colet may have disappeared but he was not kidnapped. Because if anyone had come to fetch him last night you would have been woken up?"

The proprietor nodded vigorously:

"Woken up!"

Belot turned to Perraud and asked curtly: "And what about you?"

"I left yesterday afternoon," he said in a whisper, "because she told me that neither of them would be going out again . . . like the night before. . . ."

Belot folded his arms.

"Because she had already dismissed you the night before and you had agreed? And how do you know what happened that night?"

Perraud plucked up the courage to defend himself.

"In any case nothing disagreeable, as she was quite all right yesterday. It was agreed that once they had retired for the night I should go off to bed myself. You instructed me to keep an eye on them not to keep them under strict observation. It was eight o'clock."

"Eight o'clock. Why do you call that the afternoon?"

"I was talking about the day before yesterday," said Perraud, bowing his head. "Yesterday, it was four o'clock. . . ."

"All right, we'll discuss the matter later. Stay here for the moment and not a word to anyone. Eh, monsieur? To nobody from the hotel or from elsewhere. Come, Gaillardet. Everything is perhaps clearer than it looks. I think I know too where we shall find her."

Mme Colet had been at Bellevue for an hour.

The taxi had dropped her in front of the villa Sans-Souci. The gate was open but she had had to parley for a long time at the front door with suspicious, invisible Longspès before her message was taken to M. Verdon and before the bolts had been drawn back, the key turned and the chains unhooked. It was not Longspès but his sister who performed this task. It was she who in a dressing gown and curlers received her visitor very amiably despite a huge swelling on her right cheek.

"You poor soul! So now its your turn to be in trouble? If you'll wait a minute in the drawing-room, M. Verdon will see you in a moment, my brother is attending to him. He hasn't had very much rest, poor man."

Mmc Colet nodded her thanks without a word. She looked distraught.

"I'm going to make you a nice cup of strong coffee," said the old spinster. "Yes, yes, no trouble, and the shock you've had! And coming at this hour all the way from Paris to Bellevue! M. Verdon will be pleased to drink one, too. Besides, it will do my abscess good!"

Mme Colet was left on her own. She closed her eyes and did not stir until Longspès, looking his ordinary self as if he had not undressed all night, came in to say in a surly voice, "You can come in."

In the corridor he murmured: "Your troubles are very unfortunate, I know, but will you try not to stay too long, for fear of tiring him?"

Verdon was sitting up in bed propped up against two pillows and wearing a blue braided jacket. The shutters were still closed and the lamps alight. He pointed to an armchair near the bed. "What is this news, madame! Your husband has disappeared?"

Mme Colet sat down and still did not say a word. She looked like a doll depicting Misfortune. She forced herself to drink Mlle Longspès' coffee at a gulp, burned herself and at last recovered her tongue. Yes, her husband had disappeared. She had had a horrible nightmare and had woken up with a start. Raymond was no longer there. Had he ever gone to bed? Overcome with weariness last night she had gone to bed first and fallen asleep almost at once, like a log! He had said to her: "Get to bed quickly, with your headache!" And he, who never stayed up late, she could still see him walking about the room and she had not had the strength to ask him why.

Verdon listened, putting in an encouraging word from time to time.

"So M. Colet must have left . . . of his own accord."

"It's not possible! He must have been *forced* to leave! Not like you, no, forced . . . morally! It is even more awful!"

"Have you notified the police?"

With a contempt equal to her despair she groaned: "The police? What good have they done so far? M. Tavernier is dead, you nearly died, M. de Laeken has disappeared and 'The Passenger' is still at large! Besides . . ." she cast a terrified glance at her listener.

"No," she went on immediately, "I want to find my husband on my own. Oh, Monsieur Verdon, I'm certain you can help me. You are the only one to have been in touch with those people. You managed to get away, though in what a state! But the others . . . perhaps Raymond will not be any more spared than they were."

"Calm yourself, little lady," said Verdon, with warm kindliness. "Let us think the matter out together. There is first of all one very important point. You include M. de Laeken among 'The Passenger's' victims but don't you know that . . ."

"That you saw him before being kidnapped the other day? Yes, you told us so yourself yesterday, and I thought then that *he* was 'The Passenger.' But you denied it with such energy. . . ."

"Could I do otherwise? I should have got nothing out of Miss Abbott if I had crossed her any further."

Mme Colet shrugged her shoulders.

"What can one get out of a woman who is so much in love and who is so blind? That was another idea of the police. Do you think I didn't guess that there was an inspector in there?" She pointed to the door of the cupboard, which was now closed.

"You were right. And that's why you didn't come back?"

"I wanted to see you again alone. I meant to come back this morning." Her voice broke. "But I didn't imagine that it would be in such circumstances."

"But surely," said M. Verdon, surprised, "Miss Abbott is your friend?"

"Certainly not, monsieur!" she cried angrily. "No one is my friend in this business. I received a threatening letter and I tried in every way possible to discover who sent it. Your police hadn't been able to learn anything from this Miss Abbott so I decided to get to know her myself. I came with her here for the same reason."

"I see. And were you successful?"

Mme Colet gave a sob, which sounded a little like a laugh.

"Yes! my husband has disappeared. . . . The murderer has the last word."

Verdon made a gesture which was meant to be comforting.

"I am trying to put myself in your place to be of some use to you, madame. I find it difficult, especially as I feel a little . . . odd also. But I will be quite frank. Reading through the papers of the past week there is one thing which struck me . . . or rather one *person* . . ."

"Oh . . . ?"

"You, yourself. You and M. Colet. But you in particular! You were the witnesses in the U bus on Monday. I suppose it was by chance. . . ."

"What do you mean?" replied Mme Colet, dumbfounded. "You *suppose?*"

M. Verdon's voice grew even warmer and kinder.

"My dear, let me continue. Your photo appears in the special issue of *Le Grand Journal*. It didn't get there on its own. You are reported as being present at M. Tavernier's funeral. I imagine you didn't go to it against your will?"

"Why don't you say straight away that we are 'The Passenger's' accomplices?" she replied in a shocked voice.

The bandaged head was shaken vigorously.

"I am saying you did not wait for a threatening letter to be sent to you personally before becoming interested in the Tavernier affair. And besides, you gave that letter too, to the newspapers. Don't deny that you had a motive. I swear I am speaking as a friend. But even this . . . this mistrust of the police. . . ."

Mme Colet was trembling all over.

"Of all the things! While my husband is perhaps being tortured at this very moment! But I must answer your insinuations. How could we have been in the bus, except by chance?"

Verdon replied in a new tone—the tone of a man who considers his own arguments to be incontestable.

"Oh, when one suspects that something will happen at a certain place it's not difficult to get there. When you go to see *Carmen* at the Opéra Comique you know that she will be killed in the last act."

"If I knew that she was really going to be killed, I shouldn't go. Are you going to make out that we were notified of a crime already planned, and that we allowed it to be committed?"

"Not necessarily," replied Verdon, still rather loftily. "And I realise that my *Carmen* was ill chosen. But you could have foreseen a clash between M. Tavernier and the man in grey. To serve as witnesses for one—or the other."

Mme Colet made a pathetic attempt to give her usual little nod.

"Well, I must say you have imagination! We knew neither one—nor the other. Besides, this murderer was only a common tool, I am sure. . . ."

"Then perhaps you know his boss?"

"The 'Passenger'?"

"Call him 'The Passenger' or anything you please."

"What do you mean, that I please! What else do you expect me to call him?"

Verdon was getting a little irritated. "All right, 'The Passenger,' the man who had a grudge against the unfortunate Tavernier to the point of having him killed. Have confidence! We shall get nowhere without that!"

She fell silent, obviously a prey to conflicting emotions.

"Confidence. . . . Of course, that's why I came. . . . But in whom can I have confidence? Do I still even have confidence in . . ." she gave a start. "No! Don't think. . . . My husband is the most honest man in the world!"

She relapsed into her depression. Verdon raised himself laboriously and moved to the edge of the bed as though to draw nearer to his visitor and to speak to her heart to heart.

"Tell me everything, my dear. You'll see that we shall understand together."

"I wonder if he did not do something foolish," she whispered.

"About the murderer?"

"No . . . in his business."

"What sort of foolishness?"

Her control suddenly appeared to snap.

"How should I know? I'm obviously getting silly ideas, unworthy of him. I'm basing them on impressions, which I can't pin down. On a state of nerves, anxiety, silences. . . ."

"Since the murder?"

"Since your kidnapping."

"And *before?*"

"Absolutely nothing! Nothing before Wednesday evening when a reporter from *Le Grand Journal* came and told us of your disappearance, of 'The Passenger's' letter to M. Rose and the demand for ransom. I saw him change completely. It was from that moment that I got in a panic. . . . After years of marriage to wonder if the man with whom you have shared everything has something in his life you know nothing about! When the threatening letter arrived he said to me: 'I don't want you to pay *for me!*' And that evening when we learnt about the Laeken affair, and at the hotel I repeated Miss Abbott's confidences, he turned quite pale and replied: 'I'm beginning to see what all this is about.'"

Verdon's eye did not leave Mme Colet.

He replied: "I'm beginning to see what all this is about? Why: *all this?* What did Miss Abbott tell you that could have provoked his reply? It's of vital importance, you realise—not only for M. Colet's disappearance, but for mine. The inspector assured me he got nothing out of this woman; but she talked to you?—"

"Of course! She talked to me of her love, of her Guy! She was heartbroken about 'the faint' and would never forgive herself for having complicated 'The Passenger's' transaction. She wanted it to succeed, since the life of her lover depended upon it."

Verdon repeated:

"And to that your husband replied: 'I begin to see what all this is about?' Did he say anything else?"

"Don't you think that's enough? This reference to 'The Passenger' coming up again and again? And this name, de Laeken, which suddenly cropped up, well, my husband knew it already . . . that's what it proves! How could he be in the know?"

Verdon's eye wandered.

"I'm thinking. . . ."

"You see the whole description Miss Abbott gave me of her friend as he was the night before his . . . departure fits Raymond, word for word. Even the meal . . ." she paused for a moment, "apparently he ate like a wolf that night. So did Raymond! Oh! Monsieur Verdon, these horrible comparisons which keep running through my head!"

Verdon was still lost in thought. The touch of a small hand on his made him start. He took it in his and murmured:

"You poor little woman! I was wondering how far you've been hypnotised by these comparisons and if they are not entirely the products of your imagination."

"I wish they were!"

"Then perhaps it's your husband who made connections that don't exist?"

"Connections with what?"

He returned to his first obsession:

"With the Tavernier murder."

"But as I tell you again, we could only have been witnesses of it by chance."

Verdon said gently: "I shall never mention it again if you can give me proof that your journey in the bus was as unpremeditated for your husband as it was for you."

"That's easy! We caught the first bus that came along. Raymond had dozed after lunch. I didn't want to stay in the hotel, we were going to the Motor Show."

"In that case, and unless the threatening letter was sent to you by the police. . . ."

"The police?"

Mme Colet gaped at him. Verdon's voice had recovered its self-assurance.

"Yes, indeed. Why did it never occur to you that this letter *could* not have come from 'The Passenger'? The newspapers say it was made up of cut-out words: why this waste of time when he had a typewriter, and used it on every possible occasion? They weren't cut-out words that he pinned on my pants the other evening! The police could quite well have employed this method to use you as a bait."

"But that would be disgraceful! To expose a woman. . . ."

"In the war against crime," said Verdon sententiously, "no methods are disgraceful. I will concede that that one would be ungracious."

With a frown Mme Colet ventured: "Perhaps the police suspected Raymond of being . . . mixed up. . . ."

"Certainly not. For if your husband had been in contact with 'The Passenger' he would have known at once that the letter did not come from him. You underestimate the police, my dear. They work, and they work for us! Our only hope is in them."

Mme Colet withdrew into herself. "Yours perhaps," she said in a low voice.

Her hand had tried to free itself, but Verdon held it now in a firm but gentle grip.

"But there is another explanation which I find more convincing," he said. His eye twinkled and his voice was almost tender.—"A flight."

Mme Colet snorted her disagreement. Verdon went on: "It's

difficult for a woman to believe these things! She prefers to imagine the worst catastrophe! I know all about women. I adore them! They are all delightfully foolish. But you, madame—allow me to pay you this compliment, you are not. You are not foolish and you are delightful all the same. Mind you, I'm not courting you. With this rag doll for a face, I can hardly be seen. But I'm talking seriously. You are the first woman I have ever met who is not foolish and who is delightful. And M. Colet deserves the reproach of all people of good taste."

With her mouth open, completely taken aback, she listened to Verdon who continued:

"Yes, that's the truth, and I am not often mistaken. M. Colet has played a joke on you, which he has grafted on to an extraordinary story. My kidnapping gave him the idea of feigning his own. He adopted similarities here and there, even as far as the behaviour of Laeken. It was he who invented the threatening letter. Who better than he could have left it at the desk of your hotel? There's nothing tragic about it! And I am delighted, I assure you. I can't unfortunately prevent you from being unhappy but it is my duty to reassure you! Besides, he'll come back! Once he has discovered that no woman comes up to his wife he'll come back!"

Verdon's hand fondled the little forsaken hand; he let it go when it was withdrawn. Mme Colet at last closed her mouth, then replied: "I don't really understand. . . ."

Verdon was surprised.

"Isn't it clear enough?"

"Oh, yes! Very clear. My husband is deceiving me. But is this really the only possible theory?"

"I assure you I cannot see any other."

"Yet when you thought my husband could have known Tavernier or his murderer, you didn't think then that he had run away?"

"Well no."

"And it's when you agreed that he did not know them, therefore that he must know de Laeken—or 'The Passenger,' whichever you like—that this idea of flight came into your mind?"

"Precisely."

She smiled. It was her first smile that morning.

"So you, who suffered so cruelly from this 'Passenger' or from this de Laeken,—you, whom he beat and tortured"—Verdon assented with an eloquent gesture—"as far as my husband is concerned can only put forward a ludicrous suggestion. For let's be frank: the idea of my husband running away from me *is* ludicrous. It's ridiculous! In your place the first idea I would have had is that he is being beaten up as I was beaten, and tortured as I was tortured!"

Verdon began to laugh.

"There you are, my dear. What did I tell you? You prefer a guilty husband to an unfaithful one!"

"Were you guilty, then?" asked Mme Colet.

"Do you think that 'The Passenger' is going to imprison forty million Frenchmen in his country house?" retorted Verdon. "He got what he wanted from the American woman, and I served him as 'the idiot,' to use his expression. He has no further need of anyone except perhaps to settle accounts with some accomplices. That is why we have to choose between your husband being guilty in the eyes of the law, or in terms of love! In the eyes of the law, madame, he is innocent! Yesterday, after you left, Inspector Belot talked about you and your shop in Avignon: you are honest people, my dear. Do not let us complicate a business which is mysterious enough already. I like you and would like to be friends."

Mme Colet, who had stopped smiling, now smiled even more broadly. She bent over the bed, placed her hand once more on the invalid's hand and said in her most wheedling tones:

"Monsieur Verdon, give me back my husband."

10

Belot sits himself in an armchair

Verdon appeared not to have heard. He was listening *further off*. He announced with relief in his voice:

"I think it's the inspector."

Mme Colet stood up abruptly.

"I don't want him to find me here."

"Why not, my dear?"

"Because."

Verdon laughed again.

"A very feminine reply! Yes, how feminine you are, how feminine indeed! How charming you are!"

With an expression both hounded and hostile, she repeated: "I want to go, Monsieur Verdon! Can I get out that way?"

She walked over to the long French windows, still shuttered like the smaller ones. She tried the handle, unsuccessfully.

"Longspès locks up every evening," said Verdon, "and he alone knows where he hides the keys."

"So it's a trap," she said, turning back towards the bed.

"You're the one who's accusing yourself, or accusing your husband," exclaimed Verdon, "it is I who maintain that you're honest, so why should I have laid a trap for you?"

She ran a trembling hand over her forehead and listened in her turn.

"I can't hear anything."

"I must have been mistaken," he replied calmly.

She went over to the door, thought better of it and returned. "Why did you frighten me like that?"

He laughed gently.

"What about you? You cunning little creature! 'Monsieur Verdon, give me back my husband. . . .' Where do you think I'm hiding him? In the cupboard? Last night I put on a camouflage bandage and stood in front of your hotel, and with occult passes willed your husband through all the walls and floors to 'Come down'? Seriously, my dear, what is going on in your sweet little head?"

This time there was a ring at the door. Mme Colet was listening intently and did not reply. There was a sound of voices and steps in the hall. Then a knock on the door. Longspès' head and shoulders appeared like a Jack-in-the-box.

"It's him," he said, "the inspector . . . Inspector Belot."

"Splendid!" said Vernon, "don't keep him waiting."

He watched Mme Colet, who was biting her lips. In the same tone of voice that he had used to Miss Abbott the evening before, he ordered: "Sit down."

Belot appeared.

He shook hands with Verdon, gave a quick little bow to Mme Colet, asked the sick man whether he had spent a good night and added:

"I should like a few words with you in private."

Very much the man of the world, Verdon replied:

"Madame Colet is a friend."

"So I see."

Her eyelids lowered, she seemed turned to stone.

"Furthermore," added Verdon, "she is more interested in this case than ever. M. Colet has disappeared, didn't you know?"

"Yes. And I see that instead of coming to us, she preferred to come and see you."

Mme Colet raised her head, a desperate plea in her blue-grey eyes. Belot answered it with no trace of gentleness: "We are looking for your husband, madam. As for you, if M. Verdon sees no inconvenience in your presence, neither do I. We can perhaps clear up your case at the same time."

"Inspector," said Verdon, not hiding his impatience, "you've made some new discoveries, I can feel it!"

Belot, recovering his usual amiability replied:

"Correct."

He sat down in an armchair, took a notebook from his pocket which he did not open at once, noticed that the shutters were drawn and said:

"Do you know that it's light now?"

"I'm looking after my complexion," replied Verdon. They both laughed. "In actual fact the light tires my poor eye."

"Now," began Belot, "we have received an extraordinary piece of evidence about your relations with M. Tavernier."

"What?" said Verdon.

"Someone has come forward with a statement, supported by proofs, that M. Tavernier and you were on more than friendly terms."

"Supported by proofs? I swear to you on my mother's head that I have never seen M. Tavernier either alive or dead, and that I had never heard of him until this week. Who is trying to injure me by inventing such a lie?"

Belot turned over the pages of his notebook.

"It was not I that took down the statement," he replied calmly. "And it's a very full one. I must apologise for having to give the details before a lady, but that's how you wanted it. We have been informed about a woman of whom it seems that you and M. Tavernier were both, at the same time. . . ."

Verdon had regained his composure.

"They didn't tell you too that we were suckled by the same she-wolf? Romulus and Remus were really us!"

Belot smiled. Still consulting his notebook he went on:

"I have a lot of questions to ask you this morning. For instance, that pair of one-franc vermilion that you were to take to M. Archer on Wednesday, you did show it to your clerk *the night before?* It spent the night of Tuesday to Wednesday in your safe? Do you know that the London firm which sold it to you claims that it was sent to you *months ago*, and to your home address? . . . May I ask why?"

"Oh, ho!" shouted Verdon gaily, "so that's the mysterious statement which has made you so touchy. What do you think of it, my dear?"

Mme Colet stuttered:

"The police are always suspicious of everyone. . . ."

Belot turned a trifle pale.

265

"Well, I'll let you into my secret," continued Verdon. "Just because I discover a fine stamp from time to time, I am not going to let my clients think that they are easy to obtain. You have to nurse a collector like M. Archer—keep him guessing a bit. Keep him on the bid! He wanted these one-franc vermilion, I had to make him crazy for them, covet them. Covetousness, Inspector, is probably better than actual possession. Particularly since M. Archer is not always keen to part with his money. Longspès told me about his refusal to pay towards the ransom. It doesn't surprise me. That's how I like my clients to be! As for the delivery to my home address, the explanation is just as simple. I distrust inquisitive people —and that includes my dear old Longspès." Verdon heaved a deep sigh—"Where are my vermilions now . . . ?"

"Is this rather a special case?" asked Belot.

"No, why?"

"Because we didn't find a single stamp at your home."

"It is true that great rarities seldom turn up."

"What bad luck you happened to deal with that one on the day of your kidnapping!"

"What bad luck," replied Verdon, "that you could not arrest the criminals a quarter of an hour before their crime!"

Mme Colet in spite of her dejection could not suppress a smile. Belot consulted his notebook.

"Now, this woman whom you and M. Tavernier associated with at the same time."

"No, Inspector," interrupted Verdon curtly.

"Are you sure that you never went to the rue du Ranelagh?"

"To see whom?"

"To see this woman."

"No."

"I wonder where they got it all from," muttered Belot.

"What do you mean?" cried Verdon. "Is she accusing me?"

"No, no. I'm speaking of the person who gave us the statement— man or woman."

Verdon chuckled:

"More likely a woman, isn't it?"

"So there is a woman you know well who knew about M. Tavernier's private life?"

"Pardon me! I was simply suggesting that your 'witness' was

slandering that poor wretch, just as he or she is slandering me!"

"Did you propose the Café de Marigny to M. Archer as a meeting place?" asked Belot.

"You have no pity for people who have fallen on their head. . . . Yes, sir, it was I who chose the Café de Marigny, as usual. Still for psychological reasons. What I sold M. Archer for 10,000 francs in his own home I could sell him for 12,000 at the café. Two thousand francs more because of the collectors all around. Is that a crime?"

Belot noticed that Mme Colet smiled again. He turned away and his voice was now less cordial.

"The Café de Marigny, as usual. Then why did you ask M. Musard which was the best bus to take for the Rond-Point?"

"I ought to be looking for a lawyer instead of waiting for the doctor," said Verdon. "I always thought that decent citizens who appealed to the police had a right to some consideration?"

"Innocent people have nothing to fear from us."

"That remains to be seen. Let us get on with our explanations. I always travel by taxi and I am not very familiar with public transport. I don't know which one of us started our exchange of jokes about the U."

"He assures me that you started them. In any case, you remember them quite well, they are in your statement made at the Broussais Hospital. 'I decided to go by bus. On the U Line, the famous U. Musard and I even cracked a joke.' . . ."

"Don't bother to go on. I added, and I repeat it now that the joke was hardly outstanding for its good taste."

"But why did you remember them *since the U played no part in your kidnapping?* Why should this bus appear to you 'famous' on the evening you made your statement? You were kidnapped on Wednesday morning. At that time if you only knew of the case through the newspapers as you say, what could you know about the U? On Tuesday, the murder of Tavernier; on Wednesday, the envelope found in the bus, *no details of which were published.* Therefore no signature, no 'Passenger.' Well?"

For the first time there was a moment's silence, which seemed interminable. Mme Colet bent her head down still further. Verdon said at last:

"I have no idea! Probably I was obsessed by the death of M.

Tavernier. At the moment, which was a crucial one for me, when those brutes drew my blood, they must have mentioned it."

"And you never went to the rue du Ranelagh?"

"He's obsessed," Verdon said sadly to Mme Colet, who no longer seemed to be listening to anyone. "No, Inspector."

"Mind you," Belot remarked confidentially, "the murder of M. Tavernier may possibly entail some very extenuating circumstances."

"So much the better for the murderer."

"Or for the man who gave him the idea. When questions of paternity are at stake. . . ."

"Because now," said M. Verdon, winking his one eye, "Romulus and Remus are also fathers of the same child."

"You are certainly very witty, Monsieur Verdon. You deserve an interrogator more gifted than I. I only deal in riddles. For example, those two brutes who drew your blood. . . ."

"Well?"

"They paid you a visit together during the night of Thursday/Friday?"

"Yes."

"And the taller leapt on you and pulled your hat down over your eyes?"

"Yes."

"*How did you see them?* Didn't they switch off the light before they came in?"

"Yes, they did."

"And in the pitch darkness you were able to make out that *one of them was shorter than the other?* And the other was able to leap on you and put on your hat, *avoiding a chest of drawers* behind which you were hiding 'like a frightened dog.'"

"Good heavens, it is rather extraordinary! Perhaps it was already dawn. The chinks in the shutters . . . ?"

"No, the bloodstained undershirt was discovered at five o'clock in the morning and we are now in October. Your subconscious again, perhaps?"

Verdon laughed and turned once more to Mme Colet: "And he says he is not witty! The truth is, he is not generous. He takes advantage of my state of health, of my bad night, to pile on these peculiar questions. . . ."

"You haven't replied to the main one. . . ."

"The mother of the child from the rue du Ranelagh? Confront me with your mysterious witness, man or woman! His statement will fall apart. Why don't you accuse me of being mixed up in the kidnapping of M. Colet as well?" Mme Colet raised her head sharply. "This charming lady thought of it, as she herself can tell you."

"Really?" said Belot in surprise.

"Oh yes! I am lying helpless in this bed, your colleague, M. Malicorne, hasn't left the villa all night and . . ."

"That's no excuse. 'The Passenger' didn't kill M. Tavernier himself."

Without losing its hint of irony M. Verdon's voice exploded as though driven by some inner force: "Oh, thanks for the comparison! In a minute you will make out that I am 'The Passenger' myself."

Belot smiled.

"Why not?"

"Of course, why not! And M. de Laeken is an honest gentleman whom I have imprisoned in one of my innumerable lairs."

"No, you don't hold him prisoner. You live with him on the best of terms."

"I suppose I'm hiding him in my cupboard, too," exclaimed Verdon.

"Not so far away," said Belot quietly. "Under your bandage."

11

The duet becomes a trio

During the last questions and answers, Mme Colet had woken up. She followed them from one face to the other as though she were watching a game of tennis. Verdon was still motionless in his bed and Belot in his armchair.

"Well, well," said the invalid, "here is something that interests this sweet lady. A switch! Laeken kidnaps Verdon and gets himself taken for him! I am no longer myself. I am Laeken disguised as myself!"

"No," said Belot, still just as calm, "you are still M. Verdon." Verdon was not joking any longer. He said gravely:

"It's madness."

"I'm afraid so," replied Belot, stretching his hand out to the bedside table to pick out from a pile of dailies Thursday's copy of *Le Grand Journal*, the issue that contained news of the ransom.

"Here is a rather bad photograph of you at the Brussels Congress in December. You didn't come straight back to Paris?"

"I should really let you wallow in your slander, but I shall prove to you that I am not afraid of anybody or anything. Yes, I returned via London. I made some purchases there, quite openly. So what?"

"You returned on the same boat as Miss Abbott?"

"Really? It's possible. I'm not rich enough to hire a special boat."

"You introduced yourself to her under the name of M. de Laeken."

"So that is how my legend starts? And we saw yesterday how it ended. Miss Abbott fell into my arms crying: 'My beloved!'"

"Wait until she sees you without a bandage."

"Did you at least show her my photo?"

"We've only this one, which is worthless. There was not a single photo at your home."

"I'm not a narcissist. But Miss Abbott must have shown you M. de Laeken's photograph?"

"No. Would you believe it, 'He' took it away with him!"

"Too bad. Let's be serious, Inspector. If it's true that I travelled on the same ship as your American friend, I began to realise why this 'Passenger,' this crook. . . ."

"This criminal."

". . . This criminal chose me rather than someone else as his bait and decoy. He not only tortured me this week, he must have been keeping his eye on me for months. It was a masterly coup. He has turned a victim into a suspect!"

"I admit that 'he' is clever," said Belot. " 'He' even suggested to you that you should change your existence since January, since your return from London! Your relations and your friends didn't see you any more of an evening. . . ."

"At thirty-five I consider I have no time to lose if I wish to educate myself. Of an evening, I read."

"You live in a house where you can stay out all night without anyone noticing it. . . ."

"A house which my mother chose ten years ago! During those ten years, has anyone levelled the least reproach at me?"

"You changed your daily maid's timetable. There was perhaps a risk she might not find you at home in the morning?"

"Let me whisper this reply."

Belot stood up, bent down and listened. When he returned to his chair Mme Colet suddenly said:

"Mademoiselle Guillaume is very charming."

The remark and the tone of the remark were so unexpected that two heads turned towards her in one movement of surprise. The young woman's gaze was still on the floor. She looked up and stared Belot straight in the face. Verdon took the time to wipe his eye with a handkerchief that he carefully unfolded first.

"Yes, of course," he said, "you met her here."

"We had a long chat," said Mme Colet. "But forgive me, I'm interrupting you. . . ."

"Not at all!" exclaimed Verdon. "But something tells me that I'm at last going to understand the reason for your visit. As you must be here with the assent of M. Belot. . . ."

Belot did not move an eyelid. Mme Colet retorted: "You're quite mistaken. I have already told you: I am looking for my husband. And if I am looking for him here it is because I have indeed some ideas of my own. . . . You're interested in psychology, aren't you?"

"Above all I adore women, whatever they say."

Mme Colet inclined her head. She seemed completely recovered. Even if she still felt anguish in her heart, she didn't show it.

"Women return the compliment a hundredfold! I met three in a single day—yesterday—who are absolutely crazy about you."

"Only three?" said Verdon with a straight face. "And who were they?"

"First of all your cousin, Mme Barbason—Irène. . . ."

"What?" said Belot.

Without blinking Verdon asked:

"The second?"

"Not so quick! That seems to you quite natural, as it does to me, but that's not a reason. I went to see her yesterday afternoon after I left here. She was very rude to begin with but finally offered me tea and cakes. I don't know what happened between you. . . ."

"God help me!" sighed Verdon, "nothing at all."

"She has not forgiven you. She mourned you because she thought you were dead and I did not take it upon me to disillusion her, but she avowed that such a misfortune hardly surprised her. She told me a curious story which she would never have wished to confide to the police for fear, as she said, of 'sullying your memory.' So I cannot, in front of M. Belot. . . ."

"But please do! My 'memory' begs you to do so!"

"Your cousin asserts that one night this winter she saw you get out of a taxi outside a boarding house in Auteuil and go in."

"Is that all?"

Verdon's voice had grown weaker and his breathing was stertorous. It was clear that such a long and unusual conversation was beginning to tire him or strain his nerves.

"In Auteuil?" asked Belot. "Very interesting. Whereabouts in Auteuil?"

"In the rue Jouvenet. A very quiet little street, apparently."

"I've never been to the rue Jouvenet," said Verdon. "My cousin must have mistaken me for someone else."

Mme Colet nodded.

"That wouldn't surprise me. A woman in love. . . ."

"But this coincidence is going to surprise you, monsieur," said Belot. "Laeken lived for six months in that boarding house."

"What did I tell you?" exclaimed Verdon. "One thing explains another. Each detail proves that I was not chosen by chance!"

"But strangest of all," said Mme Colet, "Mme Barbason is convinced that she followed you from your house. You went first by metro to the Étoile. You called in at the Hôtel Victor-Hugo."

Belot could not repress a smile as he said, "Where Miss Gwendolyn Abbott was then living."

"Mme Barbason walked up and down in front of the hotel for two hours! In the mud, the snow and the dark . . . from eight until ten. She thinks you must have dined there. When she saw you come out *you were wearing a monocle!* You took a taxi and so did she. You stopped at the rue Jouvenet and she returned home. During the night she telephoned your home but there was no reply."

"I disconnect the phone," said Verdon. "I like to sleep in peace. Madame, I don't believe a word of this story. I'm going to ask M. Belot to send for my cousin."

"As soon as she knows you're alive," said Mme Colet, "and that her testimony risks doing you harm, she will deny everything, of course. I must add that what she reproaches you for most is the monocle. Since she is certain that your taste only runs to chambermaids she considers this method of seduction unworthy of you."

Verdon laughed a little wearily.

"That's a fine transition to take us on to number two—Mademoiselle Guillaume, presumably? Who must have seen me at the Zoo with M. Tavernier and our child in front of the monkey cage."

"No," said Mme Colet. "She has never seen you anywhere else except at your home and alone. And never enough for her taste! She would have loved so much to have been present at one of your dinners for example, to have served you and watched you eat. But you *never* returned from your little evening outings before she left, and yet she never left herself much before nine o'clock. . . . The following day she always found empty plates beautifully clean and she only had to rinse them; you yourself took the trouble of throwing the remains down the incinerator. These modern houses are so convenient! You could have got rid of the whole meal and no one would have been any the wiser. The same thing with the bed. Let us suppose that you asked Juliette to come in the evening, not only to have the pleasure of, well, shall we say, chatting with her, but because you did not sleep at home and there would have been a risk of her finding the bed unslept in next morning? Whereas by returning from your office in the evening just before she arrived, it was easy enough to disturb it. Especially as . . ."

Mme Colet stopped short and blushed.

"If you could see the way M. Belot is looking at you!" said Verdon. "How he admires you! How he watches you! He is telling himself that he has never had such a pupil. You would send innocent men to the scaffold with the greatest subtlety and skill. . . ."

She shook her head rather sadly.

"You're wrong again, Monsieur Verdon. I'm trying to understand, I'm not trying to condemn—except the murderer, of course. I would consider 'The Passenger' very extraordinary and even . . . and even very attractive, if there was no crime."

"But there is one," said Belot.

To get more comfortable, Verdon had slipped down the bed and for a moment closed his eyes.

"That leaves us with the third woman?" he said.

Mme Colet began again abruptly: "Have you noticed the strange likeness between Miss Abbott and M. Longspès?"

"Good heavens, there's something in what you say! But don't tell me it's Longspès you consider . . . ?"

Mme Colet blushed again. Verdon laughed silently and murmured. "Dear girl!"

"Very funny indeed," she replied, "you know perfectly well that there can be attachments as binding as the love of a man and a woman. Have you never kept a dog? M. Longspès adores you like a dog. It is extraordinary how you manage to surround yourself with people who are ready to die for you: M. Longspès, Mlle Guillaume, your friend M. Durand apparently. . . . And that is how

Miss Abbott loves M. de Laeken. One really wonders why he took so much trouble and why he chose to run such risks."

"To the point of killing," added Belot.

Every allusion to the crime now made Verdon blink his eyelid. He said: "I still can't see the third woman."

"What is very curious," said Mme Colet, "is not that Miss Abbott looks like Longspès physically, but that morally she succumbed to the hold her friend had over her just as Mlle Guillaume succumbed to your hold. Just imagine, they both used almost *the same expressions* to tell me that you—and M. de Laeken—wanted them to be strong and brave. They both repeated a lesson which seems to have been given them by the same lips, by the same master. As a psychologist that ought to interest you."

Verdon, now genuinely exhausted, replied: "Above all, it's beginning to tire me out. All this is very intelligent, I had never thought that a woman could be so intelligent, but it adds up to nothing. You are embellishing and embroidering, and in the meantime M. Colet is probably being slashed with a razor, not in the arm but in the throat!"

Mme Colet hardly winced.

"But you assured me he had left me."

"I did not know then that you were working with the police. Oh, don't deny it! I did not say *for* the police. But you must admit that it comes to the same thing, and the murderer may have got fed up with it."

"And so have we," said Belot bluntly. "We may have embroidered a little but the embroidery holds good. Thank you, madame. I have only one *small* detail to add. The fingerprints which I had taken just now in M. Verdon's apartment in the rue Laffitte and in the bedroom of Laeken at the Villas Kléber are *one and the same!* Well, Verdon, are you now going to tell me of your relations with M. Tavernier?"

For the first time Belot had not said Monsieur Verdon. Verdon raised himself.

"Monsieur Belot, your obstinacy will be the cause of a new disaster. I repeat to you that M. Colet is really in danger. Believe me, madame, there was a crime before the affair of 'The Passenger.'"

"Why *before?*" asked Belot.

Verdon clenched his fists.

"But, heavens alive! *Because there is no connection!* Your mysterious statement is false and I do not believe it. You have invented it from beginning to end to get me. All right, you've got me. This story's going too far. You keep on talking to me about Tavernier, Tavernier. . . . I am anything you like but not a murderer, nor a person who incites to murder!"

He fell back on his pillows and continued in a distant voice: "I let myself be carried away by my work. . . . You cannot at the same time be an artist and make a fortune. Naturally, I preferred to be an artist. . . . You touched me just now, madame, with your praise for 'The Passenger.' 'The Passenger' kisses your hands. . . . But what of your husband?"

Mme Colet replied sweetly: "The police are looking after him, as you know very well."

"Well," growled Belot, "are you going to talk or do we have to make you?"

And Verdon, suddenly humble, replied: "I will talk, Inspector, I will talk. . . ."

12

The demon of the monocle

"Yes, it did all begin on the boat. Everything. For when I went on board I did not think of pulling a fast one that day any more than any other. I had enjoyed the Philatelic Congress at Brussels, I had made some good buys in London and I was returning prepared to take up my life as Verdon. And then on the deck I noticed a woman doubled up, looking for something. I went up to her and bent down. She raised a pair of the most short-sighted eyes I have ever seen and the long horse-face with which you are a little, but so little familiar. And then it happened. . . . Without my being aware of it, a hint of butterflies in the stomach, and I asked in a broad Belgian accent: "Are you looking for something, madame?" and that moment I took my monocle from my waistcoat pocket and put it in my eye."

"What?" asked Belot.

"That is the whole case, Inspector! Without psychology there would be no case! The accent on its own would not have taken me very far. The demon resided in the monocle. I had carried it in my pocket for nearly fifteen years. It had *never* been taken out—I mean in public. Fifteen years! I was twenty, my father was dead and I lived with my mother. I had given up my law studies to go and work with Ibert and Bélier when I met a gentleman in the street wearing one, and within the next quarter of an hour I had gone into an optician to buy one for myself—naturally, in plain glass. I thought they would throw me out. Plain glass! Not at all. Twenty francs it cost, and they let me choose a little case for it and I was given in addition a soft little chamois leather. As soon as I got home I tried it in front of the mirror. It held in my eye at the first attempt. I danced, jumped, whirled around. It held. It has always held, for fifteen years. Oh, if I had had to replace it, it would no longer have been the same thing—the same one which had made my heart beat faster. Naturally, there was no question of sporting it in public. No, in my room when I was alone and I wanted to dream and tell myself stories—idiotic, delightful stories—of Monsieur X and Madame Y, of gondolas and riding to hounds. And then I went back to classify stamps at Ibert and Bélier's and with my mother I led, as they would say, a poor but honest existence. Poverty sickened me although ours was comfortable enough. Nor had I anything against honesty, I have never thought that it could in itself prevent one from succeeding. But rich and honest seemed to be an excellent combination. But there was the demon of the monocle. . . . It was he who gave me ideas about life and, first and foremost, suggested that one can be bored with it, bored to death! I adored my mother and I could not imagine living apart from her or getting married. She was perfect. Also I loved women far too much to confine myself to a single one. To change a woman is a way of changing one's skin. . . . My cousin is an idiot, because firstly I have never specialised in servant girls and secondly, I have always respected my scale of values: on the lowest rung the daily round, in the centre distractions and women, and at the top my dreams. Not all poets write verses. Obviously I should have made a name for myself in letters. Mme Colet and the whole of the provinces would have known by heart *Peonies and Roses* by Maurice Verdon of the French Academy and I should not now be suffering in this bed with every prospect of going to jail. But I should not have experienced all that has happened this last week. . . .

"My mother died in January last year. I was very unhappy, but at the same time I thought: 'Well, there we are!' Where? I was thirty-four and with a business of my own. I realised that her death brought no change. On the contrary, I stopped dreaming and even juggling—for I was also a juggler. It is a fabulous distraction: the object which escapes, which loses its weight, which becomes a bird, a dragonfly and a pair of hands that fly with it. . . . I bought horn-rimmed spectacles, to wear in public. I kept the monocle as a souvenir . . . not even as a souvenir but as one of those trifles with which you clutter up your pockets without ever using them.

It came out of an evening with everything else, taking its place next morning in the waistcoat. Our Verdon thought that he had settled down. The most he said to himself was let us sell our stamps and when I am rich I shall travel.

"Until January 3rd this year. . . . I swear to you that everything happened in a split second. I put on my Belgian accent as I had done in Brussels with colleagues to pull our hosts' legs. But as soon as I felt the monocle in my eye, when I realised that I had put it on in broad daylight, that I had exposed it, exhibited it for the first time in my life, I shivered with pleasure and felt a moment of intoxication. I was going to play a *prodigious* joke! And yet it was quite modest! I simply wanted to fool this great horse without doing any great harm."

Verdon fell silent.

"Give us the facts," said Belot as blunt as before.

Mme Colet gave him a pleading look. Verdon retorted (he had already lost the humble voice he had started with).

"I'll tell you everything or I'll tell you nothing. And if you want me to last to the end don't interrupt me!

"I had to introduce myself. A name ran through my mind—the name of a district or an avenue in Brussels: Laeken. Vicomte Guy de Laeken. But it was not the Vicomte de Laeken who found the American's lorgnette and flung it into the sea, it was Verdon. Verdon wanted to disappear without leaving any traces, so as to be able to reappear without trouble. The farce was to continue until we arrived . . . no longer. I persuaded Miss Abbott that I could not bear women who wore glasses. Similarly before lunch, which we ate together in the dining car, I plastered my hair down with a parting in the middle and I looked ridiculous. She found me madly attractive. True I told her some pretty tall stories. All my childhood memories—Laeken's of course—it was miraculous. I left her at the entrance of the Hôtel Victor-Hugo. I was supposed to live in a boarding house in Auteuil. Then I hurried off to my office with my hair parted on the right and wearing my horn-rimmed spectacles. It was all over.

When I woke the following morning I realised that it was by no means over. I wanted to see my American again. A millionaire's daughter in love with me! But above all I wanted to go on being *the other*. I had enjoyed myself so much the day before. I thought to myself: what do I risk? Let someone recognise me with my monocle and make disobliging remarks about my pretensions. My profession will not suffer and I could not care less about anything else! In short during the day Miss Gwendolyn Abbott received a dozen red roses which had to speak for themselves, because Laeken, born of a monocle like Aphrodite from the waves did not yet know how to write properly and had no visiting cards. Nor had he anywhere to live. He could not start a one-way relationship. It would have appeared too shady and it certainly was not that. I was simply embarking on an exciting game. The same evening I left the rue Laffitte blessing my mother for having chosen such a convenient house. And Laeken with a fine suitcase found a 'distinguished' boarding house in the rue Jouvenet in Auteuil. He slept there. What an impression! The proprietor, the valet and the maid all called me M. le Vicomte and even M. le comte. I was not particularly bowled over by the title. I heard this 'M. le comte' like a proper name of two syllables like Verdon, but which wasn't Verdon. I was no longer myself but a person outside myself. The real me, now a ghost, must be sleeping stupidly in my old bed in the rue Laffitte as unaware of being alive as on other days. But *he*—Laeken, 'the count'—lolled in strange sheets and did not close an eye, so happy was he to be new born. Madame Colet, when you got married, when you ceased to be called Mlle So-and-So . . . did you perhaps feel something like that?"

Verdon did not wait for a reply but went on: "In short, Laeken while enjoying his first breakfast telephoned Miss Abbott, was effusively thanked for the roses and invited to dinner. The double life had begun! During the day, I was me and in the evening and at night I was him. The most delicious aspect was that I, Verdon, was no longer bored. I carried my joke in my waistcoat pocket all the time and kept feeling it. My customers, my colleagues, my cousins and relations had no idea how little they mattered to me at those moments. And they, too, played their parts! They represented Danger with a capital D. Not a real danger for there was nothing real in this story, but each day it became more intriguing and more exciting. I kept waiting for someone to say, 'Monsieur Verdon weren't you at the Victor-Hugo last night? There was a man there wearing a monocle who might have been your twin brother.' And as time passed the more decided I was to deny it, so as not to harm my dear Laeken. *He* had learned to write with his left hand. *He* had ordered visiting cards, clothes and shoes until he had a complete wardrobe in the rue Jouvenet. I dipped into the money for my future travels, without any regret you can be sure. No change of scene could have equalled this change of personality!"

"But . . . ?" Mme Colet asked, sympathetically—

"Yes, there was a but. There was Gwendolyn. It was all right at the beginning. I saw her when I wanted to. Besides, I have to give her credit: right until the end she never questioned me on my public life, my comings and goings, etc. You have to take your hat off to the way American women respect your independence. Nevertheless, she was so happy to see me and so upset when I did not appear, that I gradually let myself be carried away. It was a kind of gratitude, do you understand. I thought to myself: there is no such thing as perfection. It even pleased me to be punished in this way, pleased my sense of 'balance.' I was enjoying myself: I had to pay. Yes, I paid—with my person. Nothing forced me to do so. And what would have happened to Laeken? Was I to involve him in other nocturnal adventures? The fact is I am not an adventurer . . . not in the least. And that is how we went wrong. I am afraid Laeken was as susceptible to charm as Verdon. His heart was not in it. Close your ears, madame. I discovered that to avoid being unproductive at night I had to honour true beauty during the day. There are a lot of people who drink coffee in order to sleep."

"That's true," said Belot involuntarily.

"There was no question of sleeping about here and there as I had done before. I needed a pretty, pleasant partner with no other demands except the one I wanted to gratify. The difficulty did not worry me! I think I may say I have always been able to find in life the people who were necessary to me."

"That's true," said Mme Colet in her turn.

Verdon nodded.

"I realise it today. Well, at that period I still took my free meals at *Chez Barbason*. There was a waitress there whom Rubens might have painted. My cousin was furious. I broke or nearly broke with the family. It was then that I discovered Juliette. She had been cleaning my apartment for six months, but I had never had any particular reason for noticing her. I killed several birds with one stone. By raising her to the rank of favourite, by arranging for her to come in the afternoon I spared myself the necessity of going home simply to rumple my bed—you saw that didn't you, dear lady? I resettled Verdon in his private life at the same time as Laeken got established in his. I educated a little girl. Yes, with books, gramophone records, ideas of decorum and being on her guard against a society which is so dangerous to pretty girls. The day she marries she will know life. And then what a triumph for morality over money. Without the least dash of powder she was a thousand times more desirable and more charming than that great bony horse with her millions in the bank. If for twelve hours out of the twenty-four Verdon enjoyed the idea of becoming Laeken he paid him back generously with sweet memories.

"From the rue Laffitte I usually returned to the rue Jouvenet, changed my clothes and then went to the Victor-Hugo (I wonder which evening I went there direct, you must ask my cousin). I dined with Gwen—not every day at the beginning—and then returned to the boarding house. It became very tedious, particularly since I had voiced some foolish ideas in the dining car. I, who adore smoking a pipe had announced that I did not smoke! I, who have such a splendid appetite that I can digest lobster shells, pretended that I had a weak stomach. No, I did not foresee that my joke would become chronic, and that is the best proof. On dozens of occasions later I insisted that I was cured but Gwen refused to accept this. We used to dine in a little gilt salon next to her bedroom. There was a constant flow of boiled fish and noodles served in the best dishes. Oh! She was so sensitive; she went on a diet to spare me any temptations. You can't imagine what Verdon devoured at midday! And when he arrived home of an evening he did not throw his previous night's dinner down the incinerator dear lady, *he ate it*. Ate it cold."

Verdon stopped suddenly and asked Mme Colet: "Is there a little coffee left? My throat is dry."

She stood up and poured him a cup.

"I am afraid this is cold too."

"Would you raise my pillows?" he asked her again.

He drank the coffee. Belot watched every movement. Since the start of the tale there had been a look of incredulous amazement in his eyes. Verdon sighed: "Thank you," and went on, "I am not insinuating that all the faults were on her side. That would be unfair. You cannot be held responsible for your ugliness or your attitudes. But the rest of the world is not responsible either. Besides, although she could not do enough for me, she made life unbearable for all her subordinates. Hard, mistrustful and suspicious, always thinking that people were trying to exploit her and rob her. Mind you, it was possible: where should one look for money except where it is? And in this case, would not honesty precisely live in robbing unworthy Paul to pay deserving Peter? Obviously Paul would not think so. Nor did Gwendolyn. She cared for her millions, as though the half, the quarter or the tenth would not have allowed her to live incomparably better than a furniture dealer, a stamp dealer or even a Chief Inspector—not to mention a chambermaid or a hotel porter! I mustn't get worked up; this subject makes me boil. Perhaps you can begin to see how the idea of a *gesture*—a stand, was born in the brain of Laeken? A stand which would be a gesture of general value even if it only benefitted a single individual. You were wondering just now, madame, why Laeken took so much trouble, why he did not take advantage of his situation. That would have been monstrous, I ask you! He would have been behaving like a professional dancing partner, like a gigolo. He would have had to marry her!"

"Marriage was not necessary," said Mme Colet. "You forget that she was madly in love with you."

"It is you who have persuaded me of it, and her fainting fit, that piece of clumsiness! I saw her above all eager to exchange her American lack of breeding for ancient, solid nobility. I could not imagine that a woman I loved so little. . . . Whatever the truth I should have rejected any behaviour that lacked elegance. . . ."

"Elegance!" grumbled Belot.

"Don't interrupt me. If elegance shocks you, let us use the word 'correctness'—in every sense of the word.

"My idea took a long time to materialise. I began by very modest reimbursements—a tie, gloves, a blotter—that did not even pay for my flowers. The money was still slipping away and I was getting much less pleasure spending it. I could not accept any jewellery. Only the signet ring which Gwen had ordered from an engraver she knew in New York. There, too, I thought I had proof of her pretensions. I had devised for myself a magnificent coat of arms— and I had stuck in a goose. Don't you think she ought to have understood? I was furious that I had to laugh at my own joke. Oh, she laughed too. When I read her *Dr Jekyll and Mr Hyde* or *Judge Hallers* and suggested: 'Gwen, supposing I was not myself?' She would reply: 'You are so amusing, my funny darling!' Second stage: I could not accept jewels, but I could accept stamps? That is a serious, very masculine passion where a present does not demean the recipient. Like giving books to a bibliophile. Besides, Laeken owed at least that to Verdon. I wrote to myself from the rue Jouvenet. I read my letters in the rue de Châteaudun and I replied to myself immediately. I placed myself at my own disposal. The whole fraternity profited by it and I can say that I have today a very fine collection of Belgians. Don't worry about it; it's lodged with a bank in a strong box.

"But still I was not pacified. I found more and more unbearable Gwen's ugliness, naïveté, stinginess, her passion for me and her noodles. Our tastes were diametrically opposed. I adore music: she didn't. I like adventure stories: she didn't. Our conversations together became a nightmare. Everything she did or obliged me to do I held against her. His existence weighed on Laeken and Laeken weighed on Verdon. Instead of being alone in my boredom as before, I was bored twice over. I had begun to learn English. But to speak English with a Belgian accent was beyond my powers. The monocle weighed heavily in my pocket and cried out for vengeance. It was a beautiful day, on June 15th, and the women had never looked prettier. Gwen chose that very moment to talk about marriage and about Boston—and to insist that in the meanwhile I came and lived at the Victor-Hugo: I didn't look well, I was overworked, I was going to fall ill. She had come to Auteuil, had peered at the different pieces of furniture and was overcome to find me living in such humble quarters. A man like me—a Laeken! I stood up for myself: 'My means . . .' (He put on an American accent.) 'Your means, Guy? My cheque book is yours.' (With a Brussels accent.) 'Oh, Gwen, how can you say such a thing!' The discussion went on for several days. It was not time wasted. Forced to make up my mind quickly, like a general surrounded on all sides, I suddenly conceived the manoeuvre which would not only free me, but cover me with glory!"

13

Truth is stranger than fiction

Verdon, who was talking with his head thrown back, his eyes staring at the ceiling, looked in turn at Belot and Mme Colet. He did
not note the contrast in their attitudes, the inspector, impatient
and hostile, the young woman, inquisitive and enthusiastic. He
continued:

"It is giving me immense pleasure to tell you all this. Don't imagine that I'm 'getting it off my chest' as any common malefactor
would do. No, I am *realising* myself. What a wonderful comedy mine
was! A single spectator in the audience and it would have been a flop.
The public was only admitted after it was over. Perhaps it is an
idea without a very great future but at this moment it affords me
the most marvellous satisfaction. I am sorry I am so tired. I'll know
better next time."

Belot was about to interrupt him, but restrained himself.

"Thank you," said Verdon. "This was my plan, the first one that
I conceived in June and the one I should have stuck to. To begin
with I agreed to live with Gwen—not at the Victor-Hugo but at the
Villas Kléber. We had discussed it together. She wanted me to think
that the price was low and I had guessed that she intended to pay
part of my bill. Why not? since I was supposed to know nothing
about it. But above all she had given me some entrancing details,
in particular that each guest was given a private key. Once installed
there I would gradually begin to accept the possibility of a marriage
in Boston. I would fix the date of departure and Gwen would buy
the tickets. Suddenly, a week before leaving, the newspapers would
announce the kidnapping of a certain Verdon, the viscount's stamp

dealer. The 'kidnapper'—I did not know what his pseudonym would be—writes to the police and to the family. I then thought of the Barbasons: a secret entrusted to my cousin would immediately make the rounds of Paris. So he demands a ransom from the family. I had not yet fixed the amount but it would be as spectacular as it was unrealistic. Headline material for the front page of the dailies. On the eve of his departure for Le Havre and Boston, Laeken disappears. This time the kidnapper does not write to the police but to Miss Abbott. Apart from small details he sends the express letter which she actually received. His original ambition was limited to 40,000 dollars instead of 80,000. That was because in that plan Verdon did not die: the question of his ransom was shelved when the Laeken affair broke—or rather did not break. In complete secrecy Gwen was to take the sum to a private box number and to leave immediately for Le Havre. There she would find her handsome Guy, free and—according to the note—ready to marry her.

"My interpretation of Gwendolyn's character—distrustful enough to necessitate a preliminary disappearance, timorous and self-seeking enough to carry out blindly the instructions given in the express letter—meant that everything should have functioned perfectly. And the following morning at Le Havre, a few hours before sailing, the two lovers were to meet for the last act. He enters. She flings her tall frame upon him. (American accent): 'Oh, my darling, my darling!' But Guy, looking gloomy (Brussels accent): 'What have you done, Gwen? You have bought me like a slave, like a lap dog. Leave on your own! I will rejoin you when I have revenged myself on this bandit, when I have wiped out the stain on the escutcheon of my ancestors.' Gwen collapses. 'Guy! I will wait for you!' 'No, Gwen. If you don't leave I shall join the Foreign Legion and as you know that would mean farewell for ever!' A siren wails in the distance and Gwendolyn surrenders. Guy accompanies her aboard. A final kiss. The gangway. . . . The quayside. . . . In the bows a lanky silhouette waving a handkerchief. Laeken disappears from view. Before disappearing completely he will wait in a Paris hotel until Verdon is resuscitated.

"Which happens like this: Longspès receives a letter from his employer containing the precious pair of one-franc vermilion—London had just sent it to me—which says: 'Dear Longspès, my kidnapper has allowed me to write to you. Go quickly and sell this fine specimen to M. Archer for 50,000 francs. Send the cash in my name to a certain box number. (Not the same as Miss Abbott's, of course.) Someone will pick it up for me. . . . And not a word to the police. They would spoil everything and I should be put to death rather than given my freedom.' Longspès obeys. Verdon reappears. He lodges a complaint, naturally, but his vague memories do little to help the inquiry. And *as he is the only victim*, with the 50,000 francs he is believed to have lost, the affair subsides—am I right, M. Belot?

"Of course, I killed Laeken, but that was nobody's business but mine. Mine and Gwendolyn's. The poor woman would one day receive a letter informing her that Guy died as a hero, in the desert. She well deserved that sentimental wreath. The signet ring would be sent with the sad news. As for the 40,000 dollars. I flirted for one moment with the idea of buying a property on the Atlantic, almost opposite Boston. A passing weakness! I decided to split the sum in three: a dowry for Juliette, a donation to the Philatelic Society and the foundation of a few beds in a home for incurable spinsters.

"This was the plan which I took together with my luggage to Room 18 at the Villas Kléber. Gwen's joy was pathetic. Laeken's joy was easier to explain. He bought a secondhand typewriter on which to type the kidnapper's letters; two beards—one dark and one fair. The fair one was attached to a wig which could be used for fetching the money, for going to Le Havre etc. and long live Barbason! They were hidden in a suitcase. He found out about private box numbers, the Venus Agency and others; the names of his eventual correspondents at Police Headquarters—M. Malebranche and M. Picard. Verdon for his part gradually conditioned Longspès' attitude to the police—that one could not do without them but one had to be on one's guard. . . . I was going against my own feelings, needless to say! But the plan made some demands. Poor Longspès!

"Once I had taken up residence at the Villas Kléber, I could no longer change my clothes before joining Gwendolyn. Verdon and Laeken had to put up with living in one and the same suit. But it was only for two or three weeks longer! Every evening I took a taxi from the rush-hour traffic of the Gare Saint-Lazare. I removed my spectacles just before giving the driver the address of the 'Old Ladies,' I changed my hair in the taxi and put on my monocle as I left it, damped down my hair in my bathroom and rinsed my mouth because of the tobacco. To get some peace at home, I mean in room No. 18, I fell back on one of my favourite fantasies: a case against some Laeken imposters. And I typed for hours 'compiling my dossier.' These documents were actually scores of rough drafts of my future letters, which I then burned. I played my role as a lover, each day offering less resistance to the agreeable idea of departure. But in this direction things did not happen at all as I hoped. Gwen, although crazy with happiness and impatience, made a sacrifice for me upon which I had not at all counted. She declared that there was no question of leaving until those 'wicked Laeken imposters' had restored my title and my property! She took on her shoulders what I had been drumming into her for months. It was useless assuring her that my lawyer would look after things in my absence, she saw in my change of attitude a proof of intense love of which her scruples would not let her take advantage. She repeated: 'We shall leave with our heads high.' She held up her head and we did not leave.

"July ended. Usually I go on holiday in August. I would rather have died than go on a holiday with Gwen. Verdon kept his office open, retaining Longspès and Juliette—a triple refuge. Laeken racked his mind how to get his Melisande to take herself off, and could think of no way, no single solitary way. Some evenings he was so desperate that he thought of giving up the game and taking flight. These attacks of cowardice did not last long. He pulled himself out of them each time more decided than ever to complete his mission. By the end of August he had decided to demand 50,000 dollars instead of 40,000. By the end of September worry increased the amount to 60,000. However it could not go on any longer. It was all very well typing my letters, trying on my beards and practising scenes: I was going off my head."

Verdon gasped for breath. Then, like a seer recounting his vision:

"Then, on Tuesday morning, on reading the article in *Le Grand Journal* on the murder of M. Tavernier—the admirable piece signed Aumerle—I had the 'revelation.' I cannot define my inner upheaval better than that. Some people use newspapers to light their fire; this one acted for me like a spark. There was nothing immoral in it, poor M. Tavernier was dead. Yes, he was dead. . . . But if the kidnapper utilised a real crime to order Gwen to leave, she would leave! I very nearly cancelled the Verdon affair in favour of an immediate disappearance of Laeken. The express letter would have been juicy enough as it was. But I should have depended too directly on the murderer. There was nothing to indicate that he would not be arrested in the course of the next few days, and in that case it was important not that I should get caught with him, but that he should be suspect for me. I don't like murderers any more than you do, my dear lady, I should have contributed to his punishment. Oh what fresh wind was blowing up from the sea! Bursting from the chrysalis of my palace, I had become a butterfly. A liner was leaving Le Havre on Saturday; it would carry off Melisande!

"Now, Monsieur Belot, you are going to learn, hour by hour, how I have lived since Tuesday morning.

"After I had read *Le Grand Journal* I hurried home to fetch my pair of one-franc vermilion. It was at that moment in the taxi, that I invented the name of my kidnapper: 'The Passenger,' on the U."

"Why, 'The Passenger'?" asked Belot.

"Don't they call someone who often takes the bus . . . ?"

Verdon struck his forehead and burst out laughing. " 'The *regular*' —that's what I meant. And the whole world repeated after me: 'The Passenger.' "

He paused for a moment.

"All the same a mistake like that does make one think . . . But let me go on. . . . I saw Longspès and put on a worried air. Laeken retained it while lunching with Gwen. I talked with a feigned light-heartedness about the Tavernier murder, suggesting possible repercussions. Why? Because it would be learned subsequently that Laeken, like Verdon, had received threatening letters. Planned kidnappings could not affect both of them solely by a malicious stroke of chance. M. Belot, Aumerle's article on your conversation with Mme Tavernier and young Roux had impressed me. From the picture given to you of the victim this poor wretch should never have received six revolver bullets, nor even one. And yet he had received them and I was certain that you would soon discover the motives. I had to get some ready for you for Verdon and be able to offer some to Gwen for Laeken!

"After lunch I announced that I wanted to complete the documents for my case as quickly as possible and, carefully gloved (what useless precautions!) I typed the first letter from 'The Passenger.' This was the little note to M. Picard, a note of which I am very proud because it contained everything. 'Do I know myself who I am? In any case I am not very proud of the events of yesterday. I expect to do better tomorrow.' . . ."

"You won't need a lawyer," said Mme Colet.

"If my pleading convinces you, madame, I could not wish for anything better.

"At half past five I, Verdon, was reading a newspaper in a bus of the U Line, and behind the opened page the envelope fell discreetly at my feet. An unforgettable moment!

"I realised what it meant to say: the die has been cast! To mystify Gwen, and to punish her, I was sealing a pact with all the vehicles of the U Line. I will not pretend I did not feel the disproportion between the means and the objective. As though a father were to set the house on fire because his daughter insisted on playing with matches. In the first plan Verdon was kidnapped in a taxi. But without the U's there would have been no connection with the Tavernier affair! Besides, I was enjoying myself again so much! A third person was born in me, without identity, without domicile, with no past and no memories—the very epitome of the *unknown!* Who was to conquer the world thanks to a fleet of buses.

"After which as usual I dropped in again to my office. I showed Longspès the pair of one-franc vermilion before shutting them up in the safe. I telephoned Musard and M. Archer, to make my appointments for the following day: the two opposite ends of the journey during which Verdon was to disappear. Back at the rue Laffitte I resumed my anxious air for the benefit of Juliette. Strange to relate there mingled with it a real little fit of melancholy. She would grieve at my disappearance. I should miss her. For how many days? If I had a setback when should I see this fresh, innocent creature again? I kept her in my arms a little longer than usual. Pray forgive this moment of tender emotion; I was not to have another. Nothing *could* happen. That's an odd thing to say now. . . .

"That evening at the Villas Kléber Laeken still looked as gloomy as an undertaker. After dinner he took Gwen, as he did every week, to a local cinema. On his return he went back to his case. And 'The Passenger' typed his second missive, his pretty little riddle, addressed to M. Malebranche, in an unstamped envelope which Laeken, pleading a headache, went off to post in the Place Victor-Hugo. A delightful walk! It was a beautiful evening on Tuesday. The first day ended with the 'click' of the flap of a post-box.

"Am I taking too long?"

"No," said Belot, curtly.

"I knew I would interest you. Wednesday. Wednesday began with a disappointment. The papers alluded to the letter in the bus but without publishing the text nor the signature of 'The Passenger.' This did not suit me. It was essential now to give a splash to Verdon's kidnapping. I had already arranged my timetable but not the episodes of the ransom, my many earlier plans no longer held good. The new one only took shape a little later. First of all the last movements of the stamp dealer. Home to the rue Laffitte to ruffle the bed. Then to his office to pick up the vermilion pair and the Empire tête-bêche. The visit to Musard, the telephone call to the Café Marigny where I knew M. Archer could not yet have arrived. The conversation with my colleague about the U Line, using the same words as poor Tavernier just as the inexhaustible *Grand Journal* had published them: 'It's the U I want to take, and I shall take the U.'

"And I did not take the U . . . I took a taxi and was dropped near the Gobelins Garage. I had found the address the night before in the telephone directory and had thought to myself 'that may be useful.' I strolled casually past the gate. To anyone with eyes in his head, one glance was sufficient. The glass cabin, the petrol pumps, the washing place. . . . I thought: Why not there?

"It was only in another taxi on my way to the Villas Kléber that I fully realised my own kidnapping. 'Now you've disappeared, my friend!' Laeken returned to lunch with Gwendolyn. At two o'clock I wrote the tragic express letter from Verdon to Longspès and typed the long letter from 'The Passenger' to M. Rose. This time I wrote direct to a newspaper, to be sure of getting my publicity . . . and to *Le Grand Journal* out of gratitude. I wrote the letter straight off, like composing a song! There is no doubt that I was now fully caught up in the game. I posed unrealistic conditions and threatened to kill Verdon if they were not carried out. I did not make my future reappearance very simple, but I continued to have confidence in myself. I thought more than ever that I was not merely a plotter but an artist. I gave free rein to my inspiration. I remembered my rough drafts of the past three months which had ended in ashes. This time it was real and definite. War had been declared on my neighbour. . . . She must have heard on the other side of the wall the noise of the typewriter like the noise of a machinegun all unaware that these bullets were destined—after going round the world—for her. And to think that had I opened the door and handed her my paper, she would have called me her 'funny darling!' They were stupendous moments. I was to have some more stupendous ones an hour later. On the excuse of 'finishing my family tree' I went out at about three o'clock, arrived at the Gare Saint-Lazare, went to the washroom, and for the first time brought into the world one of my fine false beards—the dark one—and long live Barbason! This time I really was 'The Passenger,' 'The Passenger' whom no one yet knew but whom the whole world would know tomorrow! I sent the express letter to Longspès from the rue d'Amsterdam and without a tremor—although God knows I felt inclinded to laugh—I took my letter to *Le Grand Journal.*

"Then I returned to the Villas and did not stir again. Gwen and I played twelve games of draughts—a new variation which I had invented called 'Belgian draughts.' But the time dragged all the same. . . . But what an awakening on Thursday! I had slept as calmly as Napoleon before Wagram when the floor waiter entered with my breakfast on a tray and the papers as usual. He opened the shutters and commented on the weather as usual: 'It's raining, M. le Vicomte.' And I, refraining from opening *Le Grand Journal* on which my eyes were glued, replied: 'Thank you, Fernand,' as usual. And Fernand, upsetting the usual pattern added: 'You'd think there was a revolution in Paris, M. le Vicomte. Such a business with the buses, posters everywhere! That murderer the other day has kidnapped someone else! The streets are full of people!'

"Every word intoxicated me. And that front page, those enormous headlines, those photos! Naturally, mine, the one of Verdon at the Brussels Congress, gave me quite a turn, I had forgotten its existence; but it was hardly dangerous. And I saw you for the first time, my dear. Of course, also, the whole story revolved a little too much round Tavernier's murder. That was my fault, but I turned a deaf ear to any worry. I imagined the effect this issue would have on Gwen—and, without further ado, the sum I had foreseen jumped to 80,000 dollars!

"I had to act swiftly. Laeken must disappear the following night after the punishment of poor Verdon. After handing *Le Grand Journal* to Gwen I announced that I would stay in all day and finish the documents for my law suit. She was delighted, but also distressed: I didn't look at all well. . . . To make some noise I typed three columns of the *Nation Belge*. Then lying on my bed I imagined Paris and its millions of inhabitants, Paris, the capital of France, in an uproar thanks to me! It was the triumph of Rostand after *Cyrano*, of Lindbergh after the Atlantic!"

"Of Landru after his trial," said Belot.

"No, Inspector," retorted Verdon. "I was not a criminal. If I saw the colour of blood that day, it was my own. Don't interrupt!"

. . . and more dangerous, too

"I was sure that nothing would happen at the bus depot that evening since neither Longspès nor the Barbasons were in a position to scrape together the sum demanded. I could therefore prepare my next day's work and first of all kill Verdon. The razor slash in the fleshy part of my arm above the undershirt was authentic. Rather painful, but quite bearable: I've known worse at school! and I was to experience far worse later. I packed into a cardboard box the clothes, shirt, shoes, etc. that I was wearing on Wednesday, and added the little note about the 'spare parts.' Now all that remained was to deposit the lot in one of the telephone boxes at the Gare Saint-Lazare. I then pondered on the text of the express letter to Gwendolyn, deciding to give it the finishing touches the following day. With the disappearance of Laeken I was going to stick to the original plan: the Venus Agency, Le Havre, Gwen's discretion. I was now on my home ground. And yet it was it that was going to crack under my feet!

"At five o'clock I was in for a tremendous surprise. Gwen, back from some shopping for others brought in with her *Le Grand Journal Soir*, and what did it say? That my family had begged the police to call off the inquiry; that they would pay 500,000 francs to 'The Passenger.' That the Bus Company would lend their Gobelins Garage for this transaction! I was quite giddy with it all. How had Barbason got together these half million francs, despite his financial difficulties? By a bank loan? The sale of my business? And the police was giving up? How could they, just by being asked? Particularly when they suspected 'The Passenger' of being also a murderer. If this were true, I no longer felt protected.

"In any case I had to see for myself. By making Gwen go to bed early I had time to add to my prepared programme a little trip to the Gobelins. The last dinner. . . . After nine months, nearly a year. I wanted to give Gwen a last chance. Having told her that I had completed my case, I ordered a meal worthy of Lucullus. A vast meal which was vengeance in itself!

"Had she risen to her feet, had she said to me from her great height: 'This is not fair' I think I should—well, I don't know what I should have done, but I should have appreciated. . . . But no such thing, of course! So I put her to bed, gave her a little sleeping pill—just enough to take away any desire to leave her bed if she heard me walking about during the night. A kiss on the forehead—the last until Le Havre! It was too good to be true.

"About eleven o'clock a taxi took Laeken from the Étoile to the Châtelet, another took 'The Passenger,' wearing his black beard and beautiful beige gloves, from the Châtelet to the garage. All along the street posters of Le Grand Journal still gleaming after the rain. . . . And that fantastic question mark!

"And at the Gobelins, among the crowd, there was I, the initiator, the author, the maestro himself. I stayed there for three good hours during which the police could have arrested me as many times as they liked. I saw the reporters arrive, Barbason in his taxi, and the last U bus with its escort. I saw the truck that came with it turn round, the doors close and the police leave. I dreamed. . . . Yes, I dreamed again! Of going into the garage, stealing the envelope and keeping the promises in my letter to Le Grand Journal. What an exploit! Charge, Arsène Lupin! But one cannot charge against imaginary characters. Faced with the wall and the closed door I realised that 'The Passenger' still had a lot to learn and that he was a tyro in the profession. I consoled myself by thinking that the 500,000 francs would be easier to pay back if I did not touch them; that one must never be too greedy; that I had to stick to my Gwendolyn. The impromptu arrival of Longspès delighted me. After such a din 'The Passenger' could declare that a trap had been laid for him. Moreover, I now felt sure there was a trap and the next day's newspapers told me nothing I had not already guessed."

"Why?" asked Belot.

"Why? Perhaps simply so as not to despise myself too much for my helplessness! Perhaps out of consideration for you. . . .

"Nevertheless I lingered on, I heard you named, dear lady, and suddenly the night seemed a little cold. I knew nothing about you, but you had been very active since Monday. I confess that my departure caused me a slight emotion. Had I been followed, I should not have been surprised. There was, however, no reason for my qualms! None—except you. I was getting scared for nothing. The same as on the outward journey, I took two taxis on the way back. At three o'clock without incident I entered my bedroom at the Villas Kléber for the last time.

"I wrote my note to Gwendolyn. 'My dear, I am leaving you very early this morning. . . .'

"I tiptoed in and laid it near her dear old head. I rescued from her bag the photograph she had secretly and rather cheekily taken one day. She had refused to give it back to me and held on to it as tightly as to her dollars. I considered it unnecessary that she should take it to Boston. I put in a suitcase the typewriter, a few toilet articles, and the cover of the same suitcase. I carefully checked what I was leaving behind. I thought of fingerprints of course. But fingerprints, I decided, never interest anyone but the police, and the police will never come here. Another illusion! Then I waited, a trifle nervously I must admit, until the underground started again.

"It was a tricky business leaving the Old Ladies with a tan suitcase, beige gloves and the cardboard box. But fortune smiles on poets. In the ill-lit and deserted avenue, I put on my black beard. I preferred to by-pass the Étoile Station and to walk to the Place des Ternes. In the distance I could see Musard's closed shop. The suitcase and the gloves seemed to me terribly bright. But I wanted to lay a trail from which later I should have nothing to fear. The man whom the police were looking for so far, the murderer of Tavernier, was not me; the kidnapper of Verdon, of course, was me. But what detective, had he been out at that hour, would really believe him capable of going round in colours as striking as these? The detective would have to have been at the Gobelins three hours earlier in order to recognise the beard and the gloves. My inner voices assured me that I had nothing to fear and these inner voices have never let me down."

"Except . . ." began Belot.

"Except nothing. Had there been no fainting fit, of which no inner voice could warn anyone. . . ."

"Oh, yes, it could," said Mme Colet. "This fainting fit was the daughter of love!"

"Very pretty," said Verdon. "You always come back to the same subject and unfortunately you are always right. But the inner voices only spoke to me of the police. They did not forget that the criminal was still at large although hundreds of people had seen him in all his disguises; hadn't they, madame? I maintain that without the fainting fit the police would not be here—nor should I.

"Let me go on. In the call-box at the Gare Saint-Lazare I gave myself the great pleasure—pinching my nose as I did so—of telephoning to *Le Grand Journal*. I left the cardboard box. Chucking the black beard and the beige gloves down my faithful lavatory, I put on my fair beard and wig, glasses and grey gloves. I rejoiced at the same time: *What* a game! I put the grey cover on the suitcase and it and I were quite unrecognisable. Apparently a check is kept on the sale of firearms. A watch should be kept on false beards and suitcase covers. I sat down in a small *bistrot* nearby, got hold of a timetable and to kill time worked out all kinds of itineraries like a traveller who has arrived too early at the station. I wanted to get to the hotel at a normal hour and with no connection with the time I was in the call-box. Eight o'clock, for example. And at eight o'clock a taxi took me to the Hôtel de la République quite near the rue Thorel and the Venus Agency where my business was to take me that afternoon. I knew the hotel, for some of my foreign colleagues stayed there. You can use a typewriter there without drawing attention to yourself. I had just eaten a whole pot of jam and was about to write the express letter to Gwendolyn—the final touch to my structure, when there was a knock at my door. It was a page boy carrying a pile of copies of *Le Grand Journal*, the special edition, to be distributed to each room. A malicious young man. How quick the press is! The horror aroused by the supposed murder of Verdon bored me. True, it represented a tiresome continuation of the Tavernier murder but, firstly, I only wanted to think of Gwendolyn, and this special edition suited my book perfectly. Secondly, Verdon would certainly have to reappear one day; as, that day, the criminal of the Rond-Point would at last have been discovered—yes, he would!—'The Passenger' himself still at large, would be cleared of all suspicion. There was nothing to worry about.

"I therefore typed the express letter very calmly and posted it in the Avenue de la République. On my return I made an arrangement with one of the page boys—not the one who brought round the papers because he appeared to me too sly—another one, an innocent angel, and I arranged that he should call at the Venus Agency. This precaution seemed superfluous because Gwen would rather have cut her tongue out than talk, but after all, without extra cost it added to my enjoyment, and occupied my time. The hours to Le Havre were going to drag—all twenty-four of them! I altered my identity card. *Richard*, instead of *Maurice*. It would also have been better to replace V*erdon* by *Berdon*, but the V was more indelible than a hieroglyph. I reread the newspaper, combed my new blond locks a dozen times and practised my role for the following day in front of the mirror. 'You have bought me like a slave, you have, like a lapdog.' I lunched at the hotel. Then the ingenuous page boy and I went off to fetch the envelope from the rue Thorel without any difficulty. The envelope with Gwen's clear, touching writing! I had no need to open it. Safe in the left inside pocket of my jacket it rested against my notecase, which rested against the monocle, which rested against my heart. It was an indescribable moment!

"I was in the seventh heaven, in a silent delirium. After taking back my young companion I hid my elation in a local cinema. Don't ask me what I saw: the envelope, nothing else! Two or three hours more passed, I thought it would be a good idea to send a telegram to Gwen to soothe her, to confirm that her dear Guy would be at the rendezvous next day. I owed her that! I therefore emerged from the cinema at about five. They were selling the evening papers. And catastrophe was upon me."

A movement from Belot and Mme Colet expressed renewed interest in his audience.

"Yes," said Verdon, "I don't know whether it was my heart or the envelope which leaped in my breast. I had been betrayed: I had not for one moment allowed for a fainting fit. A frame of steel to faint! Gwen had talked, she had been able to talk! So nearly home —what a disaster! The police must already have gone from the Villas Kléber to the Venus Agency. There, thanks to my precaution, the trail petered out. But suppose someone had spotted the page boy or he himself had talked? Besides, what did the envelope contain? Blank paper like Barbason's? Everything seemed lost. No question of going to Le Havre. Gwen would take good care not to be there and I should be picked up at once. What was to be done? My wig and beard burned me. Where could I hide? I had always been too much of a lone wolf to take anyone into my confidence, especially now. There was only one way out: Verdon must reappear *at once*, and in circumstances in which his innocence could not be doubted. This meant of course admitting the guilt of Laeken and denouncing him as 'The Passenger'—but what did that matter provided no one could confuse him with Verdon? And no one would dream of this if Verdon returned to the world with the appearance of a real victim, and a victim *unrecognisable* to Gwendolyn.

"That is what I thought, and this is what I did. I played my last card. I convinced myself—once again—of the weakness of the police —if you will forgive me—I decided that they had not discovered the page boy nor in consequence the Hôtel de la République. I took the plunge and returned there. It only needed a few typed lines to put Verdon in the clear. And I had to open the envelope!

"The hotel was just as quiet as at my departure and the small page boy gave me a nice smile. I asked for my bill, pretending that I had met a friend who wanted me to stay with him. I went up to my room. The contents of the envelope showed I could have confidence in Gwen. But the danger was still as great. I typed the message: 'No further need for this idiot . . .' and believe me I typed it with conviction. I left at five-thirty, and drove to a large store, *la Samaritaine*. The suitcase and typewriter were left in the taxi. At six o'clock, just as the shop was closing, I came out still wearing my fair wig and moustache, but without beard or spectacles. I wandered aimlessly, choosing the busiest streets—the rue de Rivoli, the Châtelet, the Boulevard Saint-Michel, walking casually and wondering how I was going to reappear. I could see only one solution: to do myself an injury."

"What!" cried Mme Colet. "You yourself . . ."

She pointed a trembling finger to the bandage.

"I had to, madame. I had not dined and I was not hungry. The darkness and the crowd, became my allies and afforded me a last mask. I postponed the moment of my operation as long as possible because I had to think about the choice of a place. I remembered a sordid doss house in Montrouge which I had discovered last year, one boring evening on one of those numerous strolls following the death of my mother and which usually ended in an alien bedroom in the company of a woman of so-called pleasure. I remembered the place quite clearly—a lamp above a cul-de-sac, a stinking gutter and a bunch of tramps. What a wonderful setting for the last act! It was only logical that 'The Passenger' should empty his refuse in a dust bin.

"I will cut short this episode, I have a horror of violence. I chose a dark, deserted spot near the cemetery. I threw in my wig, and the contents of my pockets—including the signet ring. I ground my cherished monocle under my heel. I was glad that I had not been able to shave that morning and that I had not slept for forty-eight hours. As I slipped my clothes into the drain—a new suit and a good pair of shoes—I said a prayer to the subterranean gods: Let the current be strong so that all this flows swiftly down to the Seine, towards the sea, towards Le Havre! I was in underpants and socks . . ."

Verdon was breathing more heavily.

"I began by dirtying my hands on the pavement and running my dirty fingers over my body. I felt sorry for myself. My courage failed me. Then, at the moment I expected it least I gave myself a tremendous biff in the right eye. 'The Passenger' . . . 'The Passenger,' suddenly furious, did not leave me time to pity myself. A terrific blow on the chin and another on the nose and I felt the blood trickle down. . . ."

Mme Colet hid her eyes. "That's enough," she groaned.

"With head down I ran at the wall. . . ."

Belot sat up. "Quiet!" he shouted.

Verdon nodded, and in the humble tone in which he had started his story: "I will be quiet, Inspector, I will be quiet. Anyway, I have nothing else to say. . . ."

But Belot did not keep quiet.

"Where is the envelope?"

"Down the drain with the rest, alas!"

Belot jeered. "You don't say so! And the stamps—the vermilions and the tête-bêche?"

"In the safe with my collection of Belgians."

"Is that so! I thought you had described your days to us hour by hour? *And what about Tavernier?*"

"You're asking me that stupid question again, when I've told you everything and confessed everything."

"Everything it has *pleased* you to tell and to invent. You only engineered the Verdon affair to exonerate you from having had Tavernier killed. Tavernier is your obsession. In the tale you invented from one end to another at the Broussais Hospital, you could not help quoting him and talking about him. Why?"

"I was carried away, I swear it, madame," he said pleadingly to Mme Colet, "you believed me, didn't you? Explain to him."

She assumed her ingenuous little girl expression.

"No, monsieur, I did not believe you. Why do you imagine that every woman will believe you?"

"And yet you haven't asked me again where M. Colet is. Inspector, present me with your mysterious witness or with the Tavernier family. Confront me with this strange Paul Tavernier whom you praised yesterday. I insist upon this. I am defeated but I have no intention of paying more than I owe."

He flung back the bedclothes and appeared dressed in a lounge suit.

"I am ready, you see. I am strong enough to go with you, with a coat and slippers, in a taxi. . . ."

"The car's already there," said Belot, "you can lean on my arm."

Mme Colet offered hers, and Belot frowned. Verdon, who was now sitting on the edge of the bed, murmured: "Madame, you will never make me believe that if I were a murderer you would show me so much solicitude."

She replied with a smile: "You certainly know nothing about women, Monsieur Verdon."

He shook his head. "Not about the ugly ones, perhaps. But as for the others. . . . Come on let's go. . . ."

He half rose and clung on to the young woman's arm. Belot opened the door and stood aside to let them pass. They were in the little corridor which led to the hall, when suddenly, Verdon yelled: "Longspès!"

A door banged in front of them and was locked and bolted. At the same moment Verdon leapt back, jostled Belot and pulled the door of the bedroom to behind him and locked it. Belot and Mme Colet were plunged in darkness. An appalling din broke out as though the house was collapsing. Mme Colet clung to Belot. Then the din died down, changed to music, but was still terrifying in its volume: a Cossack Choir, thousands of Cossacks, singing at the tops of their voices.

"The radio," said Mme Colet. "They don't want us to be heard."

She drew away, as Belot flicked on his lighter. There was a third door which he tried in vain to open. Then he began to drum on the bedroom door. Verdon's voice rose above the din: "Don't get excited. I've one or two things to do and then I'll be back. Be patient!"

"What things?" whispered Mme Colet.

"And he'll be back?" Belot muttered sarcastically. "He won't get through the gate. Mind your eardrums!"

He blew his whistle furiously three times. It could not be heard above the Cossack Choir except by the prisoners and the neighbours. What neighbours?

"Swine!" said Belot.

He put his lighter on the ground and muttered to himself: "After all, we've only got to wait five minutes. Even without his bandage he'll be spotted at once. He's pretty badly knocked about."

Was it the effect of the air which flowed freely beneath the doors or the Cossack clamour? The flame of the lighter trembled and cast the shadows of the prisoners on the ceiling. Mme Colet murmured: "You don't really think he's the murderer?"

"No, of course not. But I don't like him any the better for that."

"I do."

"Tell me, where is M. Colet?" Belot asked surlily.

"I sent him off last night to a hotel near ours. I suppose he's asleep. I needed a really good reason for coming here. . . ."

The Cossacks thundered away: "Hoi Hoi Hoi!"

"And who sent you the threatening letter, as it wasn't 'The Passenger'?"

"I did, of course! How could I have helped you without it? You didn't want my help."

"Hoi! Hoi! Hoi!"

"Everyone's gone mad in this case," said Belot.

His eyes went from the lighter to the shadows and from one door to another. And he added: "Me, too."

15

The story of a tooth

On the previous night while Malicorne, fully dressed, had been sleeping like a log in the guest room on the third floor, Verdon had said to the two Longspès:

"My friends, I am afraid we must still be wary of the police. If I had counted on them I should be dead at this moment. And every time they meet with a setback they are capable of anything—even of confusing innocence with crime. I fear I cannot expect much from my talk with them today. I hope I'm wrong but we must take a few precautions. Tomorrow, when Inspector Belot returns, if all goes well, I will ask you for a glass of milk after a quarter of an hour, at the maximum twenty minutes. If not, listen to me. . . ."

As soon as he had given his instructions, the two Longspès examined the whole of the villa in a silent frenzy. They verified the chains and bolts on the front door, the locks of the inside doors and the latches of the shutters. At the end of the little corridor Longspès blocked the lavatory door. His sister carried a huge basket into Verdon's room, which was undoubtedly full and a green umbrella, which she hid in the cupboard. From the table laden with bandages and gauze she took several dressings and made three swabs, one about the size of an apricot, the two others the size of an enormous peach, almost as big as a fist. Verdon then grated a whole cake of yellow soap with which he filled a large chocolate box with a label saying: "Beneficiary unknown." He then studied the next day's radio programmes for each hour of the day, underlining in red those likely to be noisy. This was the tricky part of the plan: he would have preferred a record-player and a good record. But never mind. . . . Mlle Longspès, proud of her nurse's diploma, took off his bandages. He examined himself, shaved with some difficulty and pain, and then the bandage was put back. Finally, he fell asleep as soundly as Malicorne. The old spinster lay down without going to sleep. Longspès did not go to bed.

Malicorne was awakened by the arrival of Mme Colet. He went downstairs and found Mlle Longspès in the kitchen.

"Your coffee won't be a minute," she said.

She told him of M. Verdon's visitor and of the kidnapping of M. Colet. He was flabbergasted. He wondered if he had not better see this lady himself. But he was there to keep an eye on M. Verdon, that was all.

Mlle Longspès, having taken two cups and a pot of coffee to the sick man's room returned to prepare some bread and butter. Malicorne noticed her right cheek.

"Don't look at me," she said. "I'm certain it's an abscess. It's very painful. . . ."

They had a long conversation. She was really very amiable and he did honour to her breakfast. As he was finishing his fourth slice of bread and butter, the bell rang. They heard Longspès talking and then opening the door. It was Belot, who only stopped for a moment by the kitchen door.

"You can finish your coffee later," he said to Malicorne. "Sergeant Gaillardet came with me. He's in the garden and wants to talk to you."

Malicorne went out, and Belot went into Verdon's room. The Longspès exchanged glances, which betrayed as much excitement as anxiety. Five minutes later the sister appeared on the top of the steps. She saw Gaillardet talking and Malicorne listening open-mouthed. "Your coffee's getting cold, M. Malicorne!" she cried.

"Go on!" said Gaillardet under his breath. "You can come back afterwards. I'm sure she doesn't suspect anything, nor the old man. They mustn't get suspicious."

"And what about you, monsieur?" she asked. "Would you like a coffee or a little nip of something?"

"No, thank you, madame. I'd rather smoke a pipe in your pretty garden."

Malicorne returned without pleasure to the remains of his bread and butter. He was an excellent public servant who was not frightened of a rough-house, but he was nonplused by any subtlety. Mlle Longspès held her cheek; her abscess had grown considerably worse. She said:

"Have you noticed how nervy my brother is, M. Malicorne? With all these comings and goings! He's pacing up and down the drawing-room like an animal in a cage. If I can't calm him down, do you think I could switch on the radio without it disturbing the lady and gentleman? Music always calms him, particularly marches or something like that. He should have been an officer. Oh, I'll wait as long as I can because this abscess has given me a terrible headache. . . . And look at my face, I look frightful. . . ."

Malicorne thought that there was everything to be gained by pacifying Longspès. He gave his approval of marches, sympathised with the abscess and went out again. This is why after an hour's walking round the silent house with its closed shutters—a silence which made them think that Belot's theory had collapsed (could be, said Gaillardet, thanks to Mme Colet's revelations), the two inspectors were not surprised to hear the blaring radio. Malicorne merely said: "They get a bit hard of hearing at their age."

"It's because people have grown accustomed to it," replied Gaillardet. "Hearing is like drink and like everything else: the more you take the bigger the dose you need." And he added: "We're wasting our time."

They made three more turns round the house in silence, impressed in spite of themselves by the strength of the Cossack voices so admirable at that distance.

"After a 'Hoi, Hoi' which announced the end of the chorus, the radio suddenly blared out a *Sambre et Meuse*. They had reached the end of the garden when they saw the shutters of the French windows open. Mlle Longspès appeared wearing a hat and looking very distinguished in a black satin costume, with a big basket on her arm. She turned back to the room she had just left probably to speak to someone, closed the door carefully, then the shutters and walked down the steps. She was wearing a little veil. On catching sight of the inspectors in the distance, she lifted it with a gloved hand, allowing a glimpse of her swollen cheek and, with a comical gesture, mimed an extraction. Then she pointed to the house and to her ears, shaking her head like a person who had been driven mad by the noise. This hasty movement must have given her a stab of pain, for she suddenly broke it off and put her hand up to her cheek again. And she went off.

"Coquetry!" said Malicorne. "She wants to hide her poor face."

"Apparently veils are coming into fashion again," said Gaillardet. "My wife, Hortense, wore one yesterday for me, with flowers on it . . . !"

Mlle Longspès had skirted the house and gone out of the gate. She glanced at a car which was parked on the left in the direction of Bellevue Station. She herself turned smartly to the right in the direction of Meudon. When she reached the market, she saw a taxi dropping its passengers. With a groan she ordered the driver "Boulevard des Capucines, the Opera Dental Clinic. And quickly, please!"

Through the black net the chauffeur saw a huge swollen cheek in a white powdered face.

"Get in, you poor soul. I'd rather be in my shoes than in yours!"

Thanks to the zeal of this kind fellow and a Paris deserted at this time on a Sunday morning, the journey was made in record time. On the Boulevard des Capucines in the entrance of the building, which was full of offices, she scanned a huge blue and white board which said: "Second and Third floors. OPERA DENTAL CLINIC. Open weekdays 9-12.00 and 2-7. Closed on Sundays." She went upstairs.

She had been gone from Bellevue for ten minutes, the *Ride of the Valkyries* had replaced the *Sambre et Meuse*, when finally, thanks to a lull in the music, the sound of a whistle penetrated the walls of the villa. Malicorne and Gaillardet rushed to the front door, rang and knocked. No reply. Leaving his colleague, Gaillardet ran as fast as his legs would carry him to the other side of the villa; he remembered the shutter of the French window which the old spinster had pushed back before leaving. But behind the shutter he came up against a door which was also locked. Now, although still in full swing, the Valkyries could no longer prevent him from hearing or perhaps imagining other whistle blasts. He broke a pane of glass, slipped his hand inside, reached the casement bolt and the lock, but could find no key. Then he blew his own whistle and hurled himself against the French windows where the two panels met. They gave way under his weight and he fell on to an empty bed. Aroused by his calls, two of the three detectives whom Belot had sent at five o'clock that morning to watch the villa, suddenly appeared, panting. (The third had joined forces with Malicorne.) While he picked himself up from the bed they leapt to the corridor door and rattled it. A voice, the voice of their chief shouted: "Have you got him?"

"Who?"

"You mean to say you haven't got him! For God's sake, open up!"

Once more there was no key. Gaillardet took out his revolver and smashed the lock with the butt. Belot and Mme Colet appeared out of the darkness.

"Did you let him escape?" roared Belot.

"Of course not," replied Gaillardet. "Only the old girl left from here!"

"*From here?*"

Belot ran to the cupboard. It was empty. On the bed, dressings, a pair of pyjamas and a suit of clothes. . . .

"Get going!" he shouted in his exasperation. "There's another door to bash in down the corridor. Find me those two old fools! You say the old girl left from here? But there was only Verdon here."

Gaillardet swore and realised in a flash how Verdon had managed to escape. Mme Colet had sat down, white with emotion, dazzled by the daylight.

"Circulate his description at once," ordered Belot.

He rushed out to join the two inspectors, sending one of them into the bedroom to guard the French window. The other opened the door for Malicorne and their comrade. There was no one in the kitchen. . . . But in the drawing-room, on his knees in front of the wireless studying the programmes—Longspès.

"Arrest him!" said Belot. He pointed to the radio: "And turn that off! Where's your sister?"

A gleam came into Longspès' eyes. "You smash up my property and expect me to answer your questions!"

Belot and Malicorne climbed up to the first floor. Wrapped in a blanket Mlle Longspès was nursing her cheek.

"What is the matter?" she groaned.

"The matter is that you've helped Verdon to escape."

Protesting loudly she was dragged unceremoniously from her bed and taken downstairs. Everyone except an inspector left on the steps was now collected in the fugitive's room. At the sight of the gaping doors and her brother in handcuffs, Mlle Longspès burst into tears. Malicorne went over to her. Belot examined the cupboard once more.

"Verdon could not have found any women's clothes here. There were no dresses in it when I hid there yesterday."

"I took them last night from my sister's room," Longspès said proudly. "I arranged everything. . . ."

"And what about this?" asked Belot, waving a green umbrella.

"It could have rained today."

"And I suppose it was you who turned on the radio after locking the hall door?"

"Of course it was me. My sister had put it on quite low some time before and she had gone upstairs to lie down. I had only to hop over to the instrument and turn the knob. I suppose you're surprised that innocent people should defend themselves? M. Verdon has everything he needs with him. You won't get him!"

"Everything?" echoed Belot. "What did he take in the way of luggage, Malicorne?"

Gaillardet had just reappeared and it was he who answered: "A big black basket."

"There must be a suit in it. What colour was it, Longspès?"

The old man refused to reply. The inspector in charge of the old maniac raised his hand.

"Don't you touch him," screamed his sister. "Brown, dark brown! My brother asked me last night to shorten the trousers and the sleeves, I didn't know why."

"Go back and telephone," Belot ordered Gaillardet. "He won't stay dressed as a woman, it's too risky. A brown suit, the right eye bunged up and they'll find the details of his scars in the file. Notify Montrouge. The money must be planted there, perhaps in Cercu's mattress. A fortune among the poverty-stricken! That's typical of him. He'll try to recover it, so hurry up. You, take Longspès! As for you, mademoiselle, I'm not arresting you, but it's the same thing, you're not to stir from here. You will remain, Malicorne. I'll send a doctor to see to your abscess: I'm interested in your abscess. . . . Well, that was exciting for you, Madame Colet. Let's go!"

A minute later as Malicorne was opening up the third door in the corridor, Mlle Longspès was left alone in the bedroom in a state of collapse. Yes, M. Verdon had foreseen everything last night even down to the arrest of Octave (he had said: "It won't be serious, he is a man of his word"). But he had not foreseen that the abscess would "interest" the police! The doctor would have her arrested. If M. Verdon still needed her help he would find no one at the villa. So despaired the old woman whose imagination was no match for her heroism. In such circumstances Verdon would have given himself a real abscess! But if he had temporarily become *her*, she had not become him. She wept as she chewed the compresses which padded her cheek. All I can do, she thought, is to throw them away and put on some iodine. Perhaps the doctor won't be here for some time and perhaps the iodine will have had time to cure me. Besides, I haven't got such a fine set of teeth as all that!"

"Monsieur Malicorne, can I put some iodine on my abscess?"

Malicorne in a rage was still struggling with the door. He replied automatically: "It's the best thing to do."

In Paris meanwhile, on the Boulevard des Capucines, a miracle took place. A lady dressed in black satin, suffering from an enormous abscess had only to go up to one of the floors of the Opera Dental Clinic to come down again ten minutes later completely cured and dressed in a brown coat and skirt. A toque had replaced the hat and a bag the basket. A small fur covered her neck and chin. All that remained was the little black veil—Mlle Longspès only possessed the one—and behind the veil an eye still closed and the other blinking a great deal as Miss Abbott's used to do. . . . Wonderful that the costumes and shoes were the right size. And for the scars and bruises which were now turning a yellowish brown, layers of powder on a foundation of vaseline. The use of beauty creams was a closed book to Mlle Longspès, which was a pity.

The black satin dress with the hat and the basket were left outside the door of the Dental Clinic. As soon as the police learned that they had been abandoned, they would deduce that "The Passenger" had changed them there for a brown suit—but for the man's suit indicated by Longspès and not a woman's costume. Perfect!

And now for the dollars.

A taxi . . . "Hôtel de la République!"

"I should like to book a room for my son. He is arriving the day after tomorrow and I can't put him up at home. I have sent his bedding to the cleaners as I did not think he would be returning so soon. Could I see the room? As high up as possible (the fair-haired man had lived on the second floor), my son arrives from the mountains and needs fresh air. On the fifth floor, you say? Couldn't be better."

Accompanied by the head reception clerk, the mother approved the room and the view. When it was time to go down again to the ground floor she categorically refused to take the elevator.

"I should reach the bottom with my stomach in my mouth."

The stairs, therefore. As they left the landing of the second floor she missed the step, called out and fell. Her bag opened scattering on the lower steps a big box of sweets, a bunch of keys, a powder case and some small change. The reception clerk wanted to go to the aid of the clumsy woman. She thanked him, but preferred to sit there getting her breath back for a moment and rubbing her ankle. He picked up the various objects. By the time he had finished she was already on her feet and laughing at herself. Down in the hall she gave him the name of her son. "M. Jean Lompé. L-o-m-p-é. See you the day after tomorrow then!"

Taxi. She passed from her sleeve into the bag eight 10,000-dollar notes and a few stamps which, without wrapping or envelope, had been sitting for the last two days under the stair carpet of the third step down of the second storey.

"You didn't give me the address, madame," said the driver.

"Didn't I? How absent-minded I am! Boulevard Gouvion-Saint-Cyr."

And now to salvage honour!

But on reaching the Boulevard Gouvion-Saint-Cyr, the lady contented herself with entering a small café and asking for the telephone.

"Hello, is that M. Paul Tavernier's residence? Can I speak to him? Speaking? Madame Pélon here. . . . Pé-lon. You don't know me, monsieur. I should like to see you urgently . . . its about your unfortunate brother. . . . *Very* confidential. . . . Come to you? Very well. Which floor? *Very* confidential you understand. In a quarter of an hour."

A few steps towards the building where poor Étienne had lived. Almost at the door another taxi. "Quai d'Orsay, the corner of the rue Malar."

"Here we are!" The lady paid the fare and disappeared into the house. Hardly had she crossed the threshold than she experienced a need to adjust her stocking and with bent head watched the taxi. A rather heavy man with a good honest face had gone up to it.

"Police," he said to the driver, "where did you pick up that fare?"

"Boulevard Gouvion-Saint-Cyr."

"Ah! No stops on the way?"

"None."

"Thank you. You can go."

"Anything serious?" asked the driver.

"Not at all!"

The taxi drove off. Sergeant Vilain took down the number and returned to the quai. It was just a visitor for his client. From the Boulevard Gouvion-Saint-Cyr: a relation or a friend.

The "friend" had heard nothing. But everything having gone as she had foreseen, she took the elevator with a light heart.

16

The murdered man

M. Paul Tavernier opened the door. Between the toque and the scarf, behind the veil, he could make out a single black eye in a clown's face. He frowned. He himself had the appearance of a suspicious old man, gloomy and foreboding as a raven.

"M. Paul Tavernier?" asked the lady nervously. She entered rapidly as though she were being pursued. "I'm Mme Pélon. There's a nasty looking man wandering about the quay in front of the building."

"Will you come into my study, madame?"

"I don't think so, monsieur," she said without moving. "Really not. . . . You should have warned me and we could have met somewhere else. Just imagine, he spoke to my taxi driver. Such cheek. He must be one of 'The Passenger's' spies."

"He is in fact a spy," Paul Tavernier smiled. "But from the police. You probably don't know that in this case I'm being treated like a suspect."

"By the police?" exclaimed Mme Pélon.

She entered the study. Pretending not to see the chair he offered her she went on: "I'm not frightened of the police, although I prefer to remain unknown to them as to everyone else. It is the others who terrify me."

"What others?"

"The others. . . ." she replied evasively. "I know too much, monsieur! And I know the risk I run in divulging it. Are we really alone?"

Her nervousness seemed to increase.

"My wife has gone to mass," said Paul Tavernier, more weary than polite. "I am supposed to join her at my poor sister-in-law's for lunch. Our servants have the day off on Sunday."

The lady raised a gloved hand to her breast.

"I have a bad heart, you know. I can't talk to you about your poor brother until I've got rid of my palpitations. I know the man who killed him."

" 'The Passenger'?" said Paul Tavernier sceptically.

"No. No!"

She tripped over to him raised herself on her toes and whispered into his ear: "Devaux-Oudart."

He gave a start. She added at once:

"Unless you can prove to me that the flat is empty, I'm going to leave. I'm too frightened!"

"Come and see for yourself," he said abruptly.

They visited every room. The lady with the bad heart insisted that all the doors should be left wide open—even cupboard doors. Her agitation by no means abated during this investigation. Paul Tavernier, however, followed her instructions as best he could and tried to hurry her back to the study.

When at last they returned she pulled out the box of sweets from her bag and made as though to offer them—Paul Tavernier received the soap powder which filled the box full in his face. He gave a cry and bumped into the table. He felt himself seized by the feet, flung on the ground and then on to his belly. With a shamelessness which fortunately the blinded man could not see, the lady lifted her skirts up to her midriff, undid two cords which she wore as a belt, tied his ankles, turned the man over on his back and secured his wrists. A large handkerchief served as a gag. The work was carried out with disconcerting ease. After the first and only cry, Paul Tavernier repressed his groans and refrained from calling for help: he almost seemed to welcome being tied up. The lady ran into the pantry, moistened a rag and wiped her victim's eyes.

"There, there," she said, as though consoling a child. "It might have been pepper, you know."

She lifted up her veil, sank down on a chair and sighed: "What a day . . . !"

When Paul Tavernier was able to unstick his eyelids he could make out through the painful mist a really incredible sight: a jovial one-eyed clown's face, a female form sitting in an armchair with legs crossed up to the lace on her knickers. He raised himself to catch sight of his wrists and fell back.

"Mmm! Mmm!" he said, beneath the gag.

The ghastly woman replied: "Yes?"

She untied the handkerchief and used it to wipe away the foam which still ran from his staring eyes. Paul Tavernier panted, then roared: "That's fine police behaviour, I must say. Inspectors disguised as toughs."

"Watch your tongue," replied Verdon, in a dignified voice. "And respect my sex. As for the police—" he sat down again, modestly adjusted his dress, took a cigarette from the table and lit it, and recovered his ordinary voice. "I don't know yet what they want here, but I certainly was not put in charge of their inquiry. I give you my word of honour!"

"What do you want, then?" shouted Tavernier. "Money?"

"Hmm! That's an idea. The banks are shut on Sunday and I'm planning a little trip very soon. . . . What's the dollar rate? Twenty-five? I have some dollars that I must change. How much have you got here?"

"I'm beginning to understand," muttered Paul Tavernier contemptuously but alert. "If I told you that I had twenty thousand francs. . . ."

"They would do for preliminary expenses."

"And why should I give them to you?"

Verdon stood up.

"Because I am a friend perhaps. Where are they?"

Tavernier did not reply. Verdon searched him, took out his wallet and extracted some notes, saying: "You're right. It's always more prudent to carry them on you. One, two, three, four . . . nineteen. Please note that it's only a loan, which I'm going to pay you back on the spot. Here is a magnificent Empire tête-bêche, the eighty centimes rose, worth fifteen thousand. With the interest we are quits. I am not a thief!"

He replaced the wallet in the pocket from which he had taken it.

"A thief, *madame*?" stressed Tavernier.

Verdon ignored the remark. "Nor a murderer. Let's get down to

314

the facts. You must have heard of me. Man or woman, I am 'The Passenger.'"

The bloodshot eyes opened wider.

"The 'Passenger' on the U," added Verdon, more explicitly, "who is accused of having murdered your brother but who denies it."

Paul Tavernier averted his head.

"That's not my affair."

"Oh, yes, it is. I had a vague idea it was, but now I'm sure. That the police placed a detective outside your door is already a black mark, for I don't think the police are half bad. But that you submitted so passively to my attack, *that you tolerated our conversation.* . . . Come, monsieur . . . !"

Paul Tavernier replied in a tone of despair: "There's been enough scandal as it is. . . ."

"I'm beginning to guess its nature. For *you* did not believe *for one second* that I could be your brother's murderer. And yet this suspicion would have been quite natural on your part. But it is because *you*, you know *who* the murderer is. Better still, for he might have disguised himself and surprised you, you know *where* he is. You know that he *cannot* be here. Yes, this crime of which you have been either the organiser or the accomplice is also a scandal. Do you understand my interest now?"

"Me the organiser or the accomplice?" replied Tavernier angrily. "You don't know what you're saying. You don't know what we are!" He closed his eyes and added: "And you will know nothing."

Verdon put out his cigarette.

"You are making me late, monsieur, and that doesn't suit me. Listen: I shall leave very soon and with the information I want."

He took off his gloves, seized the nose of the prostrate man and twisted it. Paul Tavernier screamed: "Let me go!" and spat in his face. Verdon, taken aback, let his veil fall.

"Disgusting! I see that child's play will not be enough."

He glanced round the austere and solemn furniture in the study. His eyes came to rest on a bronze clock in the shape of a pensive woman in Greek drapery. With a scowl on his face, Paul Tavernier watched his monstrous enemy. He saw him hop over to the fireplace and pick up the clock with a good deal of effort. In spite of himself he said: "What are you going to do?"

The clock was placed on his chest and crushed him. He opened his mouth to try and get a little air: the ornament weighed too heavily. His face started to turn purple. Verdon had sat down again.

"In the fifteenth century," he said, "there were fourteen ways of applying torture. They did not know this one. It is too harmless, and we are only just starting. Are there any eggs in the pantry? How do you like them? Two or three minutes? Red hot under the armpits, you will see, it's unexpected. But as an added distraction we will go on to tickling the soles of . . ."

Paul Tavernier, who was suffocating, whispered: "It's ridiculous."

"Everything in life is ridiculous. There is only one serious matter and that is death. The death of your brother, for example. Or mine—which I shall not allow you or anyone else to advance by one hour. Four kettles, in other words nine litres for the water torture! Double, when someone important was being questioned. Very simple material: only a funnel and a jug were required. I suppose you've got a little funnel in the house? And candles attached to the feet, with the toes burning down slowly with the wax. After the *hors d'oeuvres* of the clock, would you like us to draw lots for the entrée?"

"I can't bear any more," Paul Tavernier whispered.

Covered with soap and sweat, foaming at the mouth, his eyes starting out of his head, his face looked as horrible as Verdon's. The Greek woman was placed a little further off. But as though she had left her weight behind on him he continued for some minutes like a dying man to gasp for air. Verdon raised his veil once more and lit a cigar. Two long groans told him that Tavernier had recovered his breath.

"We must hurry," he said.

"Will you untie me?" asked Paul Tavernier in a hoarse voice.

"Of course not."

"A glass of water. . . ."

"No."

Paul Tavernier shook his head as though fighting a nightmare. He licked his lips.

"I'm not frightened of your threats. . . . But I see that I won't get away with it, that it was all in vain!"

"What?" said Verdon.

316

"Everything. Everything that I tried to do for months to free my brother, and which turned out so badly. All that I planned during this appalling week so that his death should only be a tragedy and not a scandal! It's all over."

"Not for me. I know two things: firstly, that you are a suspect and secondly that your brother was shot by a man called Devaux-Oudart. *I must know the rest.*"

Thanks to his rage Paul Tavernier recovered his strength.

"How I hate you," he said, "for if you really are 'The Passenger' it is you who have made everything impossible. It is you who have turned our misfortune to infamy, stain, and downfall. Hadn't we paid enough already?"

"Paid?" repeated Verdon. "Who has paid? Who: We? I warn you that the clock. . . ."

Paul Tavernier ignored the threat.

"You wouldn't understand anything about honour. *We* come from a line of honest, just men of integrity."

Verdon burst out laughing.

"So your brother had 'let down' the 'honour' of the family and you protect his murderer who has 'avenged' that honour."

"Devaux? That unspeakable blackguard who blackmailed him for five years? Whom I should have strangled with my own hands had it . . ."

Verdon completed the sentence for him: "Had it been easier to make a corpse disappear than a living man."

Paul Tavernier slayed him with a look.

"You've had some experience with your stamp dealers!"

Verdon, taken off his guard for a moment, looked sheepish.

"There are cases. . . . Listen, Monsieur Tavernier, I have neither the time nor the wish to explain myself to you. Let us just remember that I am suspected of a crime and so are you. Let us work together."

"What!" cried Paul Tavernier in disgust.

"Oh, but you're beginning to make me sick! You have insinuated that without me you could still save everything. Which means in plain language: you could get rid of Devaux. All right, let's get rid of him. In this way you will avoid your famous scandal and I shall have extorted from him the proof that his crime has nothing to do with me."

"You don't know what he's like," said Tavernier. "He's been drunk, dead drunk, since Monday."

"One can always sober people up," replied Verdon, in a dangerously gentle voice. "But *first* I want to hear your explanations."

"It's five years now that with the connivance of his sister he'd been plucking my brother and his family. She had a child and they made him believe it was his. A girl devoid of any moral sense. But they chose the weakest and the richest!" Paul Tavernier looked once more at the equivocal creature sitting there listening to him and smoking a cigar, while he lay on his own carpet with his feet and wrists tied.

"To what depths have I sunk," he grumbled, "that I prefer to talk to you rather than to the police. . . . Well, let me tell you," he went on violently, "you who are only a rogue, an outlaw, everything I despise most in the world, let me tell you what crushes my breast more than your stupid torturer's invention! How I discovered one day when going to call for him at his office that my brother wasn't there, that he lied to his wife, to his family, *to me*. How I followed him next day and discovered the house of this woman. . . ."

"Rue du . . ."

Verdon bit his lip. But carried away by his rage which now found an outlet—and possibly by an incredible hope—Paul Tavernier mistook the interruption for a question.

"Rue du Ranelagh. A house which he paid for and where for years he kept her and 'their' son. I went to see her and she dared to talk to me of the boy. She had the audacity to pretend that he resembled *us*. Étienne had 'taken advantage' of her when she was a young girl and he was a soldier. To 'take advantage' of a whore, who was years older than himself! She accused her brother of having 'sold' her, a brother from whom she had run away, going so far as to change her identity. She made a mockery of virtue and love. Yes, of love. I ought to have hauled her before the courts. But I did not have the right—I, the head of the family, who was responsible for the honour of the dead and the living, I, my father's son, my brother's guardian and responsible to my unfortunate sister-in-law since I had married them, encouraged them and supported them. No, I had no right, I repeat, I had no right. So I spoke to Étienne. He revealed the existence of his former

318

comrade—only to give me more lies, by assuring me that he was an honest man, an unlucky creature, a 'poor chap.' How he must have been terrorised . . . ! He told him, and this rascally creature had the impertinence to come and see me. He introduced himself as a brave almost heroic member of the unemployed, burdened by a sister suffering from paranoia, a madness which dated back to her 'adventure' with Étienne, to her 'maternity' and to her being forced to be a 'woman of twilight.' He stank of drink. These were the people into whose hands my brother had fallen. . . . The newspapers are full of stories of blackmailers, bigamists, of fortunes honestly acquired and sucked and bled to death by these vampires, well, we the Taverniers, were to live one of them—we had already been living one without being aware of it, for more than four years. I should have guessed it from Étienne's depression and his increasing avarice. I don't know, I never understood his character, it was so different from ours; he was so reserved, so introverted. He loved only one person in the world: his wife. . . . It was out of his adoration for her, as he explained in full in his will, that he bore his double existence or else he would have killed himself. . . . He, kill himself! He would have married his strumpet. We should have had a gangster for a brother-in-law and a regimental by-blow for a nephew. After all, I don't know—may he rest in peace—" Paul Tavernier ground his teeth—"may he rest in peace."

"Yes, yes," said Verdon paternally, "you couldn't throw Devaux out of the house. You had to play for time. . . ."

The tall, tense body relaxed, without seeming to realise from whose lips this approval had fallen.

"Yes, play for time. . . . To settle this affair on my own. I gave Étienne to understand that I did not consider Devaux too odious and that I wanted to help in his salvation. And so at last he took me into his confidence a little more each day, and what didn't I learn! Not only whisky, but racing, an attempt at burglary and constant demands for money. Devaux met him in the strangest places, appearing like an evil spirit, threatening to tell everything to my sister-in-law, and haunting the Boulevard Gouvion-Saint-Cyr. One day he even went into Gascogne Motors and discussed the price of a car under Étienne's very nose. And my idiotic brother told me all this because I had said I was ready to save Devaux. It was unbelievable!"

Paul Tavernier shook again with anger. His voice suddenly was dry, concentrated and categorical.

"I carried out my inquiries, I collected all the useful information I could on the Devaux. At a later date I saw them separately—the girl and the blackguard. I persuaded them that Étienne had changed and I got them rattled. My plan was very simple: to exploit the differences of the brother and the sister, to pursue them *in Étienne's name*, to give them the feeling that they were lost, destined to go to jail, and that I was their only hope; to send them abroad."

He breathed deeply and calmly.

"Étienne left on a business trip. I immediately wrote a letter to the woman signed by him, with the promise of an allowance on condition that she left France with her son without delay. I added a postscript: 'I have asked my brother, Paul, to inform you of my decision.' I took the letter myself . . . and the money in the other hand. The creature was only too delighted to get out of things so cheaply. They left a week later for Spain, where I was able to keep them under observation. I dictated her reply to her. From that quarter there was no more to be feared!"

Paul Tavernier fell silent for a moment, and his hatred flashed in his eyes. "I sent another letter to Devaux, also signed by Étienne. I know it by heart." He recited it like a terrible ultimatum.

"This is enough! Marie and I have cleared up our position and we are definitely agreed. You have received a fortune from me. You have enough to live on. Unless you leave Paris and France immediately I will denounce your burglary and your blackmail about the boy's paternity. I have all the witnesses I need. I am taking with me a complete copy of your record to be deposited in England. My lawyer has the original. You will see from these resolutions that my family, including my brother, Paul, now know the truth of the matter and that any attempt at blackmailing them will only be a further proof against you."

He came rushing to my office. I had foreseen this. He showed me the letter. He stank of alcohol, but he carried his drink in a way I would never have believed possible. He played the innocent. His astonishment was certainly not put on! Such a letter. . . . I added the last straw to his dismay by describing a new, ruthless Étienne. Naturally he hadn't a penny, so I offered him some money so that he could leave. He almost burst into tears. He accepted and agreed to everything. I dictated his reply too. . . ."

Paul Tavernier's voice broke.

"Why didn't I realise that this wretch would go and gamble immediately? . . . Étienne returned. I gave him the two agreements. He was so happy, as happy as a child; I was ashamed of him. But perhaps he was only a child after all—a child you could get nothing out of. A weak child. . . . I don't know.

"All this happened last Sunday. Just a week ago."

Tavernier glanced at the clock which was still at his side. "At this very hour."

17

In which two halves joined
fail lamentably to make a whole

"And the following day," said Verdon, "Devaux killed your brother. He had laid in wait for him and followed him into the bus. He went and sat beside him. 'A very good day to you, M. Tavernier!' I can hear the dialogue—or rather the monologue, for your brother must have kept silent, entrenching himself in his delight of the previous evening and clinging to the stand you had taken for him."

"That's quite possible," murmured Paul Tavernier with indifference.

He made no effort to picture the last moments of his unfortunate brother's life, because he was reliving his own moments as Head of the Family, the dispenser of justice, the victor still unaware of disaster. He raised his bound hands to his mouth, bit at the cord and then in a lifeless tone began the final story.

"I was in my office. I heard 'his' voice on the telephone. A voice I did not recognise immediately, a voice . . . It said: 'I've just done something stupid. I must speak to you.' I replied: 'What, you haven't gone?' 'I'm going, yes, I am going, but you don't understand. I'm in a terrible situation. Come, quickly!' He was telephoning from a café in the rue de Valois. I was afraid. I thought that he had committed a robbery. I took my car. He was walking up and down the pavement with his overcoat collar turned up. I picked him up and as we drove he told me everything.

"I didn't believe him. . . . Even though he was waving a revolver! But he smelt so strongly of drink, and looked so dazed, that I didn't believe him. Putting things at their worst I thought he might have fired at Étienne, that he might have wounded him, that Étienne might have fallen for a moment! He was weeping as only drunkards weep and kept repeating: 'I am a murderer. They will send me to the guillotine!' I couldn't silence him. I had to see Étienne as quickly as possible but first of all I had to lock up this madman, this snivelling fool to prevent him from talking or causing a scandal. . . . I brought him here. . . ."

"I don't believe it!" Verdon was incredulous.

"I brought him here," repeated Paul Tavernier in his lifeless voice. "On my keyring I had the key to one of our cellars"—a ghost of a smile appeared on his lips—"the cellar where we keep the best vintages. I bought a case of champagne and made Devaux carry it as we entered by the back door. In any case the porter was busy at the other side of his lodge which looks out on the main staircase. He's there. He is still there."

Verdon leapt to his feet.

"Dead drunk. On returning from my office at midday I took him food, all this last week, . . . and the newspapers. I tortured him too, tortured him with questions. For what had 'The Passenger' and the U Line to do with this nightmare? I was the only one to know. . . ."

"Apart from me," said Verdon.

". . . that it was impossible! He answered that he couldn't understand any of it. For a long time now he hasn't answered at all. He drinks, sleeps, and shakes with fright. He has broken fifty bottles! I can't understand why no one has heard him. . . ."

His voice became almost inaudible.

"Later I rushed to the Motor Show, to the Gascogne stand and to the Boulevard Gouvion-Saint-Cyr. I burnt Étienne's will. I burnt letters. . . . This crime had to appear to be the inexplicable act of a madman. The only thing I forgot was a wretched photo in an album. . . . How could I imagine that my brother preserved a memento of his executioner, even in that form!"

"You certainly forgot other things," said Verdon, "believe me!"

"So long as they haven't found *him*. . . ." replied Paul Tavernier.

"All right, let's get going. On your feet!"

Verdon knelt down, untied the cord which bound the man's legs and tied it round his own waist again. Paul Tavernier got up as best he could. His teeth were chattering.

"You're not going to make me go down like this?" he said, holding out his hands.

Verdon caught sight of a little leather briefcase which he opened and placed across his wrists, adding: "No jokes, now!"

Tavernier shrugged his shoulders. In a tone which held hatred, exhaustion and distress he said: "Jokes! You forget that you are now my only hope. You, 'The Passenger on the U.'"

A broken old man and a woman wearing a veil made their way down the back stairs. They met no one. The clean, well-lit corridor of a luxury basement, the doors of the freight elevator, red doors marked with a black number. The place looked like a model prison.

Paul Tavernier stopped outside door No. 12.

"My keys are in my right hand pocket."

His head leaning against a crate of bottles, his eyes half closed and mouth wide open, lying full length with arms and legs outstretched like a corpse, Devaux snored and doubtless dreamed because he was groaning. The stench was beyond description. Empty bottles broken off at the neck, thousands of pieces of paper—the newspapers which in his terror he had torn up and reduced to shreds —his shoes hanging on a nail, the remains of food, rubbish of all kinds, a dirty blanket, made a perfect setting for the story hero of the Rond-Point. His collar was undone and the knot of his tie on his chest. On his jacket lapel the grasshopper shone like a monstrous scavenger perched motionless on carrion.

"Well," said Verdon. "Here we are, face to face. The criminal and 'The Passenger.' The two halves of a mystery and a mystery to each other. And how degraded that half is lying there!"

In a corner, the hat was tattered with broken glass. Obviously the drunkard had tried to destroy it. Verdon lifted up the strips of felt. The revolver was under them.

Paul Tavernier watched the diabolical creature hopping from one corner to the other, examining everything.

"What do you intend to do?" he asked.

"What do you expect me to do with a man in this state?" replied Verdon. "Get a statement from him . . . a written statement? You might just as well ask him to join Alcoholics Anonymous. Sit down!"

Paul Tavernier turned deathly pale.

"I don't understand."

"You don't understand when I ask you to sit down?" said Verdon amiably. "On the floor, there's no choice! You're on your last legs and we must think things out together."

"All right," said the other, mustering a smile. "I'll sit down or rather I'll squat. You frightened me."

Verdon untied the rope he had bound round his waist.

"I wonder why," he said with a laugh, "but I'm going to tie your feet again."

"No, no!" shouted Paul Tavernier, kicking his legs like a child and trying to hoist himself up on one elbow. Verdon stood stock still. "Hush, someone's coming!"

Exploiting this moment of anxiety he slipped a running knot round one of the ankles and joined it to the other. Paul Tavernier struggled against his bonds in silence, his breath coming in short gasps. In the meantime Verdon set to work on Devaux. He seized him by the hair, pulled him to his feet and took off his jacket as one would undress a rag doll. Devaux, unconscious, grumbled. Behind Verdon a panting voice said: "Listen to me. You have some dollars. . . ."

"Plenty of them," said Verdon without interrupting his task. He had let the man's torso slump forward and was now pulling at his trouser legs. "To have dirtied such a fine suit. . . . But unfortunately I need it. . . ."

The voice went on, with all the persuasiveness in the world.

"You take a great risk if you change them yourself."

"Even more so," agreed Verdon, still tugging at the trousers, "since they are big denominations. Well, now our friend's comfortable, I need a sheet of paper."

He came back to Paul Tavernier and as he searched him had a close view of his haggard, entreating face.

"All of them. . . . I'll change all of them. I'm sure you can save us. You can invent something, to save our honour and the honour of our children. . . ."

Verdon had torn out a page from a thick desk diary. "Oh, could I?" he replied indignantly. "But there's no question whatsoever of my wanting to. I would prefer never to cash a single one of my dollars, do you hear? To save your honour! A fine honour, I must say! And such noble principles! . . . What a magnificent display of family and middle-class values! No remorse, no regrets for a brother whose death was brought about by your blindness, but torrents of tears for your 'honour.' Down here we are breathing the odour of your virtues. The honour of your children? You wanted to settle everything by yourself. Well, carry on! You don't imagine that I'm going to sully my work by contact with your sordid enterprise?"

He began writing. Paul Tavernier, his eyes starting out of his head, burst out in fury:

"The 'Passenger' as a judge of good and evil! That beats everything! You are a monster . . . !"

"And you are a saint. Here is what I have just written. 'I never needed this blackguard and it is M. Paul Tavernier, here present, who returns him to you. *Signed:* The Passenger on the U.' My first signature. . . . I'm going to pin it to M. Devaux's drawers with this admirable grasshopper which should have been a dung beetle. . . . There you are!"

Paul Tavernier moaned: "So you are leaving me with this. . . ."

"With this," echoed Verdon, sickened. He suddenly assumed a Brussels accent: "Personally, I'm in need of a little fresh air."

He climbed the staircase again a little out of breath, his head to one side so as not to smell the fumes of the suit. At the door which he had closed ten minutes earlier he rang to be on the safe side. No one came. He opened it.

Examining the empty apartment once more he took off the toque, the fur tippet, wiped his damp forehead and murmured to himself: "Chin up." he found some liqueurs in one of the dining-room cupboards and drank two glasses of armagnac. From Paul's wardrobe he selected a dark-grey pinstripe suit, grumbling. "All these chaps are so tall. . . . Fortunately I've got some pins." The hat fitted him. In the hanging cupboard between the husband and the wife's bedrooms he pulled down a pile of suitcases, slipped Devaux's suit into the bottom one and put them all back in their place. On the other hand he appropriated a fine soft leather bag into which he packed his new acquisitions. "Gwen's dollars were a form of revenge; Longspès' clothes a present, Tavernier's 19,000 francs a business deal . . . but as for this suit and this case: I think you're stealing, Maurice! Oh! my sainted mother. . . ."

In Mme Tavernier's bathroom he attended to his make up. He covered his face with a layer of cream; fortunately it was thicker than the vaseline he'd used before because his beard was already growing. He put on the toque and tippet again and went back for a farewell glass of armagnac. Then he gazed through the window and studied the situation outside.

The building formed the corner of the Quai d'Orsay and the rue Malar. On the Quai d'Orsay the fat inspector was still walking up and down. In the rue Malar a taxi was parked in front of the back door and next to it a private car, doubtless belonging to Paul Tavernier.

Verdon tripped out unhurriedly with the leather bag; he had left the cab so swiftly earlier that the policeman could not have seen what he was or was not carrying. Catching sight of the taxi he went over to it and asked: "Are you free?" although the flag was down. The driver, who was reading looked him up and down before replying: "You can see, lady, that I'm not." He walked back to the quay and continued in the direction of the Invalides. He was not followed—either by the policeman or by the taxi. He could not suppress a sigh.

A quarter of an hour later the concierge came out of the servant's entrance and called the driver.

"You're from the police, too, aren't you?" she said with congenital bad temper which recent events had only worsened. "Police Headquarters want you on the telephone in my lodge. They're in a hurry!"

"Really?" he said.

A firm voice asked him "Hello, is that you?"

"Yes! Who is speaking?"

"Don't ask useless questions. Who is with you? It is still . . . ?"

"Sergeant Vilain, yes."

"Go and get him for me!"

Vilain ran to the phone. It was a feminine voice that came over the line.

"Is that you, Monsieur Vilain? Was there a lady who came to see your client just now?"

"Yes, but . . ."

"Ssh! She's performed a mighty deed. Go down to the basement, cellar number 12. The key is in the door. Hold your nose and go in. You will find the assassin in there."

"It's not true!" cried Vilain, overcome.

"Go on, go and see! I know. I'm the woman."

Vilain went cold.

"But . . ." he stammered.

Again the voice interrupted him.

"You should know who I am. Mme Colet, of course!" There was a peal of laughter. Then the line went dead.

When Verdon left the call-box, he spotted an old driver with a white moustache sitting up at the counter of the café downing a glass of wine and talking to himself. He asked him:

"Are you free? I like the look of you."

The driver wiped his moustache on his hand.

"The girls haven't paid me those sort of compliments for years!" he said thickly. "Is the lady an actress?"

Verdon took twenty francs from his bag and held them out to the man behind the bar.

"That's for my phone call and the glass of wine here."

"The glasses," the driver corrected. "That'll cover it all the same. You've really fallen for me!"

"Indeed I have. Let's go!"

In a bland voice, the drunkard asked meekly: "And where are we going?"

"Where?" echoed Verdon. "Let's start. We'll soon see."

He dropped back on the seat. Over his wheel the driver mumbled delightedly: "I love actresses, I do! So we'll start! And where shall we go? We'll soon see. . . ."

Epilogue

Eight days after the crime, the mystery of the U Line is solved. The murderer of the Rond-Point arrested—the victim's brother was hiding him in his own cellar!—"The Passenger's" hands are clean —"The Passenger" kidnapped himself—"The Passenger," king of jokers—"The Passenger" with the hundred faces—"The Passenger" still at large. "The Passenger . . ." "The Passenger. . . ."

On Monday morning, October 10th, the front pages of all the newspapers of the world carried a series of sensational news items which by a great miracle erred not by exaggeration but by default. Thus the reader learned that the stamp dealer and "The Passenger" were one and the same person, but saw no mention of Laeken and continued to ignore the existence of Miss Abbott. Who dictated this silence, a silence respected by the whole Press, at least for the day? What ravaged and still unenlightened soul? What millionaire? What Embassy? "The Passenger" appeared now in a more favourable light as a genuine eccentric, an amiable madman whose scrupulous probity made his flight incomprehensible. He had fooled the police at the Gobelins Garage—though the police had certainly given tit for tat —he had just assisted them in a masterly manner. Rather than prosecution, he deserved thanks and praise, said one paper. Relaxed and gay, Paris blossomed despite the first autumn mists. At lunch time as he left the Porte de Champerret Station amidst a crowd of other men, a man (people did not realise that they were at arms length from Chief Inspector Belot, one of the heroes of the day) noticed in the distance that a little crowd had gathered round a car outside the Hôtel Royal. It was a brand-new bright blue Gascogne.

Standing by the bonnet M. Colet was arguing with young Roux, while a band of reporters and photographers listened and laughed, the whole group encircled by passers-by. A M. Colet wide awake, today, waving his arms, unrecognisable.

"Please don't insist!" he kept repeating. "I won't do it."

Young Roux tried to interrupt.

"The Gascogne Directors. . . ."

"Go and tell them," cut in M. Colet, with a historic gesture, "that neither Mme Colet nor myself will accept presents of such value, and I will not get into this car until I have paid for it!"

Despite the noise of the traffic there was a click and a photographer murmured: "A perfect shot!"

M. Colet glared at him. Young Roux looked distressed.

"They'll sack me . . ."

"They'll appoint you manager of the Company," assured M. Colet, "and they will be right! But I refuse to let them make publicity out of me! I bought this car and I don't want to be given it! Wouldn't they do better to think of the new troubles facing poor Mme Tavernier? You certainly have a strange way of behaving here in the capital! Well, are you going to take my cheque?"

"Could we see Madame Colet, Sir?" a journalist asked politely.

"Sir," replied M. Colet insolently, "Mme Colet thinks the same as her husband, who has only one statement to make: he will be very glad indeed to get back to Provence whether by road or by train!"

Belot had slipped over to the wall of the hotel without anyone noticing him. As the argument looked like being a long one, he went in. More composed than the night before M. Perraud and the proprietor were defending the door to the lounge. Belot found Mme Colet there, writing postcards.

"Ah, there you are!" she said. "I could see us leaving without having said goodbye to you. You'll lunch with us, won't you, Inspector?"

"I'm afraid I can't, I've only got five minutes. I'm bringing you greetings and thanks from my chiefs." He sat down, while she nodded her appreciation. "I've just heard M. Colet, he's furious!"

She glanced towards the window and smiled like a young and indulgent mother.

"He's delighted! He thinks he's home already; shouting and storming. The holidays are over. . . . I'm sure you thought he slept

330

the whole year through? No, only a fortnight each year, poor fellow! Even on Sunday during the winter he works at his own private bench making doll's furniture, and as soon as the weather's fine he's out in the garden. What's new?"

Belot stroked his forehead.

"It's I who would like to have a good sleep. Paul Tavernier finally talked last night. His brother Vincent and their wives, who had no suspicions of anything, are prostrate. Étienne's widow has behaved admirably as ever. She understands everyone, forgives them all, and her only comment is to keep asking: 'Why didn't Paul tell me about it? Étienne couldn't, no, he couldn't!' She would like to see the famous son. . . ."

"Is it really his son?"

"No one will ever know! Paul is in a state of great agitation. As for Devaux, I suppose the state will kill him: a glass of wine on July 14th . . . and we are now October 10th! We'll dig up some reason, eh, madame? Anyhow it's no longer in my hands, it's up to the examining magistrate."

The glass door opened to let in M. Colet.

"Good morning, Inspector! How did you get in? Did you see the car? Well, sweetheart, M. Roux took the cheque, he did indeed! I'm not staying, I'm going to drive round Paris a bit before we leave. You ought to get them to give you one, Inspector!"

"I should prefer a little farm," said Belot, "near Avignon. . . ."

M. Colet became serious.

"That is exactly what we were discussing in the bus. . . ." He broke off, looked at Belot and burst out laughing—"What an ass I am! That's why you said it!"

"Unless," suggested Mme Colet, "the inspector was alluding to the diabolical power women have over their husbands? Because, if I remember rightly, I preferred the car?"

Her husband laughed affectionately.

"That's true, too! The inspector knows everything! You seem to me to have been plotting together very successfully this week. What a week! Well, I'm off. Has she confessed to you what she did last night?"

"More initiative?" exclaimed Belot.

M. Colet left with a grin and his wife lowered her eyes. A door banged and the blue car drove off noisily past the window. Mme Colet said softly:

"I read a detective story."

Belot raised his arms as though to reply: Well that's the last straw!

"Do you remember the morning we looked at the album?" she went on. "You accused me of reading them. I wanted to see for myself. . . . But it's nothing like the real thing! The suspect is innocent, the innocent guilty, the policeman an idiot and the amateur a genius!"

Belot was pensive, seeming to say: "After all . . ." She said angrily:

"You're not going to pretend that you didn't see through it all from the start? You suspected Paul Tavernier, you went after him, pestered him!"

"When I think that all we needed was to search the cellars. . . ."

Not to be diverted, she continued her praises: "You separated the two cases! Three days after Verdon's 'disappearance' you knew everything about him. Yesterday morning you put him through a wonderful interrogation!"

"You, too," said Belot, with respect in his voice, "you knew it all."

"But it was no credit to me! Nobody was on their guard with me and everyone was on their guard with you! It is true that I thought that you wouldn't succeed, not because I doubted your . . . your intelligence. Because you frighten people. . . . That's why I entered the fray."

"All alone, like a ninny. . . . And you succeeded all on your own!"

"You already said something like that to me once before, 'the considerable powers of the police . . .' Mine are much more considerable, Inspector! I am a woman, I know how to laugh without joy and to cry without grief. . . ."

Belot, still pensive murmured almost with bitterness: "What a bunch of actors in this case. . . ."

"I'm not! And I'm not contradicting myself. A woman always believes in the sentiment she simulates because through it she is serving another . . . one she values more than her own life—love, hate, the need to serve. . . ." She blushed and shook a postcard long since dry. "It's men who are always acting. For us acting is only a means; for them it is an end! What are they trying to do? To escape from themselves?" She added dreamily, "The demon of the monocle. . . ."

Belot's expression hardened. Mme Colet went on quickly: "I'm talking about 'men,' 'women' just like Mme Barbason! In any case, I am not so proud of my acting talent as all that. Miss Abbott believed in it because she needed someone to confide in, and Verdon because my threatening letter, which was signed by him, was bound to intrigue him! Would I have got by otherwise? . . . At all events we both achieved success at the same time, you and I. And that isn't like my book either: a terribly complicated story which it takes 300 pages to solve! Whereas for you it was the simple business of the Rond-Point which proved the most difficult, while we spotted all the tricks of 'The Passenger,' almost right from the beginning!"

Belot opened his hands and stared down at them.

"You have discovered one of the great truths of my profession," he said. "The crime which remains unpunished is always the most commonplace. One photo less in an album, a less drunken and more mobile murderer and we should still be asking ourselves the elementary questions. Whereas the real 'artists' never have any luck with us. This said, Verdon is still at large."

Mme Colet appeared not to have heard the last sentence. She was considering Belot's statement.

"Do you really call the Tavernier case commonplace? With all that double life of the victim, and the double game of the brother with regard to the blackmailer. It is no less surprising than the double life of Verdon! Simple, yes, from the police point of view, but commonplace . . . !"

"Commonplace," stressed Belot. "You are a purist, madame. Your comparison would offend Verdon if he heard it. You taught me just now some very interesting things about the way women are able to put on an act. But if they are true we must admit that the Tavernier brothers were no different. For them it was only a means. According to your theory only Verdon played a male comedy."

Mme Colet took up a postcard and held the edge to her lips.

"And you don't believe it? You don't believe in the monocle? You believe that he was thinking only of Miss Abbott's dollars?"

Belot leaned forward and looked into her eyes.

"You'd like him to escape us, wouldn't you?"

The eyelids quivered above the blue-grey eyes.

"When your husband mentioned confession just now, I thought he'd come to ask your help."

Mme Colet gave a start. "Oh," she said, shaking her head in disappointment. "Don't you realise that he is *really* a psychologist, that he couldn't possibly come and find me?"

"Why not?" persisted Belot, obstinately. "You treated him very kindly yesterday morning and he knows that you're not in the police."

A shadow of genuine pain swept over the charming features of the young woman: "Monsieur Belot," she said, in a voice that trembled, "please don't go on."

The inspector got to his feet. "No, don't go yet!" she cried.

She opened her powder compact, looked at her face, put on some powder and turned her sweetest smile to him.

"If I'd like him to escape you? To begin with, nobody has brought a charge against him. Apparently Miss Abbott refuses to do so?"

Belot sat down, his face suddenly cheerful.

"It so happens that his relations with the police make us anxious to see him again."

"Well, let us see whether he can escape you. Naturally out of professional pride you think he can't."

"And naturally you think he can, out of respect for tradition—that Punch is more cunning than the policeman. Particularly that puppet, that ballet dancer, that juggler who is fantastic and sensational enough! But mark you, he is not a superman. Don't forget he's only been missing for twenty-four hours! We have already found his Bellevue taxi, his first cast-offs at the Dental Clinic; picked up his second feminine disguise on the Quai d'Orsay and discovered Devaux's suit—he wanted to make us think that he had taken it with him!—in a suitcase belonging to Paul Tavernier, who unwittingly provided him with one of his own suits!"

"Which friend or girl-friend," asked Mme Colet, "will provide him with the next one?"

"They are all under observation—the old Longspès woman, the Barbasons, Philippe Durand and Juliette Guillaume. I put great faith in Juliette."

"So do I."

"I get your point," said Belot laughing, "but don't have too high hopes. She is under close observation."

"She may have some family in some remote country district, whom Verdon already knows."

"So do we."

"You don't know all his relations?"

"It's a long step from a relation to an accomplice."

"Perhaps he's simply gone in to a shop."

"There aren't many open on Sunday! We have warned them."

"Someone may have gone there in his stead. Some kind creature he met by chance."

"That will mean one more suspect."

"Or one honest tradesman the less! No reply? One up to me."

The grey-blue eyes sparkled as they had done during all the peak moments of the inquiry.

"Very well!" said Belot, "but clothes aren't everything. There's his injured face?"

"He may have a third identity."

"No romancing! There's only one day and one night in twenty-four hours."

"Perhaps he's gone quite cold-bloodedly to Miss Abbott?"

"The Old Ladies are on the look-out! Besides, I don't believe it."

"A gentleman's sense of decency?"

"No, saturation point! On that score I would myself stand guarantee for his sincerity."

"How cruel you all are!" sighed Mme Colet. "She would still be capable of doing anything that would help, I'm quite sure."

"Except change her looks."

"Then, one of those women of easy . . . whom he mentioned to us? They are reputed to be faithful to the death!"

"That's often true."

"One more point to me! And there's not only the women! We must always remember that he has joined forces with the devil . . . Dr Brayer!" she shouted.

Belot jumped.

"Dr Brayer, the devil? You don't know him!"

"I?" she said, seizing upon her new theory. "We went together to the villa Sans-Souci the day before yesterday. He is astonishingly talkative, cynical and absurd! One can well imagine those two face to face."

Belot reflected half aloud.

"Yes, why shouldn't his friendship with the Abbotts, father and daughter, encourage him to hush up a scandal? As a changer of dollars it would be difficult to find anyone better. . . ." He stood up. "I'm going there at once. It is certain that with a bird with no method but to follow his own fantasy the chase becomes a matter of chance! I'm sorry I can't keep you in my camp, madame. Thank you for everything."

Mme Colet had recovered her little girl expression. Anxious and tense she raised her face to this tall, erect man whom she hardly knew, with whom she had just spent the most extraordinary week of her life, and who was now to go out of it forever.

"Won't you wait for Raymond?"

"My work . . ."

"Aren't you going to ask me for our address?"

Half way through his bow, Belot stopped still, bent forward like a man who is a little drunk.

"It is . . . on the file," he said.

"The file?" repeated Mme Colet automatically.

Together they burst out laughing. And shook hands.